Tenants and Cobwebs

Middle East Literature in Translation
Michael Beard and Adnan Haydar, *Series Editors*

Select Titles in Middle East Literature in Translation

All Faces but Mine: The Poetry of Samih Al-Qasim
Abdulwahid Lu'lu'a, trans.

The Candidate: A Novel
Zareh Vorpouni; Jennifer Manoukian and Ishkhan Jinbashian, trans.

The Elusive Fox
Muhammad Zafzaf; Mbarek Sryfi and Roger Allen, trans.

Felâtun Bey and Râkim Efendi: An Ottoman Novel
Ahmet Midhat Efendi; Melih Levi and Monica M. Ringer, trans.

Gilgamesh's Snake and Other Poems
Ghareeb Iskander; John Glenday and Ghareeb Iskander, trans.

Jerusalem Stands Alone
Mahmoud Shukair; Nicole Fares, trans.

The Perception of Meaning
Hisham Bustani; Thoraya El-Rayyes, trans.

32
Sahar Mandour; Nicole Fares, trans.

Tenants and Cobwebs

SAMIR NAQQASH

TRANSLATED FROM THE ARABIC BY SADOK MASLIYAH

WITH A FOREWORD BY NANCY E. BERG

Syracuse University Press

Syracuse University Press
Syracuse, New York 13244-5290

First Edition 2018

18 19 20 21 22 23   6 5 4 3 2 1

Originally published in Arabic as *Nzulah u-Khait el-Shitan*
(Jerusalem: Association for Jewish Academics from Iraq, 1986).

For a listing of books published and distributed by Syracuse University Press,
visit www.SyracuseUniversityPress.syr.edu.

ISBN: 978-0-8156-1108-0 (paperback)
        978-0-8156-5461-2 (e-book)

Library of Congress Cataloging-in-Publication Data

Names: Naqqāsh, Samīr, author. | Masliyah, Sadok Heskel, 1934– translator.
Title: Tenants and cobwebs / Samir Naqqash ; translated from the Arabic
    by Sadok Masliyah.
Other titles: Nuzūlah wa-khayṭ al-Shayṭān. English
Description: First edition. | Syracuse : Syracuse University Press, 2018. |
    Series: Middle East literature in Translation
Identifiers: LCCN 2018038495 (print) | LCCN 2018041674 (ebook) |
    ISBN 9780815654612 (E-book) | ISBN 9780815611080 (pbk. : alk. paper)
Subjects: LCSH: Jews—Iraq—Fiction.
Classification: LCC PJ7852.A63 (ebook) | LCC PJ7852.A63 N8913 2018 (print) |
    DDC 892.7/36—dc23
LC record available at https://lccn.loc.gov/2018038495

This translation is dedicated to my dear wife, Judy, and my sons, Elan, Ranon, and Amir, and in memory of my late brothers, Victor, Noory, and Salem.

—S.M.

Contents

Foreword, *Nancy E. Berg* * *ix*

Acknowledgments * *xi*

Cast of Characters * *xiii*

Tenants and Cobwebs * *1*

Translator's Afterword * *373*

A Short History of Iraqi Jewry * *381*

Glossary * *393*

Foreword

When *Tenants and Cobwebs* was published in Israel in 1986, there was little awareness of the Iraqi Jewish past, and hardly any audience for Jewish writers of Arabic. The Association of Jewish Academics from Iraq—the publisher of Naqqash's novel—had by then issued half a dozen volumes by different authors: mostly memoirs, a collection of short stories, and a book of poetry. A smattering of other works had been published by commercial publishing houses, but generally found few readers.

A small number of Hebrew-language authors had written about the Jewish community in Iraq, its uprooting, its move to Israel, and the difficulties of adjusting to a new life there, but these books were pushed to the margins. Israeli literature was only just beginning to explore the past lived outside of Israel, and it was largely a European past that literature explored. Iraqi Jews were foremost among the voices claiming that their past was equally valid and equally important to the Israeli narrative.

Today in Israel there is growing interest in the past and increasing fascination with what by modern times was the most ancient, integrated, and literary of all Jewish communities. Unlike other Jews in Arab and Islamic lands, who traced their roots back, at most, to the Spanish Expulsion or Ottoman Empire, Iraqi Jews trace the beginnings of their history to biblical times when Nebuchadnezzar deported the most prominent citizens of Judah to Babylon. Those exiles founded what would become the longest continuous Jewish settlement, one that ultimately found its demise in the twentieth century.

In the decades before the settlement's end, however, Jews made significant contributions to modern Iraqi society. They dominated fields as disparate as business and music. Commerce shut down for the week on Saturday, the Jewish Sabbath, and no live music was broadcast on Yom Kippur, the Jewish Day of Atonement.

Jews were also at the forefront of the Iraqi literary renaissance; the poet Anwar Shaul and short-story writers Yaacub Bilbul and Shalom Darwishe were among those who developed modern Iraqi literature. Shaul was especially effective in encouraging other writers, most prominently as editor of the *Harvest*. Samir Naqqash is the foremost heir to this tradition.

Naqqash wrote in relative obscurity. He is often relegated to a footnote or to a mention as the lone Iraqi Jew who persisted in writing in Arabic. (In reality, there are others who continue to write in Arabic, including the late Professor Shmuel Moreh, who had been one of Naqqash's biggest supporters and had recently published a memoir in Arabic.) Until now, Naqqash has been best known for the fact of his writing, rather than for the writing itself. This new translation by Sadok Masliyah serves as a great advance toward rectifying that situation.

Tenants and Cobwebs, Samir Naqqash's first novel, continues the experimental mode of his earlier stories and plays, whose value remains to be discovered by the larger reading public. The novel brings us back to the eve of the end of the Jewish presence in Iraq. The fractured narrative captures the sense of the time and place— a neighborhood in Baghdad in the 1940s—on the brink of great change. Naqqash's style and perspective are as fresh and timely today as when the novel was written. This book is not an easy read. The reward, however, is well worth the effort.

—Nancy E. Berg

Acknowledgments

The translator thanks the Association for Jewish Academics from Iraq for granting the English-language publication rights to this work. Founded in 1980, the Association for Jewish Academics from Iraq is a cultural, educational, and social organization, whose aim is to solidify the cooperation among Iraqi Jewish academics through research on social, educational, literary, and artistic activities, and for publishing the output of these academics who publish works about Iraqi Jewry and hold cultural, educational, and literary meetings. For further information, contact assjaii80@gmail.com.

Portions of this translation, in a previous version, were published as "Selections from Samir Naqqash, *Tenants and Cobwebs (Nzulah u-Khait el-Shitan)*" by Sadok Masliyah in the journal *Edebiyat*, Vol. 13:1, pp. 49–67 (2002).

Cast of Characters

Jewish

'Abdallah Ghawi. Farhah's husband, who sets up his business in the countryside.

'Aibah. A rowdy, young rascal whom the tenants consider an illegitimate son of Gerjiyi. He is Marrudi's friend.

'Amam. A good-natured and kind widow.

'Aziz Ghawi. Farhah's son who, unable to finish high school, falls in love with Salimah, a nightclub singer.

Efrayim. Sabriyah's husband, conductor on the railway, fired from his job.

Farhah Ghawi. The loud, bitter, and sharp-tongued wife of 'Abdallah. She has three daughters and a son and works as a seamstress at home.

Gerjiyi Nati. Virtuous and intent woman with a questionable past who has returned from Bombay with her son.

Jamil Rabi. Blind musician, Selman's roommate. He is frustrated, cynical, and sharp-tongued, belongs to the underground Communist Party and expresses many of its ideas, denies the existence of divinity, and occupies himself with the question of opposites in life.

Khaduri. Tobacco vendor and close friend of Selman.

Khoshi. A rich, miserly, unappealing peddler from Persia. He marries Gerjiyi.

Lulu. Owner of the house, a compassionate but old widow whose life is devoted to her son.

Marrudi. Lulu's only son, who is spoiled.

Naji el-Jundi/Sha'ul. Considers himself a good-hearted man, adores the songs of the Egyptian singer 'Abd el-Wahab.

Sabriyah. A beautiful, high-spirited, but lonely woman, married to Efrayim.

Sa'idah. Farhah's unattractive eldest daughter, who helps her mother in the business. She leaves home to marry Karim, a young Muslim man.

Salimah. Nightclub singer.

Selman Hashwah. Religious, one-eyed peddler, in love with Sabriyah, plays the oud, and loves "the land of his forefathers." He loses his parents in the Farhûd riots and comes under the tutelage of Eliyahu Hamis, a Zionist activist.

Ya'qub/Ya'qub/'Aggubi. 'Amam's son, a shoemaker who falls into debt and liquidates his shop. He is a coffeehouse crony of Majid and the employer of 'Aibah. He blames deviant political intrigues for worsening Jewish-Muslim relations and conditions in Iraq.

Muslim

Abu Ghalib/Abu Ghallubi. Night guard.

'Alwan. Owner of a coffeeshop and close friend of Ya'qub until, influenced by propaganda, he becomes hostile to the Jews and severs his relations with Ya'qub.

Aminah Shukur. Beautiful young neighbor who maintains a close relationship with the tenants of the apartment house.

'Atiyah al-Qarawchi. Near-blind, miserable old woman who lives in a shack near the apartment house.

Fayiq. Na'imah's husband, an affluent barber.

Hamidah Umm 'Abdallah. A good-natured tenant, married with eight sons. She laments the departure of her Jewish friends for Israel.

Jabbar. Aminah's brother and neighbor.

Joudi al-Qarawchi. 'Atiyah's son, viewed as something of a rascal and considered insane in the world of those who think themselves sane. His favorite, meaningless, Dadaist word is *Da.*

Karim. Admirer of Salimah but marries Sa'idah.

Na'imah. A kind and beloved woman.

Nihad/Nahhudi. Son of Na'imah and Fayiq.

Wafiqah and *Qadriyah.* 'Atiyah's daughters.

Tenants and Cobwebs

One

1—Jamil Rabi

What a relief! Silence and freedom. A push on the stem of the pocket watch and the lid sprang open. I groped with my fingers to feel the hands of the hours and the minutes. It was two o'clock in the morning, and I was heading to the room that I shared with Selman Hashwah. He was probably asleep now. All of them were asleep and snoring. The quarter was quiet and no living soul was heard. How do ordinary people see these yellow rays now? Darker or lighter? I'll pass the time playing dominos, listening to music, and playing the *qanun*. Time will pass in illusions. I was sure that Selman Hashwah was embracing God in his sleep, God lying on one side and Sabriyah on the other.

"Good morning, Abu Ghalib," I said to the night watchman. "I heard your whistle from three alleys away. It splits a person's ears. Why don't you go to Sha'ul's Café and clear your head with strong tea that will help you catch thieves?"

My companions and I had spent the night in the café of Muhammad el-Shayi and his partner, Rubain. Even if we went to the end of the world, Naji el-Jundi would keep pursuing us. There was no escape. He was after us, chasing us like my bad luck, exactly like my shadow, as sticky as tar. Doing his stupid, heedless, and reckless things, he never left us alone for even a minute.

"Why are you so gloomy?" Naji el-Jundi asked me.

My features always betrayed me—try to explain that to sheep-like people. I pretended to smile and told him he was mistaken. "You need thicker glasses to make you see better. I don't give a damn."

1

He supported me, saying, "Take it easy and don't cry unless you are hurt." He urged Muhammad el-Shayi's son: "Please, Muhammad, may God have mercy on your parents, play something by 'Abd el-Wahab."

I stayed to the side, keeping people away from my misfortune and evil deeds. I saw the world in front of me as rays and shadows. Black beetles and red cockroaches emerged from the holes and gaps in the walls of the black alley infected with smallpox. People avoided me, but I knew what was going on behind the walls.

"Abu Ghalib! Haven't you gone yet? Be careful and don't lean on the wall."

"Don't be afraid, Jamil. It's true the wall is shaking, but I assure you, by your life, that it won't fall."

"You're mistaken, dear Abu Ghalib. You are mistaken. There's only one thing that shakes and doesn't fall."

"What is that, Jamil?"

"No, it's better not to mention it. I don't want you to curse me a thousand times and call me a heretic."

There was the problem of opposites. Most likely Abu Ghalib wouldn't understand.

"Abu Ghalib, you may not know it, but the situation is like this: nothing fits anything, everything is the opposite. You sit with your opposite, sleep with your opposite, eat with your opposite, drink with your opposite, think with your opposite, and talk with your opposite. You and your relatives are opposites. You and your God are opposites. You and yourself are opposites, and you and your intellect are opposites too. I'm leaving now. I spoke to you from the corner of the alley while you were still leaning on the crumbling wall and not listening. This also is an opposite. But I, Abu Ghalib, I am the opposite of all opposites in this world."

"Take it as it comes," he replied.

You're right, Naji el-Jundi, Naji, the singer of 'Abd el-Wahab! You are convincing, although you sometimes glower and become gloomy. Like everyone else you're moody. Tell me, what do you care?

You behave like a snob with your friends, but you're just a simple person. I am the greatest opposite alive with this chronic disease, a disease as dark and black as the unfurled wing of an ill-omened crow. Last night while I was walking on the street, my shoulder hit the back of a passer-by. It appeared that he stared at me with anger and spat out words in my face like a person spitting out a piece of gum. "Are you blind? Can't you see?" he yelled. I felt ashamed, "I am very sorry," I replied.

My first chronic disease is poverty—do you want more? Yusuf Wahbi, the Egyptian actor, played the role of a caretaker of the poor in *Les Miserables*. Like a child I excused myself to go to the bathroom to hide, to conceal my poverty and shabby clothes. The shadows of my second chronic disease have stuck to me as to you, Naji el-Jundi! I don't pardon my ignorant, savage father and my barbarian mother, though I shed tears easily.

I remember Abu Shaiba, my grandfather, who used to apply medicated patches on the head to treat baldness. When I was a child I had big beautiful eyes. One day, my eyes were infected and my grandfather volunteered to take care of them.

"Sprinkle a little of the Kuppalli powder in your eyes and you will see how your eyes will heal and blossom like a healthy rose," he said. The Kuppalli powder erased the black part of the right eye and half the black part of the left eye. It left a white dot in it and a host of crimes in my dark eyes. Ordinary people don't see. And this son of a bitch asks me, "Are you blind? Can't you see? Are you blind, can't you see?" Blind, blind, blind!

Enough is enough, people, sons of whores! The night's intoxication has evaporated. Freedom has vanished and even silence is lost. All that is left is the stench, dung smells from 'Atiyah al-Qarawchi's shack site. You too, 'Atiyah, Joudi's mom, are fit to be my opposite, though sometimes we agree. Come chat with me tonight. You serve as a wonderful example of someone who contradicts me regarding some of this world's truths, its tragedies, its ruins, and the tenants of this house.

2—'Atiyah al-Qarawchi

Joudi! Joudi, is that you? Come inside and go to sleep, damn it! Enough loafing in the streets, where people throw watermelon rinds, rotten tomatoes, and cucumbers at you. Joudi! Is that you? No, it isn't. You're asleep.

I groped with my fingers blindly and found you. The passerby was perhaps one of the neighbors. Sleep, unfortunate boy, sleep. God has ill-treated you as He did the Imams Hassoon and Hussein. I can't close my eyelids and fall asleep. Hey, you stranger, who's walking there? What's the time? Oh God! It's half past two in the morning and I am tossing back and forth on my mat, sleepless, while Joudi is sleeping and snoring.

Luckless lad, go to sleep. You have nothing to worry about. You are as ignorant as a donkey. You don't even know how to read and write. What do you know about what happened and what will happen? You know nothing about what exists and what doesn't. I want to talk, but I am afraid. I'll say awful things, and if I don't say anything, I'll die of remorse, sadness, and depression. Who would take us to our relatives? Where is the righteous person who will listen to what I have to say about my hardships and about that handsome boy of mine whose mother loves him? I dozed awhile and saw him in a dream. I said to him, "Sonny, why is this happening?" He answered, "Mother, it's God's will."

I said, "How is it that God consents that my beautiful, sober, and intelligent daughters passed away while I've stayed with this crazy man? Why didn't He take Joudi and leave me with my dear daughters?"

He told me, "Are you disobeying the Creator of the world? Oh, unbeliever! Heretic!"

When the fellow stranger set out to leave, I held him by the hand and told him, "Know that I want to marry off my son, Joudi. I want to share his happiness before I die and join my dear daughters."

Well, this fellow began to laugh at me, saying, "This son of yours, Joudi, has been married for a long time." I was so surprised and overwhelmed that my eyes popped out of my head.

I asked him, "This is unbelievable! What are you saying about my son? Say something that makes sense."

He replied, "I'm telling you the truth. They took Joudi from you and married him off to a girl of theirs. She is beautiful, praised be He who created her like a part of the moon." Then I asked him, "Who are they?" He kept silent. He didn't want to say anything and disappeared. Hey, you, Joudi! Don't you remember the day your sister Wafiqah died? Don't you remember that she was as beautiful as a rose? I used to care for her, feeling and embracing her in my heart. Suddenly, the sandstorm came; it was a black day when the wind blew and blinded my eyes. I took Wafiqah under my watchful eyes and put her in one eye, but I don't know how the storm stole her away from there and blinded that eye.

Qadriyah was as dear to me as my other eye where she was dwelling. Do you remember, crazy fool, your sister Qadriyah, intelligent and unruffled like the branch of a sweet basil? The fire broke out in the midst of the river while, oh God, she was walking on the bridge. The fire was fierce and bullets of fire, darting as high as the palm trees, slashed catching Qadriyah's head. The fire consumed Qadriyah. Where the fire took my daughter, nobody knows.

Sleep, sleep unfortunate boy! And the other eye under which Qadriyah took refuge lost out too, and since then I have been bleary-eyed. I find my way with great effort, and you, Joudi, you lie on a clay floor or on ostrich feathers? I used to spin and sell cotton to support you, beg and cook a pot of *tashrib* soup for you, and you would be satisfied after eating from the people's garbage. Then I would be forced to throw the pot of food to the cats and dogs. You know, my poor boy, that tomorrow I'll open my bleary eyes, delouse your clothes, wash them, and bathe you. This is your worn-out, ankle-length *dishdashah*. Do you remember that it had red stripes when I used to wash it in the Dhiyalah River, and now it's as black as my *'abayah*?

I am not questioning God's ways. God left me with a crazy man suffering from a grief that used to overwhelm my heart. When will the sun rise so that I can chat with my neighbors? Where are you,

'Amam Umm Ya'gub? I want to tell you about my bad luck. By my life, how good she is. There's no one like her. God gave her dear Ya'gub and gave me Joudi. How lucky she is, how unlucky I am!

3—Selman Hashwah

From what did God—may He be praised—create your pure, wine-colored complexion, Sabriyah, 'Abdush's daughter? Is it possible that He made you from butter and honey, dates, molasses, sesame oil, and tea and milk? Didn't your father feed you almonds, rock candy, walnuts and the best dates, gaimar, and date molasses? Who installed those vibrant springs in every limb of your body? Oh my God! I have been sentenced to death by hanging because of your beautiful eyes and the mole in the lower part of your radiant cheek. I am doomed to stay there all my life and never come down. What did He make? A doll in Orozdiback's department store? Oh God, what a beauty, Sabriyah! You are now on Efrayim's lap, making love, tickling and kissing him. He will attack your body forever, shower you with a hail of kisses and with the name of God. He extinguishes his wild passion inside you. The other passion will remain shining in your face, sparkling from your eyes. Coals of passion will also remain in my bed to embrace and lie next to you. They will burn me, broil me, consume my flesh and then restore my bones so they will grow anew.

I am killed either by a bullet or by Jamil's sarcastic mouth when it opens and releases trash. What does Jamil Rabi want in life? Why do I share the same room with him while we are like the heel of a shoe and a scorpion, a cat and a rat, or like the All Merciful and the Devil? For Heaven's sake, have pity on me! I have grown weak suffering from gut pains. I have endured such stress and anxiety.

Sabriyah gives me troubles on one hand and Jamil on the other. I can handle Sabriyah's madness, but how can I handle the insanity of Jamil Rabi's son? If Jamil were religious, I would say, "He is lamenting the destruction of the Holy Temple." If he had been in charge of a treasure, I would have understood him and said, "He is right, he doesn't approve of anyone, and therefore casts all people beneath his feet." If he had been the only one with afflicted sight, one would have been able to say, "This is because he bears the troubles of the world." If he saw better than me or just as well as I do, I would pardon his disdain for all creatures and me. Well, what does Jamil Rabi want? One never knows what his desires are, why my fasting and prayers annoy him, and why my introverted nature and thinking as a Jew provoke him. Why does my love for Sabriyah make him detest me to the point of wrath? Why does it seem impossible that Sabriyah should love me? Although she avoids me, she still sticks a thorn in my side and pulls it out afterwards. She fiddles with my hair, jokes and tickles me, and says obscene things to me, and causes my face to blush like a child. "May death take you away, One-eye!" she says. Rabi's son is more painful. He insults me, shoving his palm in my face and says, "Get lost! Tell me who you are and what you are."

No, Rabi's son! I am not like you. I don't gather darkness around me and compress it into a blind feeling of inferiority. I am exactly as uncomplicated as anybody else. The world is full of people with bodily defects, and if all disabled persons thought like you did, the world would have collapsed, and no creature would have survived. Is it because Sabriyah is a married woman that I don't deserve her love, that she is forbidden to love me? Does it make sense for Efrayim to be better than I am? He relies on God for a livelihood and so do I. Jamil stepped up to me infuriated, as if I had stolen the light from his eyes. He shoved his ten fingers into my face, scorning me with anger, and said, "If it's true that she loves someone like you, then I shove into your face not ten fingers but the twelve fingers of Abu Rubain's family, who are known to have twelve fingers."

If that's how it is, then you don't know that Sabriyah was made to love and to be loved. The love of the world is insufficient for her. Sabriyah is always roaming in a mysterious and ghostly atmosphere that you can't see. Sabriyah is a butterfly in gardens full of blooms and devoid of thorns. I entered paradise with her beside me. As soon as she placed my feet there, I pushed myself in and entered paradise with her, but left when my rival Efrayim came. It's lucky that he comes only once a week. As soon as he comes, Sabriyah expels me from paradise. Then I look from a distance and my passion burns out. When my rival arrives, Sabriyah retires to her room and doesn't even care about leaving the door behind her wide open. Inside, the hugging and kissing goes on, and all the tenants look through her exposed room's windows or from behind the open door. You know how biting and vicious Farhah Ghawi's tongue is. Once Farhah unleashes her sharp tongue, who can close her mouth? When she sees Sabriyah, she lets the tongue loose. "From where did God send this immoral *barbug*, this whore, to us? Does she want to go through all the young men in this house? I have a dear son and young girls. I'm afraid this barbug will corrupt their morals, but I'll show her. I'll chase her out of here, or my name's not Farhah."

The landlady, Lulu, Moshiyah's daughter, is busy with Marrudi. She has nothing to worry about except him. She barely has time to change his clothes, comb his hair, make him look tidy, and say to him, "Darling!" The sound of the whistle doesn't reach her, and 'Amam will soon hurry to rescue Sabriyah from Farhah, 'Aziz's mother. 'Amam is a good kosher woman. She never stains people's honor. She says to Farhah, 'Aziz's mother, in a low, imploring voice only heard by the blind and musicians, "Umm 'Aziz, may God protect your son, leave this woman alone to her own business. Why carry the burdens of others? Don't I have a son too? Why don't I worry about him? Do you think I'll do nothing if something bad happens, God forbid? Sabriyah is still young; she's a newlywed and wants to enjoy life. She can do whatever she pleases in her room. Does she undress herself and come to the sitting room naked?"

Do you want to know the truth? When I heard 'Amam defending Sabriyah my soul almost left me. I know that 'Amam is a good-natured and sincere woman, but she crushed me by saying what she said to Farhah. Does she understand what it means to be deprived of the love of Sabriyah, the one with the mole? It's as if the Angel of Death were to come and take my soul away. Farhah Ghawi's laughter burst like wine pouring out of a flask, and I realized that something would happen.

Then came a sound like the rumbling of an eastern wind. It penetrated the gaps and cracks of this house, whistling, thin, as sharp as the edge of a sword. Farhah Ghawi shouted like the muezzin, whose voice reaches all the sides of the alley calling the worshipers, all the way to Hamidah Umm 'Abdallah's house in front of ours and 'Atiyah al-Qarawchi's shack to our right. The sound from her lips also reached the house of Shukur's sons on the left, "But what is this indecent flirting with a one-eyed, pot-bellied man? What's going on?"

What would happen if you were in my shoes, Jamil Rabi's son? I am a simple man and I don't suffer from your psychological complexes. So I realized that when Farhah Ghawi mentioned my bodily defect, she was fishing me from a well of boiling water and raising me into the light of the world. Then I was as happy as if I owned everything.

The door was polygonal, broken apart, chipped, and as worn out as Jamil's gloomy face. When it opened, it sounded like the squealing of a locomotive. All around the room, the smell of a Luxe cigarette floated through the air. It was impossible to miss Jamil's special cigarettes. Selman heard the footsteps, followed by a soft click of the light switch flooding the room with yellow lights fixed like knives on his black-purple eyes. His eyelids twitched with a shuddering blink of sharp pain from one eye. The other eye was just an empty quarry in which bruised and sticky eyelids were attached to a waxy, gummy, gluey liquid. If only he had two dinars he would have installed a glass eye in the socket. This idea had never ceased to occupy him since he had begun to be absorbed with Sabriyah. The two dinars would have placed him on an equal footing with his rival, Sabriyah's husband. These two dinars! When mentioning his defect, Farhah would then say, "This is the one with the glass eye" not, "This is the one with the blind eye." What a difference between an attribute and a defect!

Selman Hashwah turned over on his bed, the springs producing mixed noises under the weight of his heavy body and then straightening out when he got up. He sat under the light, blinking, and his dishdashah folded, wrapped around, and squeezed his belly. Dazed, he saw Jamil as thin as a rail. He yawned and asked, "Hey you! Are you there?"

Jamil immediately threw away his shoes and began to look for his slippers through the shadows of his blackened eyes, and said sarcastically, "Haven't you fallen asleep yet? Look here, you! Watch your mind before you lose it completely. Only one more notch and it will detach."

Selman took a deep breath. He was thinking of Sabriyah. If Jamil had been as crazy as he was, he would then have experienced the sugar-sweet taste of paradise. He mumbled, "By God! Let it be, never mind—losing one's mind for her is worth it." He barely saw the face of his roommate becoming gloomy. He wanted to tell him at length about her, but the expression on Jamil's face stopped him, and so his passion collapsed like burnt charcoals in the brazier hiding dust-colored ashes.

Selman questioned himself again. What got me into this mess and made me live with him? Was it only because we went to the same school? Even at school he used to make fun of me. Who does he think he is? In my presence he smokes cigarettes on Saturday, eats *taraif*, impure meat, and above all, denies God. No, he is certainly not a Jew. Does a Communist have a religion? It isn't enough for him not to stick to his religion, he also wants people to abandon theirs and become like him or . . . .

Jamil laughed at him again. "Hey, you! Did you eat beans today too?"

"No, why?"

"So, what did you eat? Boiled chickpeas?"

Anger creased Selman Hashwah's voice, blinding his other eye. "Damn you, devil! What do you want from me now? I felt happy then you came and burst my bubble. Why do you care what I eat?" He shouted. "If I eat poison, it's my business. I don't owe you an account of what I do and don't."

"I care what you eat because you filled the room with stench. How can I sleep now?"

Selman Hashwah felt his heart stabbed by a dagger. How can Jamil understand all this, he thought. Why does he continue to insult people and disapprove of them? If I say something about his defect, I'll crush him like a worm.

But Selman was too weak to say anything. The spit would fly back into his face. After all, this would only be the spit from a reckless and dumb devil, inhuman. Revenge is tasteless and disgusting, and anger is even worse than his blind eye. Selman's idea was bankrupt and senseless. He was courageous in his battle with anger to the extent that it was transformed into slightly indifferent sympathy. He whispered, apologizing for himself and the world.

"The sewage system in the house is clogged and filthy water has been oozing out. The women are quarreling because of it. You know that when Farhah Ghawi opens her mouth, her voice flows like wine spilling from a flask."

Jamil was a prisoner of the sarcastic devil. "What's wrong with you? Why didn't you empty it? You're a big man. It would take a lion an entire year to eat you and there'd still be leftovers."

Selman avoided getting in an argument with Jamil. Instead, he said patiently, "Aren't there enough cesspool cleaners to empty the drains? 'Amam Umm Ya'qub said that her son would bring cesspool people to empty it early in the morning before he goes to his shop."

Selman received no response from Jamil and turned off the light in the room. Darkness covered everything again. Only thoughts remained, floating in his mind—in his heart and inside his belly too. They fought and rose to his throat like acids in the throat of a pregnant woman. He continued to turn over on his bed, pressing down the springs of the mattress. He felt that the acid would strangle him and that he must talk and spit his thoughts out in a loud voice so that people could hear. Darkness made him sensitive, and the acid of Jamil's face brought up his own poisonous acids from his stomach. He took courage and whispered, breaking the silence. "Jamil?"

"Shut up. I want to sleep!"

How could Selman sleep? Sabriyah was on the tip of his tongue. He was too much of a coward to utter her name in a tone of sweet melody, but despite this he felt he had to say something: "Today a woman by the name of Gerjiyi Nati came with a boy named 'Aibah. They stayed in the *takhtahbosh*, the wooden-floored room."

"Oh, great," Jamil mumbled. "That's just what we need now."

Selman was encouraged. "No one knows where she came from. They say she lived in Bombay."

Jamil silenced him in rebuke, "Shut your mouth and let me sleep!"

4—'Aziz Ghawi

I'll shave my moustache—yes, I will. Na'imah's husband, Fayiq the Barber, may be surprised at this, but I'll tell him frankly that it's a matter of life and death.

Here I am, a man with a moustache, a senior in high school. Good for nothing. The looks of the children are like arrows aimed at me. The failure of the entire world is stuffed under my skin. At the instant my mother gave birth to me, people said to her, "Congratulations on the newborn." They lied. Damn the senior year. I'll shave the moustache—may God curse it! I'll tan its hide. Enough humiliation, enough shame. Isn't it enough that I enter as a senior at the beginning of every school year and the students all stand up thinking I am the instructor? High school is a curse. To hell with it! I feel like a mouse caught in a trap. "Congratulations on the newborn" is the most artificial expression ever uttered by disgusting people to demean the creatures of God.

I spent five years as a senior in high school. A failure crawling on garbage. What stagnation and deterioration—five years of stupidity, laziness, useless repetitions, and failures. Each and every year I felt as if my guts burst inside, my words got stuck in my throat, and my thoughts turned into a shovel digging under my feet.

"Sit," I ordered the seniors of my class. This word escaped from the cracks of my soul and broke the silence I had maintained. It was only a word that would have changed my life, would have turned over my ugly life like a shovel that makes the burning charcoal into a ripe date and the barren land into fertile soil. I said to myself, "Go to the blackboard and begin the lesson."

When the teacher's footsteps approached, I wiped the sweat off my face, my voice was squashed, and my resolve halted before it was born. I believed I could enjoy a moment of forbidden pleasure.

My mother, Farhah Ghawi, was still telling me white lies and raising her head, boasting of me as if I were the jewel on the world's crown. How poor she is! She dozes in the warm bathroom from which vapors rise and intoxicate her completely, leaving her in a slumber. What a damned ill-willed and malicious woman she is. She deludes herself, me, and everyone else, pretending that all is going well, and she overlooks my life's baggage.

Meanwhile, my father, 'Abdallah Ghawi, lives in a different world. He used to wander with his merchandise among the Bedouins until he dropped his anchor in Mahmudiyah, where he's been managing a fabric shop. Like a Turkish bey, he used to come home once every three months. I had forgotten that he looked like a false pasha. He's a different kind of a liar, coated by the respect of a name. He would count his money and save it in the wooden box as a dowry for Her Majesty, my sister Sa'idah.

'Abdallah Ghawi is a hollow drum, powerless. He never asks questions, never knows what happened and what will happen to his family or what is happening around him. He comes and goes as if he has ants in his pants, never slows down. And here am I, his son, cut out of his life. Do you know, 'Abdallah Ghawi, that now I realize that I am as fatherless as Marrudi, the son of Lulu, Moshiyah's daughter? My tragedy is that I am like a losing lottery ticket. In the lottery there is one grand prize and other tickets that win something when the number is one digit above or below that of the prizewinner. My losing ticket is above and under each digit of the winning number—a bad luck embracing my existence. My life was tougher, uglier, and crueler than even my death. Reality wasn't ashamed to smash my pride and defile my innocence. I'll shame reality, or my name is not 'Aziz Ghawi, the son of the wicked Farhah.

Walking toward my bench, I felt as if I were crawling on a ripped belly. I buried my head in the ground and licked my wounds amid the laughter of these mean bastard classmates. The dirty laughter of the boys tore me into pieces, but the tail of the snake always grows back whenever one cuts it. My tail will grow in this world of vice and prostitutes. I spit at you a thousand times, senior year, and will uproot you and tan your hide.

My God! Another school year, a sixth, is approaching as fast as a starved tiger on the prowl. The students have already laughed at me five times, nicknaming me "mule," "camel," and "palm tree." Enough! I am no longer 'Aziz, the son of 'Abdallah and Farhah Ghawi—that is, unless I cut their tongues out. That's easy to do, but the hardest thing to do is to cut your own tongue, Farhah Ghawi, when you talk about your "child" and about your daughters. Those daughters of yours are as fat as camels, and still you hope to marry them off. Don't you want to marry me off too and work hard on it day and night? Go ahead and marry off your camels, Farhah, and keep on giving me my allowance. I don't want anything else from you, you dressmaker of the poorest people in Baghdad. You and your eldest daughter—how high-and-mighty she is!

The room turned into a sewing hall and the customers came and went. The room was full of them and their money, but I was empty-handed, dejected in an isolated room on the second floor, alone, embracing disappointment, sleeping, hugging loneliness and dubious women—and the fire of hell. I want a woman, people! I am a human being, world! I am a man with a moustache. I am a permanent senior who hasn't budged for five years of solitary. I stay in an abandoned room on the second floor, embracing illusion in my sleep—Sabriyah, 'Abdush's daughter; Na'imah, the barber's wife; Aminah Shukur, our neighbor; and any girl I might meet anywhere. I would even embrace 'Atiyah al-Qarawchi, that old imbecile. I would hug any woman, even if she were the devil's mother. I am alone, alone in my room and isolated in the world. I wrap my big tragedy around me and put it between my legs every night and fall asleep. I wish the morning wouldn't come. What reason have I got to wake up? Where are you, 'Abdallah Ghawi, the bull? Our meeting is on the second floor every three months. Do what you please in Mahmudiyah. Don't ask about me. God protects me. I am not fatherless like Marrudi; I have a father in Mahmudiyah who lives far away, in a different world.

5—Na'imah, the Barber's Wife

So what if I share a house with Jews? thought Na'imah. By God, I live at ease with them. No gossip, no troubles, no headaches; every one of them is a prince. No one retells gossip like "this woman came, and that woman left." They're jewels.

Silence prevailed in the courtyard, a seemingly strange silence in a place crowded with tenants. Na'imah went out of her room at the far end of the courtyard wearing a colorful dress with red roses on a purple background. She was slim, with her rosy cheek scarred with *ukhut*, a Baghdad boil, which was coated over with a red cream. Her lips were painted by the reddish *dayram* dye. She was without an 'abayah, and her hair was dark black, dyed with a mixture of dayram and henna.

Na'imah lived in a Jewish house tucked into the darkness of a poor quarter. Like a tattoo sticking to a man's skin until he died, she was ready to challenge many things that remained in these quarters. She was a contented woman, satisfied with life, and she strove to keep up with the world's progress. She used to boast of her intimate friendships with Jewish women like Dr. Marsail, midwife Na'imah, and Violette, the superintendent of the girls' high school in the Sa'dun Quarter. They lived in Karradah, 'Ulwiyah, and Battawin, where the world was different than in Baghdad. Everything was spacious. Mansions stretched throughout the area, and blooming gardens perfectly fit the description of paradise. The streets were as wide and clear as the Tigris; so clean and shiny that one could lick them. Refreshing air blew day and night carrying melting breezes with flowery fragrances and freedom.

What is wrong here? Why is it okay for Dr. Marsail and midwife Na'imah to go unveiled and it isn't for me? Na'imah asked herself.

Isn't it enough that the quarter resembles a depressing, boring, and barren landscape? By God, I'll tear off my 'abayah, cast the veil into a clay oven, and whatever will be will be. She felt relieved, freed from her black coffin, the 'abayah. She used to be like an unknown black dot wearing an 'abayah, moving along the narrow street unidentified among the other vague black dots crawling on the miserable dusty surface of the street. Now she was herself, with her own looks, like Na'imah, the barber's wife. Everybody knew her and pointed to her when she walked down the street. This Na'imah the barber's wife was happy, and a pioneer among the women of her house for ripping off the black coffin. Who else except her and Sabriyah, 'Abdush's daughter, had dared to leave the doorstep of the house unveiled, without an 'abayah? Even Sa'idah, Farhah Ghawi's daughter, didn't pass the courtyard gate and show her face in public. But 'Amam Umm Ya'gub still adhered to the fashion of Ottoman times. She was pious, sat at home wrapped in her headscarf and headband, and never left without a *khailiyah* veil or in izar attire.

The picture of the spacious courtyard was stamped on Na'imah's vision. There was an open gap, like a rip or a hole in an 'abayah for the light to enter through. Rays of light flowed from the courtyard gate. The sides of the courtyard were arranged in a straight but broken line, and the left side opened onto a furnished sitting room. Across the courtyard were wooden stairs leading up to the *kafishkan*, a small storage for bedding. Next to it were stone stairs going down to the basement, and next to this stood Sabriyah's *jamkhanah* with the glass window.

Sabriyah used to open the curtains, and through the shiny glass of the jamkhanah the contents of her small room revealed the gorgeous furniture of rich people that looked odd in such a house. Nothing was shabby or second-rate. Everything was new. Her wedding bed was made of rare wood and covered with a clean embroidered cover. The closet had three mirrored doors, and the exquisite bamboo chairs stood on the well-maintained Tabriz carpet that covered the depressed, fading, and scratched old tiles.

Sabriyah's flowing silk dress reached her outrageously red mani-
cured toenails. She sat on the bed and then stretched out on it, the
most attractive object in the room. Her beauty made even the elegant
furniture seem pale. Everything disappeared except her long, black
flowing hair above her hips, her shiny, wine-colored look, and her
soft well-shaped figure. Her limbs moved as gracefully as a fresh
branch in the breeze. All the stars of the universe flocked around her
as soon as she appeared.

How beautiful Sabriyah is! Praised be Allah who created you, as if
you were an exquisite doll of the Saray Market. But what a pity. Poor
Sabriyah was a new bride and her husband worked as a conductor
on the Mosul line. At the most, he came to her bed one or two nights
a week. He hardly satisfied himself with her before he had to put on
his khaki uniform, leave her, and go back to work. Her husband,
Efrayim, had been doing this all the time, Na'imah said to herself.

Sabriyah closed the door of her room and headed for the courtyard. Why was she swaying and making flirtatious motions? Na'imah
wondered. She must be pregnant and feeling a craving for food, or
perhaps it's a bride's coquetry. Na'imah cast the smiling light of her
eyes onto 'Amam Umm Ya'qub, who was sitting in the middle of
the courtyard stuffing sausages she took from a deep pot that also
contained dry orange peels soaked in water. Hamidah Umm 'Abdallah sat opposite her, and the two conversed in whispers, making it
impossible to hear their voices. They moved their lips only and waved
their hands.

Who cares if I am a tenant in a Jewish house? thought Na'imah.
This 'Amam is peaceful. Is there another woman like her?

Na'imah greeted the two old women, and 'Amam sounded as
calm as the cooing of a pigeon protecting its chicks.

"Good morning Umm Nihad. I see you are going out," said
'Amam.

"Yes, Umm Ya'qub. I'm going to Haydarkhanah and will drop by
the shop of my husband, Fayiq, to get some money," she said, speaking in the Jewish dialect.

Why not? Na'imah wondered. Here we have Hamidah, Jadu's wife, speaking to 'Amam in the Jewish dialect. I wish every friend and dear one would be blessed with such children as Hamidah—eight of them. Each is more accomplished than the next. They are modest and honest. When they're walking they never look at women, never raise their eyes from the ground. It's true that Hamid works in construction like his father, but they say that 'Abdallah, the eldest son, is engaged in a very good profession. I don't know what he's doing now. Ever since radio broadcasting came into being he's been sitting next to the radio and, what's more, his brother Majid sings on it too. I heard him the other day and congratulated Hamidah.

My husband, Fayiq, is a decent person but naïve, mused Na'imah. He goes from the house to his barbershop in Haydarkhanah and back to the house. He is a friend or enemy to no one and doesn't even ask me what I did and what remains to be done. Whatever I want from Abu Nihad, he says happily, "With pleasure." I've never seen him hesitate. He floods me with jewelry, money, and goodies, but I have a hole in my pocket and squander the money.

What can I do? All of the women here are my friends. Would it have made sense to offend Farhah Umm 'Aziz when she mentioned the other day that my anklets were beautiful? She liked my anklets. It would have been embarrassing not to take them off and give them to her. How could I disappoint her? By God! If any of them asked me to give her my soul, I would do so gladly.

It's good that I remembered on my way to the shop to call a porter with a wagon to move our bed to Umm Hesqail's house. What does it matter if we sleep on the floor one night? Tomorrow, Abu Nihad will buy a better bed. I can't stand living without giving gifts. If I don't give presents I get sick and need a doctor. To hell with it! As long as my husband is alive, he will provide and replace what I give. It's true he's just a barber, but God has blessed him and he makes a lot of money. He earns a lot of income cutting the king's hair. It's true that the luck of the house rests on the threshold.

Abu Nahhudi told me, "Let's move to Ras el-Garyah, it's a better quarter than this," but I told him, "No 'aini, because of the luck of this house's threshold, I won't leave even if the world turns upside down. We have struck luck and wealth here. Look at Ya'gub, the son of 'Amam—he is only a shoemaker, but behold how God made him a wealthy man. He should get married quickly since he's probably over thirty now."

I asked, "Umm Ya'gub, when will you marry off Ya'gub? We would like to share his happiness." 'Amam sighed. The sausages slipped from her fingers and landed on the floor of the dirty courtyard. She scooped up each of them as they squirmed in her hand. She again began to rub them with the wet mixture of cardamom and dry orange peels.

"I hope, Umm Nihad, that I live to see Ya'gub's wedding," said 'Amam. Inshallah, you and Abu Nihad will live and attend Nihad's wedding, but I can't do anything about it. He's swamped with work, and whenever I urge him to get married he says there's still plenty of time."

Farhah Ghawi suddenly appeared from her room without anyone feeling her presence and said loudly, "Perhaps a decent girl for him has not been born yet!"

By God! Sa'idah is a good girl. She is pretty and chaste. And a question crossed Na'imah's mind, "Should I talk to 'Amam Umm 'Aggubi?"

'Amam was still occupied in stuffing her sausages while Hamidah was conversing with her. 'Amam avoided Na'imah's comment and turned to Farhah.

"Umm 'Aziz, Farhah! How is it that you are in the courtyard? No sewing today?"

"Gracious God, there is. Why do you say there is not? Life ends but work never ends. I thought to leave the room and take a bit of fresh air and see my dear neighbors," Farhah replied nervously.

"May God cherish you and protect your dear women friends," 'Amam replied.

Then Na'imah remembered something and added, laughing, "Umm 'Aziz, my husband Fayiq told me that 'Aziz shaved his moustache. Does he want to be a girl? You have three daughters—may God protect them—aren't they enough?"

Farhah shook her head and said, "Thank you. I wish God to cherish you and your friends. *Shaku beeha,* 'aini—there is nothing wrong with that, dear. He is still very young. He's a student, and the moustache makes him look like a man. The girls chase him because they think he is responsible and mature. He cut it to avoid them. Otherwise, the girls would circle around him like flies. No dear, 'Aziz is still too young to fool with girls. He is busy with his studies."

"Shaku beeha, 'aini. There is nothing wrong with that." This is Farhah's magical, preferred expression, borrowed from 'Amam to smooth things and make matters lighter. Suddenly a loud noise came from the door of the house. Na'imah thought that it must be Nahhudi coming with the scoundrel 'Aibah, the son of the new tenant. What a rascal this boy is! May God keep me away from his sins. Maybe he is a bastard, as Ya'gub said.

"Have you finished playing in the street, 'aini?" Na'imah asked Nahhudi. He hung on her dress like a mosquito. "I wish school was open and I had relief from you for a few hours. Go play with Marrudi upstairs in the room," she urged.

Na'imah hollered, raising her head to Lulu's room, "Umm Marrudi! Umm Marrudi, Lulu dear! Umm Marrudi!"

Lulu looked down from upstairs, worried. "Help me please, Umm Nihad. I don't know what happened to Marrudi today. He woke up drowsy and in a bad mood."

"Leave him to God's protection. Why do you watch him all the time? It's not good to go to extremes like this," answered Umm Nihad.

"*Fedwah*—I am begging you. Umm Nihad, who do I have except God and him? We experienced hardships until he was born, and last but not least, his father disappeared quickly," Lulu replied.

Na'imah's eyes were quick to shed tears. How would I control them? She asked herself. Now I am facing the disaster of widows and orphans. I answered her warmly, "Don't worry, dear. God will protect and guard him for you and for the sake of every imam and prophet. I wish to see him a bridegroom, oh Lord of the Universe!"

"Help me please, Umm Nihad, tell me what to do. I've become like a crazy woman because of him," Lulu begged.

"Perhaps he's stricken with fear. I'll go and send you the mullah to ward off harm from him and pray for him, and Nihad will go up to play and pass the time with him too. Good-bye." Then Na'imah thought to herself: There's nothing wrong with doing good deeds. How does one gain recompense in the world except through doing good deeds and casting bread upon the waters? On what virtue does this world stand? I can't believe, like people say, that the world rests on a pig's head. No, by God no, it stands only on good deeds. As long as Abu Nihad is satisfied with me and pampers me and doesn't say anything to offend me, damned be the queen's father who claims that his daughter is happier than I am!

6—Joudi al-Qarawchi

Joudi's dishdashah was like a dirty swamp spread in the mazes of the neglected alleys escaping the attention of the health authorities. The water thickened and turned into a black filthy mud. The inside of one's bare feet became like dry land with cracks and holes sheltering insects and scorpions. My head was shaved with a razor and became white, sleek, and bald. My skullcap was a dome sullied with a thick layer of soot accumulated from one year to another. A forest of thorns extended on my chin and cheeks.

I was walking. I smelled like the stable of a water buffalo in Jubah, spreading its stench abroad, and my slim, handsome body with its elongated crystalline face was tall.

I am striving to reach my goal! My goal is not a man's goal—I stumbled and found it. I am escaping the fall of humanity, running away from the curse of elusive goals. I am out of my mind in a world of sages. This world is an illusion like a spider's web enmeshing the trap of their serious sins. Confusing thoughts surround me and hover over and before me like a mirage. This world is a curse. This languor, this fondness for sin—man loves to commit sins that swell like hot marshmallows, bigger and bigger like balloons. He rushes to cast nets and catches small bits of happiness, but tomorrow the great frustration will strike him. The great grief, the curse!

I am running away. I have the intuition of a bird auguring the coming of a devastating storm. It's coming. I sense the creatures that are taking pleasure in the rise of the sun. Veils of deceit and coats of leprosy drop around me. I see fear lurking beneath the visible. I see fright concealed inside the fear of animals, the dread of mute, motionless objects, and their sleep is deep. I am running away from the upcoming sweeping storm, from a flood that has not yet disappeared from the surface of the earth, rolling with eternal infinite pain. The past, the present, and the future! A cadaver is looming over my head. I scrape off the secrets of the universe. I'll throw a scoop of sand at the eyes of the wise people. How stupid are the wise, how ugly is the sleep of the stupid.

I have pissed in my pants. I have revealed my genitals to the world shamelessly. I have rolled in the garbage of neglect, along with absent-mindedness and stupidity. The stupid man calls me a madman, running after me with his crowds, throwing his garbage at me. I know secrets, but I keep silent. I claim the possession of this world's wisdom. I roam. Mine is not a man's goal. The world laughs at me and I ridicule it. I have only one word that resembles the One who made and created me. It's only one ambiguous and incomplete word. Humanity will never get any word except *Da!—Da! Da!* I'll utter it until the day I die. It's the essence of my life and hidden secret.

"Da! Da! Da!" I'll utter it, gesture toward the secret wisdom, draw it out like a weapon, expose it for eternity, and whisper it only by moving my lips.

Two

1—Ya'qub, 'Amam's Son

The person who said, "When it rains it pours" uttered a gem. It applied to the disaster that resulted in confiscating Jewish assets, demonstrations, and a solid block against the Jews of Baghdad. It came from all directions. It rained shit and piss on God's worshipers, but then it rained pearls, emeralds, and other precious stones, because the turmoil of World War II passed away after leaving hundreds of victims. Soon the wounds caused by Rashid 'Ali's abortive Nazi coup in Baghdad healed, the scar of the Farhûd's mob attacks against the Jews of Baghdad disappeared, and the sores healed. The Farhûd was a "dirty game," a British dish seasoned with Nazi spices of chaos. People knew about the event and distorted the facts. Incitement was as sharp as the teeth of a saw, and the minds of Baghdad's residents were tender. Baghdad had an army of starving mobs. Starve your dogs and they will follow you. The British starved the Iraqis, so did the allies of the Nazis who shouted, "Attack the Jews!" They turned the mob into a flock of sheep, everything was mixed up, and anarchy prevailed.

There was chaos, and the whore-like game of politics was the only victor. Despite this, some Jews continued to yell and complain, "We've had it. We were their scapegoats! Let them stick those words up my ass! We alone are scapegoats, Mr. 'Alwan, by God!" This is what people say.

With the help of God I'll see you by dusk, though I am swamped with work over my head. I am going to the market to buy some raw materials. It's only an hour's walk, nonstop. On my way, I'll go by Ishaq's grocery shop and pay the rent for the shop. To settle matters, I'll go later to that son-of-a-bitch, my partner, Nessim. He embezzled my money and cleaned me out. People say, "If you are in charge, stop stealing," but he does the opposite. The more he takes charge, the more he steals. He thinks that as long as there is plenty, the theft will not be noticed, but if you continually bail water out of the river, it will eventually be depleted and run dry.

Ya'qub, 'Amam's son, passed Farajallah Alley and went slowly along old, twisted alleys between houses with bay windows projecting out from either side. The alley, wide at first, narrowed until the bay windows almost touched each other. He passed the buttermilk vendors, the cafés, and the bakeries, and smelled the crispy, plain hot bread in the clay oven of 'Aishah, the baker. He yearned to dip a hot piece of *hannun* flatbread in a fresh glass of tea at the nearest café.

He was cheerful and clear minded. His business was flourishing and accumulating plenty of profit despite his light-fingered partner, Nessim, and he now needed a helper in the shop. Suddenly the beginning of a century-old folk song came to his head, and he crooned contentedly, "Above the palm trees, look above, above the palm trees, look above!"

He strolled through the open tan doorway and saw the oven of 'Aishah, the young baker, in the corner of the slippery, unpaved clay courtyard. 'Aishah bent over the oven, her head lost inside the wide, round opening, which blazed like the mouth of a volcano. Its bottom was full of burning coals above which were the flat loaves of bread. The wood was tan, the floor brown, the baker's clothes were black, the tongs black, the bottom of the oven was red. The smell of the baked bread intertwined with the odors of dung, smoke, dampness, and the stink of the outhouse. The smells and colors of that outhouse flared up in his nostrils and eyes.

He stepped forward smiling, happy for the world and for himself. The baker welcomed him with a smile and greeted him warmly, intoxicating him with the echoes of her voice. Her voice was that of an Iraqi woman steeped in goodness and heightened by a flowing musical echo, as if it came from a fountain of warmth trembling with tenderness. This sweet warmth was not found in any other women in the world—warmth that God bestowed on the women of this good people alone, including 'Aishah, the baker. She was on the verge of drowning in this overflowing warmth and drew him along. She said, "I missed you, Aggubi. Nobody has seen you for a long time." He was actually drowning in the surging warmth of her voice but took another step forward.

"Don't blame me, blame my work. It doesn't let me breathe, doesn't even let me scratch my head."

"Maybe you had a craving for a piece of bread, and so you came. I know you well. You come here only for the *hannunah*."

His contentment grew so great that he forgot to feel rushed. Who will save me from her sweet talk? he thought. I have no time to be courteous and listen to women.

"Have it ready fast, I'm in a hurry."

As soon as he drew near the oven, she made a sound like a frightened deer. "Oh no! What happened to the bread?"

The whole batch had dropped into the oven and got a little burned. She hastily saved whatever she could, stretching her bright-sleeved arms to the oven, paying no mind to the hot coals. The bread came out slightly burned and emitted a black smoke. "All the bread burned. This doesn't happen to me often. It happens only when you come near the oven. What do you have with you? You carry an 'Irq el-Sawahil charm, Aggubi, don't you?"

Feeling big, he laughed, "How did you guess? I have an 'Irq el-Sawahil and a hoopoe's bone charms."

She stared at him. "My goodness! I don't believe it."

"Do you want to have a look? I put them in a small leather bag and tied the bag to my forearm." He showed her his forearm and the leather bag. It was made of fox skin, spotted and sweaty, and protected its contents like an oyster shell. Two dark leather strips attached to the bag were wrapped around his forearm forming a bracelet. She looked at the bag open-mouthed with astonishment, then a sigh escaped her, and her sweet voice sounded silken with wonder, "This is why I love you," she said.

He thought that she looked down on him and wondered whether what he carried in his bag really had to do with his popular flourishing business and with women flocking to his shop. Still, the bread had dropped into the oven, and 'Aishah had announced her love for him without restraint. Joy and pride welled up in him and rose to his head. Mockingly, he began to sing for 'Aishah an old song, "Oh Uncle, how lucky I am! I am a young man."

She objected, "Enough, enough, please don't make fun of me!"

His arrogance absorbed him; thoughts boiled and bubbled in his mind as loudly as the call of the muezzin for prayer. "Look how every lady who comes to my shop is like a Persian jewel, tempting me with flattering words that would make even a stone melt. Despite this, my heart never cried out for them. Can you, the gypsy who came from the breeders of water buffalo, win my heart?"

"No, 'aini, dear Aggubi. I don't accept what you said. What is wrong with being a water buffalo girl? Isn't she a human being? Is she forbidden to love?"

He was wrong. Haughtiness is, in fact, devilish. The truth is that he would have invented excuses, even if the woman was a beauty queen, but the devil misled him regarding 'Aishah. He was surely wrong and confused at the same time. He quickly said, "No, I didn't mean that, but I'm overloaded with work."

She stopped defending herself knowing that her case with this "civilized city dweller" was lost, and then tried to rescue him from his embarrassing confusion.

"Please, move away so you won't spoil the rest of the people's bread." He obeyed and cleared the way until his rear backed into a tree.

Ya'qub thought again, do I really need a helper in the shop? He rummaged around in his mind and finally realized he had found someone—'Aibah, the son of the new tenant who had come from across the sea, the son of Gerjiyi Nati. This *nagel*, this bastard, had challenged the devil who spat at him, jumped out from his grave like someone newly resurrected from the dead, and drove the neighborhood crazy during his one-week stay there. A thought crossed his mind. I'll teach him the trade and make a man of him. But who is this Gerjiyi Nati? And his father—who was he? His mother claims the father passed away on the ship and his body was thrown into the sea. Isn't it possible that whatever she said was a big lie? In any case, I nicknamed him "the little bastard" correctly. Any one of a thousand fathers could have been his. Gerjiyi Nati avoids mentioning her past in Bombay. Isn't it possible she was a whore or a madam there? So, we are sheltering a disaster under our roof.

He was overwhelmed by the confused puzzle. It was so complicated that he couldn't solve it. If Gerjiyi lived in Bombay, then when did she go there and when did she come back to Baghdad? He wanted to know everything, but the honeyed voice of the baker suddenly overwhelmed him again.

"Here is your hannunah, Aggubi Bey. Where are you? Are you daydreaming?"

He quickly took the hot piece of bread, a little embarrassed.

"What? No, nothing happened. I was thinking of a woman who came from India, and she and her son are tenants in our house."

"Is she so pretty that you are daydreaming about her?" she teased him.

He was annoyed. "Look, my beauty, you have nothing to worry about. If you see her, she'll scare the hell out of you. What's more, she's as old as my mother."

Determined to find out about Gerjiyi, Ya'qub left 'Aishah. He would crack the nut and find out what was in it. He wouldn't stop until he knew who she was.

2—Sabriyah, 'Abdush's Daughter

I am bored and fed up, I am disgusted and on the verge of exploding!

His train has not arrived at Mosul yet, Sabriyah imagined. Right now, Efrayim is going from one car to another, swaying like a drunkard. "Watch out!" He shakes as if there were continuous earthquakes under him.

I was at the beginning of my married life, reading the book *Your Life in Marriage*, turning the pages painfully and putting it away quickly. I chose you! I chose your blue eyes, your fair, curly hair. I chose your poverty and struggle, and to share life with you in this stinking cesspool. I chose my father's rage and your love. I divorced glory and married you. Undoubtedly, your train is now traveling fast, rocking through the tunnel, while I am in the other dark tunnel, a prisoner in a bottle, standing up and sitting down and impatiently awaiting you.

I threw away the book *Your Life in Marriage* and was disgusted with the novel *Thais*, the whore saint. Instead, I read the first lines of our meeting from the pages of my mind. You were on the Mosul train while I was sitting alone in the first-class car, and you came and knocked on the compartment door. When I opened the door, the silk robe I wore trailed behind me. You thought I was a Muslim and stared at me, and then you retreated and ignored me. I laughed at you in my heart and said, "He is a Jew one hundred percent, a snake, a coward, and a virgin."

I let out another healthy laugh from all my heart. At first sight, you filled one-half of my heart, and I excused you and said, "He's right. He can't imagine how a feeble ewe takes a risk being alone with a pack of wolves." I proved to you that your innocent thoughts still penetrated the world, that thoughts didn't become thoughts by accident. I showed you that the ewe might suddenly become a wild cat, as unexpected as the sound of a siren. I know myself; I now know how to protect my honor, but in my father's home, I used to be shielded by a steel wall. Even when I challenged my father's "no," I followed directions. Regarding principles, I am stubborn, but I grow indecisive in this grave, this loneliness and cruel distress. I am like the free dove that cannot be imprisoned. I cannot help it—I warned you.

I was ready to follow you to the ends of the earth provided you quit this job and found another one. I warned you, Efrayim, that I wouldn't be imprisoned and be lonely in my room, even if the world turned upside down. I cannot. I am used to going out and having fun. If not, why did I take the risk and travel to Mosul alone and find you?

I wish Selman Hashwah would come to pass the time with me. At my father's house I used to joke with our servant, and here in this room, I see only the walls. So when is Selman Hashwah coming? 'Amam Umm Ya'qub would tell me about the Ottomans and World War I. God must have cursed me. I am encircled by the stupid old days, surrounded by senile, old women, professional mourners, insane people, and old maids of many kinds.

What does Farhah Ghawi want from me? Why doesn't she take care of her daughters and leave me to myself? Does Farhah Ghawi think I came here from the street? Does she think I am a deaf mute, unable to hear or answer? Knock it off, Farhah Ghawi! She does not know that I descended from the ivory tower out of my love for Efrayim. I was a queen who came down from her sublime throne entirely of her own free will. The stuff of my clothing is unlike yours. God forbid if I lower myself and answer you, Umm 'Aziz. Where is Selman Hashwah? Where is Efrayim?

Where is my father? My father had told me, "It's as unworkable for you to marry him as it is impossible that a palm tree could sprout from your head." I left the palm tree sprouting in his head and came to live with Efrayim in Bani S'id. I came to my love in the house of Lulu, Moshiyah's daughter, the landlady and professional mourner. She either cries or bewails her husband or devotes all her life to Marrudi, her son.

The ruckus made by 'Aibah, the little bastard, the son of the Bombay woman, had already begun. He would enter the house like a sweeping flood, but Na'imah, the wife of Fayiq the Barber, would still stay content and happy. Na'imah's compassion will be the death of me, and her curiosity chokes me. This dominating love, Na'imah's love, irritates me. The woman is sick, her sickness is devastating, and she is determined to afflict others.

"Oh, 'aini," she asked me, "Why are you so weak that you can't stand up straight? Don't be afraid to admit it. There is nothing wrong with it. You aren't the first woman to be pregnant." Then she examined me and said, "Say it, Sabriyah, so I'll know what to do for you, to buy clothes for the baby and make him a gold 'afsah charm and an anklet with a bell."

This accursed boy, this eight-to-nine-year old, 'Aibah, this unhatched chick, came to me while I was sleeping, like an experienced rapist. He opened the door of my room as the most professional thief does. He lay on top of me and I woke up to find my face was full of his sticky and disgusting saliva, smelling like rotten armpits. He bit my breasts and his dirty onion smell blew onto my face. His teeth had firmly covered my lips, and I felt as if my guts had left me. I chased the nagel out, the son of the Bombay woman, scolding him. I told Na'imah, "What are you thinking, Umm Nihad? I can barely take care of myself, how can I take care of a child? No 'aini, no!"

I thought of the cursed boy, the son of the accursed woman. What would he do when he grew up? I swear this scoundrel will terrorize the world. I swear he won't leave a virgin in all of Baghdad. And you, Efrayim, who goes from dark tunnels into the light on the Mosul–Baghdad train—I long for you, Efrayim. I long for my sisters, Amirah and 'Afaf, and for my tyrant father who taught me to be the way I am now and showed me the contrasts, the softness and firmness of a woman. Then he was sorry and said, "It's as impossible to marry him as to have a palm tree sprout from your head."

I long for Selman Hashwah. When will he show up? Selman is like a stop along your train route, Efrayim. I long to fondle him and tickle his belly, so the belly of the world will laugh. Selman plays prelude on his oud and the world is intoxicated with joy. In Efrayim's absence I grow as feeble as Selman's oud, whose melodies are buried in the grave—forgotten, forsaken, and silent. Selman Hashwah swore to abandon his old oud after the Farhûd and never play it again. He kept his promise for many years. I guess that Efrayim is now in the train putting the ticket puncher in the leather sheath of his belt and thinking of me. Once a week, Selman Hashwah breaks his promise, committing a sin by sounding his melodies for me.

I don't understand. I don't understand the nagel's action, his way of sneaking to my bed. I thought two or three times about his sneaking. I thought very hard and with great effort. Is it possible that 'Aibah is looking for a mother? But is his mother still alive? Gerjiyi Nati is not a mother. Still, Gerjiyi Nati is stronger than a stepmother. The real mother is Lulu, Moshiyah's daughter. Marrudi spits at Lulu's face ten times and gets a thousand kisses spread over him from head to toe. At the same time though, he shoves his palm in her face, wishing her death while she walks around him seven times to keep the evil eye from him.

'Aibah! It's better for you, bastard, to choose Lulu as a mother. What else can I say? Na'imah will give you gold and jewels, or maybe you're looking for a mother with striking beauty? Are you hoping that I adopt you? I've made great efforts to understand 'Aibah's terrible behavior. The thought of being an adoptive mother didn't move me; it seemed like an innocent thought attacking a world that doesn't know how to break its chains. Such thoughts are as innocent and ugly as the attempt of my father to take back the elixir of freedom after it had become a part of me. I swear this bastard 'Aibah will destroy the world as soon as a moustache grows beneath his nose.

I've had it. Soon I'll give in and explode as if I were waiting impatiently in a police station or twisting with pain in a hospital, walking back and forth, shattering my head with thoughts and killing the time reading stupid and meaningless books. Until when? I have this red dress and these slippers and one dinar in my purse. One lousy dinar. Let me relax in Bab el-Sharqi or Bistan el-Khass, my father's home!

I'm going to meet my boyfriend now. Hooray, ha-ha-ha! Is this what you were going to say, Farhah Ghawi? I don't care. Let the world repeat what you say about me, Umm 'Aziz! I know Sabriyah, I know myself better than you do. Only an animal can endure living in this rotten coop. I'm fed up, my soul has exploded, but Bistan el-Khass is close by, and Bab el-Sharqi is closer.

No sooner was I about to do something than my excitement died away and melted like a block of ice on a hot day. My father was awaiting me in Bab el-Sharqi. With pretentious looks of victory, he stirred me up and challenged the proud beauty and strength of my femininity. He cast the pretentious looks of a victor at me. He crushed me with his triviality, his selfish questions, and all the while I roamed alone aimlessly without a husband by my side. My father said, "Did you see, did you see?" My big worry was that my father's firm "No" would stomp me down. Distracting myself, I opened the hanging curtains of the jamkhanah's glass windows again.

Get to it, the day is over! It's not worth it. Soon Selman Hashwah will show up, and I'll fool around with him and lead him by the nose.

3—'Atiyah al-Qarawchi

I'm talking to you, 'aini. What are you saying, 'Amam my sister? Are you saying, "May God protect my eyes?" Is there anything to protect? True, none is above God. He filled me with the sorrow of separation and seclusion. He abandoned me. As someone said, "Because of my sorrows I became so sick that I couldn't even get dressed by myself." Nothing is above God. He looked after me with a lamp, and then stripped my strength from me and the light from my eyes, left me with nothing, and I silently endured the pain. Oh! I spun wool and sold dresses and begged to feed my husband, the madman. Every day I cooked a mess of soup and heaps of rice. I thought maybe he would eat his fill and choke to death, and I said maybe the day would come when Joudi will gain an appetite, devour the world and consume everything.

Cursed be the earth! It eats so much and is never satisfied. It opens its mouth like a lion, devours endless tons of flesh, and licks the bones. I saw all this yesterday with my own eyes. I swear by my sleepless eyes that I saw it licking the bones of my dear Wafiqah and Qadriyah, like a female demon, sitting and gnawing on them. May God keep you away from this terrible scene, a scene that tears the heart and weakens the strength.

And Joudi, I don't know with whom he was talking. He was muttering and waving his hands. He had bad luck. From dawn until midnight, the storm's dust, the watermelons, and the melon rinds that people throw at him overcame him. In the end, that rotten devil, 'Aibah, the son of the new tenant, showed up. He is just a small child, not even taller than the length of my hand, has lived here no longer than ten days, and is already raising hell. Every day he makes troubles for Joudi, shouting, "Here's that crazy fool!" The other day this rascal undressed Joudi and put a melon rind full of dirt on his head. My poor Joudi came home to me in terrible shape, stripped off his clothes as if he'd just finished draining a septic tank, angry and waving his hands.

Nothing is above God! If it were not His will, He would not have stolen my darling daughters, left me with Joudi, and made me suffer with him. That handsome young boy told me in the dream that it was God's will? I am not challenging His way, but what kind of a damned will is this? When He nags someone, He never leaves him alone. By God, He will never leave Joudi alone. He drags him away like a mound of flesh and gets rid of him like a pile of bones. He tortured me and ground me under a millstone, like wheat and barley.

Now, let's go back to our tale, the tale of the Farhûd. That day was horrible, as black as the soot of a pot. I then led the life of a lady living in a big house in Aguliyah, and my darling daughters filled the house and dwelled in my eyes, Wafiqah in this eye, and Qadriyah in this eye. They were like candles for me, and my neighbors were Jews, as dear to me as you are.

In the Farhûd I was holding my cane, standing by the door, not letting anyone enter the house. Then a man came, as tall as a minaret and so broad that he could cover the gate of the Murjan Mosque. He held in his hand a big sword like that of the Angel of Death. I stood in his way and said, "As long as I am here, no one will go through this door."

I swear by your name, 'Amam, he elbowed me near my heart, my soul almost left me, and my heart began to turn like a Ferris wheel. I fell down at the doorstep, holding my cane in my hand. How could I let go? I leaned on the doorstep, raised my eyes and saw that man—may God expel him—entering the house and approaching the courtyard. I crawled toward him until I drew near enough to grab the hem of his dishdashah. "Go back!" I told him. What happened to the world? What happened?

In the alleys, I saw blood flow like a river, and people slaughtered like animals, their carcasses hanging.

The man answered, "Go back to your home, crazy woman, this is God's will!"

I replied, "You should feel ashamed! What kind of God's will is this? Does God want to uproot the plants in his garden?"

He said, "You must be crazy, they are Jews!"

Then I replied, "And what about these Jews, didn't God create them? This world is His garden and He filled it with white, red, and yellow roses. All of them are excellent damask roses. Isn't it a pity that you're snipping these beautiful roses? Aren't they all roses? Aren't both of my daughters, Wafiqah and Qadriyah, homegrown roses for me to smell? And what a good smell each gives off, like the fragrance of a citrus blossom! Surely, when I smell them I feel relieved."

He thought and scratched his head many times while I waited impatiently to see what he would say. He was silent, wondering, and suddenly began to be restless and confused. Then I looked at the doorstep and saw him leaving the way he came, stealing nothing and bothering no one. This is it, by God who gathered us by fate.

Hey Joudi, are you home yet? Let me get up, excuse myself, and prepare dinner for the poor boy. He hasn't tasted or swallowed anything since twilight.

4—Selman Hashwah

"Cotton threads! Sewing machine threads! Bobby pins! Needles! Pins! Safety pins! Sabriyah! Bleach! Blue dyes! Matches! Jerusalem! Cotton threads! Sabriyah! Sewing machine threads! Jerusalem! Bleach! Sabriyah! Needles! Jerusalem! Matches! Sabriyah! Blue dyes! Jerusalem!"

If I forget you, Jerusalem, let my right hand forget her cunning. And if I forget you, Sabriyah, let my trust leave me, let my being deny me, let my life depart from me, and let my other eye become blind and as rotten as a barrel full of garbage.

What can fill up this belly? If my love for Sabriyah were food, if my love for Zion were food, I would have indigestion and need to go to the hospital. I would never eat any food, but I possess love for both, and a narrow border separates my heart from my belly. What will fill up my belly? I'm hungry and feel a bite of agony; my burps and hunger pangs resemble the sting of a scorpion. I beg of you Fohah, the beans vendor—ladle up another dish of beans for me, fill it up, and fill it until it overflows, for my heart has grown weak from hunger. I'll go to the bakery and bring a couple of hot sourdough loaves of bread to dip in the beans.

It appears that love also makes one feel hungry, and hunger is in my heart, jumping over and crossing the narrow border and landing in my stomach. Love, hunger, black gloomy memories have swallowed me, the beans have swelled me, my stomach has grown bigger, and Jamil Rabi's son reproached me for that. He also criticizes me for my ardent desire for the one with the mole, for fasting and praying, for my love for the land of our forefathers, and for my pain whenever the days of the Farhûd come to my mind.

Last night, at the time of the evening prayer when I returned home, I found Joudi's mother conversing with 'Amam Umm Ya'qub at the doorstep, and suddenly I overheard the word *Farhûd*. My skin got goose bumps, my hair stood up, and I almost forgot everything, even Sabriyah.

The Farhûd, Karbala, agony, and grief. It's my nightmare, my insanity, and my delusion. It's a sore in my heart between Sabriyah and the Holy Temple. A festering wound is still growing and oozing pus. So, when I heard 'Atiyah al-Qarawchi talking, my knees became weak and I almost passed out. Sabriyah asked me to play for her, and I played sad pieces from the Book of Lamentations and prayers of repentance. Then I saw the sins of my world and of my being. She asked, "What's the matter with you, Selman? Why aren't you your-self today?"

What can I tell you, Sabriyah? You make things easy for me except in this matter. If it were in my power I would bury the memory, be relieved, and relieve you. But, I'm buried in the grave of memory. Karbala, agony, and grief will accompany me until death, and I'll be crushed under them just as Khaduri, the tobacco vendor, pulverizes the *hukkah* leaves. When I run into Khaduri I'll ask him for a ciga-rette to "drink," as I am drunk with that memory.

Karbala! It is the agony of the martyr Husayn, and my grief that made me forget the dish of beans getting cold and the flies buzzing around it. I also forgot the hot bread in the oven. Then I dropped by Khaduri's place, and the yoke of the past memories broke my back again.

Karbala, agony, and grief! Breathing hard, I said to Sabriyah, "Sorrow has stormed my soul." She laughed, "What do you have to worry about? Has your ship sunk with all its goods?"

What does Sabriyah know? Sabriyah! You're like a fly stuck on a person's face. Leave her alone, I said to myself, "No one is free of worries, life isn't milk and honey." I turned my back on her and set forth for my damned room.

But she wanted to cling to me, and said, "Where are you going? Are you leaving me alone? You know what? Go ahead, talk nonsense and joke. Do what I do. If you don't talk nonsense and joke, you'll explode from grief."

What defeated, broken tones—Sabriyah was probably worried. May God protect you from worries, Sabriyah. You feel caught in traps set by me. You, Sabriyah, are a pigeon snagged in a net, and I must break, for the first time, a promise I made you. What could I do? I felt my guts ripping apart. It was not wise on my part to let her into my sad world. I should not make her share my dark night. Sabriyah was created as a butterfly to hover over the roses, while I fell in a dark cellar surrounded by wreaths of thorns. As it is said in the Pass-over story, "I was forced to escape," and I left her alone. Broken and depressed, she went back to her jamkhanah, and I heard the echoes of suppressed sobbing. My worries grew. I gathered the remainders of the past and the grief of the present and continued to toss in my bed.

Please, Khaduri, give me another cigarette. This time, I want it strong and numbing, an English cigarette, Craven A, with the picture of the cat.

Jamil came from the café after midnight; meanwhile, the beans got cold and the sauce thickened. He hadn't changed and didn't get tired of throwing stones of resentment and disgust at the world, at both the living and the dead. The cigarette was superb. Long live your hand, Khaduri, for the cigarette. Top-notch, mind-numbing. The stones Jamil threw were also numbing. As soon as he stepped into the room he asked, "What's happening? How is it that you're still up? Did that woman, whose name I'm not mentioning, make you melancholy and wake you up?"

I sat down speechless. A rooster's crow came from afar asking, "Why are you crying, Selman? Has she paid no attention to you?"

I looked at Jamil's face. My ears were full of rooster cries that kept repeating again and again. Like the source of his odd moods, it was difficult to determine the source of the cries—very difficult indeed. I winked and gazed at Jamil's face. He was crying. What a surprise! He was crying and laughing at the same time. I'm not him. I'm a simple person. When I have a stomachache, I simply know that I suffer from diarrhea, but he doesn't think that either diarrhea or constipation is a sufficient reason for a stomachache.

What a surprise, Khaduri—again, what a wonderful cigarette. Had it not been for the cigarette, I would have been dispirited and my brain completely shut down.

Jamil imagines, contemplates, and accuses poor innocent Sabri-yah. She comforted me, and though she was anxious herself, she wanted to laugh and made me laugh, but I was sick without a decent remedy.

The wicked, the son of an *almanah*, Jamil, said to me, "Take care of yourself before you start talking through your fingers like Joudi. You have been out of your mind for a long time, and now Sabriyah is driving you nuts."

Karbala, agony, and grief prevailed once more. How could I forget? When will a Jewish state be established in the Promised Land, Khaduri? Save me and give me another cigarette!

Beware, Jamil will drive me nuts for sure. He only likes to rub salt into my wounds. I yelled at him, "Don't force me to talk!" The cries of the roosters were louder than the sound of memory and deafened my ears.

"May your ass be undone! Do you have anything else to talk about save your stomach, Sabriyah, and Karbala?"

He was rubbing salt in my wounds. "You have already said it all," I replied.

"What did I say?"

"Karbala, pain, and grief."

A grave expression appeared on Jamil's crying face. Like a philosopher, he said that I was an animal that understands only minutiae, that I flew off into a mental vacuum looking for something solid. He said that I hung onto memories, Sabriyah, and the Holy Temple, and that I clung to my religion and prayers.

Is all this merely a pretense, Khaduri? Is it true what Jamil claims, that I indulge myself in illusions and adhere to them?

I said to him, "Don't judge someone before you have walked in his shoes for a mile."

Now he looked gloomy. "What an animal you are," he replied. "It's better if you don't open your mouth. Do you know what I'm talking about?"

Khaduri, for God's sake, what do you say to such a person? Words were packed in my head in layers, like your tobacco leaves, Khaduri. I had one thousand answers on the tip of my tongue, sharp and cutting. They bent my back and made me offend Sabriyah. Who would silence me and render me speechless?

I yelled at Jamil, "Look, had you or your relatives been hurt in the Farhûd, then you would have known what my life is all about."

Khaduri, do you know what he answered me? I tell you, this Jamil made a fool of me and surely drove me out of my mind. He laughed. The sound of his laughter was trembling and challenging, sharp, and stern. The voice would amaze you, but stranger than that was his determination, leaving you with no doubts.

"May God curse you, Jamil. If indeed they kill me and kill those you call my relatives, they'll be doing me a favor."

What would you do to such a person? Do you drop dung on him to make him repent? And how do you answer a person who slaps your face hard, numbs your conscious mind, and throws your senses into a world without reason or logic? I was sure I had silenced him, but he came and silenced me with his deadly slap. Khaduri, how come it didn't occur to me that Jamil Rabi is the only really crazy person in this world, when he admitted that I, Naji el-Jundi, the world and I, are crazy? My roommate is insane!

Wasn't I right, Khaduri? Why are you wringing your hands, Khaduri? Was it wrong to say that Jamil Rabi was insane? Did I utter heresy? Khaduri, I'm talking to you! Where is Khaduri? Why is he sick of listening all of a sudden? Khaduri moved uncomfortably, for he was attracted by something in the direction of our alley. The black shadow of a woman wearing an 'abayah and a veil swayed back and forth as she walked toward our alley. The woman with the black 'abayah approached slowly, and Khaduri seemed embarrassed. Suddenly he forgot me, and the full dish of beans was cold and forgotten too. The sting inside me branched out into my belly, heart, mind, and intestines. The woman and Khaduri! Why should I care? Get with it and go to the baker, then come back and eat the plate of beans.

"Cotton threads! Sewing machine threads! Bobby pins! Needles! Pins! Bleach! Blue dyes! Matches!"

5—Jamil Rabi

I have doubts about all things save my love for children, Marrudi and Nihad, as well as for Selman Hashwah. I know that Selman is mad at me, but I love him, and because of him I almost make an exception to the rule and hate this other boy, this nagel, as Ya'qub, 'Amam's son, calls him. He was given the name 'Aibah, *shame*, hinting to his being a bastard, and Ya'qub is taking care of 'Aibah and his mother,

Gerjiyi Nati, these days, announcing that he had put his finger on her unknown past.

Ya'qub says, "Gerjiyi Nati was in Bombay dancing with casta-nets. She was one of three sisters. All of them were engaged in shame-ful activities and prostitution. Their mother took them to India when they were young, then she led them to the stage and maybe also pro-cured men for them. Gerjiyi pretended as if nothing had happened and told lies. She said she was married legally; her husband died on the ship and was thrown into the sea for the sharks to feast on. Let her tell it to my ass, it may believe her!"

'Amam's son says, "How pitiful is man! He not only deceives himself but also tries to deceive the entire world." Do you know that sometimes Ya'qub gets close to the truth? It is the truth that poor Gerjiyi dared to hide about her past. It's possible that truths don't give in to the light-headedness of Nati's daughter. She doesn't know that the world is small and that whatever happens in India quickly becomes gossip for Baghdadis."

Truth will win out even if powerful rulers string barbed wire along the borders of their countries. The voice of truth will come to light by Stalin, the man with the thick moustache and the decisive tone in his voice. Like half of Baghdad's children, the Indian children are lean skeletons, plagued by hunger, disease, nakedness, ignorance, and death. I'm a child, the product of one-tenth impoverishment and nine-tenths darkness. Poverty, ignorance, my relatives, and the voice of Yusif Wahbi in *Les Miserables* ring and vibrate, and here is Selman Hashwah worshipping God and keeping 'Aibah away from boredom. Is there anything better than this good time? Still, people would say, "Selman the one-eyed man, Selman the man with one eye, Selman whose eye has been nibbled away by a mouse, eaten by a dog." Tomorrow, when he loses the sight in his other eye, 'Aibah will lead him to a pit of shit and toss him there. Then 'Aibah will gather the people around him. I say to Ya'qub, 'Amam's son, "Bravo, well done!" Maybe the best thing Ya'qub has done in his life so far was to remove 'Aibah from this house. But what next? "I'll teach him a trade and make a man of him," Ya'qub said.

Ya'qub continued to boast, so why don't you tell it to your ass too, Ya'qub? Don't you know that it's harder to straighten a dog's tail than to destroy one-quarter of the world with three American atom bombs? Maybe this will occur when Naji el-Jundi sobers up, or when the world improves, or when my relatives become prosperous, or maybe when Selman Hashwah matures. Selman Hashwah chose to be an object of amusement for 'Aibah, for Sabriyah, 'Abdush's daughter, all for illusions.

My parents are animals with a human look, and Naji el-Jundi's condition deteriorates day after day. His hand and tongue are full of tons of rubbish and jabbering. Because of him I frequented all the cafés in Baghdad, one by one, from Ibn Shayi's and Abu Rubain's to Sayyid 'Alwan's. I saw Naji el-Jundi walking in front of me; Sha'ul's Café was behind me. He arrived at Hamadah's before I did. Naji was also in Majid's Café. At last I dragged my feet, went only a short distance, and said to myself, "Run away, flee!" Then I went to the Baladiyah Café and saw the Kallachiyah red-light district in front of me and found Naji el-Jundi sitting next to me.

The mullah in charge of the music in the café was enraged and driven crazy by Naji el-Jundi. He took off his turban and tossed it on the floor yelling, "Well, what do you know? I threw my turban off and sinned. Are you the only one in the café? Does nothing exist for you except you and the songs of 'Abd el-Wahab? Let others listen to this cursed record or that damn record! Nothing exists save 'Abd el-Wahab and again 'Abd el-Wahab." And the fellows met in Sha'ul's Café coming straight from Farabi Café carrying all kinds of musical instruments.

I was sitting in the Baladiyah Café where dog fleas bit me and drank my dark blood until they became intoxicated. While I stood between the ridiculous jabbering of my confused mind and that of Naji el-Jundi, I heard a roaring in my ears as strong as an entire orchestra. The discord was not only in the whistle of Abu Ghalib, the night guard, but also in all the sounds I heard coming from all directions. I saw the other extreme contradictions crowded around me like the people in the Baladiyah Café. I wonder what people do with their opposites. I dispersed the hukkah cloud of smoke from before my eyes and then absorbed the light and dared to peer into it. It seemed to me that the guests in the café were ghosts, picking their noses. Did the black and white of my eyes betray me? Possibly, yet despite this I was sure of one thing, that however my sight may have misled me, the filthy actions of humanity would remain in one's nose, stuffing it with dry mucus that would soon turn sticky. By picking your nose, our most serious problems are taken care of. What a treasure you can find inside your nose!

But I poke into another thing. My head was looking for relief from my life, a rescue from Naji el-Jundi and from the tale about his dog. Naji's dog is a different story, or maybe it's not so different.

"I know the tale. I swear by Allah, I know it. You told it to me a million times. Lower your voice and listen to 'Abd el-Wahab's record."

Naji laughed like a woman, and cacophonous voices followed each other. This world is full of such voices and movement—the discord of intellectuals.

"I wish you bad luck, Jamil. Look—I want to give you good Egyptian-style pleasure."

I'm up to here with Sha'ul el-Jundi, or rather with Naji 'Abd el-Wahab, and I'm fed up with those who are called "my relatives."

"Look Sha'ul, look Naji! You enraged the mullah, made him throw his turban on the floor, and in the end he pleased you and played 'Abd el-Wahab's records for you, so shut up and listen to 'Abd el-Wahab," I said. On top of it, Naji laughed louder than any terrible discord of voices coming out in chunks, like the stools of someone who suffers from constipation.

"Now I'm in a good mood, and when I'm in a good mood I like to talk."

This Naji el-Jundi never stops talking, which means he's having fun continuously. Does having fun absorb his tragedy? Naji, Sha'ul— Oh Jundi! Repeat it again and again, and swallow the senseless folly of your existence, a twin to my own. I have no free time for all the fellows. I mull over my chronic disease, akin to your breathing. You never get nauseated telling the dog's tale. You should go to the mental hospital and put on chains and handcuffs like the fetters of my life. I ran away from your illusion and took refuge in the animalistic, lustful ghosts that gave birth to me and brought me into the world against my will. My relatives tossed me into mire full of the pus of ignorance, into large lakes of poverty, into leaking and stinking basements of barbarism. All this was not evil enough, and they never stopped until they blinded my eye.

Naji el-Jundi waves the dog's tail around. His dog, the witness to his idiocy and the proof of his mental instability, was, precisely, evidence of his sanity, just like the proof of the handkerchief displayed after the wedding night. I ran away from him and myself to a "fresh" illusion.

I visited my relatives today, those who had made me, those who created my tragedy, those who tortured me and blinded my eye. What should I do with my opposites? My dear! I have become blinder, and Naji el-Jundi went on and on laughing, ha-ha-ha, and his tale is becoming as stinky as a toilet. When my ears hear the word *toilet*, it clashes with a similar one in my head. Ordinary people who took off their shoes and lifted their garments to cross the stinking and muddy water carried me to my relatives. My eyes were useless. I vomited on a piece of rusty tin. The foam of my insanity surfaced on the water just as vendors' cries came from a forest crowded with devouring animals of prey.

"Sha'ul! I beg you to leave me alone. My head is splitting with pain." In vain! I continued to run away from Naji and smelled the fragrance of the damask roses mixed with the stink of rotten fish and the pungent smell of spoiled vegetables. These opposites! Naji el-Jundi's dog now falls into the toilet, and I row in a wide roomy toilet as big as Lake Habaniyah. Now I am visiting my opposites, those who made me. The dream illusion! My mother ties her eternal black headband. She has a blue tattoo on her jaw and another one on her cheek. I still remember her, and when she embraces me I see her almost clearly. She is no different from a gypsy at all.

My mother said to me, "Are you here, 'aini?" Tears appeared in her eyes. They were continuously felt, and wet. She continued, "My heart has gone out to you. All the time I ask myself, "What does he have to eat, to drink? What's he doing?" Does a person completely forget his family like this? If you came once a week or once a month, your mother wouldn't worry. Right?"

Enough! My voice will become suffocated and stop in my throat, and this woman, my mother, will talk and talk and moan. She doesn't know how to utter a single word without mourning. In essence, she's a moaning woman by nature. She's probably lamenting me right now without knowing it. Should I point it out? What does she want me to do? Does she want to turn our house into a real mourning place? She begged me to listen to her.

No, go away! I found something filthier than your jabbering, somebody who'll keep me away from you, from your shadow, from your echoes. The voice of my barbarian father is still humming in my head exactly like the noise of the 'Abakhanah power plant. It differs from those echoes in that his voice is closer to me than my own. I was frightened, certainly so. Who taught my parents to speak like this? My father is a criminal and a son of a criminal! They will soon realize that these animal-like sounds are older than the primitive languages and that they're unpolished. A continuous discord stirs nausea and provokes anger, even among animals of good taste. You hear them. Their every letter is emphatic and doubled, and the point of articulation of the letters is distorted. Sha'ul's throat is full, and his mouth fills with air when he talks. The words sound like bass in the musical range and at the same time shrilling and mocking. When you hear them you hear the groan of an ox sounding like the bark of a dog. Help! They are piercing my ears and drilling a hole in my head. The noise is louder again.

"Sha'ul, why did you start to kick out of the blue?" Jamil asked Naji/Sha'ul.

Naji continued to kick the ground with his feet. "A wasp stung me under my eye."

I heard the buzzing of the wasp. I also heard Naji el-Jundi telling the tale about his dog while he continued to kick. My mother, the moaning woman, shed tears and said, "Let me dish up food for you;

I beg you to have a bite! I don't know what you eat and drink there."
Fine, okay! Once a year I take pity on this woman and have mercy
on myself. After all, I am a poor fellow too. If I refuse she'll start to
cry and moan.

"Do me a favor, Sha'ul, don't talk! Weren't you stung by a wasp?"
Jamil asked Sha'ul.

My soul squirmed. I thought seriously about the dish of soup and
rice. My soul fluttered around. My family was on one side and Naji
el-Jundi on the other.

"Say, is the sting hurting you?" I asked.

He laughed like a woman, ha-ha-ha, and disguised the pain.
"Don't worry. So what if it hurts? I don't give a shit. I want you to
have a good time. I want to finish the tale," Naji replied.

He would tell me his stories for many hours, giving me headaches,
painful days, and years of nausea. The world could be exhausted but
not his stories. I lost my appetite when I looked at the dish. The picture of an inexcusable crime committed by my relatives floated on
the soup. In its rice there were kernels of life energy thrown at me.
With poverty my relatives made me, by force they starved me, humiliated my soul, and slipped me into the folds of this eternal darkness.

"Get up and go treat your sting in case it's poisonous. You might
die now, and I'll be accused of your death," said Jamil to Sha'ul.

Things and their opposites never disappear. I talk nonsense . . .
I, Naji el-Jundi, and my relatives . . . my jabbering . . . He endures
the wasp's sting, ignores it, and continues to prattle. I am the biggest
contradiction, can't stand what's around me, above and under me—
not even myself, Naji insisted.

"I must finish the story. To hell with it! So what if I die? You only
listen to the story and let me die afterward. The important thing is
that you enjoy yourself," said Naji el-Jundi to Jamil, Rabi's son.

To enjoy myself, yes indeed. I turned the dish of soup and rice
upside down and ran away. I also ran away to avoid Naji el-Jundi,
whose swollen blue face resembled a ripe plum. He went on and on
to finish the tale about his dog—I know him. Of course, he didn't
realize that I had already left. He continued to talk to the walls of

Baladiyah Café or to the walls of the nearby whorehouse and said, "To hell with the pain of the wasp's sting!"

Oh what a relief! I don't believe it; I actually got rid of my filthy relatives and Naji el-Jundi's blabbering.

6—'Aziz Ghawi

I got two days leave from the orphanage.

The bey came, the pasha's son. The big boss came, the black bald bull, the short and squat. He appeared like the winter sun, which shines for a while but then is covered by a mass of dark, gloomy clouds. He came with a wallet crammed with dinars. Let his wife, Farhah Ghawi, rejoice, and let Sa'idah, buried in her room, become (without her knowledge) a daughter of a notable person, enjoy warm kisses, and "How are you my dear daughter?" My father, the bull, was unable to carry his daughter, the mule, so he retreated and asked with difficulty his young daughter, "How are you, dear Bannutah?" He could hardly lift her to his chest. Bannutah had become as tall as he, and Latifah even taller than he was himself. He had to stand on a bench so that his kiss would fall on Latifah's forehead instead of her mouth.

I'm the man of the house, the eternal high school student, and here the unrestrained ugly joke was coming when my father said to me cheerfully, unable to suppress his strangled voice that resembled the hooting of an owl, "My goodness! You have grown up to be a man."

He didn't notice that I had shaved my moustache. A jug of wine danced in his belly, and so he was light-headed and began to laugh drunkenly.

What kind of talk may take place in a room where two men converse at night? In the absence of the old man of the family, I, the young man of the family on the second floor, am lonely and disappointed and go through the world's women one by one at random. The faces change accordingly, but on the same pillow.

The bed and their legs are my coverlet. I would wrap their legs between mine and rub. I would vomit down below, this mixed, sticky liquid. I would feel disgusted with myself and vomit continuously like a drunkard. But the nausea would remain.

What do I say to the old man, my father, and what does he say to me? Why don't you embrace Farhah Ghawi and sleep with her? This is an opportunity. She's yours and I long for both of you. Have you grown old? Have you become impotent? Has your desire really died out? He would say, "And what about your sisters—each of them is a mule, three mules crammed in one room."

Then I would say, "They should be educated, now that they're ripe for marriage. On their wedding night, do you want them to sit in front of their husbands like pieces of wood?"

Then, he would spit out his drunken drowsy laughter, which means either he's really a bull, or he doesn't care, doesn't give a damn. He came at night out of the blue. The lights were turned off save the light in the room of the carefree Jamil Rabi and Selman Hashwah.

I've enough to worry about, and I am not concerned about the man of this house. I'm preoccupied with my own problems, with my chronic disappointment with women, with 'Abdallah Ghawi and his wife Farhah, my uncle, "the horse," in Battawin, the uncle "horse" in Karradah, and the cousin, "the colt," the son of the horse whom I see only in his inn in Bab el-Sharqi. Then, despite this my head turns to the flickering sign, 'Abd el-Nabi's Inn, which flashes over the street of pleasure and sin. Yusif 'Abd el-Nabi is the cousin of 'Aziz Ghawi, the stud and son of a stallion.

At night, my father, the black bull, the barrel, surprises me.

"What are you doing, 'Aziz? You grew up to be a man. You need a wife!" I knew that before he did. I knew that, but Farhah Ghawi still referred to me as a child who wet his bed and in his diaper. Yes, sir! Aren't I just a senior in high school? Farhah Ghawi, the deceiving yellow snake, the poor deceived woman, is still attractive. Why don't you go to her, 'Abdallah, and embrace her and sleep with her?

My father surprised me once more. "You know, despite my old age, I still indulge in adventures in Mahmudiyah. You think I'm like you, passive and lazy, a senior in high school?"

My thoughts were confused. What should I think about and what should surprise me? How do I deny the accusation against me? My father continued to surprise me. "Go on and have a good time and be carefree. Before I married your mother, I drove the girls crazy and I had a hundred women. And when I was engaged to your mother I didn't have the patience to wait, and I wanted to have sex right away. Your mother had a pink complexion and rosy cheeks. To this day her beauty and the image of her rosy face surges forth at me."

Why don't you go and sleep with her while the other one, Her Majesty Lady Sa'idah, hides her freshness and sweetness behind a veil? Only yesterday she had unkempt hair, and now she is grown up and beautiful, and her face drips the nectar of red flowers. Had my sister Sa'idah taken care of herself, her beauty would have surpassed by far Sabriyah's, but what's the use? She is steeped in shyness in a grave-like sewing hall, from which she certainly won't be resurrected. I asked myself if I also desired my sister Sa'idah in the heat of my sexual lust. I said to my father, who sometimes resembled a Chinese sage and more often was a miserable man boasting of his shortcomings and bragging about his defects, "Okay, what then?"

He said to me in a semidisappointed manner, not like his son's complete disappointment, "Your mother wouldn't consent to have sex with me. She has been rude and loud since childhood and used to throw wild tantrums. I was spending the night at their house—I mean my uncle's house—and my uncle woke up because of her yelling. What a noise! She's been like this for a long time. Your grandfather came running and caught me in her room. Don't ask how embarrassed I was. I felt as if the Earth had swallowed me up in shame. He completely lost his temper and insisted that I step in his house only if I marry Farhah first."

Stupid and fat father! So you did all this. What a sneaky serpent hiding in the grass! You say to your son, "If I were in your shoes . . ."

May the curse be on you and on Farhah Ghawi. Both of you! I'm the tug-of-war rope between you. Each one of you pulls me to his side, and then throws me to the other. She takes me up and you bring me down. She lifts me to the level of dignified people, and you lower me to the abyss of indignity and failure, to the level of animals. Illusion and reality! My great thirst, my defeat . . . "If I were in your shoes, I would do this and that." The senior year of high school is my eternal prison. It's my disaster. I'm a child that showed signs of great ingenuity, but despite this, the child must now finish the senior year. May a curse be upon you, the senior year, and me! I shaved my moustache. But despite Farhah and me—a man in his twenty-fourth year—my father, the barrel, the big male buffalo says, "My goodness! You're grown into a man. You need a wife now."

What oath should I take to let you know that I'm aware of all this? By what do I have to swear that I knew all this before you did? Do you enjoy torturing me? Do you come here once a year to stab me with your deadly jabs so that my feelings of being orphaned deepen? Knock it off! Leave me alone with my troubles.

And the one with the rosy cheeks says, "My son will leave school sooner or later. There is no rush. He's still a young boy. Sooner or later he'll earn his high school diploma and go on to college." Let me take a break and get freed from this mouse trap. The one who doesn't give a shit and leaves the world behind his ass says, "My goodness! You've grown up to be a man; you need a wife. You're passive and lazy."

Well, you know and I know and the world knows that you stick your money in the box, lock it up, and keep me from enjoying it. That money doesn't know that I'm pretending to be a teacher while I'm only a senior in high school. All the women in the world lie on my bed. I'll no longer encounter disappointments. I ask, "How?" I utter the word "how" into the air. It clashes against my dead head and comes back as dust. How don't you know? Or rather who knows? There won't be any more disappointments and stinginess after today. I won't deprive myself of women. I'll break those who mock me, snatch the money from my uncle, the horse, and from my father, the blind bull. I'll get women by frequenting the whorehouse. Yes, I mean it—the whorehouse. Women are made of flesh and blood. In the whorehouse, women aren't a mattress, a blanket and a pillow . . . Oh, in the whorehouse!

Three

1—Ya'qub, 'Amam's Son

Even if this house were a grave and the dawn a resurrection, Ya'qub, 'Amam's son, would be the first tenant to wake up. While the other tenants were still asleep, he woke up and put on the tefillin, phylacteries. From Sunday until Friday he used to perform the morning prayer in the house, carry his basket and leave for the market. The morning shopping would last about an hour, and he would fill his empty basket with fruits, vegetables, meat, and yogurt, or *geimar*, a thick, curdled cream. There was an abundance of everything and plenty of every kind of food, as much as in Damascus and Aleppo.

Ya'qub walked with a gratified sense of purpose, and the new morning flooded him with refreshing optimism that would stick with him all day long. When he left the house, the alley looked like the bottom of a vessel dripping a few drops of water. There were only a few pedestrians in each alley, but when he came back, the drops became pouring rain, as if spilling from a waterskin.

Joudi al-Qawarchi was among those who were hit by the rain. Ya'qub saw him on his journey—an aimless journey of someone who doesn't know whether he is alive or even existing. Ya'qub let Joudi go on his way and asked himself why Joudi was created. After walking a few steps, he realized that the Creator did not create anything in vain and that maybe He created Joudi to amuse the children. These neighborhood children were special, since want and deprivation molded them. They had no fun, no movies, and no happiness. Their only

51

amusement was Joudi. It was a childish pleasure to track him down and throw stones and garbage at him.

Wondering, Ya'qub began an apprehensive search for the source of the children's endless passion and attraction to Joudi, the mad child. Why would an innocent and naive child get a thrill out of hurting a weaker human being? It was as difficult for Ya'qub to discover this "why" as it was for Jamil Rabi and the one-eyed Selman Hashwah to grasp details.

Jamil was sleeping deeply when Ya'qub made this comparison, soaring within weary, cloudy dreams, following a tiresome night at a wedding party playing the qanun. He hated parties, although they were the source of his livelihood. These parties made him confront his misery face-to-face and showed that an oblivious public looked upon musicians as nuisances who answered endless requests to play and sing. These requests were indeed exorbitant, ugly, and exhausting, and stemmed from the idea that musicians were just tools of entertainment. The greatest disaster was when the musicians were blind. Jamil would come back from every party worn out, as one buried in a grave dug by his own discontent. Then he had weary dreams, probably the result of self-inflicted curses, nightmares in whose arms he threw himself and in which he denied Joudi's existence and that of all humanity. Living in the small folds of his trivial selfishness, the source of all his stupid chronic diseases, he forgot the ugly monstrous world and persisted in asking, "Why do I exist?"

By the time Ya'qub returned from shopping, 'Amam was already up, busy preparing his hot lunch to take to work. Ya'qub was careful not to make noise that would disturb his sleepy roommate. Like a thief breaking into a house, he took off his phylacteries cautiously and wrapped them while his eyes were fixed on Sabriyah's jamkhanah located on the other side of the court. Go on and raise the curtains! If she just would raise them, he could start his day seeing her radiant face. But I'm kidding myself, thought Ya'qub. I know that Sabriyah never raises the curtains before I leave. It's impossible for her to get up before the sun enters the area facing the courtyard of the house. At this time of year, the sun usually shone there only between ten and eleven o'clock. But the light of the sun was now falling on the face of 'Aziz Ghawi, who brushed the light away—whack, whack, whack, as he did with flies—and tossed on his bed. The light, however, didn't leave his face, and so he cursed the sun, hiding his face under the blanket. He was half-asleep when he heard noises from a wheel running quickly under his room. 'Aziz's rage grew as the work began in his mother's sewing hall. Wicked Haman's daughter! he thought. Is work fleeing from you that you have to wake up in twilight as if you dreamed about it? Then he wrapped a certain woman between his legs. She was soft and agile, all flesh, and he embraced her all night, then fell asleep.

Ya'qub shouted from beneath the wooden-floored room, "Hey, 'Aibah, get up, it's already noon!" His voice boomed inside the takhtabosh and awaked a woman who immediately yelled back wearily as if she were afflicted by grief. "Your boss, Ya'qub is calling you. Hey, son of almanah, get up!" When she didn't hear an answer her voice grew even more shrill—"May God chop your head off! Get up and go to work, you're holding the man up."

'Aibah got up and rubbed his eyes with two hands, making wailing sounds. He wanted to complain, but the strong blow of a stubby hand landed on his head and silenced him instantly. He got up, opened the door automatically, and went ahead of his boss, Ya'qub, to the courtyard door. Ya'qub stopped yelling and said sternly, "Idiot! I want to make a man of you. Go wash your face and comb your hair. I'll wait for you, okay?" Ya'qub was pleased with himself. 'Aibah was washing his face and complaining after being deprived of his freedom, sleep, and childlike shenanigans.

Meanwhile, 'Aziz Ghawi slept, embracing the covers and a woman. Sabriyah was asleep too, but Jamil was sleeping uncomfortably. On the second floor, Marrudi woke up in his room separated by a wall from 'Aziz Ghawi's. Lulu watched him grumbling while opening his eyes. She stood in thought, her cheek on her hand, as silent and motionless as a statue.

Marrudi's poor father drowned in the Tigris, Lulu recalled. He was the best swimmer in Baghdad, but the whirlpool betrayed him and sucked him down like a bubble. Marrudi would be the successor to his unfortunate father. As soon as Marrudi woke up, she mumbled an invocation, "Inshallah, God willing, you wake up in good health." She walked toward him and kissed him all over as if she were kissing the tombs of the prophet Ezekiel and Ezra the Scribe.

In his rooms on the first floor at the end of the courtyard, Fayiq the Barber finished combing his hair in front of the mirror. Then he creamed his hair and perfumed his face with a large quantity of strong, sweet cologne, saying to his wife, Na'imah, "I'm going to work. What are you doing today?" She answered cautiously, "What do I have to do?" Then she suddenly added, "Why are you asking, Abu Nihad?"

"Nothing," he replied, a little embarrassed. "I was only wondering whether you were going for a visit, a walk, buying a gift for so-and-so, or bringing a porter to move our bed to Battawin, for instance. Just wondering."

She disliked his tone of voice because she detected in it a hint of sarcasm. "Fayiq, what is it? Why are you holding me to a strict account? What if I give gifts. What's wrong with that?"

"Nothing. I wondered if you needed some money."

She was appeased and began to fiddle with his combed hair. "By God, Abu Nihad, you are *ibin halal*, a nice man. Give me a few dinars, because I may really need some. It's better this way than taking the trouble to come to your shop in Haydar Khanah."

At around ten o'clock everyone in the house except Sabriyah was up. Na'imah was readying herself to visit her neighbor Aminah, Shukur's daughter. How poor she was—every one of her brothers had already left for his job, and she was alone at home staring at the walls. Na'imah passed Sabriyah's jamkhanah and found the curtains still drawn. She nodded her head cynically. Sabriyah was still sleeping. Why not? Newlyweds like to sleep until noon. Time, however, runs and snatches away the freshness of things. It passes while things are changing, and no bride remains a newlywed except this Sabriyah. It's true that for a carefree person, life is a wedding, Na'imah thought.

Upstairs, 'Aziz Ghawi woke up swearing while Jamil Rabi cursed from downstairs. Jamil's creased face looked smaller and shrunken from drinking and sleeplessness. Jamil blinked his half-opened eyes, pressed the stem of his pocket watch causing its lid to pop open, and groped the watch's hands with his fingers. It was six minutes past ten. 'Aziz's problem remained unresolved. He stared at the wall with his large cow eyes and said to himself, "I'll solve my problem. I have to find a way out."

Lulu, whose room was adjacent to 'Aziz Ghawi's, had finished washing and feeding Marrudi. She continued to fix her eyes on him, without moving. She had kept all his clothes since he was a baby. She even cherished the ribbon she used to tie his ponytail before he had his hair cut for the first time in the Kefil, where the prophet Ezekiel was buried. She kept those delicate hair trimmings in a silk cloth bundle in the decorated chest. She watched Marrudi's movements as if she were watching a rare and exciting natural phenomenon. "It will be a big happy day when your pubic hair grows. I promise to cook a huge pot of rice and lentils, as big as the washing tub, and I'll pass it out to the residents of the alley," she said.

Out of despair, Farhah Ghawi thought of many men's faces and said to herself, "It'll be a feast day when Sa'idah gets married." Then faces of men flashed in her imagination and the face of Ya'qub stood out. At the same time Sabriyah saw through the glass of her jamkhanah that Ya'qub's mother, 'Amam, was busy washing the courtyard. Farhah walked in the courtyard with a composure unshakeable even by the Messiah.

Na'imah, Fayiq's wife, drank tea with Aminah, Shukur's daughter, while continuously looking into the tanned face of the young girl. Aminah had the delicate and mild expression of a pampered child among three brothers, each of them showing an air of dignity, shaking the ground when he walked. To her three brothers she was a queen surrounded by her many courtiers. And why didn't she get married? Na'imah asked herself, wondering.

The fate of Aminah was in her brothers' hands, but who would dare mention it to them? Her thoughts returned to the other girl, to

Sa'idah Ghawi. By God, Ya'qub is a good guy, and the two suit each other. Should I address the matter to 'Amam? Should I talk about it? I'll certainly consult Fayiq when he comes home tonight, Na'imah thought.

Ya'qub sat in his shop facing the anvil, preoccupied with his work and many other things, as if he had a hangover. Irritated, he yelled at 'Aibah, "Hey you, 'Aibah, give me the glue. Bring the hammer, 'Aibah, the short nails! Give me the awl to cut the leather, 'Aibah! Come and watch how I pull the shoe over the wooden last, 'Aibah!"

He opened the drawer and saw a heap of different bills. He was pleased and spoke without having 'Aibah hear him. "What should I do with all this money?" Ya'qub said to himself. I really tear into my work. I'm bent over it like a horse over a trough. I should feel relieved, take a breath. For whom is all this toil? For my partner Nessim, so that he can steal all my profits? May he drop dead! To hell with work."

2—Selman Hashwah

Husayn died in Karbala with the waterskin next to him. Ho, Husayn! Ho, Zakariyah! Ho, Husayn! Ho, Zakariyah! Things occurred to me, unearthed from the everlasting grave, biting, hurting, and burning like a skin disease that itches, spreads, and causes pain. Dizziness follows and these things disappear and I forget myself. I forget the most priceless thing I have. Even Sabriyah is wrapped up in a fleeting and depressing forgetfulness floating on a noisy sea of my memory—furious, mad, and overpowering my mind for as long as Noah's flood.

With contagious hatred in my tone of voice and sparks shooting from my eyes, the fanatic Shi'i said to me, "Criminals! You killed the prophets!" But I am a Jew, afraid of my own shadow, never stepped on an ant deliberately.

"Sir! I didn't do anything." My color turned pale again on that black day, and I trembled like the fronds of a palm tree. I felt as if I were pushed into the past, reliving Husayn's experience of martyrdom.

Sabriyah asked me with concern and passion, "What's the matter with you, Selman? Are you sick? Why is your face like a dead man? Go to the doctor!" Jamil ridiculed me, shoved his ten fingers into my face and cursed me. Sabriyah was ready to leave, and when she said she would run away there was tension on her sweet face. I was paralyzed. My feet were sinking in the mud of memory, reaching my knees in a collapsing school building. The time was late morning and the season was spring. The heat was like death, and Karbala was sitting on a volcano whose heat increased with the rising fervor.

Sabriyah left her room when the Muslim yelled at me, "You're a bastard! Are you calling me a liar and accusing me of denying God's word?"

Suddenly, courageous words came to me from an unknown source. "I'm telling you, by the name of Allah, I never killed anyone. It's as true that you didn't kill Husayn, that I didn't kill Zakariyah." That is what I told him. Immediately, he drew his pistol and I felt I was dying for the third time on this cursed anniversary day of Karbala.

"Buttons! Blue dyes! Sewing machine threads!"

I stopped at Khaduri's place and begged of him, "*Abdalak* Khaduri, help me! I don't know what to do? I can't forget that event. Many years have passed and it is still in my mind. Sabriyah occupies my mind and so does this memory. The disaster was so grave that even Sabriyah is lost in it."

Agony and grief! Agony and grief all over Karbala. It was May 1941, Thursday. The Nazis were like worms cropping up in all places. I put my head in the mouth of a hungry lion. My father—may he rest in peace—asked me, "Are you crazy? You see the atmosphere is tense and you want to go to Karbala? Stay where you are, be quiet, and wait and see."

Rashid 'Ali's coup, the Nazis, the war against the British . . . Thursday, the first of May, and the theatrical troupe . . . I was the oud player. I left for the party in Karbala with Muslim, Jewish, and Christian singers, a violinist, and a qanun player. The singer 'Ali Dabbu was with us.

My gosh, Khaduri, I never imagined what happened on Thursday—a thousand swords, my head, and a party in Karbala, the city of agony and grief.

So what? I was not the only one. I was with Jews, Basrawis, Baghdadis, Muslim friends, and my musician friends.

Going for the first time to Karbala was the temptation of the devil. Sabriyah was suffering, and a mysterious sadness lurked under the folds of her eyes like deadly poisoned arrows. She was running away, suffering and running away. I couldn't detach myself from Thursday and Friday, in the nightmare of the first and the second days of May 1941. Chaos prevailed. Night, school, café, Friday, girls, the angel of death, death after death, and thousands of deaths happened in those two days of the Farhûd. The members of the group dissolved and were scattered. No one cared about them. I was in the café. That was on the second of May. The sun was hot as hell, and my throat was dry as a drought.

"Please, give me a little water."

The busboy in the café heard me, stared at me with blazing eyes, and walked away.

"For the love of God, a little water!" It was as if I had spoken heresy. I gasped, begged for water. Water, water, a little water! Husayn had died in Karbala. The busboy cast sharp looks at me that resembled arrows, but what a difference between his arrows and the arrows coming from Sabriyah's eyes! Husayn had been thirsty with a waterskin next to him, and this one aimed his pistol at me. The third death approached and I recited, "Hear, Oh Israel, God is one." For the third time, God sent me an angel in the shape of a young Muslim.

"I'm telling you, let go of the pistol! Let go, otherwise either your blood or my blood will be shed." One thousand deaths. Then the gates of the other world opened, and an angel appeared as a young Muslim. One thousand angels!

"Give me a cigarette, Khaduri, may God have compassion for your dead," Selman said.

Jamil's voice was haughty to tell Selman, "You should thank the Communists. If not for them, you would have become bones eaten by worms by now."

Tell me please, Khaduri! Are only the Communists good people and only the Nazis bad people? Not all people are the same. Are all your fingers the same? Are they? At the last moment one thousand Muslim angels appeared. Was it possible that God made all the Communists show up when I was to die? I was dying of thirst. Surely, this busboy was one of their offspring, not helping the thirsty with a sip of water . . . water . . . water!

Another angel was ready. Another young Muslim, unknown to the café, yelled at the busboy, "Look, this man is thirsty! Don't you hear? Bring him a little water before he dies in this heat." You see there are many kindhearted people, those nursed on pure milk.

The busboy complained, "If he drinks the water bowl will be impure."

The kindhearted person shouted at the busboy, "Wash it, what do you have the *kirr* basin for?"

I drank water, restored my soul, and escaped another death. Abdalak Khaduri! What else should I tell you? Does this story have an end? Let's go back to the beginning of the story. It was Thursday the first of May at noon, the musical group and the theatrical troupe left in a train headed southward toward Karbala, to agony and grief. The Nazis and Rashid 'Ali had declared war against the British.

"Where are you, Khaduri, and why all of a sudden do you turn your back on me? Did I annoy you? Does a story like this annoy you? It turns out you're annoyed by this story that should be recorded in history, but you don't listen; you're withdrawing from me little by little, turning your face and grumbling. All this is a sudden pain. No, you're not the same, Khaduri. You're undoubtedly hiding a secret, so is the black ghost woman. Again the mysterious woman is approaching. The black ghost is drawing towards you from the nearby alley. You're confused and don't know what to do when you see any woman. The sight bites you like a snake, and your embarrassment grows, and so do the puzzles. Who are you hiding behind the 'abayah and veil? Why does Khaduri forsake the world when he sees you? Why should I care? To hell with it all! Good-bye, Khaduri, I'll tell you the rest of the story another time."

"Blue dyes! Buttons! Matches! Karbala! One thousand deaths! Sabriyah! Bobby pins! Cotton threads! Sewing machine threads! The black ghost! Jerusalem! Farhûd! Sabriyah! Agony! No!"

3—Ya'qub, 'Amam's Son

I cut out the leather, cut and sew, line it up and pull it over the wooden last, prepare the sole and the heel, glue it, and nail it. I use the small boxlike stool, the anvil, the file, and the pliers while yelling for 'Aibah, "Give it to me, 'Aibah—take it, 'Aibah." All the while my partner scoops up the profits.

Shame is like a drop that splashes into nothing when it falls. I would cut the leather with the awl, and he would steal from the shop in my absence. When the cat is away the mice will play. I cut the stiff leather and the awl gets blunt, but the leather stays unscratched, grows in stiffness, and turns into a dry and shrunken sole.

My work grew and flourished, and orders from women increased. The demand reduced the quality of my workmanship, and so the shoes I had sewn soon tore in many places and needed to be patched. I said to Nessim, whose father never fasted or prayed, "I wish your legs were broken to keep you sitting in the shop a bit. Do you expect to profit without effort?" Yes, why not? You have me blindfolded like a donkey tied to a millstone, then you come to scoop up the money and leave. To hell with Ya'qub and the whole world!

I was talking to the wall, to someone deaf and dumb, crying aloud inside a very deep well underground. This is not the real thing. I bury myself in this chicken coop, and when I die my coffin will be made of blue and red dinar bills. Until now I was like Jamil Rabi, blind in both eyes. But why don't I at least become like Selman Hashwah and see the world with one eye? I have kept silent mostly, but once I said to 'Aibah, "Hey, 'Aibah, I'm leaving. Keep your eyes peeled, watch the shop, and don't move from it. If Nessim comes, you know how to get rid of him. You're the only one who knows how to deal with him. You're a real smart bastard, a tough guy, aren't you? You are the fruit of Gerjiyi Nati's womb."

I went to my friends Sayyid 'Alwan, the café owner, and Jadu's sons, Hamadah, Hamid, and Majid, in order to slip out of my chicken coop and breathe freely. 'Alwan began to urge me, "Well, Ya'gub, what do you say? Are you going to manage my café accounts? I notice you've been avoiding me. If the reason is the pay, I assure you I'll give you more than you deserve."

The matter was not as 'Alwan imagined, for he knew I had plenty of money, and I, Ya'qub, 'Amam's son, will never accept money from such a good friend for recording a few figures in the café's registry. There's no formality between us, no difference between 'Alwan, Majid, Hamid, Hamadah, and me. 'Alwan knows that I work my fingers to the bone and that I've earned the right to enjoy myself and do nothing from sunset to sunrise. What's more, people who drink tea and coffee and smoke hukkah always frequent the café. Mahdi el-Tubar thinks he has the right not to pay as long as he carries a dagger in his belt. Those who carry daggers and pistols think that everything is managed by deceit, and my partner, the son of a whore, is no different from Mahdi el-Tubar, not even a small bit.

I said to 'Alwan, "Shame on you for talking about money, 'Alwan, but forgive me for not being able to undertake it." He continued to beg, and I was embarrassed. I couldn't shut all my doors against a persistent friend. I was forced to agree. What could I do? From now on I won't go home until 'Alwan's Café closes after midnight. From now on . . . ha-ha! Well, one week has passed during which I felt as if I were swimming in a jug of honey, and honey is a strange thing since it steals your time before you feel it, though it prolongs your life span. I'll take a break to smoke hukkah and drink many cups of tea and coffee topped with cream alongside games of backgammon—*zneef*, *shesh besh*, *mahbus*, or *gol-bahar*.

My friends have lured me to participate in the black honeypot of gaming and ignited in me a pleasure for gambling. With every draw of a domino or toss of the dice, you take an anxious breath and dare the game, "Come on, please." Then, when you show your cards, you see you're getting a new lease on life—one thousand lives in one game, hoping and longing. Your soul jumps up when you draw a card and throw the dice, ebb and flow. Then it's joy. Your heart leaps when you see the double-six you wished for right in front of you. It's nothing to lose a dirham or a dinar in a game that gives you a pleasure worth a thousand theater shows. I have a lot of money.

I embraced the thought that I would lose the dinar. Having fun is really worth one thousand dinars. So, I joyfully played and drowned myself in the black honey of gaming and gambling. A bag of money was tied to my forearm. Then, unexpectedly, I got the lucky number. I swept up the winnings and added them to my pile of money. I had won in games I had intended to lose and was disappointed. My winnings grew to ten dinars. What an overflow! I drowned in the flood of God's grace and feared the overflowing winning. What did I do? I played a lousy game but won. I decided to cheat deliberately, but to my surprise I drew a good hand of dominos, defeating my intentions. These worked together with luck and I won again, against my will. I collected more money and was furious. I raised my eyes and shouted, "God! This is enough. Enough already!"

I got a lot of weird stares and harsh words, and my friends placed me in the same class as Joudi, because a person who would refuse God's grace is considered either a heretic or insane. My friends would never know that bounty is a double-edged sword. You have indigestion if you eat double what you can, and God—may He be praised— has stuffed me. But being stuffed and being hungry is the same. Both lead to death, so I'm afraid of being loaded.

People say, "Is this a problem? Give your money to the needy! Throw it in the street! Stand at the beginning of the alley and give a dinar to every pedestrian and tell him, 'Spend it and pray for me.'"

No, no! To refuse to take something is not the same as to throw away what you already have in your pocket. I laughed, and Majid said, "Never mind, buddy. If you are not convinced of it, that's not a problem either. Don't throw your money away, but at least enjoy it for a while. Have fun! Have an easy time! Why do you let your mother live with tenants, or why don't you rent her a house near your sister Fawziyah in the Orfali neighborhood?"

I turned down his idea. "No, my friend, the room is big enough for her. I'm used to the neighborhood and the people there. How can I leave it and leave you? People might also say, 'He's already become high-and-mighty.'"

"Never mind. Forget what I said. The problem is simple. Get married! Marriage is like an open drain. On the one hand, you'll settle, on the other, your store of money will get smaller."

"No, 'aini. I won't get married, leave my mother, and get a headache from a wife."

'Alwan yelled, "We don't know what to do with you, Ya'gub. Do you mean everything or nothing?"

I reflected slowly. I got lost in my wandering blank looks, searching for a reasonable solution while my friends stared at me. I was sitting in my dear friend 'Alwan's café, surrounded by love, God's blessing and wealth, and reflecting on the world and my life. I'm not like Jamil Rabi, and I'd hate to be Selman Hashwah. I peered down like an eagle sighting its prey from on high. The orchards of my uncle's brother-in-law, Ghahmin, were dispersed throughout all Baghdad. The palms, the figs, and apple trees stood lofty in the vast paradise of Kard el-Khatun and el-Slaikh. Bistan el-Slaikh was a heavenly charm descended to Earth and planted there. Like trees, my thoughts were rooted in it. My imagination bloomed with green melodies, flowing with uncontrollable drunken noise. Imagine me and my friends in the open space of Bistan el-Slaikh! How splendid it would be to listen to the musical troupe of 'Abdallah Pataw, the man with the twisted jaw, and to Fawziyah Muhammad, singing in Kurdish and shaking her hips and belly. Enough! I said. I've had it! Like a horse's head bent over its trough, I'm swamped. From now on I'll have a very good time, even more pleasant than the fun in *One Thousand and One Nights*.

My decision was irreversible. I would rent Rahmin's orchard in Bistan el-Khass.

4—Aminah, Shukur's Daughter

I am with a sheep, five hens, and one cock.

Come in!—ti, ti, ti, ti! Here is food, five servant hens, and a cock is stepping all over them. You hoard the grain, cursed cock that you are. I have to watch you until you finish having sex with all five hens. Then, as your habit is, you stand up haughtily, ruffle your feathers, and draw up your comb and neck. Woe to the hen who dares approach the cock! Are you afraid of the cock? You're cowards, you downtrodden hens. Do you want to wear an 'abayah and make the cock less proud of himself and bring him down? Then the cock will become as meek as my sheep, and I'll feed it clover with my own hands when it is mild and stands still. No doubt, you hens hide yourselves under an 'abayah to subdue the cock.

The hidden and the seen! You, my brother Jabbar, think you're the only one in the world, don't you? I'll look at the mirror and see my naked and smooth body. Last night, Na'imah, Fayiq's wife, removed the hair from my legs, face, and eyebrows. The waxed thread she used resembled the string of a carder. It moved back and forth, plucking my hair like this cursed cock picking silently for grains. Na'imah removed my hair, and now I have a soft, smooth, and tender-skinned body. The seen and the hidden are twins. Na'imah is for Fayiq and I am for my beloved.

We have five hens and one mute sheep. I'm a playful, clever woman, but no one knows this, not even Jabbar. He's nice and tidy on the outside but stuffed with stench on the inside. A cock and a sheep, the hidden and the seen. You, Jabbar my brother, are the camel, the man of the house where I live without wearing an 'abayah. Jabbar, you're a sheep when I'm in the market wearing an 'abayah!

Na'imah tells me stories about women, but she doesn't know that the 'abayah is the most marvelous present for a woman who lives under the rod of not only one cock like Jabbar but also three. My brothers gave me an 'abayah and five hens. My brothers granted me the "hidden," to discover the unknown about others without revealing myself. This enables me to disclose the catch door of hypocrisy without anyone knowing. I caught Jabbar, obtained my rights, and exposed the truth. I asked my brother to bring me one thousand 'abayahs and looked at him with disgust divulging the comedy inherent in man's tragedy.

Jabbar is an animal. He doesn't understand. He and my sheep are alike, a cock and a sheep. He's a cock and a sheep too. I whispered to myself so that he would not hear, "Congratulations!" And my spit on his face weighed many kilos. I slapped him so hard that his head was dizzy. Shame, disgrace, and sinful and defiled dreams overwhelmed him. Three cocks! A sheep and Jabbar is the cock of the walk. I despise overweight sheep. There is only a slight difference of hypocrisy that separates you, Jabbar, and my innocent sheep. I'm the hunter under the black dome. The 'abayah is my trap. Wearing the 'abayah, I expose hypocrisy.

Come in, ti, ti, ti! How high-and-mighty you are! Do you think you're better than Jabbar? Even Jabbar came last night with head lowered. Go away from the chickens! Whack! Whack! Whack! Hey, you, cock, let the hens eat! They'll get a grain anyway, and then the lowest hen will straddle you. I'll teach my quiet sheep how to butt after I bring you down from your heights. Braggart! I made you come down out of your world of sweet dreams, a world of lies. Everyone lies and cheats everyone else. My 'abayah is the house of secrets. It takes over the seen and reveals the real truth.

Like any woman passing by with an 'abayah, jiggling her hips in front of his eyes, I passed by Jabbar's shop in the Shorjah Market, crowded with men and women. His eyes popped out as if they had left his head. Then, he lost his mind pursuing me, the black ghost. I could be any woman in the pornographic pictures he keeps in the drawers of his locked office. I took him by surprise, found the key, and saw the pictures of the naked women. They were nude as the day they were born.

I knew you well, Jabbar. Your two brothers too. The three of you are a garbage barrel of sin and hypocrisy. Your mind has lost control as a result of the black trap, and I jiggled my hips and twisted more. I made a sign to you, and you left your shop in a rush in order to run after me, after a woman who hid the greatest stamina within and was told, "How witty and playful you are!"

I continued to shake, twist, and make a sign to you through no more than a small hole in my veil. I attracted you away from the commotion of the crowded Shorjah Market, led you into empty and semideserted alleys, provoked the lust of the animal in you, and set you straight. I stopped under a window where a woman was watching. A pedestrian passed by while I crooked my finger, then you lost the rest of your mind and came forward.

I'll hit this damned cock with the handle of the pestle. I'll break its stupid neck until it learns some respect for the rights of the five hens. Not only does it straddle them but also it leaves them without dinner. You're no better than Jabbar.

My threatening slippers awaited Jabbar, my mouth heavy with accumulated spit, and the slap that landed on his face was strong and stinging. The woman standing by the window encouraged me, "Hit him hard, don't let him off, hit him some more, and hit him on the head to make him feel ashamed a bit!" A pedestrian stopped and said that I should slap him again and again.

I wish I had told you, Jabbar, and your brothers, that I had left the house without wearing the 'abayah and the veil and that you escaped from me. Do you remember how fast you dashed away? At night you came home depressed, humiliated, and defeated, carrying your shoes in your hands and dragging yourself. Your feet were weary and weak. Why are you worried, my brother? You talked to yourself, but you really talked to me without knowing it, "If only I had known who that whore was."

The whore! Who are you talking about, you cock of the house! Oh sheep! Oh Jabbar! My 'abayah has faded. Give me a spare 'abayah from your shop and God will protect me. You were thinking, undoubtedly, of the woman with the 'abayah who turned out to be me, your sister.

I, your sister, twisted your neck, oh stupid cock, and turned it into a sheep unable to lift its head, look up, or eat the grains quietly.

You, Jabbar, were talking to yourself when you said, "That whore!" What would you do if you knew that whore was your sister? What would you do if you knew that your sister did more than this?

Well done, hens! Don't let him draw close, let him go to hell! Let him starve to death! He rides you enough and doesn't give you anything to eat. Bravo! I'll bring an 'abayah for each of you!

5—Joudi al-Qarawchi

Da, da, da!

I went too far in my journey today. My quest is endless. People think I am a prisoner of certain alleys, dead-end alleys. People always make mistakes. Their prejudice holds and controls them. It is hammered in their heads like a rusty worn-out nail, which is deep, strong, and evil. My friend with the five eyes and one beak asked me to put out the brazier. I obeyed him and heated water in a hole located in the alley. Tongues of green flames rose with force and split the ground. The burning branches gave off sparks similar to sparrow's feet—deep, swelling with sharp, piercing arrowheads penetrating the flesh.

My friend with the mountain goat horn said, "What do you see?" I stared and raised my head from the blazing heat of the brazier. I wiped the mist from my eyes and swept the dust from my mind, cluttered by the overcrowding of friends. I was completely engaged in clearing a thick black layer of air and sniffing out people's generous gifts to me, overloading, crushing my back. I saw, in pillars of flame, airy sparks coming down from beneath the Creator's feet, and the Devil's laughter ridiculed a cock and a sheep. The horizon became full of black ghosts flying with fox wings, which turned into masses of pink clouds floating forward with force greater than the crests, eyes, and heads of the wise men. The ghosts squeezed themselves into the masses, and then the wise men cast their nets in the Tigris and fished swordfish and demons and danced with rejoicing beautiful women.

My friend of the long legs with the head down said, "Have you ever seen rocks turn into candy in the eyes of the wise men?" I was confused, so I escaped to my own concerns, no one else's, and found there was a slaughtered sheep hanging in the center of a butcher's shop. The line of customers was long, extending from Irbil in the north to Faw in the south, and the butcher was cutting and chopping. One person wanted a piece of fat, the other a leg's meat, the third intestines, and the fourth, legs and feet. They wanted different things, and the butcher continued to cut and fully satisfy everyone's request. The sheep was never entirely consumed, and people pushed each other. I asked my friend with the cock's horn, "Why are people wise?"

My friend with the sheep's comb said, "Don't tell anyone that the matter is so simple. They use their intellect to transplant the sheep's comb to the cock's head and replace the sheep's comb with the cock's horn." The customers waited in line to buy a little fat, or leg meat, or legs and feet—a line that extended from Homrin Mountain in the north to el-Hammar Swamps in the south. They have Job's patience and the mutual enmity of a daughter-in-law and a mother-in-law.

"Why are there Homrin Mountain and el-Hammar Swamps?" I asked.

"So that things will differ from each other," he answered.

"Do they really differ?" I inquired.

"In the wise men's eyes," said the one-eyed man with the five beaks.

"And what's the end of the matter?" I asked.

"You are truly insane. Don't ask about things you have known since you were born!" he yelled.

A wise child, who was near our run-down site—as the wise men call it—put on my head a crown that my Creator used to wear, made of diamonds and pearls. The wise child thought that the crown was a bowl-shaped watermelon rind filled with mud and stagnant water.

My mother gazed at me with her bleary eyes and shouted, "Woe is me, woe is me!" I entered the magnificent waiting room of the palace, which my mother and the wise men regarded as a run-down place. I wished my mother had known that I don't reveal secrets. I was agitated that my poor mother was in pain for no reason and bewailed something, which she should rejoice about. I was enraged by the people's illusions and continued to wave my hand and yell my only word, "Da, da, da!" No one will ever get more than this word from me, not even my miserable, stupid mother.

6—Jamil Rabi

Ya'qub, 'Amam's son, sits in 'Alwan's Café. Naji el-Jundi frequents all the cafés of Baghdad. Selman Hashwah's mind is in Karbala, and I'm everywhere—or rather nowhere. My own tragedy, my feeling of being lost, and the need to find myself are my greatest problems. I'm still playing the game of "hot and cold." I walk in darkness and ask, like the children, "Have I reached the end yet or not?" The children would answer, "You're getting warmer." I ask the same question every minute and receive the same answer. The rule of the game is that I continue to play until I reach the end without backing off. So when will I reach the end of the game? Where are you, my luck, my savior?

The turtle takes slow steps. The ordinary people urge the turtle with the whip of the visible, and like rabbits they forget and go off into their holes. In the dawn, I staggered home after I performed at a woman's night party in a mansion in the Sa'dun area. I said to Abu Ghalib, the night guard, "Abu Ghalib, you have been a night guard many years. Explain to me, how does your night go by?"

"Well, I got used to it. It passes by as fast as smoking a cigarette."

"How is that? For the sake of God, explain."

Abu Ghalib is an ordinary person. His habit of blowing his noisy whistle is also an ordinary thing. He says, "It's simple. When you pass by me we chat for half an hour, I brew a cup of tea for another half hour, I slowly drink the tea for another half an hour, then I go to the café and have a pleasant conversation for one hour. Time passes very quickly. You close and open your eyes and suddenly find out that the night has flown away."

"And what happens when the night flies away, Abu Ghalib?"

"The sun rises and I go home."

The sun! He silenced and slapped me with the sun. I was, however, in the depth of the unseen, in the depth of myself too. I decided to silence and slap the darkness on him and said, "Well, suppose the sun doesn't rise?"

He was an ordinary person, so he was surprised and even angry. He shouted at me, "Do you think I'm insane, Jamil? What do you mean by 'the sun doesn't rise'? Is there a day when the sun doesn't shine?"

It's too much for you, Abu Ghalib, too much. But never mind. It's only between the two of us. Whatever I explain to you, you won't understand. My sun, for example, never rises with the ordinary people, and you insist that I don't see. But where is the real sun of three-quarters of the people who live in misery, night guard?

The game of deceit is nauseating and causes illness, Abu Ghalib! It becomes a chronic illness to add to all my other assembled aches and pains. But there is a better reason. Who knows, maybe if not for this better reason I could have resisted my illnesses and the other game, the more dangerous game, the game of the seen and the hidden, the game of the two extremes, of desires and contradictions. Most people don't master the rules of the game. You don't master it, Abu Ghalib.

Please think a little and tell me, isn't the stable a suitable place for my relatives? No. I'm mocking you, guard of the shortest night. I swear by God that I am telling the truth. Learn the game and you'll discover things that will stun you, make your eyes pop out. You'll find that I see better than you do.

You'll find that my father and mother and the man who treats baldness are tied to a feedbag, and you'll see that various places are especially built for groups of different "creatures." You'll find the sanitarium for mental diseases full of all types of people like Naji el-Jundi and me. The world's prisons will be crowded with dignitaries, famous people, millions of animals, as well as semihuman insects arousing so much disgust that people like you won't even spit on them. You'll see that the semihuman insects became good and innocent humans, and the graves will open their mouths to swallow those whom death has so far spared. And I'm the first person among the dead who will stand in line, Oh Abu Ghalib! But the game of unjust tyrants wants me to be blinded by these stupid children's games. To fritter away a portion of your night I stop by to converse about things you understand nothing about. But during the long night I also look for my distant luck. My games are intertwined with other people's games. I remember when I returned from a night party and realized I would not have performed in it had it not been for the game of the seen and the hidden. At this point, things became a tangled ball of yarn. I participated in the game and found myself lost in a sea of deceit. The contradictions are a fact—the visible dominates, and the hidden forces its way through.

People don't listen to me. What I say is lost among the simple people like a fart in the din of the Sfafir copper market. Simple people find excuses for making me the only victim. I have never understood why. I told you that last night's party reflected the most terrible human calamity. I mean hustle and bustle, riddles that neither the blind nor the sighted can understand. People cling to the seen. The foolish and the stronger sex are the first victim and the first deceived in the game. There are men whose eyes dance in front of women. But who are we? They, the women, are unveiled and see. But who are they? Nothing separates us from them except one night. This is the visible thing that vanishes in the disgusting deceit, in the joke. The unseen alone remains, Abu Ghalib. Did you figure it out? You keep silent, and this means you're confused.

I play the music, move my body, and feel despite my blindness. Next to me sits a virgin of paradise, a houri whose body releases a purer fragrance than a Raziqi rose. Believe me, she's a cheerfully subtle player in the same deceit. She would strip in my presence and have sex without embarrassment. The person who claims she doesn't exist just because I feel her more than I see her is insane. She's beside me, feels me, and above all, sees me.

Despite my dark glasses I'm a man. But in the eyes of the stupid and strong sex, I don't belong to their foolish strong sex. Still, I didn't invent the deceitful game. They, the simple people, did. Deceit wins in the game. The seen thing is when the houri is next to me and our hips rub against each other. Do you understand now, or not yet, Abu Ghalib? I tell you, it is as confusing as everything.

I played the music and the sound of her sighs reached my right ear; her breath blew into my face and revived my soul. In the beginning, my forearm fiddled with her swelled breasts. Then I understood. She considered me a man and continued to press against me. The game of desires and opposites! I certainly am a man. Since I am, I am a human being.

You know, Abu Ghalib, sometimes, for lack of sons, people give their dog a boy's name. In such circumstances, even the donkey may become a human being in our deprivation, the deprivation for both of us. Can you imagine this, Abu Ghalib, or is it beyond your grasp? No, surely you know this, but—I swear by my life that I am a man.

She conversed with me like a human being and what is more important, I felt human in the eyes of others. I understood. Her sighs became pants. My hand descended into the bottom of a well and she pushed me inside it. I was embarrassed. I had an erection when my elbow brushed against her vagina. She pushed me inside the well and pulled the well up to me.

You're right if you say it was like a torn feather pillow or a sponge dripping boiling water as hot as the spa springs of Hammam 'Ali. Don't say anything, Abu Ghalib! Keep quiet and hold it. I passed the night smoking two packs of cigarettes and was tempted to sip some whiskey and drowned in the lap of the well and the game. The houri discovered the game. Should I curse her or does she not deserve my curse? No, no! She accepted me as a man, as a human being, Abu Ghalib. At that very time, though, I became like an instrument. The paradox, Abu Ghalib, the irony! I do a lot of things at the same time. I hum to myself, I play, and I fulfill women's requests and smoke one cigarette after another. I drink the hated liquid, the firewater. My elbow was dipped three times in the spa spring of Hammam 'Ali, and my erect penis was crushed under the pressure of the oud cradled in my lap. My mind flew up in fragments and was lost looking for a thing without its counterpart, seen or unseen, only a transparent crystal with no two sides. My feelings were enflamed by a passion between my legs. My groins pressed at me and excited me from all sides. I felt a need to expel urine and that other sticky stuff.

Man is weak and hopeless when confronting stressful matters, Abu Ghalib! He can't withstand even a bit of hunger or even a little overstuffing. He loses his mind holding his urine. My thoughts can't withstand the pressure from below. Even when there is only a small amount of urine to hold, Abu Ghalib, it drives a man out of his mind. It controls you and seizes your entire attention. My priceless thought was competing with the drops of yellow water blocked up inside me. Such is man, Abu Ghalib, such is man! The beautiful woman who made me into a human and brought me unthinkable pleasure disappeared too. I couldn't control myself. Didn't I tell you I'm the image of myself? At that time I had already stopped hurrying my death along and had entirely forgotten death and other things. I didn't invent the game. I was unwillingly forced into it. I had forgotten the seen and the unseen and had refrained from talking to women about it.

Isn't it possible that if I asked the houri, our silent relationship would have been closer and better established? I was confused, brought down, and pressed between the ten thousand jaws of a mad and vicious crocodile. At last I left, hiding my most private secret, my suffering at holding back the urine and my fervent desire to relieve it. This was my secret of secrets at that moment.

I started to kick and didn't know on what I stumbled and who I stepped on. But I found the door, opened it, and went through to a garden decorated with lights that took away the remaining one-tenth of my sight. The females were performing in the orchestra of seeing musicians. I got lost among the most stupid and ordinary people—lost under the strong pressure and attacking force of my urine demanding to be released.

Suddenly I felt a hand tapping my shoulder. No! It was certainly not her hand, the houri's hand. It was the rough hand of a man who had kept his eye on me during the commotion, a man set apart from all the simple people.

He whispered in my ear, "Do you need anything, sir?"

I whispered back in his ear, "Yes, fellow! I want to take a leak. I've been holding it for a long time and was too shy to tell the women." He differed from the ordinary people because he had apparently mastered the game, but he was enraged by my self-inflicted torture in the cause of the beauty of seen things.

He howled his angry rebuke. "You've been suffering from holding your urine for an hour and are too timid to tell her! So why did you let yourself be in pain so long? Couldn't you have mercy on yourself? Listen, if I were in your shoes I would have urinated in the middle of the women! Do you really think one should be that shy in their presence? Listen sir, the youngest among them is a whore and the oldest a madam."

Didn't I tell you, Abu Ghalib, that this person was different from other people? Although he exaggerates and makes a mountain out of a molehill, he knows the game's secrets and deals with them in his own way. He beats me in this. Do you understand yet or not? Well, I'll leave you now so that you can think about all this and the game during the rest of the night.

I left him so that he could go to bed. Then I would get up in the morning to ask, "Have I succeeded or not?"

7—'Aziz Ghawi

El-Minzul, Gog Nazar, el-Kallachiyah—all are names of whorehouses. What do these names mean if they refer only to one thing? Disappointment, failure, frustration, illusions, and deprivation refer to me, to 'Aziz Ghawi. El-Minzul, Gog Nazar, and el-Kallachiyah mean a woman of flesh and blood.

I entered the whorehouse with fear. It was the fear of the first time and the first woman—fear before an experience I hadn't gone through yet, fear of another failure. Another failure? I'm exaggerating. The senior year of high school doesn't mean the whole world, just another failure. So the senior year is a part of it. There is Farhah

Ghawi too. 'Abdallah Ghawi and the three mules exist. I exist too, the original disappointment with human features walking the earth.

I went to the whore unwillingly, carrying gleams of my first victory achieved. I am not only a disappointment but also a filthy person, a malicious scoundrel. I went there to please you, 'Abdallah Ghawi. This is your son carrying out the first of the Ten Commandments. But I came to the whore taking a risk, Farhah Ghawi! Your baby son in diapers learned how to crawl, so here I am crawling secretly into the house of a human woman, not a dollhouse, but the house of reality, el-Minzul.

I went to the whore, gasping and shivering. She was skinny and stinky, with a pug nose like a scrawny, scabby dog. Her face resembled a painting produced by the worst painter in the world, full of mistakes, but to my joy, at least it was not the face of a pillow at all.

I was scared to death, speechless and shaken. I veered among a thousand feelings, none of which remedied the situation. She was just a piece of filth, fascinated by herself. There she was lying before me, smiling at me with her cave-like mouth releasing poisonous gas, but I wasn't up to my dream. My lust went back and forth between two poles, disgust and desire. The woman was wily and shrewd, and my attraction to her was shortening my life span and the elixir of my life. I was confused about what I should say to humble this damned woman who felt honored by the gift of my sex. You are a whore, and what am I? Indeed, I'm the real whore. Maybe this is the most suitable expression. Where are the gleams of my first victory? When will the volcano explode, you bastard, dog, and son of the dark barrel and the deceitful snake?

To take the bit from my mouth she said, "Why are you afraid, dear? Is this your first time?" It was the first time that I had ever lied in order to steal or commit adultery. I said nothing. She said again, "You deserve to be pampered. You're handsome, young, and gentle."

What a blind woman she was! Most likely she saw beauty even in defects. After all, she could allure with her pug nose and her dark black charcoal face. My bit was removed. "Am I really handsome?

Can't you see my bulging jaw and donkey teeth?" She laughed. She fiddled with my hair using her left hand, and she patted my back with her right hand, as if she were putting a child to bed.

"Never mind, your gold tooth makes up for it," she assured me.

I have more things that if she knew about, she would have held the hem of her dress in her teeth and run away screaming with fear.

"What else do I have that you like?" I asked.

"You have charming, flirting eyes. Killing but reviving."

She gazed at my eyes through a dark, cracked mirror. Most likely, she wasn't lying. Maybe I really do have a little bit of charm and grace. Was she helping me to discover a positive side of myself in this shameful whorehouse? I felt sad and said that I was probably thinking of a voice that the damned woman had heard.

"What's the use? My face is sad and gloomy all the time," I said.

"Why, 'aini? Are you upset? Is something worrying you?"

There is only one problem. Why don't I say I have a thousand, two thousand, on the way to three thousand problems! I stuttered. Tomorrow when the senior year of high school begins, I'll face the greatest problem.

"What work do you do, 'aini?" she asked.

I completely stopped at the door of the senior class, horrified. What a joke, or rather a tragedy? Should I tell her that my only employment is playing with my dick? She pointed to my Adam's apple.

"What work do I do? I'm the supervisor in the Merchants' Port."

"No. Tell me the truth and don't joke."

"I'm telling you the truth, I swear by my mother's life."

The damn woman was displeased and said, "Oh! Is it a secret you can't tell? Okay, don't tell, but don't lie to me. Nobody can cheat me."

So you're not me, I thought. What will bring me close to your sharp tongue and arrogance? You're undoubtedly smart and, therefore, you're a whore and I'm stupid, a permanent student in my senior year.

"*Maykhalif*, okay, I'll tell you the truth, lady. I work as a donkey driver, but my uncle is the pulling horse. I have a lot of pullers: my uncles on my father and mother's side and my cousin, all of them are horses. Not ordinary horses, but noble Arab horses that would please you."

There were also three mules in my mother's room. The whore would have done well if she had left for a while to laugh. I'll throw another stone at her in order to regain my first disgusting victory. I suggested to her, "Do you want to be a millionaire? Go and bet on the horse race on Saturday, this Saturday." She was out of breath laughing and I held back my desires in order to restore my courage and my illicit first victory. I'm not dreaming. Next to me lies a woman of flesh and blood, laughing, joking, and stirring the fervent passion inside me. I'm a dirty person. My vulgarity has been hidden throughout my life, making me a victim of it, but now I have learned how to use it to my advantage. Now she stood next to me.

My uncle hates me. His looks poured humiliations onto me. I know that he despises me, but today I can withstand his insults. I have a task to perform today. I'll mount you, my uncle, and constantly lash your back with whips of fire. I have overcome the first experience, the first deception, and encountered my first real human woman, a woman of flesh and bones. I was terrified, and then my courage was ignited.

Whoever sits next to you, my uncle becomes a rag, but not now.

"And what do you do for a living?" my uncle asked.

"I'm in school, still in my last year."

"Ten years ago I heard you were a senior. You are old enough. Go and do yourself some good, go to work."

What should I say to my uncle? "Employ me in your business. Let me work under you and be your assistant?" He would stammer an answer and take me nowhere on a wild goose chase, but I had come to him for a definite purpose.

"Hey, fellow! Where are you? Are you in another world?" The whore asked laughing.

"I was thinking which horse would win first place and which second," I replied.

I left her laughing again.

Annoyed with my presence, my uncle asked me, "You didn't tell me the reason for your coming." I decided to tell him the matter, to get it over with and be free.

"My mother sends you her regards. She asks you to lend us a dinar. There is no penny in the house and we're starving."

"Why? Didn't your father leave you spending money?"

"He hasn't shown up for three months," I said.

He continued to interrogate me, "And what about Farhah's work? Isn't it sufficient?" I sighed, but I didn't hide my anger at him, because I didn't want him to think I sighed because I felt sorry for Farhah.

"What business are you talking about? It has been dead for a long time. It has been a month now since she sewed her last dress."

With no hesitation, my uncle quickly took out one dinar. He's definitely a miser, but he wanted to get me out of the way, and so he gave me the dinar for the whore.

The whore said, "Oh 'aini! Who'll win in the end?"

I swear by God I was confused and didn't know whether the uncle on my mother's side or the uncle on my father's side would win. Both of them were good horses, and only one was better than the other. This time she didn't laugh. Apparently she was out of patience with me and said, "Leave them alone, come on, come on, 'aini! Hurry up! I have no spare time, people are waiting outside!"

I wanted to ask her whether she is also like my uncles with people lined up at her door, and that people are blind like her, my horses, the world, and me. When she stripped she spoiled my victory over my uncle. She was no longer pug-nosed, skinny, and as sooty as a fireplace poker. She was a woman in the image of a horse as are my uncles.

The story of how I got the second dinar, or rather the story of my victory over my uncle was the same as the one of the first dinar, with a small difference. I had learned how to utilize my worst qualities. I said to my uncle, "Mother sends her regards to you."

I felt faintness and sank.

"Slowly! You'll kill me!"

You're like my uncle, my father and mother. I'm a student in the senior year, to hell with my life!

"Ouch! Ouch! What's the matter with you? Haven't you seen a woman before?"

The overwhelming, sticky, clamorous fluid extinguished my desire. My lust died out. I relaxed for a while. I looked and saw her sooty face and pug nose again. I saw myself one more time. I discharged my inside, my soul, and nothing was left except revulsion. I spat. I didn't know on what I spat. I felt as if illness had come out of me and filled the whole world. By all means I should forget, recover. My thoughts flew to Bab el-Sharqi and landed in Yusuf 'Abd el-Nabi's bar. Yusuf is a horse, the son of a stallion, and my aunt is his mother. I decided to go there and treat myself by drinking as much arrack as I could.

Four

1—'Atiyah al-Qarawchi

'Atiyah al-Qarawchi dreamed she was in her home at 'Aguliyah. Her modest home suddenly grew large and neat and acquired a different appearance. She didn't know precisely whether it was floating on the sea or soaring in the sky, but its walls were falling away, and the fragrant gardenia flowers were white and blooming on the bricks.

Paradise! She was a young girl dragging her flowing garments, as green as chard, covering hair and hands. She was like a member of a holy caste, concealing her pride, sitting on a howdah placed on the back of an elephant. Without seeing anyone she heard a whisper guiding her—"This is where you belong, 'Atiyah. Stay where you are!"

She sat on her velvet couch and suddenly saw Wafiqah and Qadriyah standing in white bridal dresses, Wafiqah to her right and Qadriyah to her left. Joudi came. 'Atiyah saw him and couldn't believe her eyes. He looked like a gentleman, even better than all other gentlemen. He wore a neat black suit, a tie, and a *sidarah* hat. His shirt was as white as snow.

"Mother, I came to tell you that I plan to get married," he said to her. Her eyes shed tears and she said to him, "Get married, son! What do I want more from God except to see you married? Get married and then I may die and return to my Creator."

"No, Yummah, Mom, God forbid. May death be far from you! You'll live and see my children and the children of my children," Joudi protested.

"Who is the lucky girl you'll marry?" she asked.

"She is the one, Yummah," he said, pointing to Wafiqah.

Furious, 'Atiyah got up from her velvet couch. She yelled at Joudi, "Are you out of your mind? She's your sister! How is it possible for you to marry your sister?" Joudi paid no attention and mumbled, "Don't be mad, Yummah. I don't have to marry this one, I will marry the other one." He pointed to Qadriyah, who was as silent as Wafiqah and smiling.

'Atiyah became even more angry and tore off the dark, chard-colored shirt that revealed her dry, flabby skin. She suddenly became an old woman with a lean body.

"She's your sister too. This is Qadriyah. Don't you know her? Pious people!" she shouted. "Come and see who wants to marry his sister! Come and help me, I'm losing my mind! Joudi, my son, has gone insane."

Farhah Ghawi dreamed that a scorpion was crawling between her bed and the bed of Sa'idah, her daughter. Sa'idah was slumbering like a rock, and Farhah was awake watching the scorpion. The scorpion drew near Farhah from Sa'idah's bed and raised its tail. Disgusted and angry at Ya'qub for having left Sa'idah's bed with this poison, Farhah raised her shoe. Terrified, she watched the scorpion raise its deadly tail, ready to sting. She paused. The scorpion came closer. She hit it with her shoe and felt relieved.

Khoshi, the Persian, disturbed Ya'qub's sleep by sneaking into his dreams. Khoshi appeared before him wearing decorated pants and a Persian hat. He carried a large heap of something inside a bulky sack.

"Well 'Ajmi! Did you bring the slippers from Iran?" Ya'qub asked Khoshi.

Khoshi took off his hat and scratched his balding head. "I beg your forgiveness. The slippers got lost. They were stolen from me on the way. Instead, I brought a whole orchard in the sack. An orchard from Tabriz, very big and very beautiful. It has pears and pomegranates and is full of fruits and vegetables." In broken Arabic he said laughing, "Want to see? Look sir, look!"

Ya'qub jumped for joy from the midst of his shop and took off his leather apron. He clapped, hugged Khoshi cheerfully and said, "Well done! You are Khoshi, as good as your name. Open the sack and let me see the orchard!"

Khoshi freed himself from Ya'qub's arms, leaned over the sack, protecting it with his body, and shouted, "No! No see before pay. First Khoshi see money, then Ya'qub see orchard. Fair, fair?"

In the room of the two young men, anxiety rose and fell with the sound of Selman Hashwah's erratic snoring in short and long rattles. Then, with a long sigh, his snoring stopped. The bedsprings squeaked under the weight of his heavy body. A sharp groan broke from his bed, followed by a murmur of his semiclogged throat, which grew into a scream.

Jamil Rabi woke up and yelled, "Hey, Selman, wake up!"

Selman woke up frightened, wet with cold perspiration. His body was shivering and his legs were almost frozen. Terrified, he tried to shake them out of their numbness and thought he was going crazy. The bogeyman was still grabbing his throat, threatening him with a terrible death. "Where am I?"

Jamil had disturbed the stillness of Selman's approaching death, but Selman wasn't angry. Selman's dying eyes searched for Jamil, hoping for reassurance.

Jamil said warmly—a side rarely shown to Selman Hashwah— "You were talking in your sleep. You were shouting. They were killing you and you pleaded with them."

Selman was now completely awake. While his fear of death had diminished, his terror remained. "It was exactly like that every night when I returned from Karbala. They came into our house wanting to kill me."

"What do you want to do? Do you want to go to the hospital again?" Jamil mumbled.

"What should I do, Jamil?" Selman was now weeping. "Dreams are out of my control. Can you understand that?"

"You see all this in the dream only because you think about it all the time. It would be better if you only thought of Sabriyah."

＊

Sabriyah dreamed she was in the train coming back from Mosul to Baghdad at a frenzied speed. She swayed from side to side in the corridor and could hardly put her feet firmly on the floor. She was looking for Efrayim, moving from one car to another, staggering because of the train's high speed, lurching and falling forward down to the floor, and then getting up. She felt lonely away from home, a feeling she had never experienced before. "Where is Efrayim?" she asked. But nobody knew. She realized that the passengers didn't know the name of the conductor, and so she began to ask, "Have you seen the conductor?" Again she received no reply. The passengers ignored her, except one passenger who shook his head in an absolute negative.

"My God! Where is Efrayim?" Sabriyah asked. Everything seemed deeper, stronger, and lonely—a complete loss. She swayed with the train, fell down and got up, and asked about him. Suddenly a shadowy image loomed in front of her and grew into the body of a man, maybe one of the passengers, taking her by surprise. He wore a long garment and skullcap, and he stared at her, shooting arrows that pierced her soul. He pushed against her with his entire body. She was crushed with a fear that dominated her body and spun her around like a top. To scream for help or run away never occurred to her. The passengers were deaf, mute, and blind. They were pleased to see her struggling, swaying back and forth like grain between mill wheels.

She suddenly found herself escaping the grip of the devil, and as swiftly as a gust of wind, she ran down a narrow passage leading to the first-class compartment. She found the same compartment where she had traveled alone to Mosul and had met Efrayim in her transparent nightgown. She was overjoyed as if saved from a most terrible death. Her fear vanished, her feeling of loneliness left. "I'll hide there," she said as she opened the door of the compartment. Efrayim was inside lying on a naked woman. She was baffled and alarmed. Her scream was choked inside her, and before she realized what had happened, a fit of trembling overcame her. Everything began to disintegrate, scatter, and fly away. Efrayim fled outside the compartment through the window and disappeared.

"Efrayim! Efrayim!" She shouted and jumped up from her sleep, frightened.

Her consciousness was shattered and dispersed in a world of ghosts swimming in the middle of a dense and dripping cloud on a Baghdadi night. Her breathing resembled the chugging of the Mosul train passing through the narrow tunnel, damping the noise. She remained overwhelmed for a while, then swallowed her dry saliva. "The evil dream is false! The bad dream is false!" she muttered.

2—Sabriyah, 'Abdush's Daughter, and Selman Hashwah

Bab el-Sharqi. For the third time I was in Bab el-Sharqi after being in Bani S'id alone, looking at shop windows and faces. I passed Ghazi Theater, reached Dayanah Theater, then went back to Ghazi Theater. My steps were erratic; my thoughts were looking for things that existed but were no longer there. My father was angry. Efrayim was absent, and lately my plaything, Selman Hashwah, was suffering from a rare illness and had no patience for me or anybody else; he seemed tired of himself. I was also fed up with my life and myself.

The park! The black paved street pushed me there with force. I stopped at the park gate for a moment and then entered. I felt somewhat relieved and I was sure the expression on my face showed it. Ghazi Park was a meadow of sweet memories, a lost paradise of golden dreams. I took shelter in a paradise of memories and dreams.

The first of May. The second of May is grief and agony, Khaduri! My return to Baghdad and madness, the Farhûd, and the death of my family. My life has deteriorated. I don't remember anything else of my world except that memory. That memory is a fire, Khaduri, a death and reckoning. I'll be punished, Khaduri. Memory is my hell on earth. Jamil tells me to forget. He says, "Forget, concentrate on Sabriyah only, love her! This is the best thing for you to do." Jamil, who habitually ridiculed my love for Sabriyah and shoved his fingers in my face a thousand times, told me this. Certainly he was right, and I had tried. By the life of your pious father I tried it. But apparently my black luck tells Sabriyah not to pay attention to me. She goes out, Khaduri. I don't know where.

She is my shelter in this world when I seek protection, but she's either already gone or Efrayim has already come back from Mosul. My jealousy is blind and I'm disappointed, burned by envy. I have slipped down into an abyss of disappointment where darkness blinds my other eye. I have become a butcher stripping my own skin and chopping my own flesh and bones. Then I returned as if the Angel of Death were standing by my door confronting me, scattering my memories in front of me, and heating my hell.

Abdalak Khaduri, I beg of you to listen to me! I have no one else to talk to. If I keep this inside me I'll die, and who'll recite the Qiddish prayer for me when I die? My father and mother are already dead, killed in the Farhûd. Does it make any sense for Jamil, the unbeliever, to recite Qiddish? Jamil is teaching the recital of the Qiddish to Hassun, who hates us. When Hassun masters the Qiddish, he'll recite it on the radio. Even religion has become a mockery. Isn't it enough that we were slaughtered in the Farhûd? Now our Qiddish is becoming a mockery? Whose fault is it if Jamil is teaching the Qiddish to a person who hates Jews?

Tell me, Khaduri, is this Communism? If so, why doesn't the government hang the Communists too? I don't understand this. Jamil tells me, "You should pray for them. You owe your life to my friends." No, Khaduri. I experienced grief and agony in Karbala where one thousand angels—a Muslim and many other conscientious people— stood up for me. Who can deny all this? Only a bastard, Khaduri. Let's get back to our conversation now.

I laughed at Efrayim deep inside, a laughter on his behalf. Like a frightened horse, he avoided me. I said to myself that he was a Jew and he had thought I was a Muslim woman traveling alone on a train racing through the very dark night. It was taking me to Mosul, to my uncle, manager of the Mosul station. I wore my sheer nightgown. He knocked lightly on the door of my compartment and whispered in a soft voice, "Ticket, lady!" I was lying on my bed, and the end of my flowing nightgown dangled all the way to the floor. I thumbed through the magazine *Qarandal*. I was alone in the first-class compartment of the Mosul train. Alone . . . I sat on a green bench in Ghazi Park. Efrayim was with me on the bench, and I had the latest issues of *Akhbar al-Yawm* and *Qarandal*. What was happening to me? The jokes in *Qarandal* didn't make me laugh anymore. I was alone, stressed, and anxious, thinking of sweet solitude while intruding eyes stared at me in Ghazi Park. Efrayim, though, was too shy to address me.

"I have the ticket, but I can't get down from the bed. I'm lazy. Please come in and check it."

I amused myself, drew him near, and he melted and hid under the ground of shyness.

"Come in, 'aini, don't be afraid. I don't eat people!" I said.

Efrayim used to say about me over and over, "She is aggressive and has guts," and Farhah Ghawi would say even more than that. I stopped and concealed my laughter. Efrayim was motionless. He swore to me later that no thought like that had ever occurred to him. His thoughts were innocent. They didn't even clear the doubt from his mind. He hesitated for a long time. He is always stuck like a piece of hardened clay, lacking courage to express even his feelings or change his job. He continues on and on, breaking his promise to me, and forcing me into this embarrassing situation. I was alone in Ghazi Park, a prey to rude, evil eyes fixed on me from all sides. I made the mistake of choosing him, but I love him.

It was on the first of May 1941 when we took the train to el-Hindiyi Dam and then continued to Karbala. We were ten Muslims, Jews, and

Christians—maybe more. The Nazis were everywhere. Darkness and curfew were imposed on Baghdad. A Bedouin from the Twair tribe, coming from a dance celebration, asked, "Which is better, the cannon or my club?" He carried a rifle and was girded by an ammunition belt. I saw the end of his club aimed at my head and replied without hesitation, "Of course, your club is better," and in that way I saved my life.

Go to hell, Efrayim! I thought to myself. What a loser you are! I laughed at him for his own good. I called him to come in while he stood nailed at the door of my compartment, making no move.

"Come in, 'aini. Don't be shy, there's no stranger here."

Did Efrayim remember how much time he wasted to gather his courage? Then he decided to enter after a long wait. I laughed inside, continued my harmless game, and got ready. I liked these games, and because of them, Farhah Ghawi's dirty thoughts would become even filthier and more malicious. He entered the compartment and looked at the floor, extended his hand, and impatiently wanted to punch my ticket and leave. But I prepared another dirty trick and yelled, "Tell me, aren't you ashamed of yourself? How do you have the nerve to enter a place with a woman in her nightgown?"

He wanted to apologize, but in vain. His words were reduced to nothing and were lost. Then he quickly retreated, chattering like a monkey and he again stood before the door. I died laughing and rolled over to my belly, desiring him more, saying to myself, "Enough is enough! Have pity on him and free him from this tricky game he's forced to play." But I was still pushing him into the game, and he was still shaking from the frenzy of play. I put the shawl over my nightgown and said, "Come in fellow, come! I was just joking with you."

"Are you Jewish?" he asked.

"Why are you so surprised and disbelieving? Are you stunned because of my black hair hanging down to my hips or because of my eyes, my reddish-brown skin like wine, and the mole on my cheek?" His fear settled, but he still didn't believe me. "What do you think I am?"

"You don't look Jewish," he answered.

"I swear to you I am Jewish. My father is the owner of the greatest nightclub in Bab el-Sharqi, and my uncle is the manager of the Mosul train station."

"Salim is your uncle?" he asked.

"Do you know Salim?"

"Of course, I know him. Where do you think I work? Why are you traveling alone taking a risk like this?"

Efrayim's childish naïveté made me laugh. I answered with confidence, "Why? What can happen to me? I'm as strong as a man and a half."

Something else occurred to him. He was too shy to reveal it to me, and it remained hidden in his heart until we got married. He said to me, "You are the most charming female," but he was conceited. For this reason, my huge self-confidence didn't sway him. He also said, "A girl in your situation worries me. You're my responsibility, and I won't leave you until I hand you over to Salim Effendi. Your uncle is my uncle." My desire for him grew. His modesty, his shyness—I loved him despite his spinelessness with women, and I still don't like this.

My shoulder is the strangest place in the world. One celebrant in the crowd couldn't find a better prop than my shoulder to shoot his bullets from. What happened? Had the world turned upside down? It was the joke of a drunkard friend to another drunk who called him a bastard. It was just a devious game, but suddenly he got mad, drew his revolver, and used my shoulder as a shooting mount. He couldn't find any other place to steady his revolver. Then the bullets poured down like rain.

Listen, Khaduri! They call 'Aibah nagel a hundred times a day, don't they? He doesn't mind and he laughs. The man with the revolver who made my black luck miserable had become insane, so that I now die in silence, a death without a drop of blood.

The group celebration turned into a war zone. I faced death with every shot fired. I died and was resurrected, was resurrected and died again. I froze when he shot. My shoulder was a shooting post, and his rifle was an open mouth, shaking with every shot, dancing with my shivering body. I counted my minutes in a special way, pleading to my saint, Me'ir Ba'al ha-Ness, the prophet Ezekiel, the saint Shuw-wa' Kohen, and Ezrah the Scribe. Save me, all of you!

The moment was, however, shattered into a thousand splinters. Undoubtedly, my fate was hiding in a part of them. I froze. How could I play music when he was shooting from over my shoulder?

"Hey, fellow. Play and don't stop," he said and hit me with the handle of the revolver that dripped blood. I hesitated. How can the dead play music? I received another strong blow. "Look, I ordered you to play. Don't stop playing! Play, or I'll kill you!"

I plunged down, torn into pieces by random death. Khaduri! What more can I tell you? One can escape the grip of death prowling the streets, but how can one evade this other death aiming at me intentionally? I hope God keeps me away from more difficult hardship. I lifted my hand and tried to talk.

"Okay, sir," I said, "I'll play the music as you please, but take your revolver away."

It didn't occur to me that I was risking my life. Did I know what the future held for me? Was I aware that I had asked the Angel of Death to remove his sword from me when it was one inch from my throat? It got closer, the inch became less in a moment, and I closed my eyes and recited, "Hear, Oh Israel, the Lord is our God, the Lord is one!" I put my feet on the threshold of the other world's gate, readying myself.

Suddenly, an angel appeared from the crowd. He took me, pushed me backward, and brought me to this world—another death and a stranger, a Muslim angel. I was rescued.

The green bench, our bench. His and mine. It still stored the whispers of love that bled from our two loving hearts. Our bench was mute, secretive. Alone, I stayed on it. Efrayim was away traveling. No, that's not true. Even though he didn't want to leave the Mosul train and come back to me, from then on I didn't permit him to make me a target of those suspicious eyes. I was overwhelmed by a host of thoughts with poisonous thornlike teeth. The evening approached, and I had discarded the memory. Selman Hashwah was ill. Efrayim was ill too, and I was suffering even more from this pensive solitude. My ennui made the world seem ill. Efrayim said, "You've been entrusted to me, you're my responsibility," and he brought me to my uncle like a piece of merchandise. My uncle told him, "Efrayim, I rely on you to take care of her and not leave her until she arrives in Baghdad."

I hated to be under guard by force. His city was merely an excuse. He believed my uncle and himself, "until she arrives in Baghdad." I said to myself, "We'll start for good in Baghdad."

I knew it was impossible for a person like Efrayim to initiate any move. Even his thoughts were frightened, even his looks, his face blazing with blushes as red as blood when it touched mine. He was embarrassed when he conversed with me. I realized then that I wasn't the only one in love. Maybe he was too. He had a desire, but he was shy. And I? I chose him. I saw sorrow welling up in his eyes in the Baghdad train station when he came to bid me farewell. I laughed at him and for him, whispering in his ears, "I want to see you. Shall we meet this evening at six in Ghazi Park?" He hesitated, and I asked, "How long will you stay in Baghdad?" At first, he withheld his answer, and then with great difficulty he said, as if his voice were choked under water, "Two days—today and tomorrow . . ."

"Then we'll meet on both days, today and tomorrow, in Ghazi Park."

I left him while he was gathering his courage, his thoughts, and his confused love for me.

⁂

The first of May 1941. An approaching dust storm was rolling in from Baghdad. The sweeping disaster moved with a snarling appetite, and the radio spat out inflaming communiqués against the Jews, official statements made by Sab'awi and the Nazi sympathizers. Feelings of outrage increased. Jews, scapegoats, and hostages predominated in Karbala, the city of the great martyrs.

We were stopped at the poorly built courtyard of the school. Night fell, and a group of Nazis separated us from the rest. The school's courtyard was a stage for celebration, dancing and singing, but it became a Nazi extermination camp. There were guards with rifles aimed at the last sparks of life. I thought that my life was over, and I was sure that our end had come. There was no doubt about it. But life is precious, Khaduri!

Tell me please, why does man continue to cling to life even though it isn't worth a pair of shabby slippers? Take, for example, Jamil. He never stops jabbering that he and his life are two rivals, he and his life are in continuous war. As long as he is alive, he fights life and life fights him. Between the two are endless skirmishes. He has the power to terminate this furious war and is capable of putting an end to his life, which is, as he says, his most hostile enemy. Despite this he hasn't done so yet.

Life is precious, Khaduri! Our life is like a woman we love who wards us off. The more she avoids us, the more our passionate love grows. Maybe I would have loved Chahlah, my cousin, as much as I love Sabriyah now. She was sixteen, and I was more than twenty when she used to come to our home. I always liked to sit by her, and I could never have enough of her. When she talked, I was delighted. I loved to listen to her. Her voice resembled the violin playing of Salih el-Kwaiti or Abraham Selman's qanun. What would Chahlah do when she heard the news from this desolated city, from Karbala, the city of grief and agony, where my life was placed in the hands of the devil?

My fate was closer there than my jugular, and my life was more precious than dear Chahlah. I was terrified. Darkness prevailed and turned into layer upon layer, folded like your tobacco leaves. Layers of intense darkness, my premature death, and the night! I squeezed my eyelids shut, then blinked, pleading for God's mercy. I saw Him in my unconscious mind as something indescribable. Once I saw Him as a midget, then a giant. He refused to assert Himself. God was the Creator of Hitler, Churchill, and Stalin, the Creator of human sheep led to slaughter. God the angry and sad. God—you are the source of justice. Put an end to your anger! I prayed. Wake up. Why are you asleep?

The Nazi said, "He is a spy. He signaled enemy airplanes. Kill him now." The spy who begged mercy from Hitler's God, Churchill's God, Stalin's God—from God, the furious, the outraged—should be killed. An angry smoke rose from the rifle of the Nazi and was aimed at my chest from the mouth of the Angel of Death. Anger prevailed everywhere, smoke, and a sweeping disaster too. God, wake up! I prayed. Why are you sleeping?

My late father—may God's mercy be upon him—said, "Keep quiet and stay at home." I took the risk and went to Karbala, rushing to my fate, to the mouth of the rifle on my head. And death was closer to my head than to Chahlah and God. I pleaded, "God! Ezekiel the Prophet! Ezrah the Scribe! Hear, Oh Israel, the Lord is our God, the Lord is one." I hung on to a mirage while begging to extinguish God's flaring fire. "I will light one thousand candles for you, Oh God, if only I can return safely to Baghdad." Then I continued without a pause and said, "I promise it in my heart, but this is no vow. I promise, but this is no vow."

How frightened I was! Reason came to my aid even when I stepped over the threshold of the other world. Tell me, Khaduri, where would I have got the thousand candles to fulfill my vow? Even if I sold my clothes, it wouldn't be enough to buy a thousand candles. So I took a precaution and said twice, "I promise, but I don't vow." My honesty was more effective than a promise to bribe Him with no funds.

The Angels of Mercy arrived, and God's help drew near. My eyes were closed, and I intended to light one candle in Sheikh Ishaq Synagogue if I returned safely to Baghdad. One candle from an impoverished man is better than one thousand candles from a rich man. Isn't that enough, Khaduri? Suddenly, help came. Was I dreaming? I heard voices.

"Why do you want to kill him? Is this his reward for coming here to rejoice with us and give us a good time?" The voice of the Nazi buzzed in my ear.

"He's a spy. I saw him signaling to a British airplane."

"What airplane are you talking about? Where was the airplane?"

"It was here and left."

"Hey you! Don't drive me out of my mind! Don't force me to curse. In the first place, there's no airplane; in the second place, you see in front of you a squinting-eyed person who can barely see you standing next to him. So how could he see an airplane at night even if it were true that it flew here?"

"What? Maybe he heard it while it was hovering."

"Heard it? Did you hear Hitler's statements?"

I heard their argument, and fear enflamed my heart, mute pleading burned my lips. The voices—there were two of them, an angel's voice and a devil's plus a candle. Three voices, two angels and one devil, and two candles. Ezekiel the Prophet! Ezrah the Scribe! Shuwwa' Kohen! Three angels. Four candles! God's angels defeated the Nazis. Five candles! Five angels! Rabbi Me'ir Ba'al ha-Ness! Mercy! The Nazis were put to flight. The angels of mercy triumphed. They freed us, the night of the first of May 1941!

Restless and annoyed, I was sitting on the green painted bench among the trees of Ghazi Park in Bab el-Sharqi. I sang, "Oh sole traveler leaving me behind alone, why do you travel so far and forsake me?" May God not forgive Efrayim for what he has done to me! He is torturing me, himself, and my father, thought Sabriyah. As for me, I can endure suffering. I'm like a cat with nine lives.

Give me a cigarette, Khaduri!

Selman Hashwah was caught alone in the trap of the second of May in Karbala. There were sticks, clubs, and rifles' mouths, thirst, and falsely accusing fingers pointing, "You killed the prophets!"

The Nazis, and a thousand deaths! It was sunset on the second of May in Karbala, and the sun was scorching, penetrating into the soul . . .

Sabriyah was absorbed by loneliness, moving uncomfortably under malicious eyes that stared at her . . . Selman Hashwah was sucked into the traps of death—a thousand traps. His friends were scattered in a thousand directions, unprotected.

The Basrawis left for Basra, and the Baghdadis took precautions in advance. Only 'Ali Dabbu, the singer satirist, members of the theatrical troupe, and I remained. 'Ali Dabbu said to me, "I'm with you. Have no fear!" Then he started to call Jewish names sarcastically as if he were reciting a comic skit, "Hey, Shummail! Hey, Hesqail!" The eyes of the Nazis were alert, watching everywhere with angry eyes hunting for a lone woman.

In Ghazi Park at sunset, Sabriyah sat impatiently on a blue bench, overwhelmed by boredom and longing. Nets of starved eyes were woven around her, and death traps joined forces. If you escape from one trap, you would end up in another. Sabriyah said with a sigh, "What trouble this is!" Then she stood up, lost, since she had yet to find the goal of her persistent search. This goal was still in the Mosul train and in Bistan el-Khass . . .

Selman Hashwah was smoking Craven A cigarettes, nervously exhaling the smoke, covered by a rain cloud that showered a dark and gloomy memory with a grain of the red dust storm. He was stuck in a foul-smelling swamp, and his feet hung inside a giant human trap—a hell-bent scapegoat.

Sabriyah stood at the gate of Ghazi Park, stuck between two evils: Bistan el-Khass to the north and Bani S'id to the south. Which direction would she choose? She was confused . . .

Selman Hashwah was also confused how to save his life. The field was full of mines. Death was all around. Baghdad was far, and Mosul was further. Bistan el-Khass was closer than Bani S'id, but it seemed like the end of the earth . . .

Sabriyah hesitated, lost her way, didn't know where she would step next and in which direction she should move her legs. A young man followed her, but she didn't notice him. Then she heard a vulgar whistle from behind that drew her attention, and her confusion was replaced by a sort of warning siren. She sighed with frustration.

Muhsin 'Abd el-Wahid. I knew him only in the disastrous trip to Karbala. He was a member of the theatrical troupe. It never occurred to me that Muhsin 'Abd el-Wahid was another angel, the greatest angel of God, the angel Gabriel. He saw me crying in silence and suffering more than if I were a heretic. He put his right hand on his chest and assured me, "Look, Selman, don't be afraid! I'll escort you step-by-step and not leave you until I bring you home, even if it costs me my head. Don't be afraid."

Hey, Khaduri! Jamil says the Communists saved me. Do you think that the angel Gabriel is a Communist? Does this make sense?

Selman clung to Muhsin like tar to the road . . . Sabriyah headed to the right toward the lights, toward the crowd. She was no sheep or wild cat. She was a young and lovely married woman followed by evil people . . . The black face of the night coated the flickering lights of Bab el-Sharqi like a black demon, spreading ghosts of fear and death with a wide-open mouth of a beast. Selman sneaked into Baghdad. Muhsin 'Abd el-Wahid led him across the bridge like a sheep while Selman held the oud. His entire body was shivering as death penetrated into his soul.

Muhsin said to me, "Close your eyes. I'll lead you. It's better this way." I was blind even without this—blind because of the dark night, the fright, the death—and because I was leaving this world. Angry ghosts spawned in the darkness. There were pro-Nazi Kata'ib troops, arms, guards, nationalist groups, and Nazis. The guards stopped us at the beginning of the bridge located in the Karkh area of Baghdad. The guard asked us many questions like, "Where did you come from? Where are you going? What are you doing out at night? Don't you know there's a curfew?" When he asked to see our identification cards, I felt like the Earth had opened its mouth and was swallowing me up.

At that moment Sabriyah was going from one place to another in Bab al-Sharqi with self-confidence. She was fed up, angry, alone—yet together with the other people. Efrayim was far away. She felt the steps of an intruding young man. His voice interrupted her thoughts.

"My God, what a nice figure you have," he said.

She thought to herself, I taught Efrayim action, but words have gotten in the way. Still, he never said words like those to me. She avoided the young man and made regular steps toward the lights and the crowds. She neither rushed nor slowed down nor turned around. She heard nothing . . . disappeared.

Selman Hashwah didn't hear or see. He was in the Rusafah side of Baghdad and had just gone past another obstacle of death while holding onto Muhsin, who led him as if he were a beast of burden. Mute verses from Psalms occurred to him interlaced with names of prophets and saints.

The other obstacle drew near. Approaching Sabriyah, the young man said, "How beautiful your flowing hair is."

Amen! That word didn't count. My husband was absent, my father was angry. Selman Hashwah had vanished, and I didn't know what happened to him.

"How wonderful is your shining, lovely face."

Efrayim would shower my face with kisses. I desired his kisses too, but what should I do with this human animal that was preying on me?

"How charming your mole is. How beautiful your chin and breasts are."

There he was going gradually down my body parts and soon he would reach my vagina. What a big fuss is this? Sabriyah sighed. Soon he would approach her and she would be furious. Would she turn and spit in his face? Would she scream and gather everyone against him? Would she? No, she hoped, let him go on jabbering and he'll shut up.

He, however, continued to advance saying, "How delicate is your belly button."

That's it, he's almost there. When would Efrayim return from Mosul? She said furiously, "May he never return a hundred times, a thousand times!"

Immediately she jumped. A heavy weight pushed her from the back, and then the stranger faced her. She felt a sting in her breast—the sting of a scorpion, an animallike pinch with sensuous desire. She stifled her scream and envisioned Efrayim and her father. Rage almost overcame her, but she was strong and defeated it. She saw the stranger and recoiled. His complexion was dark. He had a pock-marked nose and scars on his face. He was filthy and juvenile.

"Listen, why don't I give you a dirham. Go to the movies and leave me alone," she whispered.

"I invite you to a movie. It's better for you to come along than to bribe me. There's a good film at the Ghazi Theater," he said with a smile.

What a shame, you devil! But she controlled her anger and said, "Listen, son!"

"I am not your son," he said, annoyed.

"Okay, my brother."

"I'm not your brother either."

What to do? Oh God! Efrayim had caused me a lot of pain. My father too. May God not count this against them!

"Forget it! I have no time for movies. I'm waiting for my husband. He's a police officer and bound to come anytime. What do you say? Will you take the dirham and leave? Isn't it better?"

She opened her purse to take out a dirham, but the young man vanished in the crowd. She looked at the faces. He had disappeared, melted like a block of ice over fire. She felt relieved, as if a mound of lead had been removed from her chest . . .

But the mountains of the world were still on Selman Hashwah's chest. Muhsin 'Abd el-Wahid identified himself, and the earth vomited Selman Hashwah after swallowing him. He continued to walk in darkness, carrying his cane and feeling the warmth of Muhsin's hand—the warmth of humanity, which once had bared devilish teeth.

Hitler . . . Nazism . . . Death . . . Muhsin 'Abd el-Wahid was not a man. He was certainly God's angel, Gabriel, Selman prayed. The night was intensely dark, and the alleys swallowed both of them. Selman walked and stumbled and repeated, "Rabbi Me'ir Ba'al ha-Ness! Shuwwa' Kohen! Nabi Hesqail! Ezrah ha-Sofer!" Death was beckoning but dying out . . .

Sabriyah hurried and stopped the first horse carriage she saw. Exhausted and out of breath, she mounted it and took a seat. She felt safe and commanded the driver to go to Bani S'id.

The carriage driver hesitated for a moment. Creased features twitched on his wrinkled face. Such a beautiful lady tells me to go to Bani S'id. I wonder what such a lady will do in Bani S'id. He was bewildered and pondering the matter in his mind. Finally he shrugged his shoulders and gave up. It's not my business, he realized. As long as I'm paid two or three dinars, I'll take her anywhere she wants to go, even to the graveyard. The driver whipped the horse harshly, and the carriage rushed off carrying Sabriyah inside.

In the beginning of our alley I stumbled and fell with the oud, and the silence was disturbed. The sound of the oud echoed, and it seemed that a crowd had gathered at the opening of our alley. The trembling sound started to awaken dozing death from its sleep. Bells tolled in the land of the rebellious demons that had been silent and sleeping for ages. The demons jumped from their graves. The armies of death reassembled and, this time, they possessed countless eyes. I fell, and the oud fell. I fell in the pits of the assembled eyes and sunk.

Give me another cigarette, Khaduri! I am troubling you, excuse me. Again I irritated God and recited, "Hear, Oh Israel!" It occurred to me in the turmoil of my death. My mind resembled a piece of glass that had crumbled into a heap of dust by the stones thrown at me, and my tongue became a piece of rag. Guards surrounded us from all sides. I went through the hardships of the busy world, and then on the bank of the river I collapsed entirely. This was the greatest disaster. I said to myself, "There's no way out. I didn't die in Karbala, I didn't die on the bridge, but my death will be close to our house." They would take me then, Khaduri, with holes in my body like a sieve. They would drag me in the dust, roll me in my blood and waste. I wouldn't even have a stretcher, not even a coffin.

Did I go wrong? Did I escape death, or was I a dead man walking, speaking, selling dyes and matches, and in loving Sabriyah experiencing all sorts of feelings not granted to others? At any rate, the main thing is that I opened my eyes. A neighborhood crowd assembled around Muhsin 'Abd el-Wahid and me. They recognized that I was Selman Hashwah himself. They talked about me for a while and decided, as neighbors, to let us go.

At the doorstep of my father's house, Muhsin, the greatest angel of God, left me. Exactly there, another thing had fallen—my mind! With a pounding, grinding in my head, I knocked on the door. I heard commotion inside, threatening, yelling, thundering, broken by ugly, jumbled, unpleasant voices. They then became clear and squeezed my empty stomach with the insane word, "Death, death." The door opened. My mind was topsy-turvy. Fog in terrifying shapes doubled my insanity. My late mother, a jinni with unkempt hair and bared teeth, sharpened her claws and screamed like a starved wolf, "Kill him, cut him into pieces! I'm hungry. I want to eat!" My own father was an odd and deformed wild animal. His face had one eye above his nose, and a horn grew above his eye. He had a tail like a snake, bent on encircling me. He yelled at me in a voice neither human nor animal, "You killed the prophets! You're a spy. You signaled to the airplanes. You should die, should die."

My aunt was a ghoul, a demon appearing in ever-changing shapes. Sometimes she resembled an old jinni or a mentally deformed human with an unsatisfied appetite for human flesh. I retreated screaming, barking like a dog. "For God's sake, I haven't done anything. Don't butcher me! Don't kill me! Don't eat me!" They hugged me as if they were strangling me. They kissed me, my body became like a rag. I thought they were biting me, and they went calling for Chahlah. It was in vain. Chahlah's sweet voice flew like that of a meek bird and sounded like the shrieks of an owl. The whole fright came from Chahlah's voice.

I was alone among the creatures that did not belong to this earth. I wished the world would be dissolved. If the world were reduced to nothing and what existed would turn into nothing, then maybe the most horrible nightmare would go away. They took me, and I woke up a month later. I was saved. Let my father die! Let my mother die!

Khaduri, give me one, give me one! People consider me a human like them. They think I am able to walk, talk, and smoke a cigarette.

Suddenly, the black ghost appeared at the beginning of the alley. He stopped, and Khaduri was momentarily troubled, then controlled himself. He shouted at the black ghost from the center of his shop, "Come in, my sister, Selman is like our brother!"

I recalled Khaduri saying to me, "She comes here to buy tobacco for her middle brother and says that Shihab won't smoke a hukkah unless he uses my tobacco." She lifted the veil, and I saw her brown-toned and delicate face. It was the first time that I had seen her face up close. She was truly pretty. I also remembered Sabriyah with regret and fondly called sincerely for my angelic guard.

"Don't worry Sabriyah! All the girls are stars, and you are their moon." Numerous feelings pinched me and erased the fog of my cursed memory. I felt embarrassed and yearned for Sabriyah. A sting of hunger pricked me, and I said to Khaduri, "It's about time for me to go. I'll go and eat a dish of beans at Fohah's place." I felt something was squeezing my heart because of hunger. Whenever I remember this story I feel hungry. "Please, tell me what I can do, Khaduri. I have no control over hunger. Let me gain strength and go back home. Maybe I'll see Sabriyah there. I'll do as Jamil told me and see what will happen. Maybe Sabriyah will make me forget."

3—Na'imah, the Barber's Wife

Why is Fayiq nervous? I only said to him, "I'll get a great reward in Heaven," and he got hot and bothered and said, "Stay where you are! Have you done everything else in order to become a matchmaker?"

What had I become except that? I'm no more than a normal woman who visits dear friends and likes to see the smile on their faces. What's wrong with that? I said to Fayiq, "Happy is the person who can bring two people together in a dignified manner."

He started to shout angrily, "Can you make Ya'gub get married? Don't you see he's swamped with work?"

What's wrong with that? Isn't marriage a religious obligation? Fayiq was not convincing, so I explained to him. "Why? Don't all married people work? Who'll agree to marry an unemployed man?"

"I tell you, good woman, don't get involved! How do you know that Ya'gub wants Sa'idah? You're only going to create problems and gossip."

'Amam wished to marry Ya'qub off, and Farhah wanted to hunt him down with a rifle for Sa'idah, her daughter, but Fayiq was fearful and saw all this as interfering in another's business. Sa'idah and Aminah live in their own rooms. The one is busy with sewing, and the other takes care of the rooster and the sheep.

But who will have the courage to ask dear Aminah's hand from her brothers? Why does Aminah mock me? I wonder how she can stand this situation. She is educated. She finished elementary school, believes in going out without a veil, and interprets things in a thousand different ways. Maybe those who went to school speak like her. Sa'idah left after the fourth year of elementary school.

Farhah said, "What can I do with Sa'idah? Her head can't take it in anymore. Do girls have to finish school? She knows how to read and write, and that's enough. She'll end up getting married and sitting at home to serve her husband and earn gold by sewing dresses."

One needs good luck to get married. God blessed me and gave me a man like Fayiq, but unfortunately Fayiq doesn't let me talk about matchmaking, and that makes me lose a great reward in the next world. Also, the house is quiet and needs some action. Sabri-yah is still sleeping. How happy is the trouble-free person! What do I have to worry about? Dear Nihad, may God protect him, is at school with Marrudi. 'Aibah is with Ya'gub in the shop, and 'Aibah's mother has left to wash people's clothes. Farhah is busy sewing, and so is Sa'idah, and 'Amam is very quiet. The men of the house left for work this morning like birds. Only Lulu, Moshiyah's daughter, and I stayed behind. How poor that woman is! She won't relax until Mar-rudi comes back.

Lulu said to me, "What to do, 'aini? I'm afraid for him. Every day I light a candle to the prophets so that Marrudi will come home safe and sound. My eyes watch the door and impatiently wait until the moment he opens it and walks in. I count the hours one by one, and I almost die waiting for school to be over and for his safe return. Every day is like this."

"Stop worrying, Lulu. Nihad goes to school with him, doesn't he? Leave them to God's protection and they'll be safe," I said.

Lulu pondered: "May God take care of Abu Nihad! What are you talking about, 'aini? My son is both an orphan and *walad 'aza*, a wimp. He was born after we were childless for ten years. We did everything to have him. I even put feces on my head, but as soon as he was born, his father passed away and couldn't enjoy seeing his son grow up and go to school."

My heart was broken. What should I have said to Lulu? She's a stricken woman. I ordered beads, a wolf's tooth, and three talismans to ward off the evil eye from Marrudi, and I bought him a new suit exactly like Nihad's to wear to school. I thought this might satisfy Lulu, but soon she said, "Do you know Umm Nihad, what I was thinking? I thought I would take Marrudi out of school and have him tutored at home. That is better than tearing my heart out and worry-ing about him from the time he goes to school until he comes home."

I thought that Lulu was insane, may God help her and give her strength. I said, "Let him go out, see people, see children his age, and become a man. Do you want to have him stay here and quarrel?

Lulu, don't be mad if I tell you that this child will be spoiled by your rotten pampering. You have pampered him too much." I was alone here with her and I would have to ask and answer questions. My heart would be torn hearing about Marrudi and his father.

Fayiq makes me depressed and upsets me too. Why does he keep me from earning a great reward? "I'll go out," said Na'imah. It's been a long time since I visited Na'imah, the midwife. I owe my life to her and Doctor Marsail. Na'imah is also a nurse, a physician's assistant in the operating room. What would have happened if Na'imah, the midwife, and Doctor Marsail hadn't taken the right measures promptly and removed my appendix? It exploded inside our Kurdish servant and he lost his life.

Na'imah called "the living dead," and really, in the last moment, the king of death seemed to vomit me up on the shore. Is it too much to give Na'imah a few presents? I'll bring her the silk fabric decorated with flowers that caught my eye yesterday in the market, two or three kilos of manna and a few walnuts and almonds, then I can visit her sweet and kind face. With all this, I'll buy my peace of mind and remove my present grief. To hell with the person who calls me a squanderer!

4—Gerjiyi Nati

Oh my Lord! Who was 'Aibah's father? Mr. Kelly, Mahmud Khan, or Babu Singh?

All three men were with her on the same night. Then she fell sick and didn't sleep with any of them for two months, by the end of which she discovered she was pregnant. The memory lashed her, a pang and regret, then another shattering blow. A wail of grief broke from her, mingling with the groans of pain rising from all her joints. Her bones felt crushed to powder, her spine in its folds of fat moaned. She looked at her camp bed with the brittle legs that were wobbly or broken, resting on the wooden floor of her small room. The bedstead's cording was slack. She was overwhelmed by a sharp biting smell similar to the stench of a ship's wet deck—a stinking whiff of the turbulent sea's dust-laden, unhealthy air. The palms of her hands were white, chapped, worn away by soap and water.

"My back has become as stiff as a board, and I can't move it. I shall lie down a little," she said. She sank noisily into the linen of her camp bed, and the floor of the small room trembled. Gerjiyi thought she was falling and plunging inside the shaky, sagging floor.

In Bombay she had been the castanets dancer in semireligious circles, a special black-market whore with three special men. And now she was a laundress in people's homes, living in a stinky wooden grave at the top of a house crowded with tenants. She was lost and overwhelmed with labor and misery. Indeed, "Steal with luck, commit adultery with luck, and cry for the unlucky ones." Mr. Kelly, Mahmud Khan, Babu Singh!

Like a rain cloud that makes the earth green, the days of her glory had vanished. 'Aibah asked her, "Who is my father? Why do all the people call me nagel?" He was told that nagel means someone who has no father. She made a special effort to recall, "I wonder who his father was?" A futile black cloud evaporated. The ocean breeze from the Malabar Hills, which usually blows in the monsoon season, suddenly blew up another cloud expelling the rottenness of the stuffy, stinking air of Bombay. There, she danced for the crowd around her and for the tan-skinned men. She wore red clothes and narcissus garlands. On her forehead was jasmine fragrance, and she was odorous with camphor. She danced to different drumbeats and to the melancholy and cheerful melodies of the oud. She danced in the center of the circle wearing a Punjabi dress decorated with designs and special prints. Bracelets adorned her wrists; anklets with bells shook and jingled above her bare feet. She was once a middle-sized, small-boned, and graceful woman without an ounce of fat. She didn't have bags of fat hanging from her forearms or wrinkles in her belly or hips like a cluster of dates. Her hair was plain, neither shiny ebony nor gray, nor unkempt, but it was long and thick, creamed with narghile oil. She shook her neck, and her hips resembled a cobra standing upright, twisting to the melody of the flute. She tiptoed, ran, prowled as lightly as a fearful cat.

Kelly came to the bed chamber, and Mahmud came, and Singh also came. Then 'Aibah was born. 'Aibah asked, "Who is my father?" She said, "A nagel is a fatherless son." She was again mixed up by many conflicting thoughts—yearning, joy, and grief combined with sudden pangs of despair. Everything was in vain. She tried very hard to revive her shabby memories—the features of the men, three men.

All were thin, with different shades of tawny skin, and she was a medium-sized, muscular woman. Now she was fat, full, and tan, while 'Aibah was medium-sized with brown skin. Unlike 'Aibah, the men had thin and soft lips, but she had rough lips that had thickened after the invasion of flesh and fat. Their noses and eyes were almost lost and seemed faded, semierased. She agonized recalling what her late mother used to say when 'Aibah was still in the cradle after fixing her eyes on his eyes. She would mumble with happiness, "This bastard is a duplicate of you. You're like two peas in a pod."

How did Ya'qub, 'Amam's son know? How did all Baghdad know? Confused, she thought, "As long as I don't know who made me conceive, all three are his fathers." They were a Jew, a Muslim, and a Hindu. They took up her time completely, sneaked into her life like an unnoticed puddle underfoot, like a passing fate. She was deeply perplexed, then things changed. How? She protested, and with a slight impulse of fear she jumped onto her wooden bed, its legs on the verge of breaking down, and stood on it. Does one surrender submissively, so easily, and shamefully?

The glorious days were gone, and everything was over. Why? Was business sluggish in Bombay, or was it her cursed old age? She stepped off the bed and walked to the wooden chest. Inside were the remnants of bygone glory. The dancing costumes were worn out, but they were a treasure she would not give up for the entire world. A bundle contained a folded silk handkerchief scented with ambergris and the picture of Gerjiyi, then a young popular dancer. She opened the bundle cautiously. Her eyes fixed on the picture, and the passing years flashed by like the gusts of a raging storm sweeping away everything.

She took out the golden comb and the decorated mirror with the silver frame, thrust the comb in her unkempt hair, and checked her eyes in the mirror. No! The situation was not as horrible as she imagined. Indeed, there was some gray hair. This was due to sorrow. I should dye it and make it look as before, she thought. There were wrinkles and pockets in her face. That was due to negligence, continuous hard work, and odd jobs. Oblivion! Her teeth made a clicking noise like a wounded lion. But how is the lion caught like this?

She remembered how she used to empty the pockets of her admirers who would fall before her altar with offerings of their souls and money. She would, without hesitating, kill them with kindness, play with their adoration, and suck the juice from a thousand sources. She filled up her pockets and her soul, and her lust swelled and then subsided. She was digging her own grave. Then, suddenly, she became a cat in February pining for young males and mewing for a mate. While she looked at the mirror, Ya'qub, 'Amam's son, appeared to her. She kept on looking attentively, examining, scrutinizing. No, she had not grown old yet. How old am I? Fifty? She wondered. Not yet, I'm far from fifty. A fifty-year-old woman would not have a monthly period; I do regularly. Maybe forty-five? No, that's too much. Forty? No, barely thirty-five. At the most I'm two years older than Ya'qub. So what? My sister Rajinah married a man who was ten years younger. I've deprived myself and buried my life with my own hands. It's all my fault.

She was overtaken by an eerie sweeping sound. She left the chest open with the items spread out before her. She stretched again on the portable bed holding her perfumed picture, looking at it and witnessing her past. She was a cat in quest again. She was dreaming of Ya'qub, but where was he?

5—Ya'qub, 'Amam's Son

Noon. I was still stuck in the shop, stuck between the armless chair and the anvil. I still had a thousand things to do. Everything in this world is work. Even pleasure becomes work. To burn your nerves waiting for this wicked Persian is to get yourself in a mess more difficult than hard labor. He's Persian, a blue jinni out to cheat, so judge for yourself. He would take you to the river and bring you back thirsty. In addition, he's a Jew.

"'Aibah! This Khoshi surpasses you in trickery and deception, but you're not less sly than he. I cautioned you a thousand times to stay here and keep an eye on the shop. People see you closing the shop when I'm gone, so don't use the occasion to play coins and dice games." I wished my partner, Nessim, and Khoshi the Persian were dead.

Woe is he who says to me "woe"! I wish I could smoke hukkah, drink a cup of tea in 'Alwan's Café, and play two rounds of backgammon or dominos. I wish the weather were clear so that we could go to the orchard. Three or four carriages would clatter away to the Slaikh, and we would take with us drinks, candy almonds, and nuts. The fruits would be in abundance, and we would pick the young oranges and the fresh and juicy sweet limes directly from the tree. My friends and I would be pleased. I asked the orchard caretaker to let the water flow in the orchard ditches. My friends and I would also look for a woman dancer with a beautiful face. "Enjoy greenery, water, and Eve's face. This is life!"

May people moan and groan at you, Nessim, my partner. How low and cheap you are! Since I can't stop you from stealing, I'd still like to know what you do with the stolen money. Do you stuff your pillow with it to put your head on when you die?

Khoshi's watch is slow by four hours every day. From now on, I'll arrange my daily schedule accordingly. This means that if Khoshi promises me his Persian goods at 9 a.m., I would have to meet 'Alwan at 2 p.m. There's no other way since I am forced to tolerate Khoshi's broken appointments and stupid jokes. His Persian goods are an inexhaustible goldmine, though his gold is fake—even charcoal is better. Women are excited about everything embellished and bright. The Persian slippers attract women's eyes in Baghdad though they are made of paper and cardboard instead of leather. Thanks to their stupidity, I'm able to pay the first payment for the annual leasing of the orchard, play backgammon and dominos at a loss, invite friends, pay the orchestra, and hold fabulous banquets. A thousand friends are better than one enemy. Some people complain and say, "What happened to the authorities? They're troublemakers and they fabricate things against us, the Jews. Are Rashid Ali and the Farhûd days back?" Let the Jews keep away from the heat of the fire, relax, and save themselves.

"'Aibah! Why are you sitting and doing nothing? Start a simple job to pass the time. Nail the strips on the slippers, straighten the nails, and sand the heels. Do something, pass the time! You're not making progress in this craft at all. All you are good at is playing coins and dice games. You're as clever as your mother is when it comes to vice. Now, most likely she's primping and beautifying herself to the teeth."

What does Gerjiyi Nati want? I saw her last Saturday when she looked gaudy with her hair dyed, wearing Indian bracelets. She was sitting cross-legged on a bamboo chair in the courtyard, showing off her heavy thighs that resemble tree trunks, and tanning herself while throwing sideways glances at the young men of the house. She also tried to win my friendship. The sight of her shamelessness makes even a rude person ashamed. Her eyes sent off sparks that stunned me and made my mind stop functioning.

I thought about the situation of 'Aibah's mother. What does she want? The old days are gone. They'll never come back. She's now a tenant in a chaste and honorable house, but she can't help herself. She'll manage to flood this pure house with disgrace and make us the talk of the town. So we'll have to wipe out this curse first and take care of the disease before it spreads. After I consulted my mind, I heard it saying to me, "It seems that this woman can't survive without a man." Then I asked it again, "Who'll desire such a woman with such vice and viciousness?" Even the mighty Samson can't tackle her terrible past. Now, she hides it in her fat body and her ugly face. My mind said, "Aren't there blind people in this world?"

Another hour passed, and His Majesty the Persian hadn't shown up yet. Cursed be the breasts that nursed you, Khoshi! You're a real Persian and a suspicious Jew. Why not? He's an expert in handling money. He shouldn't have a blind spot about women. Ah, here he is now dragging himself with a sack heavier than he is. What a relief!

I said to 'Aibah, pointing to Khoshi, "Hey 'Aibah! I will marry off your mother, Gerjiyi, to him!" 'Aibah jumped, shaking when he saw Khoshi, the 'Ajmi. He was first scared of him then annoyed, but when Khoshi liked my idea, he tipped 'Aibah ten fils. Then the face of the nagel laughed and promised he would not take a step out of the shop. Ho! Ho! Should I believe 'Aibah? He has extra money rattling in his pocket and he'll certainly go to gamble and then come back.

I left my shop. My dreams are truth, the truth of my life is dreams.

6—'Atiyah al-Qarawchi

How great it is when the good dream comes true! If my dear daughters come back, I'll hug them first, then sleep. If I feel relieved, and my poor unhappy Joudi feels relieved, and we get together with all the beloved ones, I'll isolate myself and stay home. I wish I had the ring of Solomon the Prophet to rub. The servant of the Master would appear and tell me, "Make a wish and your wish will come true, I am at your service!" I'd say to him, "Sir, I want neither wealth nor glory, neither gold nor silver, neither pearls nor diamonds. All I want is relief. I have no strength or sight anymore. Because of my grief, I have become dust, an animal in the butcher's hand. Sir, I beg of you to save me in life and death, by either having my daughters return, or by giving Joudi his brain back. Otherwise, let me die so that my eyes won't witness misery and my heart won't be grieved."

Does the good dream come true? Wishes are one thing, but realizing them is different. They are usually as far from each other as Bani Sa'id and Jubah. I sleep only one hour, which leaves me with twenty-three. I had become a lady surrounded by maids serving and fanning me. I found myself jerking in my sleep, then waking up with the tale of the black slave who was ordered by his wife, the princess, to separate white and black beads. If he had had the courage to disobey her, she would have killed him. I feel like that slave. I was given an ax and told to tear everything down, to tear down the rocks and the mountains and destroy myself and become crumbs like the bodies of my dear daughters.

Why, God? Why? It would have been better if you had taken me instead of Wafiqah, Joudi instead of Qadriyah. How dear they were to me! When the fire broke out at home, all the 'Aquliyah area burned down, and there was a leak in the cellar like a spring of water from hell. The angels began to cry, the people, the jinnis, and the animals too. Only God remained silent like a piece of wood, not moving.

Days before that, Wafiqah told me, "Mom, don't worry, you're atoning for the sins of the people. Don't you know that people are full of sins?"

I said to her, "Couldn't God find somebody else to make suffer for their sins?"

Qadriyah intervened. Like her sister she wore a white dress. She said to me, "No, Mom, nobody is moral enough. The people have become tyrants and unbelievers. You're the only pious one amidst libertines and a saint amid sinners."

I woke up from my sleep and saw Joudi sitting and digging in the dust of the wreckage, taking out worms and eating them. I tore my clothes, beat my brains, and yelled at Joudi, "Oh, the son of the shameful mother! Stop! Where did you learn this new vile habit of eating worms? Look, people will condemn you and you'll die in the desert!"

You think that Joudi will hear? You'd be better heard if you had shouted in a desolate desert. I cried, and my tears drowned the site of the ruin. I was overtaken by slumber and saw a beautiful garden in front of me. It had no beginning or end, and was full of blooming flowers, giving off fragrances. People were dispersed all over the garden, holding hands and walking, happy and having a good time. I reunited with my beloved Wafiqah, Qadriyah, and Joudi.

I asked, "Where are we?"

They said, "The Messiah has come. He has wiped out inequity and installed justice instead. People are equal, all of them rejoicing and loving. There will be no death anymore, or insanity and worries."

I remembered the Farhûd, and asked, "Will the Farhûd that I witnessed come back again?"

They laughed at me and said, "What Farhûd are you talking about? Don't you see that all people are brothers?"

I got up and decided to go to my friend 'Amam, Ya'gub's mother, and tell her the dream. Hey Joudi, the son of the disgraced mother! Enough is enough. Haven't you crammed enough worms down your throat? I've cooked a pot of tashrib soup for you that even the sick would desire.

Five

1—Naji el-Jundi

"Naji?" Shridah, the busboy asked.

"Yes, 'aini."

"Are you Naji or Sha'ul?"

"Whoever you want—Naji, Sha'ul."

"Are you one or two people?"

I laughed.

"May the devil take you, Shridah! How many do you see of me, one or two?"

"Well, why are you called el-Jundi?"

"I don't know; they named me that way."

"By Naji's honor, why?"

"Well, I'll tell you why. Long ago I was a *jundi*, a soldier. My fellow musicians called me Jundi. I left the military many years ago, but the nickname stuck."

"But why do they call you Naji 'Abd el-Wahab?"

"You mean, you don't know that either? I adore 'Abd el-Wahab, the musician, just as much as I worship and pray."

"Well, to which party do you belong? Communist, Zionist, Nationalist, or Dumbocratic?"

"No, dear, all the political parties are not worth one pair of shoes. My party is of a different kind. I belong to the Musicians Party."

"Explain to me what kind of a party that is."

"I, good man, belong to the 'Abd el-Wahab Party. All I do is listen to 'Abd el-Wahab and read art magazines."

The visitors in the café called for the busboy. Shridah jumped away from me and shouted back to them, "Coming, coming!" He left me alone.

Why had the fellows not come yet? They were my dear friends and colleagues. Maybe they stopped by another café.

Go to hell, Jamil! You're the reason for everything that happened. I want you to have a good time, but you're avoiding me. You run away from me and kidnap my friends and companions, when life is pleasant with friends and companions. There's no difference between man and animal in my eyes. I love man and I love animals and I love anything that the Mighty God has created. Tell me what's the difference between removing an obstacle in the way of a handicapped person, or helping a blind man, or a child, or an old man crossing a crowded street with deadly vehicles and recovering a puppy from a toilet or spreading my love to all creatures without exception?

But then there are some things that have priority over others. If I left a friend stranded for an hour or all day (and this often happens), he should know that it was not my fault, and that I received a humanitarian call to assist someone who was in trouble ten kilometers away. I would pursue a call to do a good deed even if it were a hundred miles away. My entire time is devoted to the Merciful, and I have not wasted one minute for the devil. That is my concern, so what can I do if my heart is made of a fresh, tender, and soft *shakar-lamah* cookie. I beg God to protect all His creatures so that my heart will stay healthy and beat calmly.

My brother, Hesqail, scolded me today because I didn't use the exact amount of ingredients in making Turkish delight. It didn't come out as hard as it should have. I coated the Turkish delight with syrup and it looked normal. Accidentally, Hesqail pressed a piece of the Turkish delight, and it got squashed in his fingers. The pungent pink liquid burst from inside out, as did my heart. My brother is rude sometimes and he doesn't understand. His heart becomes as hard as stone when he is angry and as unconscious as the heart of my divorced wife, the rabbi's daughter, may God keep you away from her. She wanted to undress before me and have sex at a time when I was busy saving the life of a poor dog that was stuck in a stinky man's pit of feces. I picked up the animal and let the lust of my divorced wife sink into the pit of filthy feces instead.

Hesqail said, "This batch of Turkish delight is no good. Throw it in the garbage!" How can my conscience allow me to cause him harm? Secretly and on my own initiative, I carried the heavy Turkish delight from the candy factory in Taht el-Takyah to the shop in the Shorjah Market. It was as if I woke up and saw the face of my ex-wife. Today, the opposite of everything I wanted happened. As soon as I put down the batch of Turkish delight, I started to gasp for air. The Turkish delight was mashed and resembled a piece of dough. I dirtied my clothes. Hesqail really gave me a hard time. I came to Jamil Rabi to pour out my grief to him, but seemingly he wasn't there. He had hidden himself and all my friends with him. Then Shridah, the busboy, also left me.

I was alone. Midnight was approaching, so there was no hope that a funeral would pass by and I would be able to join it and recite the Qiddish prayer if the deceased didn't have sons to do it. I had no electronic device to warn me that a creature may be in trouble somewhere, but I would run head over heels to help it, even to the South Pole or North Pole or the dense African jungles.

Feeling ashamed and with my head down, I said submissively to my brother Hesqail, "I don't care about my clothes, dear brother, but the Turkish delight will bother me for a whole year. How have I caused any harm? You should fire me from work." Suddenly his rage subsided, and he said in a rebuking tone, "Why do you feel ashamed, Sha'ul? You didn't do it intentionally; I've spoiled the sugar candies many times. Go, do your work and forget about it."

The situation is different because he's the owner and I'm no more than a worker in his shop for the daily wage of a quarter dinar. I caused him no less damage than twenty dinars. It's impossible to justify the damage by the intention. The damage is tangible, and there's no difference whether it was done intentionally or by God's decree. I'm also very careful not to cause damage to anyone; when I do, I should be punished. My brother, however, became concerned about my well-being and was so generous that he didn't let me repent. As long as he refuses to fire me, it would be a good idea for me to climb the 'Abakhanah powerhouse and jump from there. This is at least what I deserve. Otherwise, I won't be satisfied. I said to Hesqail, "I have to leave. Either you fire me, or I commit suicide."

Attempting to pacify his troublemaking employee, Hesqail said, "Perhaps you got mad at me because I yelled at you. Don't you know I'm moody? One minute I'm angry and the next minute I calm down. Come on, brother. Come on and give me your hand!" Then he kissed my hand tenderly.

Poor Mettana, the vendor of baking items, came carrying a basketwork tray on his head. The poor fellow is impatient until he sells one piece of pastry.

"Mettana, come on, my brother. Give me one with sugar!"

I saw such situations so much that I couldn't stand them anymore. But Mettana had to make a living. How much does this poor fellow earn? One fils for an item—and he has children? A quarter of a dinar is more than what I need.

I said to Hesqail, "Deduct one hundred fils from my daily wages until you receive full compensation for the Turkish delight I spoiled."

Hesqail rejected my fair proposal and said, "And on what will you live? Will you eat air? The remaining 150 fils do not go far today."

It's amazing that he knows that. Soon I carefully calculated my expenses for my art magazines, coffee, and tea, and I found that I was short one *qran*. I said, "Hesqail, do me the honor of leaving me with 170 fils. That will be exactly enough." He remained confused and embarrassed and left a sticky white spot where he scratched his head with incomprehension. Looking at me, he asked me with astonishment, "How will this be exactly enough for you? Explain to me, brother."

I explained to him my main expenditures, "Just a few cups of tea, tips, giving to beggars, and buying magazines. I don't smoke or enjoy alcohol, and I don't go to the Midan, the red-light district. I get my food, drink, and housing from my mother and father. So what's left to spend? Do I want to be rich and own the entire world?"

But Hesqail stared at me angrily and said with rage, "Brother, when will you sober up and consider what's good for you? I heard that my mother is looking for a decent and chaste girl for you. If you continue to think this way, how will you afford marriage? You have to save a little bit."

My brother Hesqail cares for my well-being, though if somebody else were to work for him for a quarter of a dinar a day, I would incite him to strike immediately and demand double the wages. I would say to him, "My brother is sucking your blood, my brother shouldn't be exploiting you." I'm no hypocrite. I'll hang myself for justice, but my brother is lucky in that respect. Undoubtedly, he chose me to work for him because he knew I put aside my private interests and fight vehemently for the interests of others. My brother, though, amazes me when he insults my intelligence. Does Hesqail think I'm stupid or crazy to believe that I can make a fortune from earning a quarter dinar per day, or buy a home and get married with such wages? Hesqail's fortune shines brightly as long as he deals with a person like me, whose heart is made of pure gold. What happened to me in my first marriage is pushing me to stay inside the fortress of this bachelorhood and never leave it.

I said to Hesqail, "Me, get married again! You think I have lost my mind? You saw what that wicked woman, the rabbi's daughter, did to me. As soon as the ink dried on the ketubah, the marriage contract, she asked for a divorce, but did anyone else do what you did on your wedding night?"

No one understands me. The good deed is defeated, forsaken, with no supporter. What I do looks ambiguous, abnormal, and not understandable. Let it be so! Even if everyone despises good deeds, I'll remain loyal to them. Good deeds are not appreciated, and people step on you without conscience or mercy. Let them say whatever they want. I'm in favor of good deeds to the last breath of my life.

Where are my fellows? Goddammit, Jamil! You ran away from me and took them along. Just wait and see what I'll do. You won't go far. I'll search all the cafés of Baghdad. I will find my friends and companions, spend the night conversing with them, and tell Jamil about my unfortunate dog, and make him happy.

2—'Aziz Ghawi

My senior year of high school turned out to be a failure, while the bars, nightclubs, and streets of Baghdad were flourishing. Baghdad's air was filthy and very cold, but the roads were cleaned and rinsed. I sneaked out of one trap, cast my nets, and walked into the trap of her eyes. Then I found my life.

As usual, I entrusted my books and notebooks to Radi, the grocer in the Sinak Quarter, and started another day of going hunting, loafing, and anticipating. Salimah was my target, my imagination and reality, and I waited for her. Time was insignificant before I saw her. It became valuable as soon as I saw her. Passing like the whispering of the wind, time became the dearest thing I possessed, and my most hated enemy. Time is now precious, trivial, and heavy.

I turned out to be a professional liar, a worthless person. I was lost by the looks of her eyes and found myself in this vast terrifying world. Meanwhile, my mother was imagining that I attended school and sat at the desk in the rear of the classroom. I deceived her; let her sleep soundly under an invisible sun, hiding behind the clouds. I have torn up the illusion of my life, ripped out my loss, and buried it at the bar of a nightclub in Bab el-Sharqi. Salimah is my life, my soul. Salimah-*choka-boka*!

She appeared in front of me while I was eating a modest lunch in the kebob shop. My food disappeared and so did other things. I nibbled the slice of pickled cucumber. I also nibbled my sweet imaginations. My mouth was filled with the distinct sharp smell from the arrack that I drank when I met Salimah for the first time. At that time, I was standing at the bar fighting for my life. Taking my time, I slowly drank my first sip from the white glass. My features screwed together and I felt the taste of sharp arrows in my throat. The wine in my cousin's bar was tastier, because it wasn't mixed with anything. My cousin, Yusuf 'Abd el-Nabi, was a stallion.

Salimah walked in, smiling, with a swinging gait, like a goose among half-drunk men. Our eyes met. She winked at me and smiled again. I had the hope of an abandoned orphan who found an adopting parent. She immediately materialized my hope, and my soul set out to pursue her. She stood at a table next to a corpulent man with a big belly. Her smile was killing me. Her teeth were like a string of pearls between her lips. So, God melted the souls of the radiant, pure angels into drops arranged in two rows between her lips. Then I knew that I was an original poet. But no, I meant to say that the pearls were cheap and disgusting. Everything else she had was unique and praiseworthy. So why did I stay a senior for five years? Cautiously, I asked the busboy in the café, "What is her name?"

"Salimah," he said, indifferent to my silent prayers. With difficulty, I controlled myself. My voice left me, retreating, becoming hoarse, and leaving me with no more than a thin whisper.

"Salimah Pasha," he said.

At the kebob shop, the waiter laughed at me and said, "Why don't you make her out to be Umm Kulthum, the greatest Egyptian singer? You seem fresh, innocent, and naïve." I was mad and felt humiliated not only for myself but also for Salimah, whom I had known since Farhah Ghawi gave birth to me. The waiter was throwing stones at me and casting rotten eggs at the imaginary crystal dome that her eyes had built in my world. "You like her, don't you?" he asked.

I lied if I claimed to know more than I did. Angry, I shoved the glass toward his face. Suddenly her look came into my soul. The fire of my anger was extinguished, and a different kind of fire broke out. I wished she would sit next to me and drink with me, not wine, but a toast to my honor and my life. The waiter said with the certainty of a know-it-all, "All things obey money. With money, not only Salimah-choka-boka will sit with you but her bosses too."

The waiter continued to defile the holiness of my temple. I realized from then on that there was nothing more than her, nothing more than Salimah. Yes, to be bankrupt means death, and he who has no money is not worth even one fils. And there I was bargaining over one dinar that I had once given to a filthy whore with a pug nose. I obtained the dinar by a trick, just as I obtained the second, fourth, and sixth dinars. Later this trick was disclosed, and my uncles expelled me. What did I do next? I watched next to Farhah Ghawi's sewing hall and only went inside when the last client left. I saw money all over the place, and Her Majesty Sa'idah was collecting it.

My mother was wrinkling the bills and stuffing them between her breasts. Sa'idah was disturbed when she saw me. I was on the verge of hating myself again. A man like me, lowering himself before women! Still, my life was mild-tempered with Salimah, and she could make all obstacles easy for me. My humiliation in the red-light district turned into pride. I didn't hesitate to answer when Farhah Ghawi said, "Dear 'Aziz, do you need money?" I did have a right to some compensation because she humiliated me and damaged my ego. For the first time, I felt I was beginning to become a real man when the magic bills that Farhah had slipped between her breasts landed in the breasts of Salimah. I'll become a man with her now, without phoniness, something real will spring from illusion.

Salimah appeared in front of me beckoning, smiling at me, making me feel I am a real human. Many unknown things overwhelmed me in her disheartening, small room. I had to be with her all the time, so that she would hear my voice praising her whenever she raised her head. Whenever our eyes met, I felt my poetic talent surge, and also my arrogance, when I was about to smash a glass on the waiter's head.

"Give me two dinars! Pass two dinars to me!" I said to Farhah.

"Aren't two dinars too much, 'aini? What are you going to do with them?"

Too much! Not so. But your child turned into a man and one dirham is no longer enough for him, is it?

"I have to pay for books, notebooks, taxis, cigarettes," and Salimah. I also thought about selling my books and my unused notebooks but later changed my mind. Farhah Ghawi should remain in the dark. I saw her hesitating and shouted, "Will you give me something or should I quit school?"

I held the two dinars and looked at Her Majesty Sa'idah. She was pale and angry and undoubtedly hated me. I certainly hated her. The hidden hatred between us was now raging in Sa'idah's eyes as if I had stolen kilos of fat from her body. I decided to be frank with her. "What's wrong with you? You look mad. Do you want to eat me alive? Did the two dinars she gave me cause you pain? They aren't yours anyway. You have become tightfisted. Should everyone working in this house give you all his earnings?"

I heard her rapid breathing. Farhah Ghawi also kept silent. She had nothing to say. She was confused, and as 'Atiyah al-Qarawchi says, "She was like a ship sailing between two cliffs."

Sa'idah was angry but silent, unusual because she usually uttered a hundred words per minute. The entire world could hear her loud, polished voice sinking down in a pit of refuse that could penetrate many thick heads and more than one hollow skull. It came from her disintegrated brain that held putrid thoughts in a giant black spider web—dead but able to think, mummified but able to move.

She was a twenty-year-old virgin bride like one from the Nile. There must be a ransom to free her. How would the knight of her dreams kidnap her without a dowry of gold? This grave of a room she was buried in!

Has the knight of your dreams shown up yet? Not yet, so you're mad at me. I'm your victim, Oh woman! Bravo 'Abdallah Ghawi, the bull, for running away from us to Mahmudiyah! Like you, I'll run away from these women into Salimah's arms.

What a great woman Sa'idah is! She is charming when angry. Her face becomes red, her lips tighter, her cheek leaner and more noticeable. Her small nose twitches proudly. The man who marries her is lucky, but men are blind, no doubt, as blind as the pug nose of a whore, like my uncles, my cousin, and Ya'qub the Shoemaker.

Sa'idah was angry at me. The silent war between us sounded its first scream. She yelled, "Beat it!" I looked down on her, but she broke into my heart. I despised her but at the same time felt pity for her. I answered her with a smack, "I wish you were dead, God willing!" Frightened, I stared at her while deep in my heart I murmured, "I wish I were in Salimah's arms." Salimah!

The two dinars were now in my pocket, but I needed a greater stock of money in hand. I looked for a job at a printing house and cut paper for low wages, but I didn't like either the job or the wages. I left and resorted to my cousin Yusuf and borrowed another dinar with great difficulty.

Salimah, though, sat next to me. My mouth was parched, and my tongue stopped wagging. She treated me like a child.

"What will you have to drink, fedwah, may I be a sacrifice for you?" she asked me.

"Why don't you ask me in the Jewish dialect, *kepparah*, what will you drink? Whatever you drink, I drink." If you ask for the soul's elixir, I'll bring it to you, even if it comes out of a spring guarded by a thousand rebels holding swords of fire. She thinks I'm a child, a regular client who comes to have a good time and leaves. She thinks I embarrass her intentionally by talking with her in the Jewish dialect.

"I drink champagne. Try it if you haven't yet. It's good for boys like you. It's not strong," she answered back in Muslim dialect.

I lowered my voice and whispered to her, "Salimah, talk like a Jew; talk like me. I'm not a client like those you see here. I came because of you. I love you."

She laughed. Did she laugh at me? Not at all. She was playing hard to get. She was a woman of few words, but she still considered me a child, "May your mother celebrate marrying you off! It's better if you go and sit on her lap."

Should I take an oath to prove that I'm a man? I wasted my youth from my freshman year in high school to my senior year. I wasted one extra year as a freshman, two as a sophomore, and three as a senior. Add it all together and you get a lot of years. This clearly shows that I'm not lying by saying that I'm a man. I swear by your breasts and eyes that I am a man.

She glanced at me with affection, sipped only a few drops, and I paid the bill. I needed a stronger drink. I was out of money and thought to drink in my cousin's bar and just charge it. I'll come back to you! I'll come back, Salimah, I must. I'll come tomorrow, every day, every hour, every minute, every second.

The vapor rose from the cooking kettle and I saw the name of Salimah written in it while staring at the empty kebob dish. I saw her picture outlined. I'm here, at noon, with blind people who don't see that my life is Salimah, who don't see that my sister is Sa'idah.

I left empty handed. I would go out to hunt for dinars. Where would I cast my net this time?

I'll go to Mahmudiyah. There's still plenty of time to go and get my father's money and return on time.

3—Gerjiyi Nati

A shelter! What attractive yellow metal, and a pleasing marriage . . . And you, Khoshi, resemble the bird that, wherever it alights, picks fat grains from the ground.

Khoshi drank the glass of orange punch with such a giant disgusting sip that it made a sucking whistle, and then he passed the empty glass to 'Amam. A deep smile appeared on 'Amam's kind and welcoming face. She said, "Congratulations! Inshallah, everything will turn out well."

Farhah Ghawi frowned with disgust. She whispered to herself, "He drank like an animal as if he hadn't drunk punch before. How awful! Even if I had a blind dog I wouldn't marry it off to him."

Everything in Gerjiyi Nati's body calmed down except her eyes, which didn't stop moving between the two men—Ya'qub, 'Amam's son, and Khoshi, the Persian. A magnetic power attracted her to Ya'qub, and an aversion mixed with fright and pain turned her away from Khoshi. A fire of thoughts kindled in her mind, fed by the fuel of the past and the present. Here in 'Amam's room there was an old Persian man looking at Gerjiyi's gold Indian bracelets with fervent desire. Gerjiyi had always been cherished and respected by well-known men. A host of thoughts stabbed her desiring heart—love, wealth, and glory stood out among them—and gratified masculinity had always kneeled to her femininity. Why had time not stopped then? What would happen if her youth had frozen in place, in her bedroom in Bombay ten years ago—or was it fifteen years?

"I wish I had died then!" she thought. Those bygone moments escaped her inadvertently and were maliciously swept up in the current and engulfed. She was consumed by the flame of those enjoyable years. She saw Ya'qub once again, and saw Kelly, Mahmud, and Singh. Had the tide of time come back after continuous ebb? Did the Zoroastrian fire die out too?

'Amam said, "By my fortune, you're a good match. Both of you are lonely. Neither he nor you have anyone. You'll cuddle up to each other and be settled comfortably."

The tenants of the house scattered, and Gerjiyi Nati's eyes slipped away from Khoshi's giant belly, moved away from his face, and hid between his legs. The frozen ice of the past had melted and cast her here. Her memory still turned fearfully toward the source, the stream of time, regretting it all. There was a great distance between the past that carried her away and her present.

She sneaked further between Khoshi's legs, concealing her initial shyness of his genitals, and became an old cat with remnants of passion. Like a cat in heat, she yearned to find a male cat, any cat. Resigned, she said to herself, "If all my wishes had come true, I would have remained in Bombay and would have been respected and honored by men."

Ya'qub, 'Amam's son, belonged to the present, and it was probable that cruel time had changed Kelly, Mahmud, and Singh, and they had grown old. She forcefully turned her eyes away from Ya'qub's magnetic charm and fixed them on Khoshi's prickly appearance. She was bound to get used to him. Suddenly her thoughts swerved, turned sharply, and she didn't know where she was heading. Was she going from illusion to reality or from reality to illusion? Would she stay away from the herds of the crowds? Would she be headed toward them and go with the stream? All things seemed the same. She was unlucky, contemptible, and a slave subjugated by the bodies of three men. She had never experienced the joy of a wedding like other people. She sighed for the loss, and so did Farhah Ghawi, but Farhah was also resentful. Ya'qub knew how to help others and do favors for people and marry off Gerjiyi. Did he know how to do well for himself? Why was he blind to my daughter, Sa'idah?

"What do you say, Gerjiyi, is it a deal?" 'Amam asked when she served coffee to the guests.

Gerjiyi blushed. She was put on the spot. She whispered hesitatingly, both convinced and unsure of 'Amam's question.

"What can I do? I do whatever you tell me to and wear whatever you design and sew for me." Then all the women uttered shrilling sounds of joy.

Ya'qub, 'Amam's son, said to himself happily, "I was right that she couldn't survive without a man. She didn't give up even this smelly, stinky Persian." He thought for a while and then was convinced that the two were as fit for each other as a lid to its pot.

＊

Farhah Ghawi said mockingly, "Shame on her! What would you say to a woman her age? She wants to have a *hinni* party too."

'Amam answered, "Isn't she a human being, poor woman? She was never married before and nobody had a hinni party for her. She wants to have her dream come true."

Ya'qub interrupted, "For heaven's sake, enough! Two old beaten people want to get married. Do you want to make people laugh at us?"

'Amam pondered a moment then whispered, "But the situation in the country is unstable, and the authorities try to find excuses to arrest people. I'm worried that it will spoil our joy."

Na'imah, the barber's wife, was first happy, then upset. She rebuked Fayiq saying, "You see how Ya'gub has been rewarded for what he did for Gerjiyi, and you didn't even let me talk for Sa'idah?" Fayiq thought it was better for his wife to keep silent, so he avoided answering her. Farhah Ghawi remembered suddenly that dyeing her daughter's finger with henna or staining her clothes with the dye after the bride and the groom finish dyeing their fingers might expedite the marriage of her own daughter. She resigned herself to taking advantage of this lucky opportunity, and her mocking voice became almost submissive:

"Let us have a hinni party for her and satisfy her desires," said Farhah.

'Amam happily agreed, "But what are we going to do for this poor woman? Will this be a phony wedding where we only pretend to celebrate in happiness for one or two hours?"

Ya'qub found the ideal solution: "The best thing to do is to combine the hinni party with the wedding night and celebrate them on one night. We'll only invite the tenants and not tell anyone else."

Na'imah was worried. Where would the couple sleep on their wedding night? Thoughts came to her assistance. She had an idea. She said to Fayiq, "Fayiq, where will they sleep? Gerjiyi only has an outdoor bed from which her legs stick halfway out. You know what? I've been thinking of letting them sleep in our bedroom on their wedding night."

Fayiq stared at her angrily and huffed, "And where will you sleep, 'aini?"

"It's only one night and it'll pass quickly. I'll sleep with Sabriyah. Her husband may be gone, and I'll have Nihad sleep with Marrudi."

"Well, what about me?"

"Why are you complicating things? Go sleep at your parents' home. It's only one night."

"And where will they sleep the second and third nights, dear woman?"

Worried again, she drew near Fayiq and smiled at him, not knowing why he was so nervous lately.

"What happened? Why are you sour and irritable these days? Isn't this just a discussion? You know, Abu Nihad, I've been thinking of giving them our new bed. In any case, we have to give them a wedding gift."

"Do you know this is the fourth bed I bought for Your Royal Highness this year?"

"So? What happened that makes you stingy, all of a sudden? You're starting to hold me to account a lot of times, Fayiq! Don't make a fuss about it, may God bless you, and you'll buy another one."

He calmed down but warned her, "If you put the bed in the wooden-floored room, I won't be held responsible."

She smiled while combing his hair and appeasing him. "I'm responsible. It shouldn't be your concern."

He freed himself from her hands sighing, "As you say, dear Na'imah . . . Well, I'm leaving." And immediately he left.

There still remained 'Aibah's problem. Where would he sleep after the marriage of his mother? The eyes of the people present turned toward the young men's room, but Jamil warned Selman Hashwah and both kept silent. 'Aziz Ghawi rejected the idea vehemently and expressed his rejection by cursing 'Aibah and including Gerjiyi Nati in the curse. Lulu, Moshiyah's daughter, made excuses too, and said to Na'imah, "If Nihad were the one, I would welcome him, take good care of him, and give him a place to sleep with Marrudi. But 'Aibah seems to be something else. He carries the devil's germs in his soul, and I'm worried that he'll infect Marrudi."

In fact, Lulu was taking care of her own needs and concealing them, since she was an introverted woman and liked to be alone inside her shell. She was still tender to the pain of her husband's tragic death and felt compassion for her son, her only hope in this world. She cherished these sentiments with no restraint, felt completely isolated in her pain, and would not let anyone intrude or disturb her, even if he were a boy of Marrudi's age. So where would 'Aibah sleep from now on?

Farhah Ghawi suggested sarcastically, "Whoever has the space should cooperate. Meanwhile, he'll sleep at everyone's place. For example, when Efrayim is not home 'Aibah will sleep at his place."

Sabriyah jumped up, alarmed. So Farhah hasn't stopped annoying me. What does Farhah Ghawi want from me? Sabriyah wondered, shivering. There are still the scratches and hidden scars that 'Aibah left on my breasts, face, and lips. I still smell the nauseating, stinky onion odor he gave off—a chilly feeling like the edge of a sharpened knife stabs and cuts me. If I agree, he'll rape me this time, for sure. It's bound to happen, and I'll be humiliated and disgraced. This Farhah Ghawi! She raises her hand to slap my honor, my feeling, my soul, but never my face.

In fact, Sabriyah was distressed at revealing her weakness. She despised Farhah Ghawi and firmly said, "No!" Her refusal branched out in more than one direction and included Farhah, her father, and Efrayim. Efrayim continued to insult and humiliate her without knowing. He traveled and left her behind. She hated him so much that her hatred intensified to furious rage. She despised him as much as possible, even more than she despised Farhah Ghawi. She sheltered ambiguous feelings for 'Aibah that she herself could not understand, mixed feelings of sympathy and apathy. 'Aibah was wretched and malicious, and Farhah must be evil. Her father was arrogant and critical. She wondered if her husband was dull by nature.

Na'imah's enthusiasm returned to her and dominated her. Why wouldn't she let 'Aibah sleep with Nahhudi in her room? She wondered. What's wrong with that?

Fayiq opened his eyes wide, dragged Na'imah to a corner in the room, and pointed to a rectangular spot where their bed stood until that morning before it was moved to the wooden-floored room.

"Look with your own eyes," he said. "Here Nihad sleeps, and here we sleep. Bravo, woman! Can't you think a little and ask yourself how I could let a stranger watch us sleeping?"

"He's just a little boy. What does he understand?" She replied defiantly.

"There's no power and no strength save in God. I hope God saves me from this!" Fayiq said, and added furiously, "Since this is the case, he should sleep with his mother and her husband. Why are you people worried about finding him a place to sleep?"

'Amam, however, settled the matter easily. "No one should worry. My son, Ya'qub, and I will take care of him. From now on, his boss will sleep with 'Aibah next to him. I'm like his mother, and Ya'qub is like his brother."

The problem of 'Aibah's sleep was solved, but it left some tenants with a certain apprehension.

A naive shyness fell over 'Amam. She was embarrassed and apologized by whispering, "The place is small, but he who loves also forgives." They were crowded in a box where everything was modest. The room was filled with smells of *salonah* fried fish and homemade pickled vegetables made by 'Amam, an expert, with the help of Lulu and Na'imah. The food was placed on the table in the middle of the room, and there was hardly a place to stand. 'Abdallah Ghawi postponed his trip to Mahmudiyah to attend the wedding ceremony and serve as a witness with Ya'qub, 'Amam's son. He was restless and so pressed between his wife and daughters that he had to hold his breath. He and Selman Hashwah occupied one quarter of the room, and Gerjiyi and Khoshi another.

Even Lulu, Moshiyah's daughter, came down from her room with hesitation. 'Amam had urged her in the morning to attend the wedding. She held her hand in the kitchen and pleaded, "Abdalek, do come! I'm worried you won't."

Lulu's face was flushed and she frowned. She felt a hot stream rising to her face, then climbing into her eyes, and a hot well of tears exploded from her. She wiped her face and eyes with her open hand, and while sighing and leaning on a shaking black wall said, "How is it possible to enjoy anything after the death of my husband? I worry enough when Marrudi goes down and plays with the kids."

'Amam offered her a glass of water. Lulu wiped her hands on her clothes and took it.

"Come down, Lulu, for the sake of your son, Marrudi. Do you want to disappoint Gerjiyi? The poor woman has nobody and we all should help and make her happy," 'Amam said.

Na'imah listened while she turned pieces of fish in the frying pan and put the stone weight back on the pieces as the sizzling died down. She said reproachfully, "No, Lulu! You have really gone too far. We seldom have a happy occasion in this house. We should all roll up our sleeves and help. Do you think it's fair for you to stay in your room alone? What will people say about you? You are not mad at Gerjiyi, are you?"

Without any hesitation, 'Amam mumbled in agreement with Na'imah. "You're right, Na'imah, may your father and mother rest in peace. The heart still cherishes the deceased person, and he'll rejoice in his grave. Isn't it so, Lulu? For the sake of God, come down, Lulu, and attend the celebration. Do it for Marrudi's sake and to make poor Gerjiyi happy."

Now Lulu sat in the crowd not caring about what was going on around her. A heavy feeling of remorse and grief filled her, and then she heard the voices of the young men. Of all the voices only Marrudi's entered her ears. She heard it, as if taking in an angel's voice, and his dead father looked from his grave, laughing with happiness. She saw him and Marrudi walking slowly in a sweet dream and stepping into a world full of joy—a world in which God hadn't a kernel of grief in store.

The dead man said, "This is your life after my death."

And she whispered, "Marrudi!" She felt relieved, and the heavy feeling inside her disappeared and was replaced by warmth and happiness. Lulu looked at 'Amam's gentle face with gratitude and thought, "How good you are, 'Amam! You do many *miswah*, good deeds.

Ya'qub turned his sight from Khoshi mumbling, "What a sloppy son of a whore he is! He comes to his own wedding wearing his patched, everyday clothes. He doesn't even know he should have changed his clothes. Shame on you and on every stinky Persian miser like you." Ya'qub was drowning in a whirlpool of intoxication, the result of one of his bouts of joyful merriment. These bouts had increased ever since he leased the orchard. He addressed the crowd, "Friends, the rabbi's in a hurry! Let's write the ketubah, the marriage contract, and betroth the couple, and then we'll start the celebration."

The guests were alarmed. Gerjiyi had demanded without previous notice that Khoshi write ten thousand dinars into the marriage contract as a dowry for her. Ya'qub said, "This daughter of a whore seems to have changed her mind and wants to spoil the deal, and now this Persian will run away when he hears about it." But Khoshi didn't move.

All the guests shouted when Khoshi announced that he agreed—all except Jamil Rabi, who leaned and whispered in Selman's ear, "Be careful, he's a swindler. Only the person who harbors bad intentions doesn't mind whether it's one thousand or ten thousand dinars. He only promises and signs papers. To hell with it! Let her go and get the money from a bankrupt bank."

Khoshi hesitated. He turned around many times until he took a silver ring from his pocket. He didn't know what to say when he put it on Gerjiyi's finger, but he repeated after the rabbi, word for word.

Ya'qub cried out, "Sound your cheers of joy, women!" Harsh vibrating cries resembling a train whistle broke out . . . Efrayim's train stopped in Biji Station. He was traveling on it, secluded from thousands of passengers. He thought only of Sabriyah and said, "She is unfortunate." She said, "Bastard!" She was alone in her bedroom crying.

Ya'qub snapped his fingers on the tambourine; Jamil played the qanun, and Selman the oud. Selman looked for a lost thing, his doll Sabriyah, the blossom of his bygone days and the essence of his present life.

'Aziz Ghawi's doll turned into a woman of flesh, blood, and bones, and singing in a nightclub in Bab el-Sharqi. His soul was an extension of hers. She gave him a new life and connected his heart to the stage. Still, he lived in anxiety. The forthcoming moment embraced the past, present, and the future. As soon as Salimah finished singing and came down from the stage, he had it all, everything. His excitement was tremendous, impossible to subdue.

There were frenzied noises in 'Amam's room, in 'Aziz's soul, in Sabriyah's eyes, and an attack of joy pressing recklessly inside Ya'qub. A sarcastic and sad joke existed in Jamil's mind, and in Selman's heart fragments of hope and promise occasionally alleviated a lost and repressed desire. There also existed composure and happiness in 'Amam's face, a sort of carefree attitude coming from the firm indifference of 'Abdallah Ghawi's nature, and a very ravenous desire that mercilessly sucked out Farhah Ghawi's freshness.

Gerjiyi's fingers were dyed with henna, followed by Khoshi's, and then came Sa'idah's turn. Na'imah insisted on dyeing Sa'idah's fingers and announced to the guests, "Lord, my generous Lord, help Sa'idah, Farhah's daughter, for the honor of every saint and prophet! Enough, get going! What are you waiting for? There's no time, the groom is here."

Fayiq's glare missed Na'imah's preoccupied eye. Ya'qub heard nothing. He was busy singing and beating the tambourine with avidity that almost tore the leather. He sang a wedding song, "We will not let the person with the henna alone . . . ." The henna was in Gerjiyi's fingers, in Khoshi's, in Sa'idah's, and in 'Abdallah Ghawi's. Farhah's heart became red with the henna, pure red.

Sabriyah's eyes were as dark as the blood pooling behind her tears. She heard the cheers of joy and the roaring noise of the Mosul train. Are you behaving like this Efrayim? Even tonight you left me alone. Won't you listen to one word I say? "So, what will happen if you take two days leave?" she had asked earlier. "Swap your shift with somebody else! I'm stuck here. Did I marry you or your room?"

"I can't, I'll be fired," he replied. "Didn't you see my bosses? They're on the verge of exploding, looking for an excuse to fire people. I don't want to give them any excuse to fire me."

Sabriyah begged him. It was not her style to beg, but she did so with Efrayim. She also fired questions at him. Still, let it be! Let him be fired if he doesn't dare to quit his job voluntarily, let him be forced to leave! She wanted him to look for a different job that didn't take him away from her constantly. But her words were in vain. He left her alone crying.

Alone, Efrayim swayed back and forth on the dirty floor of the crowded third-class compartment, punching tickets without checking them. He felt a lead ball rolling inside him, a feeling of inadequacy, incapability, and remorse.

"Why isn't Sabriyah here?" said Na'imah. "Where is she?" Selman's heart throbbed. He knew where she was in the ongoing commotion.

'Amam said, "I'll go and check in her room." Na'imah followed her, and Selman was pleased. The strings of his heart throbbed powerfully with the strings of his oud.

Salimah came down from the stage and all 'Aziz Ghawi's heartstrings trembled tensely and never stopped. His mother felt ongoing distress, and she poked 'Abdallah with her fist, "Where does 'Aziz go each night?"

She had asked 'Aziz the same question before, and he, in turn, continued to tell her every day in a threatening, louder tone, "If you want me to pass this year, don't ask me. I go to a friend's house to study until midnight. Enough failing and shame!"

It was crowded that night. Was it reasonable to think that one night would do what a whole year couldn't? Could it be the difference between success and failure? Would one night decide the fates of 'Aziz and Salimah over the course of six years? It was only a moment, a continuous moment that began at the nightclub and extended to many nights, his life's dream and hope.

"Leave him alone! What do you want from him? He knows what's good for him, to study or to have fun. He's grown into an independent man," 'Abdallah Ghawi said indifferently.

Sabriyah was overcome by languor. She wiped her eyes and saw the world growing smaller and narrower. She was escaping inside herself on a one-way road with no exit. She said to Na'imah, "I have a headache. I can't come to the party. Excuse me, 'aini."

It was useless! The road was closed and there was no way out. Where could Sabriyah run? Efrayim was traveling far away on the train to Mosul. He didn't inquire about her, neither did her father. Na'imah pulled Sabriyah up saying, "Come on, come on! Couldn't you find any better night to play hard to get? Come and you will see how all your pain will go away."

'Amam begged Sabriyah, "Come on! Why are you so tense? Do you think I don't know that you miss Efrayim? We miss him too.

What can he do? I hope he is safe and sound. He is a working man and will come back the day after tomorrow. Come on! Please, don't disappoint me!" 'Amam kissed her.

My father, Efrayim, and my sisters didn't ask about me, but right there the tenants were begging and pleading with me, Sabriyah thought. From then on I would never again beg Efrayim. Let him and his train go to hell. I wish his train would crash and turn into ashes! The first time I saw him I felt affection, compassion, and jealousy.

Despite her anger, Sabriyah took back her curse, and the effect of the wine-like henna color remained; so did her challenge. Play! Relieve yourself and don't pay attention! Put the whole world under your shoes, she pleaded to herself. I'll paint the town red tonight while Efrayim is swaying alone on the Mosul train.

Hurry up. To hell the entire world! I'll challenge them and have a good time. I'm not upset, Efrayim! I swear by your life, I'm happy. I'll gouge out the eyes of anyone who doesn't want me to have fun. Be upset, Farhah Ghawi! I'll clap, sing, and make a fuss and joke against your will and Efrayim's.

"Selman! Damn you! Why don't you ask about me anymore? You've proved to be a man with no conscience, selling friendship quickly," she exclaimed. I was embarrassing him. The poor man was abashed. The unfortunate game! It's the game of a queen descending from an ivory tower, a broken ivory game. Break down, oh Mosul's railroad! I want to get drunk. Where are the drinks? Is there only beer? You should have brought cognac, arrack, and whiskey, although people may not be used to these kinds of drinks. Well, I have a bottle of Johnnie Walker in my room that my father left, so I'll go and get it. Drink Na'imah, drink! Please drink! Why are you winking at me to keep me silent? Is it because Fayiq doesn't like what I'm saying? Men have tortured us. What can we do to these men? Get going, Ya'qub! Play, Jamil, play, Selman, play!

"Selman! You are the only person I feel at ease with, even more than with my brother. Play! Don't worry and f— the world!"

"Umm 'Aziz! Where is 'Aziz? I swear by the five books of the Torah he's missed here!" said Sabriyah. Farhah turned pale and changed colors—to green, yellow, and red. I'll upset her more, said Sabriyah to herself. I'll upset those who do not enjoy themselves and dance with 'Aibah, the bastard, who bit my breasts and sucked my cheeks and lips. He would have raped me had he the courage.

"Hey! Move the table outside!"

I'll put a handkerchief around my hip and dance. 'Aibah, come and shake it with me! Give me your hand, like this. Ya'qub, beat the tambourine! All the cowards scram, beat it! To hell with life's hardships! Na'imah, I see that you also are ready, so come and dance! Your eyes are twinkling too much tonight. I know that Fayiq is here and he won't let you dance. This devil bastard and I will swing and sway to the beat of the tambourine, the oud, the qanun, and the clapping.

I'm not alone. I am surrounded by this glowing circle of people who, except Farhah, are like the throbbing heart of love for me. Explode Farhah Ghawi! Let Efrayim alone nod his head together with the dozing heads on the train to Mosul. Let Mosul be struck by an earthquake and be burnt down!

And here Sabriyah performed on this wild red night, despite Efrayim and Mosul.

✳

Fayiq went to sleep, and the rest of the guests remained. Ya'qub said, "Don't go, friends. The night is still young, but the bride and the groom are in a hurry, and now they're hugging each other and having fun in bed. Let's have fun for another hour! Who knows what tomorrow will bring?"

The newlyweds went to the bedroom, and Gerjiyi stripped. Meanwhile, 'Aziz Ghawi sneaked into Salimah's bedroom at the nightclub, where she was taking off her dancing costume. He was drunk and eager. Salimah, his life, stood in front of him. They were alone. She was not repelled but avoided him anyway.

"When will Salimah, my life, stop avoiding me?" he wondered.

"Salimah! You are my soul, my life." He pounced on her like a mad dog, a hungry lion. "Your breasts, your face, your eyes, your lips!"

He was out of breath and angry. He bent and kissed her. She was caught between his arms. She resisted then surrendered, refusing then accepting.

"Enough 'Aziz! Enough!"

Khoshi the Persian joined Gerjiyi on the wedding bed—Na'imah's bed. The wooden-floored room shook violently.

Salimah's body shook too. "Ouch! Move your face! You are killing me," exclaimed Salimah. "The smell of arrack and cigarettes in your mouth is terrible."

And what about the smell of the alcohol on her breath? And the cigarettes? Were they terrible too? But all this is honey mixed with poison. Let's kill each other with it!

"'Aziz, do me a favor, get off me!"

Salimah began to be fed up, but Gerjiyi faced a unique and forgotten experience. She would remember Mr. Kelly, Mahmud Khan, and Babu Singh. Would those dreamy days ever truly come back? She doubted it. Nothing in this world leaves and comes back. Who could bring back what had passed?

'Aziz was content with himself, dropping his entire body on Salimah and covering her with his perspiration and saliva.

"Enough! Soon Karim 'Abd el-Wahab will come in, and then who will rescue you?" she said to him.

"To hell with whoever his name is Karim 'Abd el-Wahab! Karim, do you hear me, Karim? Let him hear me, and if he's a real man, bring him here!" 'Aziz yelled loudly in his drunken voice.

Salimah was quickly enraged, and all her body shivered like the fronds of a palm tree in a hurricane. She was frightened and began to whisper with anxiety, "You are crazy! You are crazy!"

Gerjiyi stretched her hand toward Khoshi's belly, which was as wide as a jug. She found a belt firmly wrapped around his belly many times. She pressed it, and her hand came upon solid objects absolutely unlike a human belly.

"Khoshi, what is tied around your belly?"

He was suddenly terrified but scolded her at the same time.

"It's none of your business, woman! Go to sleep and keep out of it."

"Take it off, otherwise it will poke my belly!" She said scolding him.

Khoshi's fright grew and he held his belly with an anxiety akin to that of Lulu's for her son, Marrudi.

"If Khoshi die, Khoshi not take off belt. You are crazy. It's my capital."

She flirted and asked him as if she were a bashful child.

"Then how will you take me?"

"With my finger," he said with no hesitation.

She had doubts about him. No sooner had she stretched her hand to the lower part of his belly than she screamed in a disappointing voice.

"Shame on you! May your face be blackened with soot, 'Ajmi! I accepted all your shortcomings and said okay. Now, I find that you are not a man."

He understood what she said and sat up protesting arrogantly, "Shame on you woman, Shame! I'm not a woman. Once I take opium, I become a man and a half."

※

Suddenly 'Amam became quiet. She listened closely and whispered in a hiss, "Listen! It sounds as if something popped on the rooftop." She tried to hear and then added, "Listen! It sounds like a strong thumping on the rooftop. The ceiling trembled and it sounded as if someone had jumped from the rooftop of Aminah Shukur's home to ours. Oh God, don't turn our joy into sorrow!" She didn't move, and the other guests kept quiet while everyone rushed outside the room.

Then came sounds and rushing steps descending the ladder. All the guests were terrified, thinking many things, but their lips soon opened with astonishment, "You! Why? How?"

Khaduri's face was as yellow as a big lemon peel, his body was shaking, his mouth dry. He immediately felt like kissing their hands, pleading, "Protect me, and God will protect you!" 'Amam quickly moved from astonishment to compassion. Embarrassed, she said to him, "Don't worry. What happened is none of our business. Calm down, don't be afraid, and wet your mouth with a drop of water."

The water fell deep in his throat but came back up continuously. The edge of the glass shook between his teeth, and he kept silent. Why did he do such a thing? Who would imagine that? He came down from the rooftop as if he were descending from the gallows. Suddenly he pushed himself to the door leading to the outside and ran away mumbling, "God bless you! You certainly saved me from death." Then he disappeared into the darkness of the night and the alleys.

'Amam could not understand and made a strange gesture. She called after him, "Everything may come to mind except this. You are a respectable man and own a shop, but what got you into this bad situation of burglarizing homes?"

Ya'qub said, "And whom did he, the son of the whore, try to rob? Aminah Shukur's home? I don't envy you, Khaduri. What would have happened to you had you not run away? They would have cut you into pieces."

Farhah Ghawi rushed to say, "Live and learn! Can anyone claim, from now on, that it's possible to trust people? You can't even trust your brother or your neighbor. May he be beheaded! Have you ever seen a person burglarizing his neighbors? There's no goodness in this world anymore."

Meanwhile, Selman Hashwah continued to turn over in his bed, and the springs squeaked under him. For a moment, he forgot everything. He forgot agony and grief; he forgot Sabriyah and God. So far, he couldn't grasp what had happened so unexpectedly, so maliciously. He felt pain spreading over him, the pain of his crumbling confidence in people. He said to Jamil, "Jamil! By God, I don't grasp this incident. If you tell me now that God Himself is a Communist, I would believe you. But this Khaduri is a reasonable, chaste, honorable man. Our neighbors and other people like and respect him, but now he has turned out to be a thief. In addition, he chose to burglarize Aminah Shukur's home. Everyone in her family is as brave as a lion, causing fear. Even Ammunah trusts him and removes her veil in his presence when she comes to buy tobacco. Is this the end for Khaduri? Has the world turned upside down?"

Jamil yelled at Selman, "Damn you! Doesn't your brain go any farther? Go and wash yourself with the filthy water of the *pachah* dish. You deserve it."

4—Joudi al-Qarawchi

Da, da, da! The water tanks of the city began to ooze clouds of steam from the ground. His Majesty, praised be He, got wet from the black dust. Suddenly a cloud butted into horns made of dough, and into a mountain of steel.

My friend who sees from the front and behind said to me, "The dough and the steel are one." At the spur of the moment the cloud defeated the mountain, which turned into a lump of clouds. The latter united with transparent masses of dust. A legend was born—that the clouds gave birth to an animal that crawled anywhere and everywhere. I washed the dishdashah by the fire, flaming from a kingdom of none other than His. As a result, my mother imprisoned me in one of the large rooms of the palace that had a hundred rooms and a thousand doors.

I stayed there for a while, from the day of resurrection until the creation of the world. I saw how God created Adam from a bulging nail inside Eve. Then I freed myself and asked my friend, whose belly grows out of his head, "What is in your belly?"

"Air," he answered. I understood.

A flying elephant the size of a mosquito chased me continuously, and I drove it away from me. Then a tremendous waterfall gushed out from an open spring in the cellar of the world. Millions of mosquitoes poured out. Each mosquito was the size of the world. The wise men breathed in the bugs, but I avoided them by closing my nose with the blue sleeve of my dishdashah washed in pure oil. Then I . . . I don't know, but I overheard what was going on inside the wise men's minds. I saw the voices of the insect elephant that had sex on his mind, and I smelled wandering eyes searching everywhere for a solid object resembling their raised heads and crisp brains, but I did not find any.

I asked my friend, "Why can't they find that solid object? I am in front of their wandering eyes all the time."

My friend with the one eye and the five beaks said, "Don't forget! They are wise men, and you are crazy."

Then I asked him, "What is the difference between a wise man and a crazy man?"

He said, "The difference between the wise man and the crazy man is the same as the difference between the crazy man and the wise man."

I was confused, so I decided to return to my quest, which is different from that of every other man. I saw a pottery jar, which belonged to humanity alone. It contained items that were likely to be stolen.

My friend with the one beak and five eyes said, "All items can be stolen. Don't be a wise man, please! The wise men steal everything from the jar. This one stole freedom, the other stole love, money, and pleasure. The giant jar never became empty."

I said to my friend with the two faces, "Why do the wise men steal from each other?"

My husky but invisible friend said, "So that they will be the same as others."

I was astonished at having not stolen anything myself. I became angry and stole and ate the worms to take revenge on the wise men, my sisters, and all bad people. I took what I deserved before the worms deprived me of my rights. My mother denounced my deeds. She didn't know we live in a kingdom of worms. The worms are everywhere, Mother! I steal different items than the wise men and devour whatever the wise men steal.

I'm punishing the worms while I keep silent. My unfulfilled word is sufficient. The wise men do not understand it, and my mother is saddened in addition to her sorrows and bad dreams. I pity her. Why worry when we live in a kingdom ruled and demolished by worms?

Da, da, da!

5—Naji el-Jundi

Are you listening, brother?

Thanks to the sound of the guitar playing 'Abd el-Wahab's songs, I was filled with joy. I spoke my mind and thought. Whenever Abd el-Wahab sings, the solution of the universe's puzzles becomes easy. The other day Jamil Rabi posed a question that deserved thorough thought. It's not impossible that Jamil thought he was just making fun of me, ridiculing me.

"Naji, do you see yourself among the human beings or the animals?"

This was exactly his question, a question with scope. I was not naïve, but I was a human being. I was not concerned with what Rabi's son meant by asking such a question. Although it concealed a deeper and more serious human guise, an old philosophical question, I was angry and earnestly concerned.

I can't take it. I can't keep quiet. "What is the difference between human beings and animals? Aren't they all God's creation? I belong to what God created. People and animals and everyone I see are in pain."

Jamil interrupted me, "If so, please don't repeat the dog's tale."

My anger boiled and my heart became white like bleached wheat and manna candy covered with flour. I laughed. He realized that I would tell him the dog's tale. That night I was with the dog, a group of animals, and human beings.

A person who doesn't assist an animal in trouble cannot hear a human call for help. But I don't deny that there is also someone who would kill a human being for the sake of an animal. The Society for the Prevention of Cruelty to Animals is deceitful, an absolutely loathsome deceit. Also, there is a misleading claim that man is the most sublime creature. This leads him to look down at the other species and crush them with his fist.

Everyone is equal in my eyes. I avoid falling into rude stereotyping, which traps us. My point of departure is that having compassion for an ant will lead me to have compassion for a human being. You may interpret this any way you like. Are you listening, brother? As long as your intention is good, don't worry.

She was eager. She was the Rabbi's daughter. I was supposed to plant the seeds for a fetus that would be protected by two tender hearts.

"Muhammad! Why did you stop playing 'Abd el-Wahab? Keep playing, please. Can't you see I'm speaking and thinking?"

On that night a human being was supposed to be created. As a device, God employed us to make it. That rabbi's daughter was in a hurry to have a baby, as if her father had just passed away and she wanted to name her son after him. Why should I lie? I was in a hurry to have both sex and a child. At any rate, a human being is a human being. I can't firmly form an opinion about anything unless I have a strong feeling in my heart, and this is where my conscience gets involved. I look forward to doing good deeds. Ranks and priorities classify things. I'm thinking now, conversing, and listening to 'Abd el-Wahab. Despite this, I'm still bewildered.

There's a pain in my heart. Do you know why? My nephew, may God cure him, is unwell today, and it's impossible to relax unless I inquire about his condition. Excuse me for a moment; I'm going to call Hesqail and ask about the child. Is it midnight? Are they already asleep? So what? Asking about the child is important.

Praise God! Now I'm satisfied and relaxed, but my brother, Hesqail, was frightened. He was dreaming and jumped up from his bed when the telephone rang. Despite being worried about his son he began to quarrel with me.

Are you listening, brother? People don't understand me. The old philosophical problem comes back. Jamil Rabi posed it to me without realizing its significance and dimension. I wish him ill luck. He thought he was making fun of me. People don't understand me. I have my heart engaged in all things while other people's hearts are only in one. Everyone is concerned about his own welfare, while I care for the good of all creatures.

I was wearing new silk pajamas, for the first time, on our first wedding night. She was a rabbi's daughter, stretched out on a bronze bed. She bent her knees and spread her legs apart. Her eyes were greedy and fixed on me, calling and whispering, "Come on, come on! You're too slow!"

Believe me, there's nothing faster than me when I'm called to help. Luckily, I was suffering from holding my urine and went out to a garden near our room. I thought to urinate in order to enjoy the night.

Are you listening, brother? How can one be pleasured when there is misery in this world? Suddenly I felt pains inside, coming from the invisible world and rising to my head. Hunger, calamities, disasters, death, deprivation . . . We lose such real things in one selfish, joyful, deceitful, and greedy moment. You are bound to find a bone in a piece of meat. Look for it before it gets to your throat and sticks there. No! But have courage and reinforce the feeling in your heart. Tonight is your wedding. Enjoy yourself!

"Muhammad! Please, turn over 'Abd el-Wahab's record."

"Are you listening, dear?" I strengthened my heart and made it as hard as an 'alucha, the candy that hardens when overheated. I went to relieve myself in the garden while pale and fading shadows came from our room, an absolutely romantic atmosphere akin to that in 'Abd el-Wahab's song "el-Gundul," as the voice of my genial, magical master sings. A few days ago in Baladiyah Café, I insisted on hearing "el-Gundul" and said to Jamil, the son of Rabi, "You know what I feel like listening to? To "el-Gundul," right now.

He joked, "And don't you like el-shundul, the penis?"

"How wicked you are, Jamil! May bad luck befall you! I have the heart of a tender baby, unable to harbor grudges no matter how much I'm mistreated." I answered him with forgiving laughter and then went to the toilet with those romantic breezes. A breeze emitted from her wide-open legs supported and reinforced my heart.

The toilet was a hole covered with a wooden board whose middle was cut out in the shape of a heart. We throw our refuse through the heart-shaped seat in order to fill the hole and cause the death of a soul. I heard a sound coming from inside the heart, from the depth of the hole filled with our filth. It was a wailing sound resembling more of a cry than a dog barking. The puppy made long, frightened screams, which resembled the cries of a bereaved woman. My heart did not break then, but it melted like hard candy placed on a blazing flame. I was faced with two choices: saving a life or extinguishing my passion.

The puppy was fighting hard and calling for help. This creature was going to die in front of me. A dog was trapped in the refuse while another creature was lying on a comfortable bed opening her legs in a decorated, furnished bedroom. There were two things. If one was postponed, the puppy would die, but the other would not result in bad consequences. The question was life or death against life whose seeds have not yet been sown—a matter of a soul caught in a trap of refuse versus lust. After sweet and sour thoughts rushed in and melted on a strong fire, my usual good side tipped the balance. When you are not a phony person and you are asked to take a stance after being suddenly forced into a horrible human experience, what can you do? Nothing has changed to urge you to forget what is happening in the world, even in your existence. I couldn't leave the unfortunate creature facing death while going to satisfy my wife. In a few moments the dog would sink and be lost with no good reason unless I were, God forbid, made entirely of rocks or were a dead animal myself.

I began to compete with all the everlasting, the persistent, the tyrannical, the arrogant All-Competent ones, whose real concern, like evil people, is to kill, steal, and destroy. I looked in my wife's garden for a way to rescue the puppy. Fight, you poor dog. I'll come to your rescue soon, fast as a rocket, faster than this pressing hour.

I found a stick and came back to the scene and lowered the stick to the hole. "Doggy! Doggy! Doggy! Hold the stick with your paws and climb!" The unfortunate puppy understood as if he knew what I said. If you had just seen this poor puppy, you would say that even an animal has a precious soul. The puppy wanted to get out but was unable. It was filthy, and its feet could not hold on to the stick, and it repeatedly slipped and fell. The puppy hung on, but what would I do? Again it slipped. This unlucky puppy! I burst in tears and said to myself, "God, keep it from drowning!"

To hell if my clothes became dirty. Try! Fight out, how can it fight? Why does man set traps everywhere, digging holes for his friends and others? If I see a stone in the way, I quickly run to remove it, lest someone stumbles on it. God! Give me strength and luck to succeed in rescuing a life from a terrible death!

I said to the puppy, "Fight, my friend! Hold on for a while." I rushed around the garden searching for something. I felt as if a blaze of flame were in my head, my existence, my conscience, and my breathing. Nothing could calm me down unless I could save that trapped soul from death.

The rabbi's daughter, however, burned in a different fire, a disgusting, consuming fire, misleading and blinding. There are many things that blind a man, that gouge out the eyes of his humanity, until a man becomes a real individual, whole like a live coal, consumed and consuming.

"Are you listening, 'aini," her voice reached me from the room, stung by its own live coal. Undoubtedly her legs were uncovered and propped upward. She yelled, "Sha'ul! Where did you go? Did you fall asleep in the toilet?"

I was at the peak of my consciousness and my well-being grew with the well-being of others. Should I feel the pain of every creature in pain? Was she in pain? This state of affairs deceitfully explained the truth. It was fictional justification of the truth, a terrible justification of humanity's sins in order to allow things to happen. You may be tortured by a passion for money, for example. But are you going to steal? If a man disturbs you, are you going to kill him in order to feel comfortable? Whoever Jamil is, I'll take care of his troubles and please him.

The rabbi's daughter suffered in order to have fun and wanted me to extinguish her burning lust at the expense of a creature whose flame of life would have died out, had I forsaken it for a moment. What kind of logic is that? Let the wicked woman wait awhile. No disaster would occur, but this could be an additional life I might save.

I looked around while I turned a deaf ear to her. I found a piece of metal wire that tore the lowest part of my pajamas. The main thing was that I found it. You see how God helps the straight and true person. I bent one end of the wire, shaped it into a hook and I went back to the toilet. The dog was struggling in sea of refuse but was still breathing.

I leaned on the opening of the toilet and saw a deep hole, and then I lowered the hook. The poor dog was horrified thinking perhaps that another danger was coming from above. The animal didn't understand that waiting to be rescued is like a medical operation without anesthetic. The dog began to face a real and definite death. I was compelled to chase it with the hook. Stinky, sticky, filthy splashes hit my eyes, face, and clothes. The dog did not let me do anything to help. The poor thing only kicked and could hardly move. "Doggy! Doggy! Doggy! Please trust me, I am unlike the rabbi's daughter!"

I did one thing, and the dog did the opposite, until it was exhausted and collapsed completely. The dog gave in to exhaustion and could surrender to death or to me. I was stronger than death and pulled the dog out. It was exhausted from near death. I picked it up tenderly, placed it under the faucet and let the water run. The poor creature started to shiver, throbbing like a live heart. I found a piece of canvas in the toilet entrance. I dried it, covered the puppy, and felt relaxed.

Talking is not seeing. I was happy, very happy despite my filthy torn pajamas, my dirty face and hands. I had rescued an animal and a human being, and also revealed the nature of a savage, heartless woman. This damn woman had frantic crazy attacks, as if I were a servant in her father's household, or as if she were a vendor proud of her rare goods. On top of this, she, the daughter of a crazy woman, called me crazy.

People misunderstand me. I rescued a dog and a human—what would have happened if I had planted a fetus in the womb of a barbaric, passionate, daughter of a rabbi, who is absolutely unworthy of motherhood? Would anyone feel compassion for a human being if he didn't have compassion for an animal? Isn't it true, brother?"

6—Jamil Rabi

When I was returning from the Gazil Market, I was told that brains were sold there. If it is possible to buy a brain in this market, I'll buy a little one for Naji el-Jundi and another little one for Selman Hashwah. Selman Hashwah was still thinking that Khaduri, the tobacco vendor, was a thief, and that Naji el-Jundi was among God's creatures. Where is God? Where are all His creatures? I don't see either. I'm blind! I'm . . . What is this . . .

No, leave it now! There is a time for everything, Abu Gallubi. Let nature take its course, and let's leave the situation as is until it gets worse by itself!

Six

1—Selman Hashwah

It was morning. I arose startled, forcing myself up from the abyss of dreams and nightmares. When I thought of Sabriyah, my memories became sober, my pains and dreams awoke, and there were my fringed prayer shawl and phylacteries. I entrusted myself to God's hands. Praise be to you, oh Lord!

The light from the sun sent a golden ray over Sabriyah's jamkhanah. I recited "Our Lord, the King of the Universe, who consecrated us and commanded us to don the phylacteries." I placed the head phylactery between my eyes. My eyes turned away toward the jamkhanah, as I wrapped the phylacteries around my left arm. Her room had no curtains and shed a warm glow. I finished wrapping my arm seven times; Efrayim's arm was wrapped around the limbs of a willow tree and around Sabriyah's trunk, around my soul. "Hear, oh Israel, the Lord is our God, the Lord is one!"

Hear, oh Israel! Hear, oh Israel! Hear, oh Israel! One thousand times. Hear, oh Israel, in the morning, upon lying down, in death, in my life, in grief and agony, in Sabriyah, in Sabriyah and Efrayim squeezing together. My heart was also squeezed inside Sabriyah. It was squeezed between my prayers and Efrayim, between my memory and God, while I was still suspended in the air, hovering between God and Sabriyah.

"And you shall love the Lord your God."

147

And you will love Sabriyah with all your mind, with all your strength, despite all your being. Sabriyah loves me. Efrayim loves her, and she loves Efrayim, despite all of his faults and hollowness.

"Set these words upon your heart."

Now Efrayim is placing Sabriyah on his lap. He is seating her on his thighs! I kiss the name of God on the fringes of the prayer shawl, and Efrayim is kissing Sabriyah.

"Let them be a symbol before your eyes" or rather, from her eyes. He will kiss her lips and suck my dry heart and prayer, casting me into a remote desert. Every hug, every suck, every kiss distracts my prayers. When he pinches her, he pinches me, and I scream. Then my voice dies out again, and I dissolve. Oh, my God!

"And on your way, when you lie down and when you rise up I think of you, oh God!" And I think of Sabriyah, of grief and agony, and of the land of our ancestors.

Sabriyah tosses me like a ball, making fun of me. I only exist when Efrayim is absent, and I am absent when Efrayim is here. Sabriyah speaks to me and I exist, but she does things with Efrayim, and then he exists. On his lap she can forget me, forget everything. Life also forgets me, and I spoil my prayers. I spin inside a whirlpool—may God forgive me. He is compassionate and merciful, but man is cruel and mean. I am disappointed with you, woman with the mole! I say, "I will bury my sorrows in your love," but Jamil's five fingers flare out into my face. Then, I'm forgotten and my life becomes a vacuum.

Sabriyah said, "You're heartless, you don't even ask about me."

I said to myself, "I'll try, what can I lose? I'll follow Jamil's advice, bury my existence, my grief, and my many painful memories in Sabriyah."

These memories are rising as a beast roaming in my self-inflicted wasteland, showing its teeth and ready to pounce at me. Efrayim came back, and I knew that I was playing a losing game and that I had lost my last chance. To whom should I go and talk of my grief?

Khaduri was like a flask in which I poured all my sorrows. I felt relieved from my grief for a while, but Khaduri, the wineskin, got torn. Who told you to get involved in that terrible action of theft,

Khaduri? Why? I have come to dread you. Is it not good to stay in your company anymore? It is a serious catastrophe. Selman Hashwah is unfortunate, whether Khaduri is a thief or not, whether he breaks into people's houses or climbs over their rooftops. God forbid if I go to him again. Would I be out of my mind if I did so? There are those who can cover their shameful deeds and those who can't. One day, Khaduri, your shameful sins will be discovered. This will certainly happen only when I'm with him. My bad luck will be the cause, and then who will help me solve my problems?

No, I'll never go to see Khaduri. My prayer is shattered into a thousand splinters in a furious, bloody battlefield where my thoughts fight with Khaduri, Efrayim, and Karbala. I am lost and strangled, as if I were suffering from shortness of breath in a boxlike room full of people and fried food. A sick person with asthma is in a box. There is commotion and the smell of fried food. Let me breathe, people. Give me a little air and gouge out my other eye. I'm lost! My life is an empty illusion. What should I do? I beg you, don't take the breeze away from me. A little air, I want a world with air. The world comes to an end, but the air will never run out. Air, air, air!

2—Hamidah, Hassoon's Daughter

'Amam, Ya'gub's mother! For heaven's sake, what are you doing here? Don't you know what happened to Ya'gub? May God protect him! You trust God. What other explanation is there but that they wanted to kill him? May God protect Ya'gub! How terribly poor 'Amam's state of mind was! She almost fainted. She's right. She has but God and Ya'gub.

'Amam clapped her chest and screamed, "Please, abdalek Umm 'Abdallah, help me!"

I said to her, "For God's sake, Umm Ya'gub, don't be afraid. What terrifies you? My sons and I haven't forsaken you. No one will dare bother him as long as I, your friend Hamidah, live. I have eight sons, and you have only Ya'gub protected by God, so do you think that I would let anyone even touch one hair on his head? Doesn't a thought like this make you ashamed, Umm Ya'gub? I'm your friend and mainstay. How could I let anything bad happen to him?

Yesterday my son Majid came home. I noticed him sitting and thinking. I said to him, "Hey, Majid, what's the matter with you? You're not the same person."

He said, "Keep quiet, Mother, leave me alone! My head is overloaded with thoughts about what happened to my brother Ya'gub with Mahdi el-Tubar."

Then I said to Majid, "What happened to your brother Ya'gub? Tell your mother. Tell me!"

He said to me, "Leave me alone, Mother. That incident depressed me beyond words."

I felt that something was wrong, but you know me, I'm your sister, 'Amam. No one can put me in his pocket. No way! I began to kiss up to him hoping to get him to talk, and I didn't stop until he opened his heart and told me what had happened. He told me the whole story, lock, stock, and barrel.

It seemed that my sons Majid and Hamid and other friends were sitting with Ya'gub in 'Alwan's Café passing the time playing backgammon. Suddenly Mahdi el-Tubar, may he be dead, came in, infuriated, and spoke without even greeting them. Ya'gub, may God keep him safe and sound, told him, "Sit down, Mahdi!"

Mahdi answered him, "Leave the backgammon and come with me, I want to have a few words with you."

Ya'gub could not leave his friends. He said to him, "Talk, Mahdi, all the people here are our friends. There is no stranger among us," but Mahdi became agitated.

Majid told me, "I saw Mahdi's eyes shooting fire as if he meant to do something bad. He grabbed Ya'gub with his hands and pulled him up by force." All the fellows rose to their feet to hear what Mahdi wanted from Ya'gub.

Mahdi asked, "How much do I owe you in the account?"

Ya'gub replied, "About five or six dinars." Mahdi said, "Cancel it!" Majid continued to watch them and listen, and Ya'gub pretended he did not understand.

"What do you mean?" Ya'gub asked.

Mahdi answered, "I mean cancel it."

You know how bold and brave Ya'gub is. He asked, "Why, sir? Am I a charity?"

Majid said that Mahdi was in a very bad mood and out of his mind. It was as if he were saying, "Aren't I a big shot, like the greatest thug of Baghdad, Abu Jassim, who is like a braggart beggar from Karkuk with his dagger in his belt? Who'll dare say no to him?"

Mahdi began to shout, "Cancel the debt!"

Ya'gub replied, "No, I won't."

After haggling and bargaining, Mahdi said to Ya'gub, "What? Are you afraid that 'Alwan won't have enough money? You should know that he looted in the Farhûd and killed Jews, and I protected them."

So, listen to this, 'Amam, but forget what you hear and sweep it under the rug as if you didn't hear anything. It is said that 'Alwan really did loot in the Farhûd. I heard that too. Didn't you know? I don't know if he really killed anyone or not. Only God knows, but you know what Ya'gub answered? He said, "Mahdi, it's shameful that you would like to destroy my relationship with 'Alwan for just a few dinars. If you want, I will pay your debt, but to betray my brother and erase the debt from the account is out of the question. Impossible."

What can be done? Ya'gub is bold and tosses himself into the fire. Majid told me, "Even I was surprised how he dared to talk like this to Mahdi el-Tubar."

Mahdi slammed the table with his hand. "You insulted and disobeyed me. You'll see, I'll teach you a lesson."

Suddenly he left the café, and Ya'gub returned to his friends, who asked him, "Ya'gub, what's this all about?" He told them, "Keep on playing and screw it."

They said to him, "Didn't you hear what he said? We're worried that this Mahdi will do something." He said, "Am I one of those who gives a damn about what he says? Let him do whatever he wants! Let him circumcise me, if I'm not already circumcised."

Don't be afraid, 'Amam! I swear by the life of 'Abdallah, my husband, and Ya'gub, that as long as I live no one will be able to get near him. I quarreled with my son Majid and told him, "You should be ashamed! How is it that your brother Ya'gub was threatened and you kept silent?" I also said, "Now this minute, before it gets dark, take the revolver and your brother Hamid and go to Mahdi. Talk with him mildly and try to get him to make peace with Ya'gub. If he agrees and submits to your gentle words, let it be; otherwise, kill him and give yourselves up to the police!"

I already have eight children. If one or two of them die, it's no big deal. You're a good woman, though an unlucky one. Who do you have except Ya'gub and Allah? If something were to happen to him, God forbid, what would you do?

3—Jamil Rabi

It's a pity! Brains are not sold in the market, and the sewage cleaners are busy.

Abu Ghalib—do you know a first-class sewer cleaner who can take care of my sewer? The two sewers are beginning to emit odors—the world's and mine.

There were events that warned us of a flood. It rained cats and dogs. Button your overcoat, Abu Ghalib, and set your watch according to mine. I'm afraid the sun won't shine tomorrow. It's dark, so how will you see your watch and tell the time? You can see I'm the winner.

I don't need eyes. I look at the time by the tips of my fingers and smell the odor of the overflowing sewer with a strong absorbing sense, like a dog's. Today, Naji el-Jundi's dog sunk into the toilet, but Naji was too preoccupied to notice. He's getting married. It's a waste of time for him, and I have been barking but no one heard, or rather I was heard and told, "May you be afflicted with many diseases and be dead in the filth!" They were getting even with me. Time is my enemy, my first opponent, and Naji's. Naji gives me his troubles while it passes slowly for me and fast for the dog. Still, both Naji and the dog are like filth. Naji el-Jundi's life goes by with no purpose, and I'm vainly stuck in mine forever. Tomorrow she'll divorce him just as his first wife did.

Do you bet, Abu Ghalib, that tomorrow she'll divorce him, or he will divorce her to take vengeance on his first wife? The two are related. I'm sinking. Tonight, I was rescued from an illness, but I was afflicted with another illness. I got out of filthy swamp water but fell in the outdoor toilet. Have I reached the end yet?

My fellows were fed up and didn't answer. I interpreted their silence by asking many confusing questions. In our house lives another man. I don't know what to call him. I tried many times to compare him to a human being but I didn't find any resemblance between the two. Believe me, Abu Ghalib, I wanted to compare him to my mother and father, but I failed. He doesn't even look like an animal. Is it important that human beings and animals get married in this world? Man opened his eyes to this filthy custom so that the tragedy of reproduction could continue. Today I heard a sound of laughter, the sound of a death rattle. I also heard crying. Then I asked myself how all this could happen. Why does a man cry, sneeze, and gasp when dying? Why does he laugh and fart? From a conventional point of view you'll see these things in a clear manner and be moved by this joke. You'll go to the wedding and laugh in the meanwhile.

When you play the qanun, one string resounds, the second cries, and the third vomits. When you strike man's string he laughs. Why? From my blind viewpoint in a blind moment—which may be the sharpest of all moments—the illogical picture will become clear to you. We walk and talk like machines, torture others, and are tormented in turn. We are born, then we die. Everything is mixed up and jumbled in front of you, like a comedy performed by Ja'far Laqlaq Zada in the Farabi nightclub. Getting married has become so fashionable these days that even Naji el-Jundi is getting married, and Gerjiyi Nati and this anonymous person from Persia have already gotten married. I don't even know on what basis this nonhuman man-thing from Iran was called Khoshi, which means *good* in Persian. All this has inspired Laqlaq Zada to perform more funny, ugly, inspiring, and stimulating shows. I feel pity for Selman Hashwah with his mind in Karbala pulling toward Sabriyah with the strong, twisted, hemp rope of illusions. Now he blames the entire world. Sabriyah failed him. How unfortunate she is and how miserable a man he is!

You know, Abu Ghalib, if I had the power, I would castrate every male animal and human being in this world. You may say about me whatever you please. What is this dirt and ugliness? Human beings are machines moving in ugly spontaneity. They are toys in a theatrical play seen by more than one spectator or witnessed by the invisible eye. As such, it's claimed that their Master created the universe in order to enjoy the human comedy and roar with laughter until His insides burst.

God continues to deceive Selman Hashwah, and Selman Hashwah deceives Him. God has agents and advocates in this world. It's not the fault of the person who has a loud voice. It's my fault. Would Naji el-Jundi be able to rescue the dog from the refuse again? If so, Laqlaq Zada's shows would improve, and his great entertainment would be performed many times.

I wish I were wrong. Usually, I'm like you, Abu Ghallubi—wrong. As you imagine, the broken wall won't ever collapse, and the sun will definitely shine every morning. I'm mistaken. I imagine that in my dreams, I'll cover the nude children with blankets and put flesh on their bones or debunk God's legend and be truly worthy of reaching my goal.

The contrasts, Abu Ghalib, the paradox! Does Naji el-Jundi think that rescuing a dog from the bottom of a toilet or giving a piece of bread to a beggar or reciting the first chapter of the Koran over the dead will straighten out this messy world? Naji el-Jundi himself is a gross example of the disorder of the world, an entire scene of this world's insufferable comedy. He needs to go through death himself, a salvation.

I'm not only mistaken, Abu Ghalib, I'm also perplexed. The opposites have baffled me. The visible and the invisible and the joke that cast you in the middle of the outdoor toilet have puzzled me. We have become two overflowing sewers, two misfortunes, this world and I, as it is said, oh Umm Husayn, we were afflicted with one misfortune and now have become afflicted with two!

When I was in the café, neither Naji el-Jundi nor the dog nor the humming of the record player existed. I asked myself, "Who are you?" Na'im the Lame was playing cards with Abu Khlaif and Manni, the Assyrian sewer cleaner. I told Abu Ghalib that the cleaners were busy these days because it's been raining. Around the game table a group of people with nothing to do were sitting and watching.

I had nothing to do either. I sat at the table, not watching the game but hearing the curses pouring out from Na'im's mouth every time he took a card from the pile. Oh what rain, or rather, what bullets! Every curse was like a storm. He blasted the notorious Rabbi Yosef Hiyyim, and little by little, slandered all the important people along with the rabbi.

I was also haunted by the incident of banned leaflets, which a young Muslim, belonging to a certain political party, gave me to distribute. The young man was eventually hanged. What a pity! It is I who the blind people only see as blind, while my comrades are lucky whenever we gather together in a meeting of the underground party. Na'im discharged his bullet-like curses, beginning on the lowest steps of the ladder up to the highest ones, reaching the sublime throne. What else should I tell you, Abu Ghallubi? He tore down every holy saint and prophet and reshaped them anew. Not even a Jewish or Muslim saint or a Jewish prophet was spared, but he continued to lose, and nothing changed. I distributed the leaflets and nothing changed either, but what happened? Na'im's bullets penetrated into my heart like the refreshing cold water of Shaqlawah Springs, as if I were Lulu and Marrudi had been given an award at school for being the first in his class. I was as pleased as if Selman Hashwah had woken up in the morning and Sabriyah was the first thing he saw while her husband was away on the Mosul train.

It was in vain, as if man's fate on Earth had been written on the forehead of Na'im the Lame. He cursed and railed against the world, but to no avail. I rejoiced secretly that his luck stayed topsy-turvy in this manner, but he's stupid after all. He labored and suffered climbing the steps of the ladder, but when he approached the sublime throne, he stopped short and could not even revile his Creator.

Why didn't he dare? I took a risk when I distributed banned leaflets and exposed myself to hanging. Did I really take a risk? Maybe not. Maybe it was my real mistake or maybe it wasn't. The opposites in life, Abu Ghalib, the opposites are everywhere. They were dark, and so were my eyes. It's possible I thought the man was a military officer, but he turned out to be a police officer. Naji el-Jundi was absent, busy with the game—the filthy human game of deceit, unable to pull me out of the messy refuse. I said to Na'im the Lame, "Do you know why you are losing? It is because you are only hanging onto the tail of things. Go up the ladder a little bit and slap the Creator with a fat curse like a big chunk of frost. Then you will win."

The messengers of God are everywhere, even around the card table in Sha'ul's Café. They play a trivial and foolish game and want to keep it as comedy and entertainment. The man with the loud voice was one of His agents, a gifted messenger. Had he a grain of sense in his head, his desperately hard life could have been won. He would have mourned the world for seven days, Abu Ghallubi. The advocate was mumbling in a voice no one heard except me whenever Na'im the Lame, may God obliterate his name, shot out his barrel of curses. He did not dare raise his voice at Na'im, but it wasn't high-pitched when he addressed me. Rather, it was like the voice of an advocate pleading in the court, akin to the cruel voice of the world: "Why do you want him to be rude and disrespectful to God? The God who blinded you can also break your legs. Aren't you afraid of Him?"

Can He overwhelm me? God is scared of Na'im the Lame. Where is the sewage cleaner, Abu Ghalib? There are two overflowing sewers, the world and I. Why? What do I want? I'm telling you it's my mistake, not His. I'm not a believer. Why should I mention His name when I don't believe in Him? If so, why does His name occur to me every moment? Why do I use Allah in greetings and appellations when I say, "May Allah save you," "For the sake of Allah," "Allah is generous," and "'Abdallah," which means *God's worshipper*? Is this just another filthy habit, like copulation in the human and animal world? So why am I so pleased when a heretic slanders and curses Him? Does this mean I admit He exists but I don't admit acknowledging Him? Does this mean I blame Him for my personal tragedy, and because of this, try in vain to retaliate against Him? What about my relatives, my grandfather, forefathers, human injustice, and reactionary governments? I am confused, Abu Ghalib, I am lost!

You remember the hubbub of the women in the party, Abu Ghalib? It was worse than not understanding anything. And what about the banned leaflets I gave to the police officer? Did I give them to him by mistake? Was it to challenge him, so that he might hang me or bring me closer to my end? I am the opposite of myself; I am my own worst enemy.

"So it is possible there is right and wrong with the two opposites together. The officer called me and said, "Come here, boy, where did you get those leaflets?" I would be lying if I said I did not dread him. I would be lying if I said I was not afraid. I would be lying if I denied I was shaking from panic. Fear forced me to lie. So I said to the officer, "By God, sir, a stranger ran into me on the street, gave me fifty fils and told me these were movie ads for distribution." The officer confiscated the leaflets and tore them up. He seemed to be a decent man. Maybe he believed me. Maybe he was a member of the party or simply a nice person. He said in a fatherly manner, "Never mind, son, but don't do it again. Don't take leaflets from strangers when you don't know what's written on them." I simply lied. My potentially treacherous side tipped the balance and I lied. In doing so, I betrayed my conscience and myself. I betrayed Yusuf Wahbi's call in Les Miserables and I enjoyed this endless game. I have approached my goal and intentionally walked in the opposite direction.

Well, what do you say about this? Am I a believer or an unbeliever? Am I a leftist or a reactionary? Am I urging death along or escaping it? You are bound to curse me a thousand times, Abu Ghalib, and say about me, "What a terrible unbeliever and heretic he is!" All the while, you wear an overcoat protecting yourself from the rain, while I am vulnerable and miserable going to my room like a wet dog with its head lowered to the bottom of the garbage bin. Naji el-Jundi is busy tonight and so are the sewer cleaners. People give me death wishes and say, "May you drown, may you be infected with six thousand diseases!" Good-bye, Abu Ghalib. May God save you!

4—Ya'qub, 'Amam's Son

The bracelet! I stretched my hand to my forearm and could not find it! I was out of my mind. The bracelet—where was the bracelet? Did the ground swallow it? My charms are a pair of sticks and a hoopoe's bone—the prosperity and fortune of the world!

Why wasn't I afraid of Mahdi el-Tubar, among the most dangerous thugs in Baghdad? Mahdi is an immoral person, but I didn't care about his threats and disregarded what he said. After all, I did have the bracelet. Somebody informed my poor mother about what had happened, and she died without spilling a drop of blood. I came home and saw her scared and pale. She begged and pleaded, "Kepparah, I beg of you, quit this business and don't make me die." She made me take an oath a thousand times to change my ways. I swore to her a thousand times that nothing had happened and that Mahdi el-Tubar had come to me, and we hugged and kissed and made peace.

My mother still did not calm down. She likes peace, avoids trouble, and is against taking risks. She does not know that man's life is itself a great risk and that the person who wants to be safe should stay at home, go into his room, and lock the door behind him. I am not among those who would not take a risk, sit at home, and look at the faces of Gerjiyi and Khoshi, the Persian.

No sooner did I help Khoshi get married than he, the brother of a whore, disgraced us and denied the favor I did for him. And now he won't bring me sacks full of merchandise. Those slippers of his were an inexhaustible gold mine. So I did a favor for the wrong person, and in return he cut me out of the golden eggs his fertile hen laid every day. I gave in to my mother's tears and said to 'Alwan, "Did you see what happened? Would you let me be killed on your account? No. I quit this business." 'Alwan understood me well, but

I still do not understand what is happening to me and to my profits and prosperity these days.

The bracelet . . . Now I remember. I took it off yesterday before I washed my arm and changed from my work clothes. As usual, I put it on the window. Majid, Jadu's son, came in like a thorn pricking me in the throat. He was in a hurry and didn't let me check around thoroughly. "Come on, Ya'qub, hurry up! There is no time. The guys are waiting. Hurry up!" He rushed me out. I lost track and forgot the bracelet.

'Aibah, you are a dog, the son of a dog! The boy whose mother gave birth to him from a thousand men. Where's the bracelet? By God, I will stuff you back in the womb of your mother if you don't give me the bracelet back. 'Aibah! The bracelet is mine, where did you put it? Did you give it to a mother prone to vice all her life? Did you sell it to play heads or tails? Just tell me what you did with it.

The bracelet! It's my luck, my fun, my happiness, and my ticket to a good time, my friend, my love, and my wealth. What did you do with the bracelet, 'Aibah, the boy whose mother took a bath in a hole full of muddy water before conceiving you? Give it back! If you don't, I will roll you in the dust, I swear to God.

I lose control when I am angry. My anger was like a storm, cruel, sweeping, and destructive—a flood overflowing Baghdad. I lifted the chair and shook it before him. He ran away from me. I threw the hammer at him and missed. 'Aibah went away, and I followed him with my curses. My voice filled the world and the entire marketplace gathered around my shop heard the story. They were astonished but no one was indignant for me. They began to calm my anger. They urged me to steer clear of evil and only watch over my honor. The payment for the rented orchard was due, but no one had found the bracelet yet. Seemingly, somebody had stolen it. For the first time I didn't have the installment for the orchard's rent. What should I have done?

One person from the crowd said to me, "Ya'qub, this is not the way to handle the situation. Calm down, please. You scared the boy, and now he is afraid of you. Calm down a bit and use tact and persuasion and maybe he'll tell." I would not have given up that bracelet for any kingdom on Earth! And 'Aibah is afraid now, running away from me. Where will he go? He has nowhere to go, not even a grave to sleep in. My good, pious mother sleeps at night with her arms around him. Is this the way people are repaid for a favor? Is this how Khoshi compensates me? Is this how 'Aibah and fate reward me?

'Aibah, come back, don't be afraid, I won't hurt you. Come back! Just tell me where the bracelet is. Have no fear, I was mad but now I've stopped. Don't you believe me? There are people here, they'll protect you. Look, I put away the shoe tools! Look, I'm closing the shop! I swear by the soul of my father I won't beat or harm you in any way. Believe me! I'm telling you and taking an oath by God that I won't do anything to you. Is there anything greater than God to take an oath by? Here is a dirham if you would just tell me what happened to my bracelet last night.

The people and I didn't stop persuading him. He was scared and didn't dare come closer. I kept tempting him, like luring a loose hen into a chicken coop. Night fell, and I wouldn't budge from the shop because of 'Aibah, the bastard. Then I ran out of patience, and the heat was on. I didn't go to the café, and I didn't join my friends, but I continued my negotiation with 'Aibah, the dog. "Come on! This is enough. You've imprisoned me here. I'm telling you I won't do anything to harm you, I swear by God three times. Is there a greater oath than this?"

Relief through God was in 'Aibah's hands, but he kept me waiting. What's more, the bracelet was still lost. Finally, he gave up and granted me God's relief. He drew near the shop, frightened. Before he entered the shop, and in the presence of a few witnesses, he set a condition, "First of all, don't hit me!"

I almost got mad at him once more; with great effort I controlled some of my rage but yelled at him impatiently, "Didn't I swear by God? Do you think I used the name of God in vain?"

He calmed down, entered the shop, and confessed. I collapsed on the spot. So it was not enough that Nessim, my partner—I wish he were in the grave—stole my money, he also stole my luck, prosperity, and the people's love for me. He's a criminal, an unbeliever, and a heretic.

'Aibah claimed that Nessim, the *gawwad*, pimp, had raided my shop in my absence and had sent him to bring him a spit of grilled meat—may the spit get into his eyes! He had gotten rid of 'Aibah so that he would be alone and free to steal as he pleased. 'Aibah was absent five minutes, only five minutes. Oh yes, 'Aibah plays tricks on me, swears by the prophets and wants me to believe him! How could I believe him swearing that the tar was white? More likely, 'Aibah had been delayed by a bunch of hooligans playing dice or something like that and he forgot himself. Anyway, what difference did it make for my partner, Nessim, whether it was five minutes or five hours? He has quick hands. A minute is enough for him to steal a jewel from your nose, and here he had already stolen my wealth, all my luck in this world. I was devastated. The bracelet went bye-bye.

What can I get out of Nessim except denial? The bracelet is gone for good! The bracelet is gone. The son of a whore! Didn't I warn you, 'Aibah, a thousand times to keep your eyes wide open and watch Nessim when he comes to the shop? He sent you away, and you obeyed him.

What's the use of talking to 'Aibah? There's an open space between his ears as my words enter one ear and go out the other. I'll have to buy another hoopoe's bone and a pair of sticks for good luck. As long as I'm alive, I'll always buy the best, and it'll take a long time to find a real hoopoe's bone or original pair of sticks. There's only one real bone for every thousand or even million fakes.

Beleaguered by the pressing problem, I felt exhausted with frustration, and paralysis fell through me. Where would I get the installment for the orchard's rent? Should I ask my mother to borrow it for me from Farhah Ghawi? Farhah is stuffed with cash, but would she interpret my request as a desire for her daughter, Sa'idah? Would she see this as a commitment on my part or a simple financial debt?

To hell with it all! In any case, I won't tear myself down, I'll go to my friends and forget my sorrows. Let my partner go to hell with the shop and the money!

5—Sabriyah, 'Abdush's Daughter

What Should I Do, Oh God?

Sabriyah drew a sigh of boredom from the depth of her heart. The ennui was becoming unbearable. She longed for her former life, although she had buried it of her own free will. It was an abbreviated sigh. Between reading a chapter from a novel and listening to a song from the radio, she ate some nuts with a few raisins.

Efrayim brings me nuts, raisins, and love when he comes home once a week from Mosul, Sabriyah said to herself. I get sick and tired of the nuts and fed up with the black raisins, while his love remains a mystery. I hate him when he's absent. I wish he wouldn't return, but when he does he fills me with passion and yearning. I live one day of every week and die the following six days. I'm not treated like a wife, rather I'm a humiliated and abused mistress, a disgusting part that becomes whole only when Efrayim comes. He's a coward and he is low, but he certainly is attractive. Love makes me collapse and makes my resistance falter. I'm empty and isolated because of boredom and yearning—and neglected. I ask about falsehood and truth, about true desire and false, beguiling, and misleading desire, while at the same time nursing and cherishing a longing in my heart for Bistan el-Khass, that place of truth and reality.

Truth and falsehood! Sometimes one is not at ease with reality and so escapes into the unreal. Then the unreal deflates spontaneously and disappears, and in the spur of the moment, the image of the pleasant and the innocent relationship that ties me to Selman Hashwah fades. This has been a fluctuating relationship built on crumbling sand to fight scrawny, empty reality and to pass the time laughing and joking. Suddenly both of us got tired of the game, and a breach spontaneously formed between us, a breach not really of our creation. The warmth of our relationship vanished in the cruel and cold Baghdad winter. Consequently, we became estranged, but a killing boredom, a stupid reality, and other things remained.

I sighed. The house looked more miserable because of rain gathering in the courtyard. There was a mess in the alley, and the odor of garbage became intolerable. It nearly choked me. It accompanied me from sunrise to sunset and stirred my yearning and affection. My shadowy self stepped away from it, but my shadowlike steps hesitated when I approached Bistan el-Khass. And Bab el-Sharqi stirs my fantasy even more! The retrieved meadows of memory in Ghazi Park faded. The cold and rainy showers stopped me from going there, and so did the annoyance of the roughnecks there and the immoral pursuits of youth. My fear also urged me to keep my distressed longing a secret.

There are no words to describe this house. It offers gentle words and contains precious people, goodness, white angels—'Amam, Na'imah, and Selman—but I remain a human looking for another human like me. In a sad moment, I'm distracted by a sweet hymn coming from another world. I'm entranced by the rustling of white wings, but fully divine goodness in the shape of an angel does not materialize. I remain a human and can understand no one except a human of my age, my level, and with my ideas about Bistan el-Khass.

It was afternoon, and the rain took a rest. Sunny visions like ghosts cast pale, dreamlike shadows on the wet ground. My stress was as painful as falling rocks settling on my chest, heart, and head, and tears burst from my eyes. My father taught me not to be weak, but I'm growing weak. Still, I'll never give in. Giving in a little bit is the beginning of a total collapse.

What am I talking about? Is there really a reason for this? I just long for them. I only desire to see those who shared my flesh and bone, my blood type and my life. Blood will never turn into water. Even the gravest mistakes cannot erase that. My father made a mistake and so did I, but both of us are right. My father made a mistake and so did Efrayim, and this caused troubles to fall on my head. They and I never avoid repeating these mistakes, but each of us is right.

This is a lie! When avoiding mistakes, one runs into imaginary obstacles, out of cowardliness, just for the power of staying miserable, while stuck with the consequences of those mistakes. It's a cursed reality that resembles the repulsive odor penetrating these alleys, like the meaninglessness of my life inside this jamkhanah, an emptiness among a superhuman goodness engraved in people who

can't see that a human's life is a sudden cry, who don't know how a
human's life should be. My father taught it to me but kept me from it.
He denied me. I wonder what happened to my sisters 'Afaf and Amirah. Something inside me hardened, while warm and cold accosted
me at the same time. It wasn't like sitting in Efrayim's lap, when both
of us wrapped ourselves in a passionate night and I emptied my anger
by loving him, realizing that my love for Bistan el-Khass was a sham.
Is there another in this world afraid to reveal love to her father and
sisters?

More tears fell uncontrollably, and she sighed heavily. Shadows
struck the redness of her cheeks . . . The red coat fitted her very
well. She put it on, buttoned it, and wore her high-heeled shoes. She
had two dinars in her purse. It was muddy outside. She felt beaten
down, depressed, and weary. Her shoes sunk in the mud, and brown
drizzle stained the hem of the coat that covered her pride and dignity.
She was overpowered by nostalgia, going from one meadow of love
to another. She was ambivalent and wet. The showers of mistakes
poured down from clouds of illusions.

I will never give in, she assured herself, but despite that, it was
Bistan el-Khass I longed for. I drew near it with hesitation. This is the
street. My house is there. This is where I opened my eyes. My personality, thoughts, feelings, and memories were formed here, making me
the way I am now.

Would she come closer to the home where she grew up and was
shaped? She was bewildered. What if someone saw her? Yearning
whispered to her. What if someone leaves the house now? What
would they say about her if she were discovered? Would they say she
came back defeated?" They would retaliate and shout out, "Why did
you come? You wanted Efrayim, so go to Efrayim! We don't know
you or recognize you." She was frightened, but her feet continued to
stride forward.

Father, 'Afaf, and Amirah, I miss you all. By God! I always missed
you very much and my heart sang, "I passed by the lovers' abode."
My home is here, and I breathe a fresh and fragrant air. I enjoy the
trees, and the scenery restores my soul. Two decades! What can I

say? Can a person live two lives? Can one split a life into two equal parts or must one choose only one thing, one love? Why do some people think the two are only bound to contradict?

I took more steps forward. Wasn't it enough so far? They'll see me before I peek at any of them secretly. I'm unlucky this time. I feel disappointment, a slight sorrow, and fear. Shouldn't I be returning? I'm getting close to where I grew up, a forbidden place full of danger. I moved my feet from the paved and clean floor free of mud, but it was stickier than glue. I hardly turned my back, could barely believe my eyes. Only a few seconds of silence and bafflement passed, and there was hugging.

"Sabriyah, my sister!"

"My sister, 'Afaf!"

A burst of hugs charged with memories squeezed our breasts like a sponge. A giggle, a sigh, a glow, a laugh, and a sigh followed each other, chaotically mixed up. "My sister, 'Afaf!" "My dear . . ." "My sister, Sabriyah . . ." A disbelieving giggle mixed with crying and sighs.

"What a surprise! Who showed you the way here?" It's inscribed in my heart. How could I forget the way? My father denied me, while you forgot me all this time.

"By the name of Allah, you were always in our minds day and night. We longed for you. We missed you. We swear by God we missed you!"

With a cry of joy and a hint of reproach, I said, "If you had really longed for me, you should at least have asked about me."

'Afaf was never relaxed. She gasped as if she were running a long-distance race.

"I swear by father's life and by God that I came to fetch you several times. I asked and was told in Bani S'id where to look for you, but I couldn't find your place."

Should I believe her? Sabriyah wondered. 'Afaf has always been faithful. "And do I remember everything myself?"

'Afaf giggled, with tears and gasps, off and on.

"Everything. Of course, my sister, Sabriyah."

"Do you remember? Our fun included pinching, tickling, and bad-mouthing each other. We joked by pulling hair, kicking, and whispering about the knights of our dreams. I used to talk about a light-skinned young man from the Orfali family. He used to kindle my dreams. But I was never taken by fair hair," Sabriyah reminisced.

"Do you remember what we used to do at school? We drove the Arabic teacher, Mrs. Shafiqah, nuts. She used to look at us through her glasses while writing on the blackboard."

"You were a devil and still are."

"And Madame Hafiz, the English teacher! Do you remember how she stammered the letter *r* in 'the rare men' and 'I want a synonym for the rare man?' I answered, 'You mean another man?' And the entire class burst out laughing."

"Damn you! Why are we crying?" Now I was crying with joy and laughter.

"Come home! You can see how the weather turned out clear because you are here." 'Afaf pulled me by the hand and eased me forward.

I was frightened. My pride was still a mask—my father and the mistakes. How could I see him?

"You remained as stubborn as a Kurd, remember?"

There was a giggle as drops of sweet and moist memory poured again down our cheeks.

"We called you 'the brat,' and we used to call Amirah 'the camel,' because she was huge for her young age." My diary was entrusted to 'Afaf. If Efrayim reads it, he would say that I was a woman with a past, but everything written there was a lie, or just bold dreams and wishes.

"Where is the camel?"

My sister 'Afaf giggled.

"Who? Amirah? Maybe she's playing hopscotch with Dellal Msaffi at our neighbor's house."

"You mean it? Is she still playing hopscotch? Isn't she afraid of getting her monthly visitor?"

She is a playful child. I wonder if she is afraid that her . . . will fall off?

"I missed her, by my father's life, I missed her—by God the Truthful. I also miss my father, all of you, all of you."

"Come inside and you'll see all of us."

I hesitated but didn't stop weeping. A malicious arrogance suddenly appeared on my face.

My sister 'Afaf pushed me, poked me with her fist, and pulled me with force.

"Damn you, come in, don't stand on ceremony!"

I laughed and wiped my tears.

"Are you still bad-mouthing?"

My sister 'Afaf, my dear sister, also laughed.

"What is this? May a disaster strike you, Sabriyah! Now, after being married you've started to get worried about bad-mouthing; I'm just blessing you, come in!"

"When we love we curse each other. I haven't forgotten. Is my father still mad at me? Did he really forget his own best instructions?"

"I swear by the five books of the Torah, my father's heart is as white and pure as the snow. He's crazy about you."

"And Mother? Does anyone see her?"

"Shut up! Don't talk, should someone hear you!" She jabbed me.

I understood, and my other sister screamed from near the garden gate.

"Father, guess who came? Come and see who came?"

I faced him again. He taught me to be strong and taught me tenderness too, and between those two things he taught me how to avoid mistakes. He ran toward me now, opening his heart and arms.

"Sabriyah, dear Sabriyah, my daughter!"

Things that were suppressed were now set free. Tears of joy poured—tears of remorse about the past, tears of regret for man-made sorrow, drops of happiness for restoring what had seemed lost.

6—'Aziz Ghawi

No, no, no, no! Those damned noes! Salimah—no! My school—no! My mother—no! The newspaper—no! My life—no! When will I hear "yes" instead? Leave me alone and don't talk to me! If you have poison, bring it to me to drink. But if you have Salimah-choka-boka, come and sit next to me and chat with me from now until sunset.

Salimah, Salma, Sallumah, Salamah, Sulaymah—no matter how you call her—she is everywhere, in my food and drink, in my madness and inspiration. I sing, "Oh dear Sulaymah! Oh dear Sulaymah!" and write her name in all the styles of the Arabic script. She blows like a spring breeze, touches my soul, immerses, intertwines, and increases, but does not change. I hate her out of excessive love, a bitterness that tastes sweet. I long for her, "People's eyes have fallen asleep, but how can my heart sleep?" Now she kills me, now she feels compassion for me. Now she avoids me, now she slaughters me.

Sir, do you want to hear a real good poem, the most truthful poetry about the most honest woman? It comes from awareness of sufferings: "Pay no attention, abandon and avoid me, and drink from my tears to the last dregs."

I get drunk from you, Salimah. I see my life linked to your image in the wine I drink. You are my life, and my life becomes drunk from my tears, so let me say the verse like this: "Until the last dreg, you get drunk from my tears." Listen! Isn't it better to say, "To calm my heart, don't be scared, step on it, and don't dread my death." No, no, no! I'll say the verse to myself and follow the rules of Arabic grammar, for which I wasted five years in high school. Is killing me a crime? If she commits the crime of murder then she's not guilty. My life is always committing a crime against itself. Therefore, let's follow the grammatical rules in verse and say, "Step on my heart, don't be scared, and don't be afraid to kill me."

Bravo! 'Aziz, the son of Farhah and 'Abdallah Ghawi, you're a poet—a poet of innovation and failure, of lamentation and sorrows, of pain who created all poets, a poet for the world, for Salimah. Salimah is the world and the world is Salimah.

The editor of the newspaper *Crazy to the Third Power* told me that my poetry was that of adolescence and instead it needs to address everyone. He is stupid and doesn't know that the world reaches maturity when it sucks from Salimah's breasts and perches on her lap. Only then does the world become a branch and Salimah the root of being.

"Is there somebody among you called Karim 'Abd el-Wahab? If he is truly a man, let him show his face! But if he is as cowardly as a woman is, it's better for him to run away. I swore by God to drink his blood," 'Aziz thought.

I held a charm that starts with the letter *S* for Salimah and Salam, peace. But where is peace of mind? Salimah threatens me with a pimp by the name of Karim 'Abd el-Wahab. No, no, no! My *S* is not the first letter in Salam—it is the first letter of *devil*, Satan in Hebrew, English, and numerous other languages. A thousand Satans. Salimah is of Satan's breed, exactly like me. We are cousins, the devil's offspring. So why do you deny your origin and your cousins and brothers, Satan?

"Where's this Karim 'Abd el-Wahab? Let him come!"

Between Salimah and me nothing will stand, not a thousand revolvers or a million Karim 'Abd el-Wahabs. I'll fight for my life with wine, tears, and blood.

I bathed my eyes in her sight. She sat on a dirty table in a modest restaurant and then disappeared from view. Amid tears I reached out to her, but she had gone and left me sighing. And another sigh escaped from my chest. I inhaled and stopped the series of sighs. Then my lungs filled up, and she settled again in my heart, soul, and veins and spread everywhere. She drenched my being. No! A thousand noes.

How can the soul hate its owner? The soul is playing hard to get. My soul is like a pretty, pampered girl. No, impossible! Salimah doesn't approve of me because I'm a "child." I'm a child in her eyes and in the eyes of Farhah Ghawi, but I'm myself, whereas the world is like an old man with a bent back. Salimah and my mother think I'm only a child, but Farhah Ghawi adores me. Why then doesn't she become Salimah? The world can go under while my face is buried in Salimah's breasts.

Money! My stupid, insane friend told me, "All things heed money." I was as blind as he was and believed him.

I reached the bottom of my lowliness and followed my uncle's friend, a horse like my own uncle. I said to him, "My uncle sent me to you. He bought a lot of goods, but he doesn't have cash for the down payment and he asked you to lend him ten dinars until tomorrow." I had ten dinars, ten dinars more from the treasury of Miss Sa'idah. I asked her for the money at a bad time, though her belly was stuffed with about a thousand dinars that I could have snatched, but I felt bad for my sister's sake. What's more, Farhah Ghawi would have cursed and scolded me. I was content with a small amount of leftover cash that certainly nobody missed, but I thought it would be helpful. By doing so I proved that despite my lowliness I had human needs and rights.

You see, Salimah, how good I am! Although the entire world is unjust to me, I sing the hymn of Saddiqah, the saint, and pray with her to God: "Oh Lord, the worshipped God, make her compassionate to me." But Salimah's heart is like a hard rock, with no compassion for me.

Sa'idah shrugged her shoulders, ridiculing me when I took the dinars. She said to me with scorn and arrogance, "Stick them up your ass." While Karim sucks her blood and stains her ripped, shattered honor and self-respect, still Salimah is my life and my life is a whore. She is my soul, a contemptuous whore devoid of mercy. She's my enemy, drawing her shameful sword against me. Her greedy master sucks her blood, money, honor, and humanity.

I hit the dirty, shaky table with my fist. It trembled and the porcelain dishes flew in the air and fell between the legs of the chairs and tables, scattering shattered pieces. I looked at the shop owner and said, "Don't glare at me, fellow! There's nothing to be sorry about. They were disgusting dishes, hastily repaired and glued. How could anyone eat from them? I did you a favor. How much do new dishes cost, one dinar, two, three? It's nothing and don't worry, just say how much. I have a lot of money and will pay for the new dishes. Let the customers eat from new dishes!"

But my soul was loathsome, too, and torn into a thousand pieces. How could I trade it for a new one? If money was, as they lied to me, the main thing, I would have robbed a bank and asked my mother to sew a dress for Salimah made of one-dinar bills. If people didn't really like to be humiliated, Salimah wouldn't have stooped before thieves and before those who injured her honor. She would have said to Karim, "Get out, beat it!" If people were reasonable they would love the person who worships them day and night. Then Salimah would say to me, "You are my soul, my life," and she would expose her breasts before me. But man is crazy. Salimah is crazy, and 'Aziz Ghawi is crazy. Is there anyone who can fold time and condense five or six hours of my life into one minute?

A derisive sound reached me, saying, "Yes, there is. Death can fold up your life in one second."

"No, sir. You don't understand everything. Death can't do anything because I'm actually dead now. But five or six hours from now I'll be revived. I'll be resurrected," I replied.

"What kind of a dead man are you? Don't the dead sleep and keep quiet? Go and take a nap during those five or six hours until you're revived. Take a rest and give us relief from your headaches," the sound suggested.

Why do people mock me while an entire generation is being tortured every minute of the day? I'll break off with those lofty bygone days until I reach the end of my repeated tour each night. I wouldn't replace my great, terrible torture for all of Solomon's treasures. It's surprising to see that both Salimah and Solomon are alike—thousands of female slaves kneeled to Solomon who sat on a throne of pearls, but Salimah is luckier, because every one of her heartbeats praises her name. As long as Salimah is there, the throbs of my heart increase, and my heart remembers her 1,000 times a minute, 6,000 times an hour, 144,000 times per day. One, two, three, Salimah, Salimah, Salimah.

Time is motionless. I stood up staggering, and neither the ground nor the living creatures could stand me. I was annoyed by an insect on my outfit, coiled within myself and within Salimah's ghost, expelled by one street and rejected by another, blocked by a wall and bounced off by another. Like the insect, I lived and died in the strings of a net made of an unbreakable material. Inside the net there was the lie of my father, 'Abdallah Ghawi, the black barrel, the foolish old man. This old man was raising hell in Mahmudiyah.

I am his son, the young man, the adolescent whose slight attractiveness I discovered one day in a tarnished mirror in the Kallachiyah when I kneeled down before a woman, a whore many years older. The bartender in the nightclub had managed to be alone with her, and I almost threw the glass at his head. I adore her. I sacrifice myself as a scapegoat for her sins despite the fact that she rejects my passionate love, receives me with coldness, and threatens me with a man of low morals—a procurer. Call me a fraud if my father could even get a blind bitch in Mahmudiyah. Who knows, maybe the blind bitch would not approve of me either. How could Salimah approve of me then?

Salimah, Salimah! When I see her she becomes the greatest joy of my life. She glares at me sideways, pays no attention to me and laughs at me when I turn my back. But I see her smiling and ask myself, "Why don't you show friendliness to me?" Do you love and forget once? You're weary of it all. Are you scared of something? Are you easily taken in? Be like me! I'm firmly grounded in my senior year of school, grounded in your love, firmly grounded in disappointment and failure.

"Give me a quarter bottle of arrack," I ordered the waiter.

I sipped the sharp arrack and finished an entire bottle, above the limits for drunkenness. I swaggered, and Salimah, like a cane, supported me. I followed her to the room. "Salimah, Salimah!" I fell at her feet and then buried my head between her legs. "Salimah!" I cried and moaned like a child in his mother's arms. She patted my back with silent affection, and her fingers fiddled with my hair. I was bewitched, but suddenly she jumped away, frightened, and yelled, "Stand up!"

Slightly indifferent, I said to her, "We were okay, are you like this world and the world like you? Every minute you're in the arms of a different man."

"Hurry! Stand up in case Karim is coming!"

Then there was the one named Karim.

"Where is Karim? Let him come!" I shouted.

Karim entered. Salimah screamed in fear and ran away pleading, "Karim, please put away the revolver, put it away for the sake of God."

Stretched on my belly on the ground, I wetted the ground with my saliva and tears. Karim stood above my head with Salimah facing him. He pulled Salimah's hand away from my collar, "Get out of my way, please! Let me shed the blood of this dog! I don't understand what he wants from you."

I want to save my life, merciful people! By God, I want my life. Now I'm rolling in poverty and agony.

"Karim, be reasonable, please," she begged.

Let him . . . Let him rescue me and grant me death!

'Aziz said, "I am telling you, get off me!"

Free me! Come on, fellow! I'm begging for it! Come on and hit me! Why haven't you shot me yet?

"Karim, for God's sake, don't end up doing something stupid! The show will begin soon. I have to go. Karim, what's with you?" Salimah asked.

"This dog, this son of a dog, has worn out my patience."

You're right, if I weren't a dog, I wouldn't be so humiliated. She embraced him in my presence, smiled at him, rubbed her face against his, and I was paralyzed. I don't have the presence of mind to fight against the betrayal of my life. I was tired.

"Leave him alone! He's a dumb brute. He's drunk and doesn't know what he's doing." I was escaping from reality, exhausted, begging for a moment of death.

"Would you do me a favor and take him home?" Salimah asked Karim.

Was this a comedy or a tragedy? Karim didn't laugh—rather, he was astonished. "Salimah, would you please repeat what you said? I'm afraid I didn't hear you well. Should I take this dog home in my car?"

"For my sake. Don't you love me? Let's get rid of him!"

I didn't hear anything except fragments of madness. I hoped my brain was just tired and that I didn't understand what was happening.

Karim hesitated. "How would I know where his house is? I wish his house was destroyed."

"He'll show you. It's okay. Do it for me."

"Never mind, I'll show you. Do it for her sake and take me to my mother, Farhah Ghawi, and to my sister, Sa'idah Ghawi. You see I'm tired. I want to rest," I whispered.

*

In the dark of the night, Karim 'Abd el-Wahab took 'Aziz home, away from his beloved. He was tossed back and forth inside the car like a piece of stone. Karim cursed and asked him with rage and scorn, "Where?"

Chewing over his words, 'Aziz answered, "To Bani S'id."

The car stopped.

"Where should I let you off?"

"Here in the alley."

"Get out!"

'Aziz couldn't get out of the car, and Karim had to drag him as if he were pulling a dead man, all the while reciting a full prayer of curses on the dead. Karim lifted 'Aziz onto his feet but he collapsed. He lifted him again, leaned him on his body, and held his hanging arm that stuck from behind his shoulder and neck.

'Aziz, the drunkard, was sluggish, and Karim yelled at him, "Damn it, move! You brother of a whore! You've plucked my heart out. May God pluck out yours!"

'Aziz breathed heavily, "No, brother Karim. I can take your cursing, but don't make off-color remarks about my sister. She's not like Salimah. My sister Sa'idah knows her worth. She's decent."

Karim, said, "Since she's so pretty and decent, I'll take you to her."

They were in the alley.

"Well . . . where?"

'Aziz closed his eyes and was like a donkey knowing its way to an open gate.

"This is the gate and my mother's room is next to the waiting area."

Karim left him slumped in front of the gate and stepped toward the room. Upon hearing an unexpected knocking at the door, Farhah Ghawi and her daughter Sa'idah jumped up. They opened the door wearing robes and saw a neat, handsome young man. Karim's eyes wandered from the woman to the girl. Then he calmly and politely said, "Come and take your son. I brought him home drunk from the nightclub."

7—Aminah, Shukur's Daughter

On the day our "Indian" neighbor married the Persian man, I realized on my own that I was living a crooked and immoral life in a minefield. Though a secret affair can disclose things, it can also be snuffed out easily. I taught my miserable sheep how to butt. Then it butted the wall and broke its horn. The cock is sick with puffing pride, and there's no cure. The hens run away and steer clear out of fear. I'm a female close to animals, especially sheep, cocks, and hens. I toss grains and prepare their food. I serve the animals. My 'abayah is a collector of facts but it's also a source of delusions. The mirror is my book. I scrutinize and read puzzles in it, thinking day and night. Confusion and questions overcome me. Am I really this female human being? Was I created for the animals, with the animals, on the same level as the animals? Did God create Adam to humiliate Eve, the cock to humiliate its hens, and Jabbar and his brothers to humiliate me?

The ram doesn't humiliate its ewes, so why doesn't Na'imah live with animals? My mirror is my book. I scan it. My body is open to fear, anger, and hatred, so I'll be angry and rebellious. I have failed to be strong, and my sheep was weak too. It saw me, became afraid of the cock and left. I was afraid too. I was without my 'abayah, and fear clung to me, never leaving me even when I covered myself with the 'abayah, the black dome. Na'imah never told me female tales. She told me tales about humans. She didn't need the black 'abayah that's worn only by a woman performing her own funeral.

The 'abayah is a permanent mourning dress for those women whose rights have been taken away. Jabbar, my brother, forgot the insults and the spitting he got from me, but he didn't stop looking for the whore in order to empty the brunt of his poisonous anger and go on with his dissolute life. He's like a reckless cock, like a tyrannical, ill-tempered, and merciless beast. Na'imah told me the tale of the clumsy sheep that stumbled on the "Indian" woman's wedding night. Na'imah has pores. She's like a vase with holes in it, leaking money and secrets. She is a good woman but she doesn't know that some- times goodness kindles the evil fires. I said to her, "How could you believe that? Who else was it but this poor Khaduri? He ran away from an angry gang after a quarrel, and they followed him. Then he knocked on the door, half-dead and short of breath. I felt pity for him and let him in. He's a neighbor and a good person, and we're his customers. When he realized I was home alone, he was embarrassed. Also, what would one of my brothers have thought coming in on us? So he jumped from our rooftop to yours. The poor man didn't even look at me." I also said to Na'imah, "I beg of you, Na'imah, don't tell this to anyone or else no one will save the poor man from my broth- ers. If they hear what happened, they'll imagine a lot of things, and blood will flow in the quarter."

Na'imah hates any mention of evil and blood. She even boycotts the Feast of Immolation when sheep are slaughtered. Seemingly, Na'imah has forgotten that we live in a slaughterhouse for human victims, but she won't do anything about it. I reminded her of the fact and plugged the hole that spills evil secrets.

Hey, ti, ti, ti! Come! Come! Why is your haughtiness growing day after day? Isn't there anyone around to smash it down? I'm fed crumbs like hens and live under the mercy of a rude man. What a wretched life is this! Let's face it, I'm not as good as people think. Jabbar will see what a courageous girl I am. I can cross seas of blood and step on slaughtered bodies of men. The spitting will vengefully flow down my brother's face and pierce his honor with a sharp knife. This honor of his! It's his conceit standing up like a cock's crest over a sheep with a broken horn. I'll slaughter it on the feast as a sacrifice against the slaughtering of thousands of lowly sheep, driven in degraded droves to the human slaughterhouse. You, Jabbar, stain your false honor by your own hands, whether I'm unveiled or have a thousand 'abayahs.

8—'Atiyah al-Qarawchi

I would have liked to take a nap and be awakened to see that everything had changed—the plentiful world full, people living in harmony and love, and hearts cheerful and happy without hatred, greed, bloodshed, or sorrow. I wish I had been a single girl who got married and then gave birth to two nice daughters who would take the sorrows from my heart. I would name the first one Wafiqah and the second Qadriyah. Wafiqah would be the apple of one eye and Qadriyah the other. If someone asked me how you get peace of mind, I'd be able to answer immediately. I wish I had been a single girl, gotten married, and given birth to a nice boy in addition to the daughters. His name would be Joudi and he'd turn out sensible, wise, brave, and protective of his family. He would always look out for me.

While I was sitting and wishing, suddenly I saw Joudi, the same Joudi. By God, he hasn't changed. I saw him sitting on the heap of garbage, picking and eating.

"Joudi, enough! All the worms of the world have ended up in your stomach. Haven't you had your fill yet? That's enough now!" I was sure that Joudi had come into the world to protect me. I need good luck, but where is my luck? My luck! How blackened you are like the soot and the oily fat of frying pans. I sit and wish and say to myself, "Wouldn't it be better for me if I were to die?" Death is easier and more merciful than this disloyal, cruel, and tyrannical world.

Seven

1—Naji el-Jundi

I divorced my crazy wife and finally felt relief. I had experienced so much pain that it made me hit the mezuzah with my slipper and spit at it. I said to God, "I tried my luck twice but found it lacking. I'm a good man, so what did I do to suffer like Job?" Divorce gave me relief, though, Naji el-Jundi said to himself.

Naji said, "Muhammad! Please, let's hear 'Abd el-Wahab."

2—'Aziz Ghawi

Hell! The disgrace was made public, thought 'Aziz. My rival entered my house and was honored by my family. My mother played host, and my sister welcomed him, while all I wanted to do was find my lost self.

'Aziz shouted, "Salimah!" The yelling woke up all the tenants of the house. A terrible fear seized Lulu, Moshiyah's daughter, and she embraced Marrudi tightly, protecting him from known and unknown danger.

"Salimah!"

'Aziz let out a frantic shout like the shrill cry of a woman just bereaved of her husband. It came from his tortured soul, roaming and looking for another soul, for a balm, for a lost fragment of her, for a mind he no longer possessed. Fear silenced and dominated Farhah Ghawi, Sa'idah, Latifah, and Bannutah. With ratted hair, stormy red eyes, and a frown on his face, he descended the stairs

178

wearing a dishdashah, asking only for Salimah. Salimah had stolen everything from him.

Jamil's sleepy eyes blinked, and he said to Selman Hashwah, "That animal has begun, and soon you'll hear the sounds of spilling, breaking, and screaming. The best thing for me to do is fill my ears with a wad of cotton, pull the covers over my head, and fall asleep. As for you, run away before the situation gets worse."

"Salimah!"

A door slammed, and a woman's voice came begging for help, but to no avail. Sabriyah turned over on her gorgeous bed, annoyed. Her hands mechanically began to feel next to her and did not find Efrayim. He was still in Mosul, and she was alone, irritated, and angry because of the commotion, and because she was left without protection. Sighing, between sleeping and waking, she said, "What should I do? The situation in this house has become so unbearable that no one can sleep. As soon as I get up, I'll go and stay at my parent's home until Efrayim comes back."

Solid objects began to fall with sounds of smashing and crashing coming from the women's room. The women's noise grew stronger asking for help, pleading, crying with fear. Sa'idah screamed, "What do you want from us? Get out of here!"

'Aziz bombarded her with his angry voice, "Whore! I'm your sore spot. You want me to leave so you'll be alone with this pimp and you two can have fun with each other." He stared at Sa'idah's face. Farhah trembled.

The other two sisters recoiled, and the eldest screamed, "You should be ashamed of yourself and have respect for your old father. What a brazen person you are! Knock it off! Get out!" She wept.

He was a beast frantically preying. His mind was completely absorbed with the inability to conquer Salimah for himself. His fingers were like octopus tentacles preying on Salimah, but at the same time, she was his predator too, taking him away from his family, alienating and insulting him. His hand tightly seized the tail of Sa'idah's hair and pulled it with the force of bitter defeat and hatred.

She screamed, "Father, come! Come and see what your son is doing to us!"

He was the open mouth of a volcano, "Damn you, your father, and the world!" Farhah drew near its spouting fire, stones, hell, and lamentation. She was entirely a different Farhah Ghawi from the one people knew. "I beg of you 'Aziz, avoid evil! I wonder what she has done to you. It'll be okay. I swear everything will be the way you want. Please, calm down."

"Keep away from me. If you don't, I'll be your death."

He wept. Salimah! Every creature was his enemy. Sa'idah insulted him and exposed her enmity. He yelled at his second sister and went out of his mind with Sa'idah, pulling her hair. "Salimah! Just wait and see how I'll drink Karim 'Abd el-Wahab's blood! Whores! How can you let a person with low morals in your house and then flirt with him?"

A pair of scissors flew across the room, and Farhah Ghawi's sewing machine shook. Farhah rushed into the courtyard yelling, "Help, help! Isn't there anyone in the house to help me? I don't know what happened to my son. I lost him. I don't know what they did to him!"

Na'imah ran out barefooted. "Surely, he's bewitched," she said. "Don't you see it on him? Pour a little urine and smear it over him. Meanwhile, I'll get dressed right away and go to the mullah, who'll take the spell from him and prescribe a charm."

'Aziz screamed, "Oh Salimah, let me be a dog and the son of a dog, and my sister a whore if I don't drink from your blood and Karim's."

'Amam begged her son, Ya'qub, "I beg you, get up! They are upset; these women are without any protector. I wonder what he was given to drink that drove him so crazy."

Na'imah came back carrying urine in a bowl and gave it to Farhah, whispering, "Take it, 'aini! Rub it on his hands and legs. It would be best if you have him drink some."

The roaring bull heard and yelled, "Go away! Otherwise, I'll pour the urine over your head and the head of my whore mother."

She withdrew very quickly, and the urine bowl dropped from Farhah's hand because of the uproar. It spilled between the room and the courtyard. Ya'qub came in furious, held 'Aziz, and yelled at him, "Who made you? You've devastated the lives of your mother and sisters."

'Aziz pushed him away so that he could follow his sister. Shrouded in a black 'abayah, she fled toward the gate of the courtyard. He caught her at the doorstep, and she screamed. He kicked her, and she shrieked. He spat at her face and screamed again, "Whore!" She fell and wailed like a professional mourner.

Ya'qub caught up with him and said, "Be ashamed of yourself! Show a little respect and dignified behavior to your sister and mother."

'Aziz confronted him with his blazing eyes and shouting, "Eat shit and shut up! If you are good for something, you'll marry Sa'idah, and if you truly feel like protecting her honor, then take her, bury her."

Suddenly, Ya'qub let up and retreated like a wounded man. He said to his mother and everyone else, "Is this what you wanted? You see what kind of trouble you got me into? It's none of my business to get involved in other peoples' messes. I have enough problems of my own—the shop, the damn orchard rent, my partner, the son of a whore, and you want me to be involved in this mess? Come, 'Aibah, let's go!" he called. "Damn these people!"

3—Jamil Rabi

Well, what did I tell you, dear Abu Gallubi? Didn't I tell you that Naji would divorce her? The first time he turned out to be crazy, and this time she was crazy. I'm right—nothing fit anything harmoniously: everything has its opposite. Everything is an opposite to something else. No one can get out of this maze, away from this spinning propeller. The opposites are in control. The circle is closing, becoming a ring. Baghdad is worked up in turmoil. What do they want? I went along and was engulfed with them in the current, not guided by sight but pushed by waves of crowds and uncertain desires. People in all shapes and of various degrees of intelligence want to survive. Although life is a senseless, comic, and mechanical game, people stuff it with a thing called desire, wanting the comedy to grow into a tragedy, and they commit crimes to satisfy desires. And desire is another disease. I'm telling you, if one insists on having something, all the people will suffer as a result.

What does 'Aziz Ghawi want? He's a microcosm of this world's insanity, its desire. All is needed to bring destruction to this world is a conflict of desires that grows into a revolution. Everything becomes completely confused in a jumbled mess of contradictions. The world is rolling in its own blood. The reds die, the blacks die, the whites die, everyone dies. Only the color red remains. The red is blood that will soon turn black. Black means mourning, orphans, and widows. All this is because of people's contradictory desires. Everyone wants, but no one knows what or why. My mother and father—what do they want? I have lost the essence of desire. Sometimes I don't know what I want either. I'm afraid to know what I want, or I'm lost in the desires of my intertwined, complicated opposites. It's never easy to have desires.

Abu Ghalib! What do you want? I know what you want. You desire the night to go by quickly so that you can go home to your wife and children. Your night is different than mine. My night is like the nights of many miserable people because of desires different than theirs. Though their desires don't come true, that doesn't stop them, whether they are weak, cowards, or stupid. They still strive for an illusion.

And Selman Hashwah, what does he want? Selman Hashwah is a sucker. What does he think? Am I not a human being just like him? Am I not able to fall in love with Sabriyah like him? Rocky hearts are apt to be smashed at Sabriyah's feet, but I see myself as people see me. I'm blind, and this means I'm imperfect and weak, but people don't realize that I have insight that withstands pain and turns my back on illusions. Otherwise, I would suffer. Does this mean that I labor and don't attain my desires and try to crack open a hard nut, though the inside is almost certainly empty?

Naji el-Jundi wants modest things like Selman. People can be classified into ranks, Abu Ghalib. Naji el-Jundi's rank is low. He's satisfied with listening to a song of 'Abd el-Wahab and telling the story about his dog. But do you really think listening to a song of

'Abd el-Wahab is enough for him? If you think so, you are, as usual, mistaken. Don't be mad, Abu Ghalib! We're all mistaken sometimes. No one is better than anyone else. The opposites, Abu Ghalib, have the upper hand even when desiring a song that may end in a massacre.

The other day a disaster was about to happen in Muhammad Shayi's café because of two songs and a damn stupid desire, between opposites, Naji el-Jundi and Yahya the Butcher. You know Yahya, he adores Umm Kulthum. The night she sings he slaughters a sheep and distributes its meat to the needy as if he were celebrating a wedding. Many people commit suicide because of a small desire that swells into action. Blood is shed everywhere on account of insatiable and rejected desire. And here Naji clings to 'Abd el-Wahab, and Yahya's life depends on the night Umm Kulthum sings.

So how would you reconcile these opposites? Yahya clings to his life, and Naji wants to hear the songs in the film *The White Rose*. The "rose" almost became red when an argument broke out between Naji and Yahya. Yahya is a butcher with his mouth and his hands. In a loose-tongued moment, he started to insult the religions of the world. In this world there are a lot of advocates of opinions, political ideas, honor, religion, and God. But the best thing to do, Abu Ghalib, is to sew one's mouth shut and keep silent. The life of the person who talks becomes miserable, for as long as there's someone watching over you, you can't even fart.

Radi, the advocate for religion, was present. He stood up and slapped Yahya on the face very hard and said to him, "How dare you curse religions?" I was astonished how Yahya the Butcher, held back.

Meanwhile, I wondered how Gerjiyi Nati could stand Khoshi two full months and live with this thing who came from Iran, unless of course, they're from the same stock. She is also somebody from Bombay, but this useless Persian is called Khoshi, *good*, with no justification. He's certainly a con man. What does Gerjiyi Nati desire? What does this Persian swindler want?

There are big things that grow small until they're lost, and there are small things that grow big until they're written in history. Yahya the Butcher received Radi's blow quietly then rose, and nobody felt his departure. Another chapter in the human comedy was to be written in Shayi's Café, a chapter based on the opposites—songs of Umm Kulthum and 'Abd el-Wahab; Naji el-Jundi; Yahya the Butcher; and Radi, the advocate of religion. As it turned out, Yahya came back quietly with a revolver and shot Radi in the shoulder. You see the joke here, Abu Ghalib. Lucky coincidence is sometimes good and praiseworthy, capable of saving people from desires and fickleness.

For example, Radi was born with stooped shoulders and had to lift them by putting high cotton pads under his coat. He was safe when the bullets went through the cotton shoulder. But who would save Yahya from the people now? They wanted to see a quarrel in which the true sparks of our wishes come out and the onlooker with the arrogantly twisted mustache would be pleased. Muhammad Shayi had desires too, but he was a decent human being, more reasonable and truthful. He stood up and faced Yahya the Butcher and shouted, "Nobody touches him! By the prophet Muhammad, no one comes any closer to him." What did Muhammad Shayi want?

A good desire is generated by the sparking of contradictory, dull, and insignificant desires leading to bloodshed. There are many other desires. Only one quarrel caused by conflict of desires could have escalated into bloodshed, and the world would have been destroyed.

What do I want? Can I truly ask and wish? Do I have anything to give? And if I don't have anything, why don't I invent a lie for Shridah, the busboy, who works in all the cafés of Baghdad? Like Naji, Shridah came from Tarab Café to Sha'ul's Café. He brought me a wooden board, and on the sides he hammered nails and ran a wire through the nails. He thought he had made me a qanun. "Teach me how to play the qanun, for God's sake!" he said to me. His qanun was as deceitful as people's desires, but I don't carry my qanun with me. I taught him half the deceit—the first musical notes. Shridah wanted to learn how to play this string instrument on a board with wires at a time when everyone was very busy doing something. All people have strong desires.

What does Habishah, the madam, desire? Well, madam's desires are answered quickly. The madams do whatever they please whenever people are killed in Baghdad's streets, victims of people's damned contradictive desires governed by the opposites.

Abu Ghallubi, do you know what I want? No, you don't know. Do you think I know? Am I not a paradox myself? I was born a needy Jew well before they blinded me. As long as I'm a Jew, the authorities will call me a Zionist, and against my will I'll also stick another attribute to myself—Communist. Real Communism and true equality is death. In addition to what people attribute to me and what I attribute to myself, I support Hitler too. Weakness is bound to be uprooted from the earth. I lead the column of the weak people who should be swallowed up by death. It's better to die if you can't even wish anything, because of the opposites in life that are the obstacles!

I'm a coward, a chicken! I've been tossed into the human game against my will, and I remain an echo of all things, of all opposites. Why wasn't I born in Nazi Germany and driven to the gas chambers? The human animals in Nazi Germany differ from humans whose baldness is treated with red Kuppalli powder, which also takes away vision. The matter would have been different because dust storms don't blow in Germany, nor do eye infections sprout up. Surely, I would then be able to see. If I could see and live like a human being, why would I want to die? This is another dilemma with more chaos, but all people want a mirage. In reality, I'm blind and see only by virtue of illusion and desire. Do I desire to know reality or do I strive for a half mirage?

Why are you scratching your head, Abu Ghalib? It's a difficult problem, a very difficult problem. You have no business daydreaming. Go and enjoy a cup of tea and a cigarette and don't think! Be aware, Abu Ghalib, that thinking is the source of all catastrophes. Don't you agree?

4—Selman Hashwah

I don't know what to do with my life. Thoughts are loosening in my mind. A dam collapses and bursts inside me, releasing a furious stream flowing internally. I have a different opinion every hour. Every minute I feel different. I lost Sabriyah and I moaned. When the Jewish State was declared in Palestine, I recited, "Blessed be He who has kept us in life." I envisioned sinister memories as realities, while walking in Baghdad, and my body pricked me with pins and needles. I felt happy and sad, elated and depressed, calm and frightened. I changed colors every hour.

"Please Foha, don't ladle a dish of beans for me!" What can I do? I don't feel like eating. I'm stewing in my own juices. Just this month my belly shrunk two inches; I'll be flesh and bones before next month. Jamil asked, "What's the matter with you? Are you lamenting the destruction of Beith ha-Miqdash, our Holy Temple? The Jews now have a state, and they'll build it up."

He mocks me. He knows that I'm caught like a mouse in a trap. He also knows that my castle has collapsed and that I'm buried under its ruins. Above me are huge hills of miserable reality, smashing down. Sabriyah! Sabriyah was the sweetest illusion by which I survived and became happy. But God, praised be He, thought she was too good for me and He took her away. He took my illusions and shattered them completely, and then I was forced to descend from my ivory tower.

Should I or shouldn't I go to Khaduri? No one can endure their own sorrows and joys without having someone with whom to share them. My silence rattled inside me. Loneliness reduced me to nothing, and I became nonexistent in the human whirlpool. I lost my identity in the crowd, existing no longer. My sorrows cut short my happiness, and a sharp plough turned me over. But I'm looking for open ears to listen to me. I want to do the simplest thing a human being does—speak and converse so that I can get my being back. I've missed having an attentive ear since Khaduri jumped off the neighbor's open rooftop. Last night, I passed by his shop with a lowered head. I was confused and hesitant. Should I stop by? Should I not go by to see him? I saw the black, ghostly presence in his shop and I lost my senses. I could not understand. Kaduri was conversing with Aminah in a free and friendly manner, as if nothing had happened.

What impudence! What insolence! How did he have the gall to look at her? I was not two-faced. I dashed off as quickly as the wind, but my whole body felt cut off.

"Needles, pins, matches!" I whispered to her in a low, sad voice.

Sabriyah was imprisoned in the tone of my voice, like a muzzle, and I was imprisoned with her in the turbulence of stormy, terrifying Baghdad. My memories became twins of the present, spirits animating a dead body that I saw in front and behind me, leaping, climbing, rising from the past, moving between yesterday and today. Ghosts were behind and in front of me. These truths were eating away at my reflections. Then I disappeared.

"Dye, sewing machine threads, cotton strings!"

Eliyahu Hamis stopped me. I gave him matches but he did not go. Ever since I have known Eliyahu Hamis, he has never stopped longer than the time it took to pick up a box of matches. This time he stopped. I had a lot of things on my mind, and I admit that I forgot: "Didn't I give you the change? Excuse me, I am absentminded."

Eliyahu laughed at me. I had already given him the change for one dirham, but he didn't budge and put his hand on my shoulder. He said cautiously but firmly, "Walk with me, I want to talk to you."

I was surprised and overwhelmed. A feeling spread over me, like the legs of a centipede, a feeling that takes in all of the thoughts and desires of a man. I knew Eliyahu as a quiet person who never raised his voice unless there was either an emergency or a shadow of hope. I followed him like a sheep, a dog out of breath starving for a piece of bone, and I had been speechless ever since the presence of Sabriyah in the house had eclipsed like the moon of the Muslim month. When a sense of shame defiled Kaduri's deed, I forgot my words. I lived in silence, not hearing the noise or commotion in the house and the street. Except for Jamil Rabi's sarcastic and ridiculing talk, nothing reached my ears.

Eliyahu Hamis dragged me down twisted alleyways as quiet as my silence. He led me there promising to tell me something I had been waiting for impatiently. He wanted to talk to me, but he didn't know that wanting to talk to me gave me exactly what I had felt ashamed of asking for. Nevertheless, my curiosity grew stronger, making me human again, if not humanlike. I resembled a famished dog running after a piece of bone—a dog whose patience was tired by searching and not finding anything except the murmur of silence, my silence and the silence of those who avoided me. Damn this silence! I'm filled with silence. I'm hungry for a human voice to talk to me, come near to me and know I'm human too.

Eliyahu Hamis tempted me. He continued to put his hand on my shoulder, sending currents of a seldom-felt feeling, as though my importance was restored. I remembered the warmth of Muhsin 'Abd el-Wahid's hand leading me to safety on the most terrifying night of my life, and my body sensed the sweetness of Sabriyah's tickling me, and when she used to lift me to the top of my sweet dream. But Eliyahu took his time to talk, and I had to implore to him, "Go ahead, say something, I'm anxious and I feel pangs in my stomach."

I wondered if talking needs a special place. Did I have to run after him for an hour? True, I didn't know then that the gems he let out of his mouth and for which I had waited a whole hour would turn into an atomic bomb exploding inside me.

Eliyahu Hamis told me things that plucked my heart from its root. He dropped his words into the pit of my stomach. They were irreversible. I felt chills running through my limbs similar to what I felt the first and second days of May 1941 when I was overwhelmed by a deadly cold I had. When I opened my eyes I saw the long kisses between Sabriyah and Efrayim and their lips cleaved together. What does Eliyahu want from me? I felt like telling him: "Find someone else for your calamities. Isn't there anyone else to recruit for your strange tasks except me, Selman Hashwah?"

My shoulder was a shooting post in Karbala, and since then I have been taking precautions and avoiding troubles so much that I don't even go near Kadduri. And Eliyahu Hamis wants to put me in the barrel of the gun? My mouth was parched and I said to him, "No brother, God bless you, leave me alone! Baghdad is full of Jewish youth. Could it be that Baghdad has run out of them and only I remain? Go and find someone else."

He didn't let me go. My answer didn't stop Eliyahu Hamis, who saw more importance in me than my matches. This quiet young man suddenly became a chatterbox who bombarded my ears with verses of horror chosen from the books of Job and Jeremiah, the prophet of anger. He warned me, and I fell to pieces. He didn't give me the right to leave, and in doing so, he entirely annihilated my being. After surveying the Jewish history of all periods he said, "Take your time, think about it, and let me know tomorrow."

"You are a martyr!"

Following the rhythm of the bed's springs, back and forth, one side to another, Selman continued to stare at his life, the mirror of his doomed past and present. He had fallen into Sabriyah's arms. Sabriyah had stepped aside and said to him in the biting tongue of Farhah Ghawi's hostility, "You think of yourself as a human being, don't you? You're only a one-eyed man!" Then he had escaped to Eliyahu Hamis, waiting for him with open arms. The Farhûd happened then and now another one was looming, moving into ambush position.

Surely, Eliyahu Hamis didn't want to frighten him, but he openly said, "If a Farhûd happens again, what will you do?"

What would Selman do? His insanity had protected him during the first Farhûd. Several times he had succeeded in avoiding death on the first and second of May 1941.

Eliyahu said to him, "The precious vase can't be saved every time."

Fear sneered at Selman, showing its teeth. He lowered his voice and called his roommate, hissing, "Jamil, Jamil!"

Jamil answered angrily, "Shut up and go to sleep!" Selman's tongue was paralyzed. He was mute, frightened, shivering, and lost. He wondered how his father and mother had been killed in the Farhûd. Either no one had seen it or no one had agreed to tell him. People still wouldn't tell him how his parents had died.

Why? Sabriyah! Why? Oh Baghdadis! Why did you burglarize people's homes, Khaduri? Selman asked.

In a collapsing school building where the clean air of the city didn't emit a stench, Selman was accused, "You're a spy! You killed the prophets." They were pro-Nazi, and he was a Jew. Years had passed and the blood of Jews, Muslims, and Christians was shed on the bridge, but he was still a Jew. Although he was thought to be a coward and wouldn't even tread on an ant on purpose, he was accused of treason. Why? A hostile air, which Jamil explained to him, encircled him: "Reactionaries, imperialists, and mercenary governments feed the uprisings."

"Is it possible that the disaster of the Farhûd could happen again?"

Jamil replied, "Everything is possible. This is a dirty government. The people here are agitated, and the government wants to channel the people in a different direction."

We're the scapegoats! So, why do the people dance to anyone who plays the music? Why are the people so naïve?

"Is it reasonable to suppose that next time we'll wait until they come and slaughter us like sheep? We should train ourselves to use weapons to protect ourselves." Selman recalled Eliyahu's warning.

Frightened, I pleaded. My Lord! How will I hold a lethal weapon in my hand? Protect me, my Sabriyah! Protect me, Sabriyah! Protect me from myself! My castle has turned into a ruin; I'm smashed under it, trapped under the heap with no air. And what about "The State" there? A defeating terror and many forests of gallows are set up, separating "The State" and me. Another Farhûd is looming on the horizon, and I have no air to breathe. Protect me, Sabriyah! Give me an illusion, the most beautiful illusion, the sweetest one! Save me from my filthy life, from the gaping whirlpool, from the barrel of the gun.

Sabriyah didn't hear, didn't answer me. She was, in fact, not at home, and the rest of the tenants were asleep. They were deaf, mute, and blind. They heard nothing and saw nothing. No, that was untrue. Eliyahu Hamis listened and saw. He found me, but he would protect me by fire, by firearms, by bathing me in the sea of glaring fire. The Farhûd was coming, was coming, the Farhûd!

I imagined Sabriyah in the forthcoming Farhûd. What would she do? I tried to block my mind, my imagination. No! I'll protect you, hold the gun and the machine gun and protect you, my Sabriyah, even if you are in Efrayim's arms.

Out of downfall, bankruptcy, despair, and torment, I wept like a child. I was no longer afraid to toss myself into a sea of fire. I addressed myself in bitterness, "To hell with it! What have I gotten out of my life? I'm not an uncle to a boy or girl. I have nothing in life. I resemble a donkey with a rope around its neck roaming in the streets. Do I have anything else in this world? No! Nothing is left. I'll go out of my mind again, so going into the Zionist underground is better for me. Going to them is better for me."

5—Farhah Ghawi

Let the world be destroyed and tumble stone by stone. Everywhere I turn, darkness and blindness take over. What is written on my forehead is as dark as the night, colored with ink. I am both the man and woman of the house. I am the hardworking, the unfortunate, and the miserable one. I face three hardships, three daughters, three enormous burdens lying on my heart like a mountain, and my overstuffed, weary husband can't do anything—not even tie his shoelaces. It makes no difference whether he's home or not. As far as 'Aziz is concerned, I was entertained by dreams as tall as a mast with the hope that I would become proud of him. What should I do? Should I strike my eyes out for sorrow? What a misfortune! The evil eye has befallen us, and ever since grief entered our house, it never left. What do people want from us? May their houses be destroyed! I'm constantly with the blind tenants, Lulu's persistent cries, Sabriyah's insults, and with the evil eye of Gerjiyi Nati or her vulgar Persian husband, and with Ya'qub, the dirty dog.

My dear sister! Did you hear what Ya'qub said to his mother when my son, 'Aziz, asked him for Sa'idah, his sister's hand? He was alarmed and said to his mother, "Look what he's getting me into." Ya'qub is no better than Sa'idah. Every one of my daughters can beat him and more men like him. He feels ashamed of Sa'idah. Do I deserve evil for my good deeds? You know his gray-haired mother came to me with her head lowered, begging me to give her a hundred dinars. What for? It became clear to me that her son, Ya'qub Pasha, wanted to pay the rent for his shop and the orchard. He didn't have one fils to pay because he'd gambled away all his money. I wish he'd die, since a person like him deserves to be wiped off the face of the earth—may death not be far from him! Still, I have good intentions. I took a hundred dinars and gladly gave it to her, and in the end he was unmindful and said what he said. Well, it doesn't matter. I swear I'll disown myself if I don't give him a hard time about returning the money. I don't care if he steals. I'll press him about what he said.

Let the rest of the tenants be driven away, Farhah wished. My poor 'Aziz is confused and lost. They stole him from me! They stripped him of his sobriety. During the daytime, he strikes out against his sisters, and at night he gets drunk. He doesn't think straight or understand. There's nothing in his head except Salimah. Karim saves whatever can be saved. He carries him every night on his shoulder and doesn't leave him anywhere except at home. What would we have done if not for Karim 'Abd el-Wahab?

Imagine that my son, 'Aziz, were drunk and Karim were not around. It's the middle of the night in this wild, stormy, and scary Baghdad, and 'Aziz is alone and drunk, not knowing head from toe. He lays on the sidewalk at a street corner in Baghdad, the preying beast.

Sa'idah says, "Karim is a decent person. We are four women with no one to protect us. Karim is the only one who cares. Who would accept 'Aziz's spitting, cursing, and insulting? On his heart he carries 'Aziz unconsciously and consoles us, soothing our pain. The rest are indifferent, as still as stones, do not care. Where's my brother? Where are my cousin and all my relatives? These are only names without bodies; they are absent. What's more, a person you don't touch or feel is absent. They are absent."

My husband, 'Abdallah, said he would return from Mahmudiyah after I nagged him: "Enough, come to Baghdad and leave your damn shop. What are you doing alone among savage people in Mahmudi-yah? Are you waiting for them to get mad, attack you, loot the shop, and kill you? Leave everything and come back and stay in your house. The house has become a ruin. Come and solve your son's problem, take care of your daughters!"

If it were not for good and conscientious Karim bringing 'Aziz home every night and bearing him on his shoulders, he would die. Would any other stranger agree to do this? That stuffed mutton of a husband would come back, sit at home in front of me wearing his dishdashah, eat, drink, burp, and sleep, doing nothing.

My fate was black the moment He determined my fate. That moment was cursed. I have mules, sheep, and crazy people at home, and I have fallen into this trap. What did the whore do to 'Aziz, my beloved son? Suddenly things are turned over in his eyes: the whore becomes the saint of the world, and his mother and sisters the whores. This is sleight of hand, magic itself. What did Salimah do to you, 'Aziz?

Poor good Na'imah left her house, her son, Nihad, and her husband, Fayiq, and wandered with me from one fortuneteller to a mullah, from one soothsayer and stargazer to a sheikh.

"Don't worry, dear. I'll not sit still one minute until I find a solution for 'Aziz," said Na'imah. She showered 'Aziz with dinar bills, one after the other, and insisted that I not spend even one fils from my pocket.

My son, 'Aziz, come back! Be sober and return to your loving mother and sisters. Believe me, we love you. No mother hates her offspring. You're the apple of your mother's and sisters' eye. Salimah tempted you. The sheikh, the fortuneteller, and that fat demonic woman mullah confirmed what Na'imah had said about Salimah bewitching you.

Salimah, the whore, the poisonous snake, gave him the *damghah*, ground stone potion, to drink, and stripped him of awareness and willpower. I hope Salimah drinks the poison and tastes death. If she had been under my control I would have made her drink poisonous *salwah* with my own hand. How will I give 'Aziz the *butlah* charm to undo the other spells when he has no appetite to eat or drink? The other day he was calm for a moment, so I begged him to take a bite. I kissed his forehead with all my soul and prayers and said, "Let me bring you tea with milk, abdalak."

She had put the butlah in the cup of tea. He stared at it continuously and then he shoved the glass aside and shouted loudly, "Salimah!"

There was so much hatred hidden in ʿAziz's feather pillow that I can't see any improvement. On the contrary, his condition worsens every day. But Naʿimah hasn't given up hope yet. Saʿidah did, though, and her life became hell. Life was a living hell for us too. Why didn't my brother, my cousin, my relatives, my husband, the stuffed bull, come? My call for help was dashed in the storm roaring around us. The storm of panicked anger! Sweep all things away! Destroy the fortress of the cowards! Level the houses of the worshipped wealth! Let the plague, prisons, torture, mutilations, the gallows, and the graves come! God knows what He is doing. The conscience and feelings of my relatives, my cousins, and Yaʿqub, the dog, are dead, so what about me? What do I expect? Am I waiting for the resurrection of the dead?

6—Ya'qub, 'Amam's Son

There was the gurgling of hukkahs, nervous tension, and a growing curiosity of eyes and ears fixed to a gambling table in the fading light of a café. It was a forgotten night in a forgotten quarter. On God I relied! I drew a domino piece. Dominos concealed torpedoes and rescue boats. The way of drowning and rescue were both hidden and strewn about. Luck was blind and it came at random, but sometimes it acted on a purposeful plan, in a strange way subjected to its own will. It came as it pleased, and God forbid you should disobey it. Time was a continuous game of dominos, and I was tucked away into both the passage of time and the game.

Craning her neck, my mother said to me, "I beg you, abdalak, don't let me be worried about you. Come back early and don't hang out! Can't you see the situation is getting worse in Baghdad?"

The lost bracelet! My damned partner took advantage of me, stripped me and made away with all my wealth. I pawned the shop's rent in a game of dominos, relying on God. Ishaq the Grocer ran after me, and I ran away from him, hiding in any hole that could protect me from his shameful dunning and dinning.

The desired domino didn't show. I wanted double-four and drew a double-blank. Where was my luck? I drew double-blank only. No money, no jackpot. You, all of you, fell under the control of a dominant double-blank piece. "Damn you," I said to myself for wanting to get the shop rent for Ishaq the Grocer by winning at dominos! A short while ago, I raised my head to God and said to Him, "Knock it off! Enough drawing double-blank."

A breach was opened in the heavens. At that time, God's ears were still open. He responded to me, wrote down my request, approved and sealed it too. Now He punished me because I denied His grace. So I surrendered to His will and accepted it. Good, I deserved it!

"Welcome, welcome, Mahdi! Welcome, my brother, have a seat! The cigarette is ready, and the tea will come soon," I said.

The world is weird. The orbit revolves on a crooked axis. It revolves and turns over all the objects in its way. It makes animosity turn into friendship, a wealthy man goes down, and an impoverished man goes up. I declared bankruptcy but Mahdi el-Tubar, the most notorious thug in Baghdad, was suddenly turning into a friend, and Mr. 'Alwan was endangering our strong ties, placing them between the two filthiest blades of a pair of scissors.

No, Mr. 'Alwan, no! Politics is like a whore dividing twin brothers. If the main artery connecting the twins is severed, bleeding occurs.

"Zneef! I win! I am through with my pieces. Your coming, Mahdi, brought me good luck." Now I covered the expenses for the rolls, tea, and the hukkah. Let's hurry up and play until morning in order to cover my shop rent," I pleaded.

My poor mother waited and was sitting on pins and needles, but time got lost in a continuous game of luck. Sometimes luck winks and shines, and sometimes it frowns and hides its face. The world is a profligate whore. Farhah Ghawi is a sneaky snake, my

partner is a hairless mouse, and my luck is permanent, as a blank
is double-blank.

But the filthiest thing in this world is the ugly and childish old
whore called politics. Challenging the devil, Farhah Ghawi insists
on wanting the only lucky blue card in the deck, easily blown by the
slightest breeze. With all its tools and supplies, my shop is like an
unmoved stone. The anvil alone is heavy enough without the hammers, the lasts, the leathers and nails, the armless chair, the heaps of
ready shoes, and 'Aibah and me. The blue card, though, is a twisted
chain with steel rings dangling from heaven. It's as powerful as a
mountain that can lift my shop with its equipment and turn it into a
feather blown by the cruel wind of fate.

The piece I drew was a double-six. I won one dirham, but the blue
card wins the two thousand dirhams on which my life depends. The
blue card plays the hypocrite, then procrastinates, and never turns up.

The fate of my shop is worth a hundred dinars, and my entire fate
depends on the other side, on the immortal indefinite—the shabby
and the refurbished, the impure and low, on that sinful whore called
politics.

"Drink, Mahdi! If you don't get involved in politics, you'll hold
the fort as the most honorable and decent person in the world."

Majid, Hamid, 'Abdallah, their mother, Jadu, Muhammad Shayi,
and many others, including innocent, honest, and pious people, are
ethical too. But the stream sweeps us, and 'Alwan situates himself
at the source of the stream. He holds the bowl and forces people to
contribute money for the beloved gypsy whore, politics. He collects
money for the refugees and for saving Palestine. A revolver strapped
on his hip plus the energy of bad thoughts supports him.

He said to me, "I swear by Allah, I almost killed this baker at
the beginning of the street. What's his name? I told him to donate
money, and he told me, 'By God! I have no money. I have ten children
and they come first. How can I feed them?' He's a Jew and a dog,
and he denies bliss. I swear I was almost ready to empty my revolver
on his head, but then I said, 'No, Ya'qub made up for him. Although

Ya'qub is worried and poor, he proved he doesn't behave like a Jew. He's more respectful than his brothers in the faith.'"

But I am a Jew, 'Alwan, my friend for life. I pretended not to see what you did in the Farhûd. I did not move a muscle against you. In general, it's better to distinguish among things and not mix them up, but you're no good in making distinctions. There are still burning coals of friendship inside. There's nothing more discomfiting than having an old friend hold you responsible for what you didn't do. "An abusive Jew, a dog." No, 'Alwan! No! No, Qadri! No, Farhah Ghawi! No, Nessim, the dog! No, the most sinful whore in the world!

Again I drew double-blank. I was looking for my life inside a humble game, and inside I wandered into a despised and completely vile one. I'm drawn into this game and have turned into shit coming out of the rear of the game in the universe's shithouse. My poor mother has lost her mind by now, looking for me in unknown places full of mines and traps laid by the damn whore. No, 'Alwan! I may be a Jew, but I'm not a traitor. How could I betray a homeland containing soil holding the remains of my father and forefathers? This land is made of us, 'Alwan. We lived in it before you were born. When you were sperm, we had already completed compiling our Talmud, our Jewish law. I was here in this land before you, twelve centuries before you. Before the beginning of history, my first patriarch was born here, the second married a native, and the third lived in it. Our matriarchs, Sarah, Rebecca, Leah, and Rachel were from this land. Where were you then, 'Alwan? Would I betray the blissful land, for which I would sacrifice my life, 'Alwan?

With his eyes peeled on my every move in the game of dominos, my friend Hamid said, "You're making a lot of mistakes, Ya'gub. You shouldn't discard this piece." I laughed and said to him, "Hamid, don't be naïve. If the whole world is a grave mistake, can discarding the right piece make it right? Everything is messed up. This is a drop in the bucket, a drop of the sweet water of the Tigris in the Dead Sea."

Again, I wanted to win the shop's rent in a domino game. Why was I fooling myself? I could say that I was cramming my life into this small game of a large one designed by the sinful whore who spread all her sins, her filth, and her disasters in man's way. With the valuable blue card I could shut up Farhah Ghawi's loud mouth and finally admit that Nessim, the son of the whore, had defeated me by deceit and malice. My shop, the source of my livelihood and wealth, was lost together with the bracelet, my world, and myself.

7—Gerjiyi Nati and Khoshi, the Persian

"The opium, woman! I become a man and a half with opium," Khoshi bragged.

Khoshi makes fun of me, thought Gerjiyi. He thinks I haven't seen men in my life. I experienced many real men of all races, you son of an unbeliever! I was a lady in Kelly's lap of luxury, a slave in Mahmud's lap, a small child in Singh's lap. It was paradise in the lap of Kelly, Mahmud, and Singh. I was happy with all of them and felt the smell of the trees, the cardamom, the sandalwood, and the clove. My head was full of various scents, and I managed to put together a delightful life whose scent diffused in the air like the sweet smell of a brazier. I used to feel the world with Kelly, Mahmud, and Singh, embracing all races, origins, and religions.

My good life went by swiftly and time brought me to embrace a man heavy with filth. Now there's the smell of rotten coconut in my nose, the sour taste of wine in my mouth, and of food so spoiled that a starved old dog wouldn't touch it. Khoshi's belly has grown protruded, and his hard, sticky bulge has eaten away at my own belly. Beneath the bulge there was that thing shrunk as if a dog had barked at it. One thousand spells of witchcraft are not enough to drive fear away from his heart.

From what kind of species have you descended, 'Ajmi? What is your religion and who are your ancestors? Hurray for me! How could I stand him for two whole months? Tonight is chilly, inviting, and next to me lays one thing, neither male nor female. He's like a sewer emitting stenches and leaking all over, but a thick girdle full of coins under lock and key enriches him.

I . . . I'm a living unit called "I." I'm a pot in which all kinds of humans are subjected to an amazing flexibility. It melts and toys with people's stupidity so that the "I" will survive. I reach the "I" with different, valid passports beyond this country of imbeciles, beyond the barriers of class and sect.

I . . . I am . . . I have money. I want money. I take money. I am the bull's horn, which supports our world made of money, in which money controls everything. The demon eats it, and I eat it, even gobbling it. I am the demon! I'm Khoshi.

My odd story is written in books and inscribed in the sultan's records, said Gerjiyi to herself. The past is an attractive gray mare, and the present is a wild black mare. They race in a closed and narrow arena comprising existence. The gray mare is always the winner. It battered my entire head with its hoofs then neighed. My body shrunk, and the present retreated under the knocking hoof. Often, my present was defeated by my past. This has happened to many people. People would live longer if it were not for the present. Singh looked neat, experienced, slim, and tan with a bright, clean Indian outfit. People were humble and dignified, and love was sincere there. Singh pampered me, and I was like a small child with narcissus in her braids.

One day I asked Singh, "Where does your spending money come from?" He smiled with innocence and piety, the same way when he sat on the floor and I lay on an ebony bed covered with a velvet carpet. Singh was an ordinary man, and I was a goddess to whom he offered his secrets in ceremonies of idol worship. Pouring his sublime secrets into my heart, he said, "I'll show you my treasures."

He took me to the cellar. In Bombay, there are cellars full of precious treasures and secrets. There are also millions of bony human beings in dire poverty. Darkness and light were mixed together. The cellar was as terrifying and dark as a black lock of hair spread over a white cheek. We descended the stone ladder and were lost in a vault beneath the earth full of treasures imprisoned in the darkness full of gold like Khoshi's sock.

There were the wood scents and camphor . . . and the secrets. The vault opened, and a bright light split the darkness. My sight was dazzled when I saw the glittering egg inside the vault, and my eyes were astounded. What a hidden pearl, a big egg-like pearl. But I am not so hidden a pearl to be fascinated by this hidden one.

There are millions of human beings on Earth whose hunger eats their fat and flesh and drinks their souls. I experienced hunger in my life, but circumstances made me forget my hunger. Now, I recalled that time of confusion and asked Singh, "How much is it worth?"

"A lot and a little," he said.

I didn't understand. He protected my ignorance in that dark, dense treasury that sent bright rays driving away the fear and glitters of its dreams, hopes, thoughts—and sometimes man's humanity.

"A lot because it means power, support, and security, and a little because it's piled and hidden forever in this secret room."

I recalled being hungry. What would happen if I did a good deed for which millions of human beings would praise me? Millions would anoint their hands by touching my garments everywhere.

"How many people would satisfy their hunger and survive if this pearl appeared on Earth?" I asked Singh.

Singh kissed me warmly and said, "You're tender and kind but still a child. The pearl would be lost among one million starving bellies. It would live one more day and die."

For a moment I thought that Singh had a stone heart. I had been devastated by hunger, but Singh taught me that quenching the thirst of one person is more effective than the vain dream of saving millions of wretches. He was right. He realized this while showing his teeth that resembled white pearls after being polished with charcoal powder and salty cream.

"Despite this, the egg-like pearl can still cure the passion sparkling in your eyes, so take it," he said.

Satisfied but bewildered, I poured down the strong, sweet wine. Because of the shock of the dream, I was frightened and didn't know whether to believe or deny what I had seen. My hand didn't have the courage to reach for the vault. Singh preferred me to millions of human beings. Maybe he was just a gentle but deceived enigma.

"Take it, go on!"

I extended my hand, dreaming. What was inside this magical, shiny egg-like pearl? One million pieces of bread, a million chunks in which my life lies? The pride of a hungry woman in the remote past, with rusty pride aimed at self-possession, not only for herself but also for others as wretched and blessed as she was. Is it easy for us to climb to the top of hopes in one moment?

"Will I be able to do with it as I please?"

"Do whatever you want with whatever is yours."

I had a meal in my pocket to sustain life for one day. This means a million thanks, a million bits of pride, a million protests against cruel hunger and deprivation. This was my humane and naïve dream, my humane dream in an inhumane world where hundreds of millions of people like Khoshi live.

The pearl was lost on my way. Singh was the smartest and wisest human being. He taught me how to live. I was a queen; I was fortunate, despite what might happen . . .

Khoshi, the gold mine, emitted rotten odors, but nevertheless became real.

The present! Suddenly the wild black mare kicked my head and began to run as swiftly as the wind, leaving the beautiful gray mare behind, gasping.

My sigh provoked my vicious lust, and I said to myself in despair, "Cool off, lady of the empty tales."

I was strangled by a rotten gust escaping from the stinky Khoshi.

Gerjiyi is moody and irritable. She'll drive me out of my mind before I can run away. She's like a drill making a hole in my head.

"Khoshi, your lower part is good for nothing. At least go and wash yourself. Your smell is killing me. Are you afraid the shower will rinse away gold water from your body?"

"No, woman! It's not gold water; it's pure gold I spent all my life toiling to collect. Do you want me to give you my life's savings? You want me to give away with a ladle what I earned with a soup spoon! No, woman, no!"

Where should I put my own money? Don't people here wash in the same room where they relieve themselves? What if someone were pressed to relieve himself and needed to go to the toilet while I washed? Wouldn't he attack me and then take possession of my savings? There are many public baths in Baghdad, as many as in Tehran, or even more. I was on my way to a public bath once, and because I was terrified, I ran back.

People take baths together here. I saw ten pairs of eyes, ten traps desiring my belly. I was carrying the wealth of my life on my belly alone. People carry their souls inside, but mine was carried on my body. You see, little by little, people will drown me and my life will be lost. There are also private compartments in the public baths, but you can't get rid of your dirt by staying alone. You must also rid yourself of the load on your belly, and here lies the disaster. You stupid woman, I want my belly to rise and become harder, not to go down and become soft. So, plug up your nostrils, Gerjiyi, and sleep! This is all I've been wanting for two months. I ran so swiftly that a thousand dogs couldn't reach me, and you know the city is full of a thousand crazy dogs. Gerjiyi Nati is another crazy, loose bitch. The time has come, the time has come, Gerjiyi Nati!

*

I had pearls and gold coins and now I have an ugly man who lives off yellow metal and what comes out of a creature's rear end. The past and the future! I feed this ugly man and still nourish the present—the wild black mare. What did Khoshi bring except a stinky used-clothes hanger? It's likely he snatched the hanger from a helpless peddler in the hubbub of the Haraj Market, or else he bought it for a quarter of its price. Khoshi blames me for the hanger and says, "Woman! Khoshi brought a hanger for his skullcap. Do you know how much the hanger cost?"

Let him hang his rags on it, so that everyone will know his misfortune. They stuck me badly with him, and my life has become useless with this inflated jackass. Once I came to him suddenly and saw a pile of yellow coins in front of him. He was counting them but forgot to close the door. He's no man. I wish he'd make up for it by renting and furnishing a home for us. The ugly man opened his gaping mouth wide, hugging the glowing pile of coins while his saliva dried out from much drooling. He lost his breath.

Then he yelled at me frantically, "How did you get here? Get out, woman!" Refusing to budge, I said to him, "May you be bereaved! Are you afraid of your wife? Spend a little money and don't worry, it won't decrease."

Like a camel he kneeled down on his golden pile, enraged, "Leave! Damn you! This is my capital. No one see it except me. Out! Out, woman! Gerjiyi die and not see!"

Shame on you, leprous dog! Singh taught me how to live for myself. I wonder where Singh is now—alive or dead? Where is Kelly, and where is Mahmud?

Khoshi was hollow and heavy with the shining precious coins in his head. He suffocated inside a shroud tied firmly around his belly while Gerjiyi was overburdened by the present. Stray desires shouted out like sparks of fire, then turned into dry alfalfa hay spread throughout her heart. Once the alfalfa was green but had turned yellow. The yellow gold wrapped around Khoshi's belly hasn't lost its gleam despite the darkness and the offensive, stinky sweat.

Like two plump mountains, the two were squeezed into a bed where Fayiq and Na'imah used to sleep. With every move they made they bumped into each other, and the wooden floor of the takhtahbosh shook and screamed like the sound of a saw piercing the ears.

"Take it!" A whisper from the distant past became louder and harsher and went through Gerjiyi's mind. The takhtahbosh was a small room, a cell where the Persian man's hand warded away others from his belly, which in time rose, grew, and swelled to the ceiling. Khoshi resembled a woman about to give birth to quintuplets.

Gerjiyi remembered thirsty, starved, slim yellow idols—while in Khoshi's head, the numbers were running and combating each other in a continuous war. His eyes couldn't close to sleep. Singh had told her, "Take it! Take it!" Nothing had impelled him to say that except a sense of generous dignity.

"Khoshi, why are you so strangely quiet?" she whispered.

He grew quieter and snored intentionally. This woman never falls asleep, he thought, and I wanted her to doze for a moment. As soon as I lifted my head, I heard her calling, "Where are you going, Khoshi?" I wrapped the leather bag around my belly wondering how many qrans I had spent. I told the peddler I would not pay one fils more than a qran. He said to me, "What can you buy with a qran? Take it back." I opened my hand but I put the qran in my pocket. Let's say I spent more, say sixty qrans, one qran every day. That makes a lot of dinars in two months.

Gerjiyi shouted, "What's happening to you tonight? I thought you had already fallen asleep. You are tossing and turning and won't let others sleep."

"I am sleeping, woman! I swear by the devil and by what lies on my belly, I am sleeping," Khoshi replied.

He braced himself and shut the bolts on his body to keep them from trembling whenever he gave out a dinar. How can Gerjiyi believe I'm asleep? he wondered. If I swear to her now that I'm awake, could she think that a person is talking about sleep while sleeping? I was mistaken. I had to make her get used to the fact that I talked in my sleep.

God pointed to the chest where Gerjiyi, the silver woman, put her bracelets and other antiques. Yes, I spent dinars, she admitted to herself. How can God consent to spending money? I didn't know whether it was reality or not, whether to deny or to believe. Singh urged me, "Take it!" I would obey Singh tonight and take it. Khoshi's soul resembled the impure soul of a dog sealed with a thousand locks.

"Hey, Khoshi! You stabbed into my belly. Move over a little and go to sleep."

Khoshi held back without saying one word. He thought that she was crazy without a doubt, and he wondered how could he go to sleep when her gold bracelets were on her chest, and his belly was vulnerable?

Sleeping was death. It made his body drip qrans like drops of blood brought to a head. Two months had passed, and his investment hadn't yielded. Still, his palm and fingers fiddled in her fatty, feminine flesh. What a pleasure! Here and there he took away a few dirhams from 'Aibah pretending he was a loving father. He tried to convince the child that sweet and sour and sesame candy only cost two fils, but the bastard child was not convinced. Khoshi snatched 'Aibah's dirhams away and received a thousand curses for it. But was there a decent profit?

His belly trembled despite his protective girdle. It was cold, and he called for his woman to warm him up. He was shivering. His protective shield was bound to become thick and dense in order to protect him from the severe cold penetrating into all of his bones, despite the heat of the mountain of flesh heaped next to him. But he no longer desired the heap.

She heard him moaning and shouted, "What's with you? Why are you moaning? I wonder what your thoughts are. Don't they ever come to an end? Hurry up and go to sleep! I hope rocks fall on you."

Why did his damn voice betray him? He saw the opportunity slipping past him. He had missed it long ago. An hour passed, and commotion broke out in the sleepy house. It came from Farhah's room and mixed with the whispering of a stranger—whispering usually heard at this hour of the dark night. Gerjiyi got up and went to the courtyard to relieve herself. She was fed up. She heard Singh calling her to take the pearl and fought the drowsiness gathering in her eyes, trying to drive it away. And now the usual night noises began.

She rose and saw a young Muslim man and Sa'idah Ghawi whispering to each other. She also saw 'Aziz Ghawi in the throes of death near the doorstep of the house. He was short of breath, moaning in rhythm, "Salimah, Salimah, Salimah!"

Gerjiyi knit her brows and shouted out toward Khoshi, "Enough, go to sleep! May death take your soul."

Khoshi jumped. How did he miss the opportunity that night, the opportunity of his life? It was a betrayal of the mind, uncalculated trouble, and a wrong thought that had led him into stupid cowardice. That was the difference between making big business and small business. Making big business was the opportunity of a lifetime.

She had gone to urinate and would come back in the blink of an eye, he thought. I had hesitated, but it seemed she had gone to urinate and to relieve herself. She would come back soon, and I would hear her footsteps before I opened the chest. He only heard a noise coming from the woman's room intertwined with the voice of the strange young man. He hit his head and said to himself, "The bracelets would have been in my hands by now, and I could have left."

She came back ten minutes later. His opportunity for life had gone to the bottom of the toilet in ten minutes the way her body waste did. And God . . . He created the world in seven days. How long did it take God to create the yellow metal? It certainly wasn't longer than the time it took Gerjiyi Nati to do her big business.

On that night, I would have been successful, he thought. Indeed, he would have succeeded. Thick, sticky saliva dropped on his chin, resembling a piece of bulging dough. Tonight! Tonight I'll succeed.

He feigned death, and the hubbub died out outside.

The crowing of a rooster came from the neighbor's house. That was Shukur's family rooster. Next to Gerjiyi sat the open mouth of a cave in which oxen mooed and vile-looking water dripped out as slowly as syrup. "Now he's asleep," Gerjiyi thought. Then she sighed like a sleeping person. Khoshi thought she started to doze. He turned over on his metallic belly and tried to sleep on it but couldn't stand the stiff pains he felt. For lack of another choice, he turned over on his back with his wide paunch pointing toward the low ceiling. He snored loudly and let out harsh-sounding, stinky air.

Gerjiyi held her breath, frightened. She neither grumbled nor felt disgusted. Singh's voice came again with grace, confidence, and sincerity, not requesting but ordering: "Take it! Take it!" The hand she extended toward the hidden pearl trembled constantly and then lowered cautiously little by little all the way down. Another gurgling sound and the man fell asleep for certain. His moneybag could sleep now in the commotion of his troubled death, while she pretended to be asleep, but her hand was still awake. Her hand crawled as slowly as a turtle, made one step and stopped, and lingered after making another move. Finally it perched on his paunch. She said to herself sarcastically, "I'm going to sleep while hugging my sleeping husband." Then she laughed. What a difference between this man and all others! Her palm struck the inhuman mound. Everything was there except a human being—a man, the flesh, the belly button, and the hair. He's not a human being at all. Rather, he is a rough, dry, elevated, thick layer of flesh. "Take it!" she urged herself.

The skinning! Did you ever enter a slaughterhouse? No, but a sheep has been slaughtered in this house. Gerjiyi saw the butcher skin the sheep and felt that she would know how to skin such a hide. The hide overturning logic is the core, and the core is the pulp . . . I'll skin it and shake his big penis later. Her short, sturdy, grapelike fingers crawled and quickly embraced the metallic pouch.

This woman wanted a man. Now she lusted, and the two months she was married could not convince her that Khoshi was not a man with or without opium. Even while sleeping Gerjiyi wanted to have fun.

Suddenly his thoughts were disturbed, feeling that an abnormal action was taking place on his belly. His gaze was fixed on his belly and her hand. He was frightened, and all his limbs were numb, all his life was stuffed into that belly. He felt fingers fiddling next to his soul and became terrified. The woman was approaching a prohibited area where no foot or human hand except his had been allowed to step.

His warning siren was loudly at work and woke up every part of his body. It was awakened immediately. He forgot about Gerjiyi's bracelets in the chest and jumped astonished, "What happened, woman? Are you tickling my belly?"

Gerjiyi answered, "Oh, 'Ajmi, shame on you. You lied and only pretended to be asleep."

With unusual presence of mind, he realized what was happening, leaped out of the bed, and in a giant step drew near the door and said, "Woman, you want to steal the capital of my life? Woman thief. People of Baghdad thief. God forbid if Khoshi should see women anymore. God forbid if Khoshi see Baghdad. Khoshi, return now to Iran."

Like a horse lashed with a whip, he ran away in the middle of the night holding his belly.

8—Joudi al-Qarawchi

Da, Da, da, da!

Unexpected diseases fettered my feet and made me sit in my palace for a few hours, or many generations. Like the wise men, I suffered from a fever, and my mother was seized by the wise men's anxiety. The wise men are everywhere with fever and anxiety. I tried to reach their world through the path of my disease and the hallucination of my fever. Then I stopped by a river whose current was made of pure human blood on which a head, rotten skulls, body parts, and bones were floating. On the other side of the river a war was raging between dust particles coming out of the earth—the one and only source—and scattered in the air. The war was indecisive. One particle would attack the other like sparks igniting inside the skulls of the genial wise men. The other particle would retaliate and destroy it as fast as the speed of thunder, using dusty but sealed atomic equipment. Soon the particles would stick together and crumble into a thousand splinters, and the air would resemble a dusty area and a battlefield.

The wise men scared me. I asked myself while retreating to my fortress—the fortress of immortal wisdom unseen by their world—what do the wise men want? They lost the answer in the chaos of their vehemence, and so I couldn't obtain what they had. Instead, I enjoyed the visit of my faithful and pious friends, and after hesitation freed myself from the confinement of the wise men's fever. Suddenly, the burning fire inside me turned into water that flooded around me and drowned me. Am I wise?

My mother shouted anxiously, "What should I do with you, Joudi? You're sick and perspiring. Cover yourself and sleep or else you'll catch more cold air, create trouble, and make me a mourner."

"Has the wise men's soot and mourning run out?" I asked my friend with the appearance of a giant ant, "When does the wise man's illness stop? The wise man is burdened with the troubles of the past, present, and future. When will he overcome and free himself from anxiety?"

My grasshopper friend said, "Let me congratulate you for coming back. You returned safe and sound from the wise men's world."

I was very happy. My friend gave me the answer I was passionately yearning to hear. We understood each other in the clear, unambiguous way characteristic of wise men. But wise men can contradict each other.

My mother, for example, dreams of a son who protects the family and avenges it, but soon she refutes this terrible dream with an angry denial when I make good on some of it. She sees these in my deeds but doesn't know that protecting the human family is a fairy tale. Revenge, though, exists as long as I, Joudi, am alive and insane, and as long as worms and insects are produced in this world by all things and are available to me.

My friend with the belly growing on his head objected: "You're exaggerating in a way that only wise men do."

I asked him, "Where did I make mistakes?"

He said, "Regarding the wise men's minds, the wise men's consciousness, and all the wise men's motivations." Only then did I realize why the sandy towers of the wise men's houses had collapsed, and why the sand was twisted into ropes, and why circles of worms landed on human necks and rushed the wise men in the worm's domain. The lambs were transformed into pigs, wolves, and hyenas invading the world of the wise men and the whole world. Even our neighbors were not spared. I heard the barking of the rooster, the trumpeting of the elephant and the shrieking of an owl everywhere. I couldn't understand. I stood up to flee my mother's spacious palace, too awesome for breathing. My mother shouted, "Damn you, you're sick! Where are you going to loaf now?"

Let me go back to my world where wise men's illnesses don't exist, Mother! Everything is sick in your world. I'm only healthy as long as I don't put myself into your terrible world. I hunted my goal, not your goal—the lost goal of humanity in a furious world in which dust particles fight each other. Your world showers down insect worms that afflict the hidden entrails and change everything.

I'm running away, so let me save myself from the wise men's world. Let me wave and argue with my friends in a hidden whispered voice uttering an incomplete word that those who suffer from too much reason and from the whips of the worms do not grasp: Da, Da, Da! The worms eat everything, but I only devour the malicious worms that eat the wise men's reason.

Eight

1—'Amam, Ya'qub's Mother

At night the ghosts are many. The night is a dark hiding place for humans and ghosts . . . The ghosts are many. They are human and nonhuman. Tonight is like a thick forest. An animal's barking is coming from the forest—horror, fear, happy, and nightmares. It was not late yet, but 'Amam, Ya'qub's mother, began to worry. She was alone in her room under a downpour of terrible thoughts. There were piles of lasts in a corner next to an anvil, hammers, and nails. When she looked at the tools in the darkness of the night her anxiety grew. The gold mine and bounty had run out, and these were the remains. 'Aibah had gone back to his mother, but Ya'qub had not come back yet. Baghdad was a desert of danger and fright. The night was a devilish trap—a kiss, a sigh, whispers, hopes, and secrets. Aminah, Shukur's daughter, was not alone in her room. She, the black ghost, was a fresh body. She kissed Ya'qub's lips and said to him passionately, "There's still time. Don't leave."

No! His life was not worthless. He was astonished that she didn't hold him back this time and succeeded in getting him into trouble through his involvement with her. She was a daring woman, equal to ten heroes. He said with embarrassment, "This time neither you nor I will be safe. They'll chop us to pieces."

He was ready to leave. There were two human ghosts hiding in the dark between 'Atiyah al-Qarawchi's empty ruin site and Aminah's house—a Jewish man and a Muslim woman, holding hands. In Shukur's home there was a Muslim woman and a Jewish man intoxicated by the sweetness of a forbidden wine, the wine of love. There was also a Jewish man and a Jewish woman in a nightclub in Bab el-Sharqi separated by a barrier of two biting things: deprivation and disaffection. 'Aziz was leaning on a table where he had poured his whole life out while Salimah sang on a stage filled with liveliness, jubilation, and applause.

Sa'idah Ghawi said to Karim, while her hand was pressed in his hands, "How will 'Aziz come back? Who'll bring him home?" Karim squeezed Sa'idah's hand harder. "You and I are the world! Why are you digging through a buried past, worrying? 'Aziz isn't the same now," Karim replied, "It seems he has washed his hands of Salimah and sobered up a bit."

But, in fact, 'Aziz was searching for Salimah everywhere while he was sitting at his table. Her face became transmuted into the faces of the audience. He looked over through the gaps between the walls and jumped on the table holding his glass. She was on the stage, and time was torture. He suffered. Likewise, 'Amam, Ya'qub's mother, suffered from bewilderment and anxiety. "Na'imah Umm Nihad, what time is it?" Her answer shook 'Amam. It was after ten o'clock, and Ya'qub was lost in a place where wolves were howling everywhere. 'Amam gasped, "What should I do? Bring him back safe, God! My guts are being torn from my body!"

The night! . . . Hiding places! . . . Fears! . . . Dreams! . . . Love! . . . And hatred! . . . All of these converged in one stream, but Aminah was equal to ten courageous men. She maintained her pride in Ya'qub's company despite danger. A victorious feeling came upon her: I'm asserting myself and demand justice, she thought. Let Jabbar and his brothers go to a thousand hells.

The other hidden ghost in the 'abayah said, "Karim, let's go inside!"

After all, Karim was a man. His fingers sent electric shocks over Sa'idah's breasts and revived a lifeless, barren land.

Karim said, "What's with your father? Whenever he runs into me, he glowers and ignores me." Sa'idah smiled, but her smile faded in the darkness of the night . . . "Your father . . . He's a man!"

My brother too. She felt a taste of bitterness in her mouth, and her thoughts swung between Karim on the one hand, her father and 'Aziz on the other. The latter were men made of paper while you . . .

She whispered to Karim, "My father is stupid. He only eats, drinks, and sleeps. My mother is the man of the house, and she treasures you."

Sa'idah pulled Karim inside while Ya'qub drew a domino in a crowd sitting around a table in the café. His heart was eager, and he drew a domino piece. "In God I trust!" he said, as if drawing it out of the deepest folds of his heart. But luck betrayed him. He glanced at the domino, his enthusiasm deflated. He was disappointed. Double-blank! Double-blank again! He rushed into a war where the only victor was defeat, a war of failure and destruction. The crow of ill omens! Oh crow! There were many black crows in this world and 'Abdallah Ghawi was a crow and the son of a crow, like my partner, exactly like me, Ya'qub thought. I overlooked the destruction of his family. I was oblivious too. I was watching my partner and blind to 'Alwan's activities.

Ya'qub drank his black bitter drops of coffee noisily. The taste and the color matched what was in front of him. The world became treacherous. He felt heat rushing to his head when he remembered 'Alwan as saying that the Iraqi Jews including Ya'qub himself are ungrateful for the bliss of this country and called us outsiders, and the government of Baghdad called us traitors and caused us much suffering and hardship.

My poor mother is worried because I chose to make a losing game of my life—or rather, I didn't choose it, Ya'qub thought. My partner, friends, our government, and the filthy whore named politics threw me into the game. I glanced at the café's waiter shuttling from table to table and held out my empty cup. "Pour, bitter black coffee!" The bitter drops of the black coffee came down from the yellow spout of the dark coffee pot, burning like the world's treason.

He sipped the bitter black coffee while 'Aziz Ghawi sipped the sharp, intoxicating wine. Innumerable fingernails scratched the cells of 'Aziz's brain, and mosquitoes bit his mind.

"Salimah!" 'Aziz screamed. He was confused and didn't know how to remove that viper mosquito. How could he? He dreaded the idea of removing it, because he had nothing else to cling to. Salimah was his entire life, and he saw her multiplied a million times, in all things, but she eluded him. He laughed while crying so deeply that he held the sorrows of the world.

Karim is now with my sister, he thought. Karim is a pimp. My mother is a madam, and my father is a fat pimp. Now, my father the big shot moved to Bani S'id and he realized that he is not such a big shot, but simply a useless, good-for-nothing imbecile father. So don't be fooled by the corpulence of the so-called 'Abdallah Ghawi, the empty, black barrel, the dumb braggart, the runaway failure. His pugnacious noises are as flippant as the rumbling noises in his stomach when he snores in his sleep, knowing nothing about what is going on in Farhah's room. Who had failed to remove my mother's virginity before he was bound to her with a marriage ring?

Who said males are the stronger sex? I'm driven mad by a woman, the most disgusting woman, the lowest—or rather the greatest—as well as by the poisonous snake who dominates 'Abdallah Ghawi. When I swallow the portion of my death from this cup, Farhah Ghawi swallows 'Abdallah Ghawi's personality and empties him entirely of his manhood, leaving him a useless and hollow waterskin.

Aminah, Shukur's daughter, was in her room vengefully taking arms against prideful cocks. She was spitting in her brother's face by kissing a man in her brother's home. She insisted that Ya'qub stay, but he insisted on leaving. Ya'qub opened the door and slipped out with caution. But just as her brother Jabbar left for the alley, he saw a ghost leaving his home, certainly the shadow of a man. Startled, he stopped for a moment and glanced around him. It was difficult for his mind to grasp what had caused that sudden confusion. Then he rushed in pursuit.

Ya'qub ran fleeing a death that was following him, an imminent death. Run, run! Aminah was crazy, crazy, he thought. God created the night for hiding, so these twisted alleys will protect me. Jabbar certainly won't be able to catch up with me. He'll never recognize me in this darkness. But what will Aminah do?

Ya'qub continued to run, and Jabbar was a bomb-like boulder rolling down a steep slope at maximum speed while Aminah was on the verge of facing death and destruction.

Thoughts of death and destruction rose in the soul of 'Amam, Ya'qub's mother. It was already eleven o'clock, Ya'qub hadn't come home yet, and the police were arresting people in the streets. My God! Where should I look for him at night? She wondered.

She carried an oil lamp and went out, but to where? Baghdad became a wolf ambushing Jews. Why? Did God tell you to come back at midnight on such days and have your mother worry about you? she wondered. An evil idea occurred to her and plunged her heart into a frozen pool of water. She was troubled. She was entirely frozen. God forbid someone should provoke him on the way home and accuse him of something and throw him into jail. The oil lamp shook and swayed in her hand. She prayed humbly and earnestly, "Oh God, please, don't let anything bad happen to him! Let me die before a bad thing strikes Ya'qub. Take my soul instead!" She stood in front of Hamidah's house, frozen, not knowing what to do. Should she ask for help?

No one will help you except God and your legs, Ya'qub said to himself. Run! The strength of his feet helped him to run, and he disappeared into the dark twisting alleys. Jabbar lost him, and Ya'qub was short of breath when he stopped running. He thought as he gasped, "What would dear headstrong Aminah do to save herself from her brother Jabbar?"

'Amam stood in front of Hamidah's home like a beggar, not daring to knock on the door and ask. What would she do when her heart was chopped into pieces, into small parts of the unknown? Morbid thoughts beckoned, killing her in cold blood.

Ya'qub withdrew another domino piece, another bubble of fate. His head itched violently. He took off his hat and began to scratch his head vigorously. "I wrote two lines," he said, and then he sang, "You were peeing, and now you're shitting." He mocked the world responsible for his worsening situation, but a fire began to burn inside him, and his heart shriveled in the flames.

'Amam was lost in a giant vacant bubble, agitated in a devouring and raging horror. "God, don't let . . . Don't let . . ." She wrestled to force out the sound dormant in her throat. What should I do? She wondered. I need help. I'm up against the wall. Where do I look for him at night?

She stood near the house of Hamidah and shouted, "Please tell me, Hamidah, did your boys come back?" The door opened, and Hamidah saw 'Amam's face looking pale. It was even paler in the reflection of the dim oil lamp. She was horrified, "What happened, Umm Ya'qub?"

'Amam, afraid, jumped with fright and said in despair, "I don't know what to do or where to look for him at night. Ya'qub hasn't returned yet."

Hamidah glanced at her and comforted her, "God forbid, nothing bad will happen. Don't be alarmed, there's nothing to worry about. My boys have just come back. Perhaps he forgot about the time and stayed with his buddies in the café. He'll return soon."

No. Something bad must have happened to him, 'Amam thought. Does it make sense that his friends came back and he stayed behind at the café? Where do I go to fetch him at night? She began to cry, so did 'Aziz Ghawi in the nightclub holding his life.

Salimah avoided him. He never stopped drawing a picture of her through his tears, but soon she disappeared in the air. I'll write her name in ink, charcoal, and blood so that neither air nor fire can erase it, he thought. Blood! She could drain my flesh, extract the blood from my body, and pour it into a pail in front of me. I picked up a fork. The fork pierced my palm, and I began to write her name with red letters—with my blood—not in imagination but in reality.

Aminah heard frantic knockings on the door, saw sparks flying from the eyes of her brother Jabbar and asked him fearfully, "What happened, Jabbar?"

Angrily looking around the house he gasped, "Who was with you?" Jabbar felt that he had been tricked in his own home, that his honor was stained with a shame so black that only blood could wash it away. His yelling resounded in the darkness of the night. "I told you to report who was here and what he was doing."

With anger and dismay, she said, "Jabbar, what did you say? Are you crazy?"

His voice reached all the areas of the huge alley.

"No, I'm sane. I saw him with my own eyes. Tell me, who was with you?"

Aminah said to herself, "Jabbar is a sane man, a violent, enslaving dictator, a hangman, and a murderer. A female enslaved him at the market and she used him like a rag. I was that woman. I realized what he was like and said to him, 'No, no, you won't make me a slave any longer, Jabbar! I'm your sister and the time of female slaves and mistresses has passed. I'm a worthy human being. I'm not a sheep to be driven to the slaughterhouse, humiliated with my head downward.'"

Jabbar yelled, out of his mind. "Your lips are shut and that means you confess your guilt. You are ashamed, you have nothing to answer, you're a disgrace, a shame. Is my honor just a game for you, whore? You're defiling my honor! I'm Jabbar and I will cut off this humiliation and wash my honor with your blood."

He took a knife . . . This man means business. He'll kill me, she thought. This is, in fact, a slaughterhouse, and the butchers of the slaughterhouse are men, and the sacrifices are innocent human sheep. What a pity that my youth was wasted under the roof of a person who buried me for twenty-five years and now also wants to wash his honor with my blood. Yes, his honor was blackened by his outbursts, behavior, and his mistakes. He followed her with his knife. I held my 'abayah in my hands.

Run away! . . . Run away! . . . But where will I go? Run away! He'll kill me—he's a butcher on the verge of committing a murder against my life. Run away! Run away . . . But to where? He'll kill me. He pursued me. She shouted from the bottom of a pit of defeat, then her voice died down.

"Jabbar. Calm down! Jabbar! Don't kick me out of the house with fear and humiliation."

Run away! Jabbar's voice was brazen: "Then it's true. It's true then, but your death is near. You can't escape from me."

The butcher wouldn't catch up with me. I'd run away. I didn't know where to go but I had saved my life and protected myself from him. Being lost was kinder than his sinful hands raised to cause my death. I was a slave and a victim, a slave and a victim!

In this world there was loud noise, a commotion in Baghdad, a persistent clamor in our quiet, forgotten alley. It continuously reached 'Atiyah al-Qarawchi's ears. She was tossing and turning on a carpet that didn't cushion her ribs. What had happened? Why, as soon as the night falls, did the noise of feet, whispering, and screaming never stop in the alley? What had happened to people? What had happened in our alley? What had happened to the world while Joudi was sleeping?

The world was awakened and so was night, fear and death, barking dogs and howling wolves, in the midst of false tranquility. 'Amam's feet sank deep into the depths of the unknown. The oil lamp gasped and danced with her trembling strides and movement. 'Aziz Ghawi got up staggering. Out of disappointment, fatigue, and drowsiness, Ya'qub swayed and paused under a dim light at the beginning of the alley. He began to count a handful of rusty, heavy, red, white, and yellow coins. It was heavy change that nevertheless amounted to less than a dinar. Where did his piles of dinars go?

The world is a prostitute. Politics is a prostitute. Treason is a prostitute. Salimah is a prostitute. Sa'idah my sister is a prostitute, 'Aziz yelled. Jabbar yelled too, "Look, whore! Do you want to run away from me? Where are you escaping, whore!"

There was a long, dark tunnel in this world where men determine fate. The world was full of helpless females ruled by butchers, crazy, stupid men. Run away anywhere, Aminah! Jabbar's knife entered the door above the hook latch and stuck into the dry wood of the door.

She was as soft and scared as a terrified chick fleeing when set free, a shooed-away chick stoned and chased by hungry jackals. No, the jackal would never catch hold of her. She put on the 'abayah, her trap, the cloak of her disappearance before a blind fate controlled by a man equally blind, by a foolhardy and predatory tyrant.

At the turn of the alley under a yellow light, Ya'qub counted his rattling change and said to himself, you're a sheep, 'Abdallah is a sheep! 'Abdallah's son is a sheep, and Sabriyah's husband Efrayim is a sheep. They're all a herd of sheep, and the world is the butcher.

Suddenly, he saw his mother, lost, stumbling alone in the night, carrying an expiring oil lamp. When 'Amam noticed him she relaxed, stopped, and took a deep breath in order to keep from fainting. She was exhausted. Ya'qub drew near her, supported her, and bent his head to hers. He hated many things but loved his mother. She stammered for a while until she released the words, "Why did you leave me with a broken heart? I didn't know what was happening to you, but finally you came. Don't you know, sonny, it's not safe? The police are arresting, jailing, and hanging people. Come now, I pray that God doesn't take from you what you've rightfully earned."

Like a fleeing deer covered with an 'abayah, but with the face seen, a black ghost passed by 'Amam and her son. Ya'qub glanced at her and was relieved. He pretended to distract his mother. She noticed however. "Alas! Why is the sister of the Shukur brothers dashing away on such a night? I know her brothers are quarrelsome and create problems but I wonder if anything happened to them." 'Amam looked troubled, and Ya'qub walked home with her.

2—Aminah, Shukur's Daughter

No return! I'm simply an 'abayah traveling through the unknown paths of a jungle inhabited by men, thought Aminah. The world is full of men, rams, and cocks. I camouflage myself with my black veil to save myself from a death that awaits everywhere. Who am I and where am I going? I don't know, but I know that I'm setting forth toward a dead end. This is the road in the forest where I walk with an 'abayah, a woman without identity looking for an identity stolen by men. Five hens, a cock, and a ram follow me. Jabbar goes everywhere, behind and in front of me. Behind and ahead of me there are mistakes that have become difficult to correct—except by killing, death, and blood.

How great and respectable you are, Jabbar! For two and a half decades you've been raising an ewe, feeding me in order to eat me. But my flesh is bitterly inedible. The taste of the bitter apple will live in your mouth until you die. Why are you everywhere, Jabbar? When you lost your mind, you threw it into a basin of stench, and your male animal nature has been swimming there ever since. Do you remember how you felt when I was veiled and you followed me to the market and then I spat in your face? You wallowed in humiliation and wouldn't forget it for even a moment. Be ashamed until your soul departs you. I burst open my fetters and escaped. Then I fled from delusion and nothingness because of your oppression. But it turned out that my game of cock and sheep was like me, an illusion. I'm looking for my lost self in a world ruled by men. Is it right for me to do this in a world full of men like you, Jabbar? Am I the woman at whom people spit? Run away, run away, Aminah, I said to myself! My way is dark, frightening, and complicated. There are a thousand roads, but is there one and only one road leading to safety?

"Where does this train go?" I asked of men. They stared at me with eyes like Jabbar's, having the shadows of thirsty death. I heard a voice calling me *ukhti*, my sister, and I was scared should it have been Jabbar's. How odd was it that Jabbar had discovered my way? Did he really catch up with me? When I was about to run away the voice said, "Don't be afraid sister! I see you're scared and in trouble. You're like a sister to me, by the prophet Mohammad."

Should I trust him? I questioned myself. It didn't matter if I really was his sister and he was a man or I was a ewe and he was a ram. I was out of my mind. Was it right for me to be Jabbar's sister? How was it that the ghost of "the whore," disguised as an everyday woman with an 'abayah had continued to foil him and had known how to strip him down?

Tonight the whoredom of the world is piled on Jabbar's sister—on me, "the whore"—and blood fills up a bathroom in which human sins and fictitious whores are invented by courageous brothers.

"Why are you troubled, sister? Where do you want to go?" the passenger asked.

What did it matter if he was a cock with his real sister or a ram with another sister wearing an 'abayah hiding her identity?

"Where does this train go?" I inquired.

"To Basra, sister, and where are you going?" he asked.

What does it matter where I was going so long as the road would lead me to one road without return?

"To Basra, brother."

"Go and buy the ticket fast, sister, the train leaves in a quarter of an hour, but I'm afraid you have no money."

I had twenty or more dinars that I kept in my chest. It was my life savings that I earned bit by bit, which slowly destroyed my youth. I was a servant of men and animals, a black ghost inventing games that had no place in the world of tyrannical males who controlled nine-tenths of my six years of schooling. May God protect you, Jabbar! At least you let me learn how to read and write before you said, all of a sudden, "You're a grown-up woman now." Then you imprisoned me at home in order to kill me.

I looked around for a woman but all women were strangers hiding in 'abayahs like me, a sad black ghost in the middle of a grove of trees. These women were just like parcels, baskets among other items for Jabbar. They walked on drowning roads and through fire—roads with no return. They were slaves until death in the middle of roads and whorehouses.

Na'imah would shed tears of blood for me. She was lucky; she skillfully slipped away from the imprisoned animals in a cargo wagon into a gorgeous, large passenger wagon, where real people sat unveiled together with their brothers and husbands. I, though, was looking for my identity, staggering alone with no human image before me.

"Move!" I heard someone say. I shook and trembled with fright. My body was shaking as I stood. The speed grew faster as I deserted Baghdad and Jabbar, the illusionary game, death, the slaughterhouse, and my being lost amid black packages piled among men, not drawing near to anything.

I was alone in the world covered with an 'abayah. Still, I knew how to read and write, possessed twenty dinars, breasts as round as watermelons, some bread and dates for food, a train ticket to Basra, and a female body with no identity.

"Why are you standing? Sit down!" said the voice of an old woman with a wool 'abayah. Of course, she was not alone. She had sons and grandchildren, and on all sides were gifts. She removed the tin can that was beside her in order to make room for me, and I sat down.

"Are you alone?"

I answered that I was not lonely when alone. My relatives had died, which happened to many women like me. The person next to me was inquisitive and of the same sex; perhaps she was of a little higher class—almost a person. I envied her.

"So you have nobody."

Not at all. I had . . . I don't know what. The last butcher I had died yesterday. Don't be afraid! I . . . I have twenty dinars. I know how to read and write. I know, yes I do! It's as much worry to be a woman alone as to be with Jabbar. But I was fleeing from a still bigger fear, because I didn't know what would happen after death. You're saying that Baghdad is a paradise. You went there for a visit and did not see the slaughterhouse and the butcher. Well, then, the paradise may become hell, to last as long as men live there.

"We're from Samawah, but we have lived in Basra a long time. What are you going to do there since you don't have relatives or know anyone?" She was making me confront my fate and offering me chicken with rice and onions. I had dates and bread. But I was suspicious and my deep fear stirred me from time to time. I knew I could betray myself for food. My dinars had lost their value with the increase of dread in a city ruled by men, cocks, and sheep. I found my dark fate tossed between idiocy, tyranny, and masochism—a ewe in the arms of a butcher or the arms of a brother sheep. I was not his sister. My flesh wasn't edible, though it was as good to eat as date syrup. What are you doing here? I'm a beautiful female. I carry the source of my livelihood in my body in case there's no other choice.

The rulers of this world are imbeciles because women's bodies store inexhaustible treasures.

No, no, no, no! Like people, I was dreaming of having only one permanent sheep or choosing only one butcher husband without a knife to kill me. The woman said with a compassion I had never experienced with Jabbar and his brothers, "Why are you crying, 'aini? Don't worry, the world is still kind."

She was fooling me with words, and her thoughts were meaningless. This woman invoked fear in me, then soothed and put it to sleep like a child. How's that? Is there another way other than the path of no return? She continued digging in my soul, and I invented stories and legends for her. I didn't really lie. Until then my life was a lie, but from then on I would try to put sincerity in it. At those moments my life was overwhelmed by a great, fearful puzzle. I had missed my chance. Jabbar was everywhere. What could I do? Instead of one Jabbar I could run into a thousand of them in Basra. The grave was a secure place, but Jabbar had kept me from my own, leaving me to the vulnerability of a collective grave. The world was constant fear produced by men. I was a woman and I was lucky that my livelihood was in my body and the world was hungry, eating me as food. Oh my God, why were there so many butchers for me in this restless world?

Southward! I had been traveling for hours; my anxiety left me then returned. What would I do now? I thought of many things and said to her, "You're right." What would I do in Basra? I was afraid. "By the way," I asked, "don't you need a servant in Samawah in exchange for food and lodging?"

Something collapsed inside me. Why did I say that? Was I looking for an alternative to something I had lost? Did I want to choose a contemptible identity from among more despised identities, to be a female drudge, a slave or a prostitute, or a dead body with holes in my chest as simple as a servant? But I wanted much more than that. I wanted protection, my mother! I glanced at the graves I had avoided. Jabbar and death had split me apart from my mother. Where was my mother? In her lap, I had found shelter then wept, found calm, and felt safe.

A rough hand slipped out of a wool 'abayah and stretched out to hold me. Her voice said, "Why a servant, 'aini? You look like a decent woman. There are a lot of injustices in this world. Come home with me, 'aini. You are welcome, and I will take care of you as if you were my own daughter. The world hasn't run out of good people yet."

Was it true that my mother was resurrected? I didn't know but I wet her with my tears and wept bitterly. Who knows? Maybe I was really lucky. Should I give my new mother a chance? Of course, a lot of luck is necessary when a woman is lost in a jungle of butchers. Samawah! It came with a promise of motherhood, but the lost identity was still in an unknown place. I would never surrender to him, to Jabbar. Let him look for me until the last moment of his life! Let him chew his bitter cud until his last breath!

3—Sa'idah Ghawi

The scissors jabbed my hand! I stuck my hand, and the filthy blood gushed out. "What's the matter with you, 'aini?" my mother exclaimed. "Recently you've been stumbling and pricking yourself and bumping things. Be careful, please."

Despite my furious anger, my sweet, dreamy absentmindedness was washing over my feelings. I became preoccupied. Yesterday when I fitted the robe on the customer, I pierced her belly with a pin. How can I be careful? I'm always daydreaming. I've lost my mind because of that man. "Latifah! It's your worry now to find a husband," I said to my sister.

I stared at her in an ill temper as if she had defiled my holy things. She was jealous, very much so in fact. I slapped her, she pulled my hair, and we almost started fighting. I cried, not because Latifah had pulled my hair, but because she had jabbed the edge of the scissors into the heart of my holy temple, Karim. She's cruel.

"I wish a plague stroked and choked you, Latifah!"

"Enough, leave your sister alone! You made her cry. What do you want from her? Leave her alone to her sadness, to her lonely seat. Let her bewail her fate in peace," my mother cried.

My mother took my side. She patted my shoulder, but her touch only stirred my yearning for Karim. I didn't know how good life could be until I met him; his magic chased away the illness of my life. Since he came into my life I've been healthy amidst others afflicted with the plague.

My mother yelled hysterically at Latifah, and Latifah yelled back, "It's your fault. You've been encouraging her. 'Aziz is right. We're ripe for marriage. Why else do you bring a stranger to our house and let him sit with us until midnight? Do you think people are blind, that they can't see what's going on here? What will they say about us?"

Latifah is hard-hearted. She forced me to have a host of unfamiliar thoughts. I fought a furious war within myself, but there was no winner or loser. What a foul, poisonous rage had stolen into my sweet dreams! My heart was blind until a resounding passion opened my eyes, and bells rang and sang from nowhere, conquering my heart.

People are blind whenever they want to be and have sharp eyes when it serves their needs. Everyone looks for his own good. My father burps, sleeps, and wears a dishdashah. He's like a woman who can't do anything by herself. He can only say, "Farhah, I'm hungry."

"Does your hunger ever end? At least go to the café and sit there with people, lazy bum," and when I told him to go out and bring some dried fruits, biscuits, and chocolate, he peered at me with astonishment and said, "I'll go in the afternoon. Is Karim the con man coming soon?"

I looked down at my shoes and didn't intervene until my mother finished to rebuke him. She dominates him, and he can't open his mouth in her presence. "You have no say over who comes and goes. Those who come are visiting us, not you," my mother replied.

He mumbled an answer, and my mother couldn't hear his voice. God forbid she should hear him say, "May the grave of your father be dug up, Farhah!" Then he would slip away from her like an escaping snake slithering away after its teeth and poison had been extracted.

"Ouch! The needle almost broke in my thumb. Is this love?" Sa'idah screamed.

'Aziz's image passed like a shadow. 'Aziz is pitiful! Being deprived makes him feel crushed and then madness follows. What a big difference between us, Sa'idah wondered. My sharp sight peered forth from the remote corner of darkness, but so did 'Aziz's. How so? He was blind and had nothing except Salimah in a world bounded by the four walls of a whorehouse. But Ya'qub saw me, and 'Aziz said to him, "Marry her!" I was then half-blinded and prayed that Ya'qub would agree. The image of Karim had not seeped into my consciousness yet. So actually, God worked in my favor by blinding Ya'qub, who didn't accept me as a wife.

This world is strange! Ever since I met Karim my mother has said, "Every delay has its good side." Ya'qub has lost his shop and life but I'm still in control.

Karim said to me, "Pretty. You're pretty!" Where's the mirror? I blushed like a red and delicious Persian apple. My chin was dainty, and my lips resembled a rose bud. My lips puckered out and everything around them shivered with pleasure. I trusted Karim and opened my eyes to the view of the tall brownish man before me. He was neat, the collar of his shirt was always bright and starched, and a carefully knotted tie hung down. His suit was expensive and recently selected, in the best taste. He had ten to twenty suits, and I never saw him wear the same suit more than once. He had a Parker fountain pen in his coat pocket, and behind it was a white handkerchief sticking out with sharply folded corners. What's more, his cologne gave out a refreshing fragrance.

"Bring me the scissors, please." I looked for my scissors. Where did I put them? Not long ago they jabbed my hand. Where did they get lost? Did the devils under the ground kidnap them? What serious thoughts were in my mind and how absentminded I was! Where were they? Could it be that the earth swallowed them? For sure, Latifah must have hidden them away.

Latifah cried, "Are you blind? Here they are in your hand. You're daydreaming and accusing me of taking the scissors."

My mother was on my side again. She hit Latifah. There were many reasons I was disturbed, and while I thought of Karim, Latifah paid for my thoughts and absentmindedness. The tip of her tongue was an arrow aimed at me, one that she wasn't shy about shooting. "Karim is a Muslim and you're a Jewess. Be reasonable! If you don't watch yourself, what will happen to us and what will we do?"

The curse, a thousand curses! Love is stronger than all curses; it sets obstacles for humanity. Love blows hot and cold feelings. Love is blind but can see. But Salimah isn't blind. She is an agony in my heart. She captured 'Aziz's mind and turned 'Aziz into a tired skeleton. As Karim said, "Your brother is weary, but still he hasn't given up yet."

A sweeping storm subsided, passed away, and left behind destruction and ruin, silent sadness and bafflement. The nothingness and the emptiness in the house were in 'Aziz's soul. He had broken into small pieces; he came home with his head fixed on the ground, then left again. And Salimah? This woman became a burning coal in his conscious mind, a devastating jealousy in his heart. Ouch, another prick! I hid it. I can live without the stones of Sodom and Gomorrah, which my sister Latifah is throwing at me.

"Do you want to see what will happen to you?" said Sa'idah to 'Aziz.

I left home wearing a veil to visit my uncle, and when I came back, my mother said, "Is your uncle's family well? I wish that death would strike all of them! Why don't they reciprocate your visits?"

"They are well and say hello to you," I answered.

I carried Salimah's image in my mind—an ordinary and cheap woman who causes pain to men's hearts. My brother . . . Karim . . . How strange fate is. I burst into tears in front of Karim.

"Why did you suddenly burst into tears?" he asked.

"Karim! You have to leave Salimah. Either me or that whore."

'Aziz was unfortunate. He works as a busboy serving the drunkards and the boisterous customers at the nightclub. "Don't you see how he brought himself to this hellhole in order to see Salimah?" Karim said to Sa'idah.

Salimah, Salimah! Who is this Salimah? I was jealous of a cheap nightclub dance! How strange fate was! I was frightened. My mother said, "Hurry and try the dress on the customer."

How did Salimah come into our lives? From where did she come? Why does Latifah give me a hard time about Karim? Why did God create Muslims and Jews? Why didn't He create them only as human beings? And Salimah? Should I regret that she turned out to be like a thunderstorm on a bright day? I cried in front of Karim.

"Stand straight, please?" I asked the customer. The customer was as slender as a camel. Salimah was a simple and cheap woman. But Salimah had the power to torment more than one heart and to control my brother's mind. I was sure of that. I wept before Karim again.

"Why won't you answer me? I swear by God if you don't leave Salimah, I won't speak to you anymore," I pleaded with Karim.

He feigned laughter. His touch was like electricity running through my body, "You and the world, why do you upset yourself about something that doesn't exist? Why do we, living humans, bring up the past and dig up the graves of the dead?" Karim replied.

The needle pricked my ribs! I blushed out of shame this time. My mother looked at me severely. I understood her look that said, "Be careful!" Did I have the power to concentrate or would I prick the customers? There was always the danger that Latifah would throw her cruel and painful arrows and stones at me.

4—Selman Hashwah

Everything I see is yellow. Does the yellow of the *shaih* dye color my one good eye? Sabriyah, why is your face so pale? You're calm and sad, unusually so. It doesn't seem right for a wind-up doll's springs to suddenly stop and turn pale and sad. What's wrong? Efrayim has come back and stuck to you day and night. Your wish has come true. After all, you prayed, made vows, and lit candles to have these things happen. It's true that Efrayim was forced out of his job, but the cruel wave of discharges included him and pushed him directly into your arms. This cursed trend of dismissing government employees has cut Jewish livelihood. But our people's disaster, branded with yellow, turned out in your favor and brought Efrayim closer to you, so that he won't be away from you anymore. I'm the one with the eyes dyed yellow, the color of illness, the color of death. I see it everywhere, in your face and voice, Sabriyah! Are you sick or are you, like me, fearful of a forthcoming Farhûd attack?

"How are you, Selman?" she asked. This question came from her mouth, disheartened, cold, and sick. The grief leaked from my chest like radiator steam. My life was lost in a basin full of yellow. I was half-sick. I looked at the world, and my heart became dark. Nothing was left to make life worth living. It was devoid of plenty and bereaved of joy. The sad world was lying under heaps of dusty memories, and love had become an orphan with no more than a spark of life, set to disappear in the anguish of grief.

"Do you remember what we used to do, Selman? Where have those days gone?"

My heart couldn't withstand Sabriyah's moaning, and I was surrounded by a desperate hopelessness. We were fed up. Life had shortened our breath, and I didn't even eat half my food; sorrows consumed my belly, and my flesh had dissolved and fallen from my body. Now I avoided people. Fohah, the beans vendor, used to make a profit on me, and sometimes I was her first customer, but I no longer passed her way. It was enough to smell the beans and run for my life lest Fohah called me . . .

"Khaduri, I beg of you, bring me back the items I entrusted with you." I had entrusted my merchandise, the tray of needles, pins, and matchboxes with him. I was running away from one of many deserters in Baghdad. Khaduri was not like before. Ever since the black ghost escaped, he had been quiet and fearful. I didn't have a long conversation with him. I was a fugitive.

When a Jewish merchant was tried in a puppet court about a mule the authorities had seized from him, he was beaten even though he told the truth. He was asked, "Are you a believer or an unbeliever?"

He answered prudently, "Neither. I was fed up with my mule and left it." Then he fled the country to Iran.

Hundreds of Jews ran away to Iran because of false accusations against them and the threat of imprisonment and hanging. In our house there were runaways of different kinds—Khoshi the Persian and Jamil Rabi. What a smart man Jamil was! The black ghost also escaped, but to where and why? Dear Aminah is indisputably a believer, but I was a deserter, running away from myself to them.

"Please Khaduri, give me a cigarette!"

Eliyahu Hamis waited for me. I stopped talking at length with Khaduri or asking him about dear Aminah or about what happened after she had run away. Maybe Aminah was conspiring with Khaduri to steal from her brothers and share the spoils with him. There was no doubt that the Zionist underground put forbidden items in my merchandise tray, weapons of disaster. Those have heaped disasters on my head, but I swear by your life, Sabriyah, that I'll sacrifice everything to make your pale, frightened face shine again. I'll bear the people's disasters and mine, sacrifice myself so that your sweet smile and the brightness of your wine-like face will never die out. Even if you are in Efrayim's lap, my Sabriyah, I won't let anyone touch a hair of your head as long as I'm alive. My secret of serving the Zionist underground and your pain come to me. I can't talk because I took an oath not to, but if I do talk I'll be in trouble and cause trouble to many people. I'll be hanged.

Am I really doing something bad? Karbala and the Farhûd are still in the back of my mind, and I see those who escaped the whirlpool of the Farhûd without saying a word, as well as the flood, the jaundice, the honey, and my rough barren road. Where will I anchor when I'm entirely surrounded by dust that holds within it a dream as unfulfilled as a mirage. Eliyahu Hamis is saving me from this mix-up. He tells me, "Go ahead! I'm walking in front of you. Hang the tray on its cord and call out your merchandise. Follow me and talk to yourself until we get there." The tray was heavy, very heavy. I wondered what they put inside it.

"Needles! Pins! Matches!"

To hell, what did I have in life? Let them put what they please! Life is no longer worth living. Sabriyah is sad. Well, if you're sad, Sabriyah, it means that the world is really destroyed and that you don't know what's going on, as if you're in the dark. A long time ago, the world collapsed, and you're sleeping in its ruins as unaware as a cave dweller.

"Strings, sewing machine spools, dyes, and more strings!"

My feet became spindly strings because of fatigue. I knew that Eliyahu would lead me to the mansion near the dam, a secluded and safe place. As long as safety prevailed there, why did he worry about his fellow members? Why risk such safety, that we can only dream about? All the standards of sense were lost together with the importance of words. Everyone was persecuted without distinction. We were deprived from eating rice with 'adas, lentils. The Jews stopped buying lentils after the Jewish millionaire, 'Adas, was hanged in Basrah. Those who went to buy it from the grocer were taking a risk.

Jamil told me, "I hope the Communists, not the government, hang 'Adas. Do you know how much money he had? Five million dinars. That much money could have brought new life to all the needy of Baghdad."

More gallows sprung up immediately, and tatters of flesh hung down from them, swaying in the air. They were bodies of Communists. The jaundice! The police school looked yellow in the background and provoked horror. In the other world all the hanged people would assemble around a yellow table. The hanged people were Communists, Zionists, and simply pedestrians who accidentally met their deaths, including 'Adas. I wonder what those martyrs would discuss—the wealth of 'Adas or the hangmen?

"'Adas and the hangmen are alike," Jamil said.

Wasn't Muhsin 'Abd el-Wahid also a Communist? He was a great angel of God. And if 'Adas was as Jamil claimed, then how could anyone call the hangman a victim? Here the standards were collapsing again.

We're in the yellow zone, Jamil! The yellow people are worthless. If you don't believe me just look at Sabriyah's face and compare it now to what it was. Her face flashed and then became dim because of falseness and tyranny. The jaundice was spreading and taking over.

Sabriyah, don't be afraid, you'll never be harmed, because I'm stepping now into the fire of a world consuming both the green and the dry. The greedy yellow oppression has stolen the cream and honey from your cheeks. I have consumed my own fat and felt disgusted, and my nostrils inhaled a stench coming from behind the shacks near the dam—the smell of fried fish, the nausea of anxiety, and the terrible smell of the tiny jirri fish. Still, I wondered how it would taste.

You're right about some things, Jamil, but I'm right about everything concerning me. I'm replacing the red past with pallid yellow. The yellow dye, the *shaih* plant, Oh people. The earth here is made of brownish clay, not sandy, but I see it as a vast, yellow island. The mansion in the yellow sea is also yellow. What's more, mansions dot the landscape like pimples discharging pus under the skin. Is there a truly safe place in this empty space near the dam? Fear is an ostrich that buries its head deeply in the sand.

"I beg you Eliyahu, I'm falling apart. Is it much farther?"

He signaled me to keep quiet, and a minute later a gate in a stone fence swallowed him up. I was as close to him as a tail, which I've been all my life. What would I be at this mansion, in the depth of my own yellowness? My road was full of coals and thorns after the destruction of the world.

I walked slowly to a hall where there was a group of youths. Jerusalem was in my throbbing dreams. Sabriyah, too. The warmth was swallowed inside a whale diving into the bottom of a frozen sea. Don't be afraid! All of these people supported me, and the fabulous carpet in the mansion should have been enough to drive my fear away. Still, a hidden shivering was tapping the root of my existence—youths in the mouth of a canon! The road loomed like my own pair of eyes, half-black, half-yellow, awakening the eye of fear forever.

I said unwillingly, "They're crazy," but I didn't know why they were crazy. However, I hovered over reality. Then the truth of this reality was whispered to me with an ambiguous flapping wing sound, that of a miraculous bird fleeing humanity. My life appeared to me like a yellow lie made of fear through which I was forced to endure. I was pushed and driven through it, carrying my dreams, hopes, black memories, fearful present and future. They designed my fate for me, drew it up in Baghdad, in the United Nations and Israel, but I didn't know what my fate would be.

I'm a coward, a peaceful man, one who avoids trouble, and if ever I get control over my life, I will vow to hide in the hole of a wall like an ant or a worm, just as I've done since the agony and grief of Karbala. The members of the Zionist underground, however, were forced out of the whorehouse of Baghdad. "Get out," they ordered. "The police will discover you no matter where you hide and they'll slice you to pieces. So get out, Selman, shoulder your rifle, and protect yourself and Sabriyah."

"Come, guys, let's go!" the leader of the group called.

I crawled from the frozen sea bottom to the shore, shivering, and defeated. I walked behind a group of Jewish girls and boys who didn't look particularly sad or strong. I alone seemed like a giant, but a tall and slender one. I went as if I were dragging iron shackles linked to them and cried to myself, "Save yourself, Selman!" Had I released myself from the yoke, I could have run as fast as a gazelle to any safe place. Doubting my eyes, I asked myself, "Will these youths protect us if—God forbid—another Farhûd occurs?"

I entered with them to a place resembling a cellar, the half underground exactly matching the half above. Though the dam stood very close, a little light managed to pass through a window into the upper room, the lower half remained in darkness. Beyond the window was a garden leading to an open space. Why wasn't the window closed? Was it to moderate the fear?

Then the head of the group said, "Do you see that mattress hanging out there? Every one of you should aim at it. I want the bullet to hit the center of the mattress!" He turned to me, "Get ready, Selman. Assemble your rifle, load it, and shoot!"

I shivered. Why did I choose this? Wasn't it enough to learn how to assemble and take apart a rifle? Did I have to shoot it too? "Let's see, you courageous man! Don't be afraid. Be bold! If we don't drive fear away from our hearts, how will we be able to defend ourselves?"

This damn black pipe—the bullets, piston, and hammer—all of them mean death. By the rifle my father and mother died, and the drunkard used it to shoot from above my shoulder in Karbala. With it they wanted to kill me when they accused me of signaling to the British airplanes, accused me of killing the prophets, even though I didn't see the planes or hear their noise. There is killing in front and behind, though God commanded me not to kill. Still, man kills and makes various kinds of equipment to kill, and I remain the easiest target to destroy. But I'm unable to kill.

The rifle leaned on my shoulder while my arms swung, and I cradled agonizing thoughts. The target was a mattress on which there was a spot of light coming from a window behind it. A horrible, raving fear guided me. "Don't kill," it said. But the youth urged me, "Shoot!"

Prove you're brave and fearless! I encouraged myself. But I was a peaceful person, and it was better if I threw away this damn tool and ran. But to where? I was driven and deprived of free choice with a horrifying ambush everywhere I went. The horror was a light spot stuck to a mattress whose center was a target for my shooting, the sole target. Shoot! You'll fire at fear's heart.

I was shaking in the empty space where my destinies lay asleep and far away. I shot in the direction of fear, at my dark destiny, gathering all the lost fragments of courage from my God in Heaven, from the yellowness of Sabriyah's face, from the dark, miserable memories churning in my mind, from this terrible fear that they were forcing on me simply because I was a Jew. The mattress, the bright spot, the fear to be killed, was the worst enemy, the devilish seed of fanaticism and selfish inclination that has prevented us from living. I've never crushed even an ant in my life. I swear by the life of the pure Sabriyah who should live in innocence like an unborn child, and by the unborn children who haven't yet opened their eyes, to close my eyes and open them only after I kill fear. God, Sabriyah, the right of man to live! Go ahead—go ahead!

I held my breath. The light ray above the mattress shone on my head. It was a white spot containing the deadly germ of fright coming from a window looking out on life. Then I closed my eyes and was surrounded by darkness, but the light was inside my rifle—a red light that would kill fear. It pierced the darkness of my heart with a popping sound, and my body trembled. I opened my eyes and immediately slumped down.

Oh my Lord, what was happening? I saw everything yellow. Sabriyah's cheek was still pale. All the faces around me were pale and yellow. There were sounds of moaning and howling outside. I was secluded in an empty, yellow space with only a country woman and two children who lived in one of the dam's shacks. There was also a spot of blood.

The country woman slapped her hand to her face and shouted, "My children, they killed my dear children! Woe to Nashmiyah! I was only walking on my way. Where did the stray bullet come from that hit my son's leg?"

I was astonished and asked what had happened. I didn't kill fear, instead I bottled up a large amount inside myself.

One of the youths came gasping and screaming, "Hurry up! Hide the weapon and flee! Your bullet came from the window and hit a child. Luckily, nobody else was there. Hurry up before people gather!"

Oh my Lord! I completely collapsed. I saw the red blood overflowing on the world. Woe is me! I had made things worse. I wanted to overcome fear but instead I shot a human being—an innocent child. I was a killer or at least a partial murderer from now on. I had never intentionally stepped on an ant, but now I had injured a child with the right to live in peace. Every child had the right to live in peace.

My face lost all color over a swooning body, which nevertheless resisted the pressure to faint. I felt hands pulling from all sides and I seemed to be a heavy and an enormous package—too heavy with fear, blood, and murder, a bundle of horror brought to the light of life. A cry from a member of the Zionist underground reached my unconscious. "Take him fast, don't lose any time!"

Another person interrupted, most likely Eliyahu: "He's as motionless as a stone. Let him regain consciousness first."

And a voice that came from nowhere uttered weakly, "Eliyahu, it doesn't matter if he's in this condition, take him out through the back door and drive him in my car. He'll wake up later. Don't lose time! The police will arrive here soon, and we'll be in trouble."

Then I didn't see, hear, or remember anything at all for many hours.

5—Jamil Rabi

The opposites are mixed up, and everything is equal in man's law of the jungle. But there's a difference between the human and animal jungles. I have proof of this. Naji el-Jundi is a good and peaceful man despite his stupidity and silliness, and my relatives are victims who joined the animal jungle according to the law of the human jungle. They cause harm without being aware of it, then the law of the human jungle dominates.

One day a man stood under a streaming shower with his head upward and mouth open. He was asked, "What are you doing?" He answered, "I'm drinking clean water before it falls on the ground and becomes impure." I called this man crazy and now I'm just as crazy as he. I wait for the rain to fall to enjoy a sip of pure, clean water.

Where are you, Abu Ghallubi? There was no trace of him in the alley tonight. I didn't hear the cacophony of his whistle despite having ears that can pick up any discordant sound in the world. Abu Ghalib was not in any other alley, so he was most likely ill for whatever reason, and he wouldn't show up tonight. Reasons are sometimes excuses, but they produce irrevocable results nevertheless. The consequences of Abu Ghalib's absence tonight are known—let the thieves enjoy themselves! Was his presence tonight going to change anything? The world was chaotic anyway, and I was in a hurry.

I pressed the stem, and the cover over the watch sprung open. I touched the hands of the watch and realized it wasn't wrong. I had broken my promise and returned to Selman Hashwah. He had been sleeping for three full days and nights. During this time, he neither ate nor drank. I questioned him, and he told me the whole story. I was overwhelmed and surprised at how Selman, scared of his own shadow, was capable of doing such a thing.

The world is strange, and the strangest thing is that I became an important factor in all of this. I held the fate of many people in my hands. If the life of 'Aziz Ghawi was now in the hands of a whore by the name of Salimah, and if the life of Lulu, Moshiyah's daughter, depended on Marrudi, then I now controlled three lives. I could put an end to their lives by just saying one word to the police, or I could let them survive by keeping quiet. The life of Khaduri, the tobacco vendor, was also in my hands, and so was Selman Hashwah's life, as well as my own destiny.

I'm a fornicator, a semimurderous Zionist, and a destructive Communist, but I fill my mouth with clean drops of rain and stick to silence. Khaduri is a hero. He's no adulterer. Jabbar is the real adulterer. How could Abu Ghalib understand these deceptions when other people understood them as facts and called me blind? The intertwined game of opposites infiltrated and embraced Selman Hashwah, my companion, who was driven reluctantly into dangerous, misleading, and childish games. Selman's illusions produced a kernel of truth that is lacking in people. I'm going to take a risk for this terrible truth for Selman's sake. I wonder whether he'll be lucky and manage to save himself. I'll tell him, "Run away!"

They told him, "Run away, Selman," and he obeyed. There was nothing worth living for in this world. Dear Aminah fled, so he fled too, despite fear. He lived in continuous fright, hanging around near its gates. Go ahead, Selman, and break through the gates and penetrate into the depths of fear. You may find your safe place there, but my own problem remains to save myself from preying paws. If you simplify matters there's no problem at all. I'll inform the police about myself and everything will be over. I'll save my life and shout from the highest minaret in Baghdad, "Hang me, hang me! I'm a Communist!"

Still, I have suddenly become an important person with many responsibilities. And who would teach the tricks of the trade to

Shridah, the busboy in all of Baghdad's cafés, once I die? Who would finish my job? I've been teaching Shridah how to play the qanun on a piece of wood and rusty wires. I taught him a tricky technique that he was eager to learn. He learns easily. But it's impossible to distinguish things while playing tricks. Is it possible that a worthless creature like me could hit and hurt someone? Could it mean that deceit in this case could also produce honest things of serious outcome? Shridah's illusion is completely different from Selman's because it doesn't bring death. Shridah follows his desire created by his situation and another reality appears out of it. Suddenly, I've become important because I saved Selman Hashwah from death and made life enjoyable for Shridah.

I drive away delusion, bringing life out of deceit. But I'm still the biggest opposite in this world, lost in a welter of opposites and chaos. I postpone my own death again and again and try to give life to people from my illusion. People don't appreciate me, call me "blind, blind." But what can be expected? They're the blind ones; they can go and convince Selman Hashwah to eat after I teach Shridah a qanun lesson.

6—Ya'qub, 'Amam's Son

"Majid, my brother! What will be the end of this world?" Ya'qub asked.

I silenced Majid. I hurt and embarrassed him. 'Alwan continues to deny my part in Iraq's bliss, enraging and demeaning me with an unholy oath he took together with Qadri, my previous partner Nessim, and the gypsy called politics, to ignore me as if I were a useless domino piece.

And here is my father lying in his grave, cultivating the soil of this land as his forefathers did. It is a good fertile lineage with roots that go back to early times, making Baghdad's fertile layers of land. The remains of my forefathers are like fertilizer. The time will come when my father will pull me to him, and I will turn into soil. Let 'Alwan know that I am the son of my forefathers—the continuation of loyalty. I belong to this good earth, the earth of my first ancestors. I wonder if some day 'Alwan and the peasants will realize this. Ever since I opened my eyes I've been reared here with my many brothers. But my decent friend Mahdi is not enticed in the slightest by the naked, gypsy whore of politics. Never does he poke his nose into such a life of treachery; he's above it, uninvolved.

But hearts become tarnished and need to be cleaned and polished. "Majid! Leave it to God. Maybe He has a Brasso pad to clean and polish all the suddenly tarnished hearts."

Does God have Brasso pads? Hearts became shadowy, faces gloomy, and thoughts troubled. I remember my adventures with my friends when I used to swoop down on the joys and pleasures of life like an eagle. What good days those were! Did I know then that they would one day disappear? People often ask me, "What will happen when the good life disappears?" My good life proceeded in many directions, from right to left, from east to west, from up to down. My life used to be a shower of love, happiness, friendship, and calmness, but now it rains down hatred, misery, sorrows, and gallows.

Those who still cherish love are a handicapped group—gloomy, silent, not knowing what to say. Hatred is a flood. 'Alwan's voice roars everywhere, and I wait for God to send down a basket of frond leaves with magic cleanser that would polish people's hearts and eradicate the accumulated rust that eroded the steel ties, which united friends and poured love. I recalled my troubles, and my mother then took a deep breath that shook the world and the pillars of His throne.

Ashes, ashes, Ya'qub said to himself. I've become ashes. Do I remember the pachah dish, the stuffed small and large intestines, the stuffed chicken cooked overnight, the beef every day, the big fish on Fridays, and the flickering glory that disappeared? Now, my mother, 'Amam, is without a drop of cooking oil or a piece of meat, only bone marrow to suck. Now, I'm like a starved dog looking for a piece of bone.

May God curse you and your orchard, Chwailah's son! I hurt myself with my own hands, so I'll have to look for ointment. We were two at home and then became three. Glory flew then and Khoshi, the Persian Haman, the villain vizier, vanished. Aminah escaped, and Gerjiyi Nati gained Aminah's chickens. I was smart when I said that this woman couldn't live at all without a man. I knew that. The whore went and picked up a bum from the street as old as her son and enticed him, became intimate with him. She has been living with him and sending 'Aibah the devil to burn in hell. At this my mother said, "Poor 'Aibah, he's a complete orphan. You took care of him all this time, so this time do him a miswah and let him stay."

I replied, "What *miswah-khiswah* nonsense are you talking about? Once I, Ya'qub, was well off and blessed with bounty; now Ya'qub is dead and in dire need. One mouse can't squeeze through a small hole, let alone two mice. It goes without saying they won't fit." My mother is burning with benevolent deeds as pure as oil. She isn't afraid to cry and beg for things like these. She pleads, "Abdalak! Don't disappoint me! He's an orphan, poor child. Where will he go? Is it right to leave him in the streets? Trust God! Allah is generous! You'll see how He will provide you with living expenses and wages for 'Aibah."

My mother is as good-hearted a woman as an angel, but she thinks that God dangles daily bread for His worshippers in a basket of palm leaves. But I pretend to be ignorant and believe that He— praised be His Name—will hold out a Brasso pad cleaner to cleanse rusty hearts, instead of daily bread. I'll make my livelihood from winning in dominos or backgammon or by selling wooden lasts lying in my mother's room like the memorial statues of a forgotten hero.

May God blacken my face and shame me for this. When will I stop sticking my festering wound in a pit of rotten filth? My life has crumbled, and my insides have been eaten away and hollowed like a stinking sewer that needs to be covered to keep its suffocating smell inside. My mother pleaded with me, "Abdalak! I'm embarrassed about asking you to go to your brother-in-law and talk to him, but maybe he can find you a job with him in the factory. Isn't it better to work for low wages than to be unemployed?"

My mother was not in the habit of asking for such a thing. I realized then that the situation had become unbearable. The stuffy smell had spread in spite of my attempt to avoid it by playing zneef, mah-bus, and gol-bahar games until midnight. Is this where I'll end up—getting on my knees to people? I raised my head to God instead of lowering it out of respect and said to Him, "Enough, enough pain!" The small window in the vastness of His heavens did not open as it had before. It stayed nailed shut. He then opened the window just to pull my heavy basket filled with His bounty, though He has never shoved it open again. So I had no choice. I dragged myself to my brother-in-law, the manager of a candy and drink factory in 'Ulwi-yah, and lowered my head before him.

"Will you work as a laborer?" he asked.

"What's my job?"

"Sticking labels on the bottles and wrapping chocolate and candy," he said with embarrassment. The job fits 'Aibah.

"Is there a better job?"

He scratched his head and suggested, "There's a porter job. Can you carry boxes?"

I asked for a better job, not a worse one. I put a stop to his suggestions, as I did with Majid not long ago. Sometimes one doesn't have the power to choose, and I kept silent. I had no choice and I chose the dull job at the candy factory in 'Ulwiyah next to the Alliance Club—sticking labels on bottles and wrapping candy boxes, earning as little as half a dinar each day. Then I went back to my friends and stayed until midnight as an escape. I drew a domino and nothing changed—I drew the piece without the dots, the double-blank.

"Majid, what will be the end of this world?" I silenced him again. The situation in this case was very different. What I chose here was worse than death, so why did I choose the job? How could I accept it despite myself? One thousand times damn this ugly, childish, gypsy whore and damn 'Alwan and people like him!

7—Sabriyah, 'Abdush's Daughter, and Na'imah, the Barber's Wife

I stood confused at the intersection of error and desire, thinking of Efrayim, my love and burning trouble. A nonhuman child is growing in my womb. I'm pregnant with a fetus of sorrow you never made, Efrayim. It's the result of choosing you, the impregnation of my true love, life, and destiny. The hammer of my unabated reality is striking on the anvil with true might. Love, truth, falsehood—my beliefs are compromised now. The steel around me cracks a chink in my armor.

The wild cat continues to meow inside me. It suffers from pain, then faints and awakes again. When it disappears, the confused person in me remains and licks the wounds of my sufferings and confronts my exhausted patience. I am fed up; there's a limit to my patience. God! What did I do to deserve this punishment? That's it. I'll go crazy in this prison grave. I chose Efrayim. I loved a handsome and a fair-complexioned man as immobile as death. But he surrendered to his own lowliness. He lacked ambition. I chose his submissiveness together with his love. Oh, this grave, these buried creatures in it! Life is a stinking prison. My vengeful fetus consumes my flesh, blood, and bones. I forgot my life in your lap, my fair-complexioned animal! I let the starved, preying, wild animal eat me while I was numbed with love. The hammer didn't stop beating upon my heart. When the hammer strikes, it breaks apart the strongest welded seam, and the bond is released. I was drowning in the fragments of my being, my love, my mind, and my feelings.

"Fayiq! Why are you gloomy and not answering me?" asked Na'imah. People need your help. Where are your eyes? Can't you see? Why is your nervousness growing, Fayiq?"

Suddenly, I saw a storm blowing violently at the world, infiltrating into this safe quarter. What in the world was happening? Everyone in this house was unaware that the devil had suddenly entered the house as an unwanted guest and never left. I, Na'imah, the crazy woman, thought that we had enjoyed a good life because of the good luck the doorstep had brought us. I had believed that bounty would never cease from this house and that eternal peace and serenity would always prevail.

"At least answer me, Fayiq. Why are you staring at me as if you wanted to prod me into life? What have I done to you? Isn't what is happening in and around Baghdad enough? The curse reached this calm and content quarter only a few months ago."

"Hey Joudi! Go and piss on the doorstep, maybe evil will depart," Na'imah yelled.

"Why are you looking at me like that, Abu Nihad? Don't you like me? What's wrong with what I said? Have you become blind and deaf? You seem to see and hear nothing. Salimah's image sticks in my mind, as an ordinary and cheap woman who causes pains to men's hearts. Can't you see what's happening in this house? Ya'qub, the son of good 'Amam, has gone bankrupt and left his shop. 'Aziz, Farhah's son, has disappeared with no return. The Persian swindler has abandoned Gerjiyi who, out of grief, left her son behind, and Sabriyah's husband was dismissed from his job and has been sitting at home idle before his wife. 'Abdallah Ghawi returned from Mahmudiyah like a bereaved woman, and even dear Aminah, like a blossoming tree among her seven brothers, was uprooted by the frantic storm. She flew in an unknown direction, and only God knows if she is dead or alive. And you, Fayiq, are you still silent after all this? What has happened to people? Why have peoples' hearts become as hard as rocks?"

"You, dear Nihad, go to the doorstep and piss on it! Maybe the devil will give up and leave!"

Why did God create love as a crime and an evil deed? Didn't He say to humans, "You are free?" My father said to me, "Sabriyah, if you decide that your life will be guided by reason, then you're free."

Since God made man rational, this father of mine taught me accordingly, and I chose Efrayim out of free emotion and reason. I had desires and feelings and I enjoyed the independence to run my life freely in order to love him. I also loved my relatives, winning love from both worlds. But my sin is that I'm only a human being made of flesh and desires. Though I have a brain, I live and feel reality, and my control may waver. I'm susceptible to change. I'm a human being—I live, think, feel, and respond to what happens around me. Look! Even these motionless creatures have begun to move strongly again.

Struggling people are like coals blazing forth. You, Efrayim, you're the only one who doesn't budge or make a change. You're like a feather in the wind blown by an evil destiny. I've buried my suffering in the bosom of your love, but you've been traveling on a train with no final destination. The jamkhanah is flooded with my tears. I was content with very little and wanted to stay near your blue eyes and light-colored hair.

My love and roots are also in Bistan el-Khass, despite rejection. What would I have done without my roots? Is love a sin? The possibility of leaving is still dreadful to me. No, I'm not my mother. She chose and changed her mind, then chose again. She's flighty. She chose a different man from my father, but I chose you and that's all. I chose two natural and flawless loves—you and my roots. Whatever happens, I'll never be my mother, even if my belly becomes swollen as a result of the child robbing me of my delight. My love cracked in my heart, and I became weak. Everything has changed, except these two loves. I feel sorry, Efrayim! I loved you. I loved the living human in you. Death is horrible, so steer clear of it, Efrayim! Otherwise, I'll be wearing mourning clothes and living on a fragment of ineffaceable memory.

❊

"I'm talking to a wall, aren't I?" Na'imah said to Fayiq; a wall with ears sealed by ten large spoons of fluid and eyes spitting fire and flames at my face. Fayiq's face was the gloomy and sad face of life.

"People are suffering, Fayiq! Is it right to draw back your hand when help is urgently needed? Oh people! A small good deed will save whatever is possible!" He stared at me with exaggerated cruelty not in his nature. "Am I talking to you, Fayiq? Am I just a bitch barking?" I was certainly hostile to his stiffness and stubbornness penetrating his heart and soul. "What's happening to the world, Fayiq? Please listen to me! If your heart has truly become a rock, it should have softened. Don't you see people needing help? You're deaf only when people are in trouble."

"Hey, Nahhudi, go and piss on the doorstep again!" The devil that entered our house has disturbed the peace. He's very evil, stubborn, and impudent, and doesn't surrender easily.

The evil devil was not satisfied with Nahhudi's trickles on the doorstep. Once the doorstep was good and clean. What changed it? The devil, yes, the devil! The armies of the devil have invaded us. There has been no hole in Baghdad into which the devil and his aides have not entered.

Sabriyah said to herself, "Enough, my mind, my heart! Let the bubbling overflow the pot. Righteousness is only steam released by my brain and the vapor descends back on the stream of humanity like drops of rage falling into a filthy basin of sin. People are thirsty, quenching their desire in the poisonous basin. Happy desires were deflated and turned into sighs of grief by an ugly, evil witch."

Calamities and suffering came. Sabriyah thought, "I wanted Efrayim to leave his job, but what a difference between what I yearned for and this? I was nurturing my rosy dreams in the throes of my suffering. Then he came and turned into a pharaoh instead of savior."

"Efrayim! I was spending my time within four walls, and when you returned you became the fifth wall. I had married you to receive your name and life, but you left me with the name and without a life. In the end, I became fed up with your poverty, light complexion, and everything else. Nevertheless, I knew that your weakness wouldn't frustrate my love for you. Still, my other love is in Bistan el-Khass."

People are selfish. Our two loves have struggled with each other, each desiring to have it all, absolute love or nothing. But absolute love is an illusion. I ignored your ignorance not to lose you, so that the absolutely misleading greed and selfishness wouldn't win and possess everything. Do you all know that we're bound by love in a land without roots, without memories or childhood? Well, I chose you and you're my husband—chose you out of imperious need despite the situation. I, on the other hand, avoid absolutes and derive all my strength from Bistan el-Khass. Had our relatives not given us money for survival we would have starved to death.

You came from a low, bland background. If it were not for me you would never have been my husband. I am the one who chose you and loved you despite your poverty. I fully realize now that your face was no promise of bliss, so you must make up for it by changing your behavior. Don't force me to make mistakes and act selfishly in trying to seek the illusion of the dream in my despair. It's everything or nothing.

*

"I need a hundred dinars," Na'imah said to Fayiq.

I was intensely worried because the world's troubles were making my skull split. There was a scar, similar to a Baghdad boil, the size of a dirham on my head. 'Amam was tense, and so were Sabriyah and the tenants. I needed money for a bribe to move mountains. The police searched Dr. Marsail's home and arrested her husband because they found him binding the black leather strips of the phylacteries around his arm like Ya'qub when he says his morning prayers.

"You're communicating by wireless," they said and took him away. I owe my life to Dr. Marsail and to the midwife because they removed the worms from my stomach. The stress was overpowering.

Why has Fayiq now become cruel like our government? The devil's fire is flickering in his face. Could this just be my imagination? After all, it's a fact in Baghdad. I blinked my eyes, and then fixed them on him. There was no mistake; the devil's exhaust came out of Fayiq's nostrils like black smoke rising from burnt food. For the first time I feared him.

"Okay, Fayiq! I only want eighty dinars."

Anger started to blaze on Fayiq's face. His troubles flamed out like burning coals, and I was a victim of the conflagration.

"Okay, I can get by with fifty dinars." His face became bright, and mine delighted. I held my breath while he breathed quickly. He was silent while I spewed forth.

"Only thirty dinars. What can I do? It'll be enough for the time being." But he turned his back on me and drew away. I could see only his rear and back, and not his front and his hard breathing.

"What about twenty dinars? But what are they good for? Twenty dinars is the last word."

I was disgusted though careful not to lose my patience. I was bargaining with him and still he hadn't answered me. Suddenly I lost my patience and went to him and shook him like a tree trunk with ripe dates. "Fayiq, you make me explode. I can't stand it anymore. Couldn't you find any better time to stall except today? Can't you see people are in trouble? Consider me a beggar and give me the twenty dinars and get it over with!"

Baffled, he turned to face me and moved backwards. The veins of blood in his neck suddenly popped out, and he fixed his eyes on me with a strange look that made the blood flow from head to toe. I was frightened at his anger and retreated while spitting on my chest to drive fear away. I mumbled, "Oh God, Protector! Oh God, Protector!"

I feel humiliated and ashamed because I love you, Efrayim. I yearned to carry my head high and be proud of you, but you lowered yours. I longed for a woman's life with a perfect man, but I have lived neither a woman's nor a man's nor life completely. Half of my life with you is like a prison, and the rest is impoverishment.

I felt that my lungs were being suffocated and I burst into bitter tears. With his head down, Efrayim sat beside me drowning in his incapacity. He lowered his head as if he were looking at a field of wheat in the harvest season. A rainy cloud covered his eyes, and the wrinkles of his face looked gloomy and sad. It was a complete picture of failure, devoid of hope.

"I can't stand life any longer, I can't bear it like this," I moaned. "Find a solution, either you go to work or . . ."

I heard a defeated and restrained sobbing. It was his sobbing. His blue eyes were bathed in tears. I was in the grip of blame and despair, and he was crying in front of me as if he were a woman. I wiped his tears in order to soothe his insecurity feelings and to control myself.

Like the sad melody of a guitar, I moaned and groaned in front of the fifth wall, Efrayim, and begged him, "Divorce me! Divorce me!" Suddenly the fifth wall trembled with his blue eyes bathed in tears. Baffled, he said, "Sabriyah, do you realize what you're saying? What does this 'divorce me' business mean?"

What did I hear? And what did Efrayim hear? Undoubtedly, I disclosed to him a secret that had gotten bigger ever since I began to frequent Bistan el-Khass again. Suddenly he accused me with conviction, "Your relatives are the ones inciting you against me. They couldn't stand the sight of me from the beginning."

And what did I hear? Efrayim suddenly controlled his tongue in order to hurt my other love. The faults! He blamed my relatives. Efrayim wanted to force me to raise my voice against him, and at the same time I was forced to rush toward the impossible. I yelled at him but restrained myself midway.

"Look Efrayim, don't try to confuse matters. You know I have a good head on my shoulders and no one can influence me. I left my relatives voluntarily and followed you, so why are you accusing them? Think about it! For two years you left me alone buried in this room. Only God knew what was happening to me, and now you came and sat opposite me. I swear by God that either you find a job and support me with dignity and respect or I go back to my relatives. I can't take it any longer."

His body shook out of fear, and he saw the world as a door closing before him.

The curse! People say, "God is a provider; He closes one door and opens a thousand." But where are God's doors? Who is closing them in Efrayim's face? He looked at me and his face became serious.

I was the last door and I would give him up. This I would do—as persistent as I was scared.

No! Oh God! Efrayim was furious. Violent fear seized him. I would do what I was bent on doing and leave him. He mumbled while turning his face to the ground.

"Did I ever turn down an available job? You want me to carry a pail and work in construction or carry a cane and call 'Nazzah! Nazzah!' like a sewer cleaner?"

I was enraged and shouted at him, "You have two choices, sit at home or work at my father's nightclub."

An unexpected scream stuck in Efrayim's throat, but he spat it out at my face, "I won't work in the nightclub. I told you a thousand times I won't work for your father. Do I owe you anything to force me to work there?"

Shouts followed each other continuously like a chain clanging. I shouted at Efrayim, "Well, since you're not indebted to me, enjoy this room and be in it all the time. If you find a job by yourself, then come to me at my father's home."

Efrayim shouted after me, "Sabriyah, come back, don't be a child, Sabriyah, Sabriyah!"

I walked out in anger, and Efrayim collapsed alone inside the jamkhanah, his face buried in his hands.

※

Na'imah burst into bitter tears again. Fayiq's facial expression broke out in the flames of devilish madness. He was enraged. He spat out the flames, ordering me, "Give me my shoes!"

What was happening in the world? Fayiq was surely possessed, or the devil had certainly controlled him. The devil was everywhere, and trials and tribulations were spreading like a flood. Didn't Nahhudi piss on the doorstep of the house again? The devil was stubborn and didn't surrender easily. He provoked and possessed Fayiq, then he provoked him again. Had something like this happened before? Fayiq didn't answer me, only asked me to bring him his shoes.

I raised my voice, "Listen, Fayiq, get your shoes by yourself and give me twenty dinars now!"

Fayiq said, "God forbid!"

This was certainly a whim of the devil. Fayiq sighed to no avail. Indeed, the devil was stubborn. Fayiq yelled, "That's enough! All this time I've been avoiding evil by not answering you, thinking maybe you would stop. Hand me the shoes and let me get out of here before things get worse."

I screamed at Fayiq, opposing his devilish victory, "Fayiq, don't drive me mad! I can't imagine why you would say such a thing. Is it true what I heard or am I dreaming?"

"Yes, it's true. You're the one who made me lose my mind. It's give, give, give, give, until I've become penniless. Because of you, I had to sell the shop. You've destroyed my home. May your home be destroyed!"

No! Fayiq would not give me up at this critical moment when all the doors were closed before my good friends. Undoubtedly, Fayiq was joking, I thought. He was testing me and acting like the devil. I smiled at the devil's face to please him and flattered him by my friendliness. I said to him, "Abu Nihad! Only this time. I swear by your life only this time. Have pity on them! Don't you see what problems they're facing? All of them are my dear friends, and I'm trying desperately to help them. Isn't a real friend tested in troubled times? You only want to avenge? Oh, Abu Nihad, you're making a fuss and making a mountain out of a molehill. Postpone our revenge and give me what I need, and let's not worry about tomorrow. God is generous."

Fayiq yelled at me, "Do you want to see how I make good on my threat? You'll see, if I step in this house again, I won't be allowed to touch you."

I yelled back at Fayiq, "No, I won't let you go. Do you think you scare me with your yelling? Come on, let's see you go and not come back!"

Fayiq left running. I cried for a while, then stood up nervously. In confusion, I collected my jewelry and called, "Nihad, come 'aini, let's go to your grandfather and grandmother and let your father take care of himself. As long as he behaves this way, he's bound to discover that his body is tasteless even to dogs. Come, sonny, let's go and put an end to these quarrels."

8—Lulu, Moshiyah's Daughter

Lulu came back from Sheikh Ishaq Synagogue exhausted and collapsed on the dirty, neglected bed. She didn't take off her 'abayah because she was short of breath, tired, both sad and happy. She felt her life had been stolen from her, doling it out to others through numerous good deeds. What can I do? She wondered. The anniversary of the death of Marrudi's father came. I took a meal for the needy, lit candles, gave one dinar as charity for reading the Eshkabah prayer for the repose of the soul of Marrudi's father and another dinar for reciting the Imshemberakh blessing prayer for Marrudi. Marrudi was playing marbles with 'Aibah in the middle of the alley. The well-mannered boy, Nihad, went with his mother while 'Aibah, the bastard, the son of the Indian woman, stayed here. It's my bad luck that 'Amam performed a miswah and let 'Aibah sleep in her room.

Lulu was overwhelmed by sadness mixed with apprehension and anxiety on account of 'Aibah, the devil's offspring. The carrier of the devil's seed was bound to make additional trouble. The devil had an amulet to protect him, but Marrudi was a soft sissy. She saw Marrudi in the alley squatting on the ground and aiming at the marble. He missed the target and rolled the marble toward the mouth of the sewer. She was sad and sorry for him. 'Aibah, however, hit all the targets. She was dismayed again. How could Marrudi overcome the devil? Marrudi almost cried, then he immediately got angry. He spat at her, cursed, and then hit her. It's not my fault. Lulu thought.

Despite this, I gave him one riyal, though the cost of one marble is only one fils. I asked him sweetly to take it, but he only replied, "May God inflict you with a defect and strike you with an arrow!" I begged him to come home, but he refused. I was about to enter the house when he called me. I answered, "Yeah," and then he cursed me: "May a calamity befall you and a millstone fall on you!" Then I heard him laughing with 'Aibah. I was both sad and happy.

All the world laughs when Marrudi laughs; he laughs at me, and I rejoice. Yet there is a dark spot in my heart because Marrudi is learning from the son of the devilish woman. 'Aibah will ruin him. One thousand times I told him, "Don't play with 'Aibah." But he cried, and I cried for him, reluctantly taking back what I had said. Still, I didn't want him to play with 'Aibah.

I was exhausted lying on the neglected bed. I had nothing to say, stretched out between life and death, both racked with pain and soothed by hope. My life was a candlestick whose wick burned for Marrudi and his late father.

The light of Marrudi's wick was flickering and then gasping with each puff. After Lulu nursed Marrudi, the milk in her breasts dried out, leaving love and memory, but she hated the memory, and Marrudi mistreated her. She never complained about his disobedience as much as she dreaded the fact that he disobeyed the invisible power that commanded a son to respect his parents. She feared the anger of this power and implored God to forgive him—I am content with him even if he cuts me into pieces with a cleaver. She felt pleased and safe whenever she thought about Marrudi's growth—and I live for his sake and for this feeling of safety and joy. She affirmed this, but she felt the stab of a dagger. I pray that God will not put me to death until I see Marrudi married. His time of maturity was approaching. Would she still be alive and witness his Bar Miswah, his binding of the phylacteries? She wondered.

A sigh absorbed her being and took her out to a sea of pleasant and captivating dreams. The water became like rose water with diffusing fragrances. The shores were pebbles made of gold, and on the sea shore there were blue marbles glistening in serenity. "Marrudi," she whispered his name like an invocation to God. I will hold a fabulous Bar Miswah party that all of Baghdad will talk about, but make sure to keep away from 'Aibah the devil, because he has the impure sting of a wasp.

'Aibah stings. He stings, and Marrudi is like a young bachelor who has come of age. At the same time Lulu was tired, pulled by the two poles, was scared, dreamed, then was cheerful.

She suddenly fell asleep in her 'abayah, taking calm breaths.

9—'Atiyah al-Qarawchi

I wonder how one could cure this dilemma. Haven't they said that our Savior, the Mahdi, has come? So where is he? Those who boasted about his coming are liars. What's happening to the world? What's happening to our quarter? What's happened to people? I really forgot what my daughter Wafiqah told me the other day. Oh God, was it Wafiqah or my other daughter, Qadriyah, and was it the other day or a month ago or years ago? Oh my God! What has happened to this world? What has happened to my mind? Have I grown old and senile or did the world go crazy and make people go out of their minds? Did I sin by sitting and begging for Joudi?

A dignified stranger came up to me, and I thought he would make me rich and give me a whole qran, but instead he pinched me so violently on my ribs that I slumped to the ground. "What did I do to you, sir, that you want to bring death on me?" I said to him. "If I die, who'll take care of Joudi? I'm a woman and have no one except this crazy Joudi. I'm doing this begging so he won't starve to death."

The stranger lifted me up and dropped me again to the ground and said to me, "Get up, you one-eyed woman! Get up and disappear from here. Don't you know that begging is forbidden?"

I fell to his feet and implored, "Where should I go, sir? My only son will starve to death."

"It's better if you go away. Otherwise, they'll hang you with your son," he replied.

I was scared of him. He took my money and left. By God, I was scared. The other day I saw somebody hanged in Ghazi Street—a goat, I thought at first. How would I know that they had begun hanging people like goats?

I asked the people standing there, "Aren't goats hanged by their legs? Why is this one hanged by its head?" How should I have known it was a human being since the head was covered with a black bag and the body was shrouded, and I didn't know what was written on the shroud.

They laughed at me and said, "Are you crazy? It's not a goat, it's a man!"

So I was afraid the stranger would go ahead and hang me and then hang Joudi. I had collected about a dirham from begging and let him take it so that he would leave me. Isn't that better than hanging me and Joudi, my poor dear son?

I went to the wholesale farmers' market and gathered in my 'abayah a load of rotten vegetables from the garbage. I planned to cook vegetables stuffed with rice for Joudi. Then I came to the site of the ruin. When I opened my 'abayah and saw scorpions and snakes I was amazed and thought I was out of my mind because I had picked the vegetables with my own hands. I wondered what had happened and how the vegetables had turned into reptiles, ants, and cockroaches.

Damn the devil. Help! The whole alley is inhabited by demons, oh God! Who told me so? Was it Wafiqah or Qadriyah? No, I've grown forgetful. Umm Nihad was the one who said, "I'm leaving the alley. I can't stand it any longer. The devil has entered the alley and refused to leave."

Now I understood what those loud screams were every night. May the devil be cursed for what has been done to people! He has visited them, and the situation became chaotic. I forget, wasn't it Wafiqah who said the other day, "Mama, why did you forget us, Qadriyah and me?" Then I said to my daughter Qadriyah, "Dear daughter, don't scold me. While you and your sister Wafiqah are enjoying paradise, I'm being grilled in hellfire."

Life has become like a circle narrowing around us. If you just saw how down 'Amam is, your heart would break for sorrow. There's a hubbub, people are hanged by their necks, and the devil has come to dwell among us, setting out to prune God's garden of innocents.

Dear daughter! If you could see the situation here, melancholy would take hold of you, and you would go crazy.

Our God has been merciful for making Joudi crazy. If he hadn't been crazy they would have hanged him from his head. I warn you, it's a lie that every goat is hanged by its legs. What legs are they talking about? I see people hanged by their necks and heads. Yes, definitely by the heads. I'm going out of my mind; this world is enough to drive anyone crazy. Either one becomes crazy or turns into a goat hanged by the neck. What should I do? Well, I'll go to sleep. That way, maybe I'll have a good dream and die before waking up.

Nine

1—'Aziz Ghawi

I was in the studio of Jalal, the calligrapher. I kept examining the deep-rooted chameleon-like colors of his created beings, while a changeless dark hue has been hammered like a fixed nail into my head. As I examined carefully one example of Jalal's calligraphy, following his hand with my brush, to my astonishment, it seemed to speak, "Salimah."

Salimah was likewise obedient to my dying feelings. A strange ambition resembling an uprising or a rebellion sparked in my mind. Through many years I've been fixed in one place like a mountain, unmovable forever in my failure, in my dispirited soul, in my surrender to my roots. I felt nausea welling up from all directions and was ashamed of myself. Likewise, I felt emptiness, similar to decayed bones, buried and rotting in my mind. 'Abdallah Ghawi, Farhah Ghawi, Sa'idah Ghawi, and the last year of high school piled curses like hills of dust upon my dead body. I recalled Salimah, my sister Sa'idah, and Karim, and felt ashamed of myself.

"You're incorrigible," I said to myself. "You can't be budged, you stay in one place forever, and you do strange things. When you die you may resurrect a body that is now buried and another soul may assume this body, but your soul will take leave for good. So where will your resistance lead?"

The thought as to where this question might lead frightened me, so I evaded it in my mind and fixed my eyes on my brush. I saw the brush stumbling and hesitating, then the canvas tore. Surprise!

Surely, the strokes were not sure. The style of Kufi calligraphy is unfit to express the modern words *surrealism*, *existentialism*, and *engagement*. I'm the last word as an innovator of modern calligraphy, the creator of "intermixism." I overcame my failures and became a successful, innovative calligrapher.

I said to Jalal, "Why are you confused, master? Employ me and I'll show you what I can do."

What impudence! I had insulted him. I humiliated a master praised by the creatures of the changing color, the changeable skin.

Never look for your roots! I'll deny my origin. I'm now a pioneer of intermixism, but it was invented out of deep despair and stillness. Do you know why I worshipped a dull whore named Salimah-choka-boka? I didn't worship her body alone, but also the terrific denial of her roots. She still spits at anything that may lead to stability and could "intermix." She is able to "intermix" mentally and socially. Salimah killed me with her intermixism and made me a bridge for others against my will.

I used my spilled blood to create a different life for myself as an innovator of intermixism, and I shall live this life even after leaving my weak body and pulling out the nail stuck in my head since birth. Listen! The truth is I don't know how to draw anything other than the name Salimah, the trustee of my essence. I shape, color, mix, and then destroy pen strokes that used to be fixed in form. I draw the word *Salimah* in all the usual and the unusual styles of calligraphy and send it into the whole world in endless styles, homogeneously and asymmetrically, expressing probability and contradictions. Naturally, my greatest rival, Karim 'Abd el-Wahab, is a part of it. This rival of mine has a thousand hands meddling in my life. He has seized my soul in the dark deaf silence of the night and continues to steal my origin, roots, honor, and sister. He has burned incense in every corner of my accursed house and branded his odor onto the skin of my beautiful chaste sister, defiling her honor.

'Abdallah Ghawi expressed his triviality and pettiness by mumbling the cowardly words of a curse. That full black wineskin has a mastery of words. He's my father, the creator of my tragedy, while the poisonous snake, my mother, sheds her old skin for a new one and comes out refreshed and vital. In the absence of 'Abdallah Ghawi, I was the man in the unfortunate Ghawi family. On my paralyzed back tread the moving feet of people who enjoy themselves and cause only tragedy to me.

No! I'm no longer a scarecrow called 'Aziz Ghawi. I can act, though it's late. Who knows what will happen if I stay passive. Will a resurrection fall on my shoulders and I'll be the only one dead forever? Will God die or be fed up with His game of creation and destroy it with His shaky old hands?

No! My name from now on is al-Salmawi, 'Aziz al-Salmawi. The word *Salmawi* is derived from *Salimah*, from that filthy scar. The scar of shame is both near and far, and I'm both empty and full of it. It's a mark whose fire is more horrible than this world's fire. It devoured me, and nothing was left except dust and vanity. The wound healed suddenly yet it continued to strike in my dark side. I found myself like Berlin and London after World War II, the victim of a nervous twitch.

The calligrapher inspected my style, studying it carefully, while I watched all around me. Jalal didn't understand my innovation and the changeable colors of chameleons. He continued to scrutinize, then I checked around me and found only the vomiting of drunkards, filth, banality, and nausea. Was I a sadist or a masochist? Am I selfish or self-denying?

I drew Salimah inside me and her name was on my canvas. Actually, my style of calligraphy confuses the most famous calligraphers in Baghdad. What's the rule I followed when drawing the name of Salimah with my blood? I was alone in my confusion, trying vainly to rid myself of it. My father, 'Abdallah Ghawi, used to light a cigarette for me and get lost with me, cry for my crying. Soon it became clear that he was only crying for himself. Let him cry for himself! From now on I am 'Aziz al-Salmawi.

Suddenly the calligrapher said, "How did you acquire this style of calligraphy?"

My heartbeat stopped for a while then pounded quicker and stronger, and my mouth dried out and all my glands ceased to secrete. Would my master be surprised or would he mock and ridicule me? I mumbled through a gritty mouth and rapid heartbeats, looking for something I had lost—something I had missed all my life.

Where was the blind bitch woman who can replace Salimah? 'Aziz asked. Let everything in me be changed, even my thoughts and dialect! I mumbled again. The rusty nail had loosened and wobbled through my mind—the nail of my deeply rooted stillness, my withdrawal and failure.

I squeezed the head of the nail between the jaws of the pliers and began to pull.

"Ouch!" I felt the terrible pain, which went on to aggravate my entire life—the last year of high school and that arrogant Arabic teacher, the son of a bitch, an Egyptian by the name of el-Aydarusi who never changed his suit or scent. Every day his suit reeked of Bint el Sudan smell, which either aroused me or made me hate him. I was then just plain 'Aziz Ghawi, Jewish, stupid, and retarded. I used to stand in front of him as stiff as a piece of wood. My mouth would become parched, and my tongue and my heart would land a series of cruel blows to my chest.

Beginning today, I am 'Aziz al-Salmawi, a man with no identity, emerging from the depths of death and rebelling against it, looking to find himself. Salimah's wound has almost healed. It was my only weapon against my death and devastation.

A core of humanity kindled deep in me, like a human in process to be resurrected or a thunderclap in the dense darkness of night.

I said to the calligrapher with a voice full of dread, "Isn't it good?"

I kept quiet for a while, taking precautions—as I was inclined toward being steeped in the past as it occupied my emotional life. I, the artist, forgot about my defeated desire. In this moment of lofty, bewildering silence, Salimah now dwelled in my hands. May she perform miracles and bring me a one-eyed bitch instead of one who is blind. Suddenly, the silence was broken, like the popping of a cork that sealed the mouth of the flask imprisoning a rebel.

Jalal mumbled, "On the contrary, it doesn't resemble any known style of calligraphy at all. I don't know what to tell you. Maybe people will learn to understand it and see the importance of its beauty."

People! Did any one of them understand me? I tell you, I lost my resolve, and because of my clinging, I deviated from the reasonable. This is my blood, and I spilled it for this word. I clung to it and immersed myself in the inventiveness of calligraphy just for this word. What will be after my death? I used to see Salimah in a thousand images here, so the answer about how I've arrived at such a style should be obvious. Salimah is a thousand examples of it, and my canvases are drawn sincerely, not for gain, but with both ease and suffering. She was my soul, now separated from me, and now only an exhausted and mysterious feeling pushing me, urging me to live.

"Oh my master! What can I tell you? Do you believe that I wrote her name with my blood? Look at it carefully! You're an artist. You may find out many things in my calligraphy—love, despair, hatred, suffering, hope, even death."

Jalal cried, "My God—you're a born artist!"

It was the first time in my life that I had drawn, and the satisfying pleasure of a calligrapher overpowered me. I mumbled the word "Salimah" as if I were praying, with trembling lips. Then I said with concern, "Do you mean you'll employ me for good?"

"Yes, I will, and you'll sit in the shop and work for yourself. There's plenty of work to do, praised be God. You'll give me a portion of your income. If you're lucky, people will understand you and you'll become famous."

I turned around and suddenly saw a white light shining in the street and embers glowing amid dying ashes—Salimah . . . Jalal!

I leaned to kiss Jalal's hand, but Jalal moved away and withdrew his hand and said, "God forbid! God forbid!" I wiped my tears and wept for happiness.

Miserable scenes filled my mind, so there was more than one reason for me to cry. There were creatures that lived in a dirty house in Bani S'id who until yesterday claimed to be my relatives. They poured garbage on my head, either intentionally or by accident. There were also first-class horses winning in the races—my uncle on my father's side, my uncle on my mother's side—and my cousin Yusuf 'Abd el-Nabi never tired of scolding me.

I declare now that I disown you all! I've changed. I am 'Aziz al-Salmawi, though I'm not a real human yet. I'm still like a wandering dog. Another reason for the change is my work with the best-known calligrapher in Baghdad. Such was the beginning of my doglike life on a bright day; when the sun sets the dog will live like a bat.

My scar has healed, but the scar is still fixed in me as the last sign of my own persistence. With black wings in my heart I hover at night over the miracle—Salimah. She has killed and revived me at once. I have pulled out three-quarters of the rusty nail rooted in my head, and only a little piece remains.

I asked Jalal, "My master, do you know of anyone who has a room for rent in the Sinak area?"

My master laughed and said, "There are a lot of rooms for rent, many like garbage. Do you want a room with only four walls or do you want one with a nice-looking chick too?"

I didn't understand what his intention was and asked him, "What do you mean by 'a nice-looking chick'?"

"I mean a face with pink, rosy cheeks, swelling breasts, a marble belly, and a clean pussy."

I thought of the whore with the pug nose and the nauseous whorehouse. Events that took place in Farhah Ghawi's room between Karim and Sa'idah made me retch.

"No, my friend! Don't get me involved with a whorehouse and the red-light district. I became a pimp against my will," I replied.

My master and my partner, the artist, guffawed. "Look, 'Aziz! Why are you talking about pimping and visiting whorehouses? I'm telling you that her pussy is clean and pleasing. Go to Araksi, the Armenian girl who lives above the shop. She'll rent you a room and come to you at night, hug you, and sleep with you most willingly. Don't worry! She's no whore, just a decent girl who works as a nurse in the hospital."

Decent? Was I hearing correctly? "She's also a nurse . . . She'll hug you at night and sleep with you," as if the whole world were pimping and trading in beef and paying no attention to what happens at night in the room of the coiled, poisonous snake, Farhah Ghawi.

2—Selman Hashwah

Eliyahu Hamis looked all over the room apprehensively. Nobody was there except him and me. The entire house was desolate. People disappeared quickly, and those who remained inside spent all their time in their rooms face-to-face with their pain. In the walls of my room were hundreds of ears that suddenly grew, giant ears like those of apes perked up. Eliyahu and I saw them.

Eliyahu's voice was strangled in his throat, and his mouth drew near my ear whispering to me, "Selman, I want you to be ready before six. Wear your robe, headdress, and headband and be ready. They'll come to take you soon. The main thing is that there's no obstacle in the way of the border and nothing will go wrong."

I froze. I didn't want to hear anything. Talk to the ground, not to me, for I'm already dead. But despite my fear of imminent death, I grasped Eliyahu's whisper, and his soul slid into the valley of another death, one death was included with the other, and I was escaping from all deaths together toward ensuring one that would end all discussion categorically.

Echoes of Jamil Rabi's advice vibrated in my malfunctioning brain: "Throw yourself into the fire and don't be afraid."

To hell with it! To suffer one hour is better than suffering every hour all the time. Life has become rotten, not worth living, but does Jamil care? Jamil is a Communist, and I'm a Zionist. Does he look out for my well-being? Or perhaps he wants to throw me into a pit so deep that I won't be able to climb out.

I wiped my face of the stinking sweat of fear and heat. The fear was to blame for making me go too far in my suspicions of even those close to me. Still, I recognized that Jamil mocked me, shoved his fingers in my face, and liked to tease me. But why would he want to hurt me? If he had truly wanted to get me in trouble, he would have informed the police about me. My life was in his hands; that was fear. This life was like my one blind eye.

I was as torn as a shabby rag, wearing a dirty dishdashah and not shaving my beard for a week. My belly hung down when I was lying on the bed pressing the springs of the bed with my enormous weight. I was alone when I faced fear and death and wanted to have a human being to hold in my arms, someone to give me new life.

Eliyahu Hamis was like a bat that had vanished suddenly. The disappearance was swift but not complete. He had left behind his skill in setting off deadly bombs, and he was pleased to explode them on my body only, killing me. The fear also killed me, so I've suspected others ever since my first death followed me in Karbala, and later more deaths pursued me in a series. But Sabriyah doesn't mean death for me at all.

I missed her when she was absent and my destiny was hanging in the balance and contained the danger of death on both sides. My Lord! Which side should I choose? How should I bid Sabriyah farewell? Might I die tonight? Had inescapable death come already? I was a Zionist against my will. I may be a killer. To top it off, I was fleeing across the border illegally because I had become, in the ruling opinion, a traitor and a spy.

While I was standing at the intersection of the roads covered by a dense smokelike fog hampering my vision, I asked myself, "From where did I come and to where am I going? To paradise or hell?" Was I going to my great death to save myself from a chronic illness like the blood that had gushed out when I came out of my mother's womb, winking and flashing my one eye? Would the dawn bring heavy breezes with fear? Would this fear become dense and turn the air into a solid shield facing my lamentation and me and provoking sighs, only to cast me afterward into a desolate land where I have no root or identity?

Answer me, people, for God's love. I listened in silence charged with the croak of the invisible devil, then turned on my bed while rhythms of the bedspring arose. My upper and lower teeth chattered and my head moved in rhythmic vibrations. They left me alone and went away. How would I pass the time until six o'clock? My patience would erode by then.

The world seemed afflicted with severe jaundice. It was deteriorating every second. All the yellow things continued to chase me. The yellow color was absorbed into all colors and dominated them. It resided in the dryness of the greenery, in the hardships of life and death. The objects were yellow, the sand was yellow, so was the chamomile, the turmeric, the urine, the banana peel, and the fat that floated on the tashrib dish. I licked the tashrib soup. To hell, consider yourself sentenced to death. Give up! I had an urgent appetite for food, especially for the tashrib. I wished I had a dish of tashrib; I would crumble and sop bread in it, then devour it whole and get up and go to the gallows courageously.

Once I took out my penis and found it yellow. It was leaking yellow urine. My dishdashah had yellow stripes. My mother used to treat my hand with the yellow cream, Taramandi, and the pus was yellow. The wound discharged light yellow pus in my leg. My stool was yellow when I was very young. With courage I would climb the gallows and nothing else would remain in the world except this yellow color. The noose of the rope, the piece of wood, and this human scarecrow whose neck was caught within the noose—it meant death.

Suddenly, the springs squeaked, and my limbs trembled. I couldn't control my mouth and even the roots of my hair were shaking. Control yourself. My limbs!

The drunkard shot over my shoulder while I was playing the oud. I wonder what I might play for Sabriyah if she came and said to me, "Hey, Selman, play for me!" And what if she hugged me tenderly and whispered, "I'm bored and want some enjoyment. I want to hear you play."

The drunkard said to me, "Play, don't stop! If you stop I'll kill you!" A spray of bullets zoomed out of my neck. Would I play a lamentation for her? No, no, no. A bridal song? No. A lullaby? Never. I would play the oud then.

When the situation in the country became serious beyond solution, and confusion and fear prevailed, the outcome was the color yellow. How did one translate the color yellow into a musical melody? Trembling? Death? Sabriyah's love? My ambiguity? My confusion and insanity! Who involved me in this mess?

I wish they had hanged you, Eliyahu Hamis! No, why do I curse this poor yellow fellow? How is it his fault? Would the outcome have been different than this? They led me to this situation. I loved the land of our forefathers. My heart yearned for the new Jewish State, and I tried to swim in a limitless sea until it finally burst. The sea was a dark, unthinkable blood color. Did the red replace the yellow? No! God has decreed, and our fate is sealed. May God be your protector!

From the beginning, things were predetermined and signed with black ink, and the climax came when a stray, blind bullet was shot by yellow fear and hit an innocent child from the country by accident. What's the matter with me? Was I crying? Why shouldn't I cry for what has happened and is bound to happen to me? The yellow fear! I wanted to overcome fear in order to see things in different colors, so I dyed my hand with red, with blood. We, they, and I became alike. We dyed our hands with henna, with each other's blood. Their hands were plunged in my blood and that of my parents too. My hands were stained with the blood of a miserable, innocent child whose face I haven't even seen. Have mercy on me! My mind is slipping a notch. There's no way out. Such is my destiny, and whatever is written on our foreheads will happen.

What? Where was the tashrib soup? I want to relieve my anger in the yellow tashrib, to wolf it down and gorge on the yellow. What will be left? Do I want to change my fate by force? In any case, the red would still face me. After all, we dyed our hands with flowing human blood. The authorities provoked it. So did I, but there's no escape. I washed my hands a thousand times, but the blood of my relatives and the blood of that miserable child have flowed in my mind like a red spot invading my soft flesh. My flesh and blood became like a burning coal devouring everything fresh. Where was the tashrib? The yellow? No matter what it is, the yellow is better than the red.

Sabriyah's face appeared to me as I saw her last time. She was pale, withered and ill, yellow. My face was now doubtless—like hers. I'd like to protect you in the next Farhûd, Sabriyah, but I can't even protect myself. Who will protect you if, God forbid, the red liquid gushes out again and my hands have become stained with the child's blood, while their hands have bloodied the hands of my parents and mine? The red spot is like a scar in my mind. Where will you escape? Your fate is written on your forehead and brows—a terrible feeling.

Jamil, the smart bastard, was right when he told me, "Escape, don't be afraid to throw yourself into the fire!" The fire is certainly red, but when it burns it changes color. Still, should I burn myself in order to burn away this bright red color? Sabriyah, the oud is hung on the wall in the dusty red bag of velvet fabric. In the red bag are innumerable melodies, all muted. Sabriyah, you are far away, but I know what I would have played for you. I don't even know how I can see you before I leave at six o'clock when I am forced into the haze of my blind fate. My life was a sham, a thousand deceits, a jumble of failed attempts. So, I have no willpower now, and my eyes shed tears. You were my last resort, my God, and I fell back on you, Sabriyah. I loved you. I matched error with delusion, then rid myself of all illusions.

I saw her while fixing my gaze on something hollow wrapped in a red shroud. This hollow item contained infinite, intimate melodies, and from them I tried to compose one that was both harmonious with the color yellow and that would express my redness. My memory had rotted away. My submission to fate was the result of others' wishes everywhere, not my own will. I had no freedom and heard only my predestined fate, although everyone had participated in determining my own fate except me.

Suddenly, the significance of the red changed in my eyes and overwhelmed me like a flood breaking out of the dissolution of my dusty, hemorrhaging oud. Then my heart beat with love and affection. A strong, passionate, sweeping red color attracted me. It was the oud, the firstborn of my own creation. The oud and Sabriyah. But what would Efrayim say? It's a suppressed desire in my heart that I want to carry out. It's in my thoughts. To hell with it, let him say what he pleases! Sabriyah, I'll leave all the melodies with the red shroud—my love for you, my invisible destiny. My hands and the tyrants' hands are stained with blood.

I resembled a limp rag, a body without bones. My legs were paralyzed, and my head was confused and foggy from the nightmare struggle with Sabriyah. I took heart and rocked while embracing the oud as if it were Sabriyah's soul. My olive-sized tears quickly fell on the red, dusty bag leaving a spot in which blood and dust were mixed. And the oud? It felt as if my mind were pricked by a pin and my head pierced by a bone—heavy load, oppressive, and solid. Still, I would do what I wanted to without anyone's intervention. The oud was the last thing I left behind for Sabriyah. It would always remind her of me, whether I was dead or alive.

The jamkhanah contained my rival. Efrayim's yellow face and hair wandered aimlessly there. I would talk to Sabriyah's husband for the first time, while I carried my oud in the red bag and saw the yellow color in the face and hair of my rival. I would say to him with a courage I lack, "Efrayim Effendi, this oud is mine. I haven't used it since it was first hung on the wall. Sabriyah liked it and bought it from me before I left. Please, give it to her when you see her and tell her that Selman conveys his regards."

I left the oud in the jamkhanah with a part of me. In doing so, I left Efrayim bewildered and I sniffed Sabriyah's fragrance that lingered long after I had left. This would stay with me and nourish me in the dangers of tonight's journey, a mysterious and decisive journey, a journey of fright, of life and death.

I indulged in the depth of my unknown elusive life but didn't notice that death waited in ambush for me. Have mercy on me! I wanted to die. I wish to die and have it over with. Death was more compassionate—so what of the bones? I was just a case of bones anyway. I wished to sleep and wake up only when the Messiah came.

This Messiah was hours away from here, and the way to the Messianic kingdom was full of ghosts, demons, and evil spirits. The Messiah I mean was in Iran.

No more than bones, bones—oh Jews, Muslims, and Christians! Those in history who have led herds know that this is a lost herd of cows that overcame obstacles in the desert, not knowing whether they were going to be slaughtered or end up in a green pasture. But I couldn't wait. The slaughter was far off as well as close by, just a breath away. The pasture was far off but close by and it turned out to be only a sip of water. I threw a stone behind me as a sign that I wouldn't return. Time stopped; returning meant the gallows. The hands of each of us were stained with the blood of the other.

What was Jamil doing now? What was Sabriyah doing? There, in her room in Bani S'id I left her illusion and reality—the bloody memory with the two faces. Every red face has two meanings.

Do you remember the night when the oud fell from your hand, Sabriyah? Spears of fear were released from it like the open mouths of death. I heard the oud screaming during the night along with the scream of death surrounding you.

I heard the scream of death now in moments of paralysis while Sabriyah moved slowly and sluggishly and leaned on crutches striking my heart. I wondered if she was free to recall the melodies crammed in her memory. I also wondered if Efrayim would tell her about the oud, whether he would give it to her. What happened to the peasant boy, to his legs? There, in the glorious mansion near the dam, the members of the Zionist movement muzzled the mouth of fear. There was no reason to take pity on them. They had money and concealed what happened leaving me only with fear. I suffered like someone whose sister was a whore.

They said to me, "Your life is in danger, and you have to leave the country." Jamil said, "Don't be afraid to throw yourself in the fire." Let Jamil be in my shoes so that he can know what it means to dive into a sea of fire. Khaduri, the tobacco vendor, said at the wedding night of Khoshi the Persian, "Have mercy on me! Protect me, and God will protect you!" On that night, one thing led to another, and a lot of awful events took place. Could Khaduri be a thief? Until now I couldn't believe it. No, I swear by the One who created all the various fears in me that he was not a thief. Who would believe that I, Selman, who was afraid of my own shadow, would end up shooting a poor boy? And now I flee to the border and go through these frightful dangers, against my will and despite the trembling and shivering in my heart.

Where was Khaduri now? If he were here, I would have felt relieved from my troubles and taken heart a little by talking to him. In God's name, protect me! I was scared and felt terrible when somebody bumped me in Karbala. I stopped seeing the yellow and the red, saw only the black, intertwined by faces with tense eyes, listening, silent, waiting, and frightened.

Have you ever looked carefully into people's eyes? Sabriyah's eyes were flirtatious. They fluttered, then subsided and turned into sorrow as deep as life.

Khaduri's look was lost and fixed on the beginning of the alley. When the black ghost appeared, his eyes turned aside, but where was Khaduri now? Once, he burglarized Shukur's home at night. I didn't have the chance to look into his eyes because I was preoccupied with the true intrinsic nature he had suddenly revealed. God reveals hidden things. After the black ghost left, I noticed Khaduri's anxious glances. What was happening here in the dark? Why was I going slowly to cross the border? Have mercy on me! I was shivering. Where was Khaduri, the tobacco vendor? If he had been here, I would have sought his protection. Now, after all, I was surrounded by blackness and with troubled eyes reflecting all that might happen in the world.

Khaduri, Khaduri! His looks resembled Khaduri's, staring at me. Was he a Jew or a Muslim?

The unknown and the dangerous, fearful journey was a bond between us. A bump—what's happening? Another bump, a sharp and abrupt turn—the driver was crazy, and I went out of my mind. The Angel of Death must have been following us. Oh Rabbi Me'ir Ba'al ha-Ness, the saint! Oh Ezekiel the prophet! In what direction were we going? Were we closer to you, oh Ezekiel the prophet? Or were we closer to Jonah the prophet, and Nahum el-Qoshi, the saint?

Have you ever seen a person who doesn't know where he's being led, to the north or the south? Would we cross a river or go through mountains? It didn't matter if we fled; the main thing was to arrive there safe and sound.

Where are you, Khaduri? Give me a cigarette, Khaduri! I owe Khaduri for his numerous favors. He gave me hundreds of cigarettes, for God's sake.

"Give me a cigarette, Khaduri!" I made demands on the kind and type of cigarette—Craven A, a strong cigarette that makes you doze. "Bring it now, Khaduri! I need it. Where is it, Khaduri? Give it to me, Khaduri!" And Khaduri gave me a cigarette, but in the end, I turned out to be the bad person. Khaduri used to treat me in a pleasant and tender manner, lending me his ears. If Khaduri hadn't listened to me, I would have exploded long ago. He would always satisfy me when I asked for a cigarette, "Give me one, Khaduri!" But I mistreated Khaduri by avoiding him and only went to him when in need of help.

"Bring me my tray of goods! Give me a cigarette, Khaduri!"

"Here is a cigarette, Selman."

No, no! It doesn't make sense, my ears misled me, my mind deceived me, and my eyes met his. His eyes were calm, with the handkerchief hiding a part of his face. His eyes smiled, and my eyes seemed to be tricking me too. This was a mirage of the mind, echoes of my fear and insanity. I only hoped that my life's dream would become a reality.

"Selman, don't you want a cigarette?"

I dug in my ear to clean it so I could hear him well, wiped my eyes, and fixed my eyes on him, and there I was, crossing a dreadful border in order to make a more startling crossing. My surprise was great at finding Khaduri, but it was more amazing that Khaduri was with me in this shipment of people wandering in the wilderness.

"Why, Khaduri? Why did you take risks and throw yourself into the fire, Khaduri? I'm forced to leave the country, as it is written. But what forced you to burglarize people's homes and take a risk for a dead end? I want an explanation." The exhaustion of walking made me lightheaded, and I didn't know whether I should laugh, cry, shout, whisper, or not say anything at all, but I evidently fell out of the whirlpool of my absolute fright and ended up curious and confused.

But I stuck to Khaduri. "Why so, Khaduri? For the first time, you offered me a cigarette without being asked." I put off accepting the cigarette because there were more important things to do now. I craved a cigarette, but smoking was forbidden now. "Why Khaduri, why? And Aminah? And what about your scaling the walls of her home that night? What about taking the risk of throwing yourself in a sea of darkness?"

Khaduri had said quietly, "Just wait until we cross the border safely, then I'll tell you the whole story."

I wondered what happens in man's innermost being. Everything is changeable and contradictory. I craved a cigarette, and now I was asking somebody who seemed as far away as Sabriyah and Jamil Rabi, as far away as the gallows.

"Later, Khaduri, I'll lean on you and close my eyes. If, by the help of God, we arrive safe and sound, wake me up and give me a cigarette. Also, tell me your story."

It seemed that I didn't know anything of what was going on in the world. Jamil was right when he used to shove his ten fingers in my face laughing at me—may God bestow His bounty on Jamil, 'Amam, Ya'qub, and every good human being I left behind in Baghdad! As for Sabriyah, I wish that God, may He be praised, bestow on her the fullness of His bounty. Was I going to doze off on Khaduri's shoulders?

3—Jamil Rabi

My mouth was busy drinking the thick, grainy coffee. Only one exclamation, no sigh. The sediment of everything sunk to the bottom. I have sunk to the bottom of the cup with the unwanted sediment, like my existence, Abu Ghallubi, I have been talking to deaf walls. The unfortunate illness of the night guard had lasted for a long time. I threw myself on my bed; the other bed was free.

May troubles stick to you, Jamil, I said to myself. Even Selman turned out better than me. He's a Zionist and he took his illusion to the finish line. I wonder if he cursed me now and shook the holy mezuzah to bring about my death. Well, it didn't matter what Selman Hashwah thought of me now; I've sunk to the bottom of the coffee cup, amid scum and dregs. Was I fooling myself, thinking I had done so much for the cause? Did I believe I was a true Communist? What had I done for the cause so far? Did I save poor children? Did I succeed in making the hand of a Jew hold that of a Christian and a Muslim?

You only think you do good, Jamil. But in fact, you do nothing. The mouth of the furnace is greedy, thirsty, and sucking up coffee while you are left at the bottom of the cup with Naji el-Jundi. Your destiny has stuck to you like the outline of a shadow, Jamil thought to himself. I went to the feedbox and found animals ruminating the feed of the distant past, and then got tired of dice, the visible and invisible, the opposites, and then was led by the nose through an absurd game—the game of mechanical human machines.

I would pluck my strings, laugh, sigh, and fight with myself. This machine is full of paradoxes! My qanun needed to be tuned up, but I was tired, saying nothing, not moving. The *sol* sounded like *si*, and the *si* sounded like *re*, and the *di* flat. And the half tune sounded like a three-quarter tune. I hadn't lost every game yet; I was still splashing, stumbling, falling, and getting up. I pleaded with Naji el-Jundi to remember to fill his rotten life with the melodies of the qanun.

He said to me in a voice similar to the hooting of an owl, "Since the incident with Yahya, the butcher, and his shooting, all the cafés were closed in my face. They said to me, 'We don't want headaches and problems, man; you come to cause problems and troubles, and because of you, there'll be shooting again, driving the customers away from the café. You'll lead us to bankruptcy rather than making us wealthy.' So in which café should I sit with the boys? Where will I listen to 'Abd el-Wahab?"

I answered Naji in bewilderment, "Put troubles on the back burner, pay no attention! Aren't you the one who said, 'Pay no attention to troubles?'" He was on the verge of crying in my presence. I held back when he tried to kiss my hand. I was floating with him on the surface of the refreshing wine of the world. Naji's hopes were withering now, sinking with him like the coffee sediment, and I was caught with him amid the everlasting mud of it. I still have a ghost of "someone" who likes to do favors and provide the needs of others.

I said to him, "Okay, talk more, provided you stop telling me the old story of the dog." Well, what would it matter if I heard Naji el-Jundi's story a hundred more times as long as he enjoyed himself on my account and felt human because of it?

I'm left with the boys only, 'Aibah and Marrudi, holding their candy, sesame sweets, and money. But both food and money are destined to spend the night with me and wait in my pocket until the next day. In the meantime, let the two boys dream of paradise lost. By bribing them, I enjoy a consummate pleasure in my life, play with the two boys for a few moments, then go with Shridah until his last round in the cafés.

Such a string board of rusty wires could only produce strangled sounds, echoes of the melancholy melodies of *Hijazkar*, *Saba*, and *Rast*. I was still a ghost of someone, and I cast this ghostliness into the weak heart of deceit, within death, so that Shridah could remove the deceit in order to master playing the qanun, to become a human being, not only the ghost of a human being. But whether a human or ghost, we let the world continue in its madness. Was it because of the season, the eggplant season when people got crazy, or was it an accident? Or was there something in the world's madness and in Joudi's craziness that ordinary people and the blind didn't understand?

4—Naji el-Jundi

Is a man forbidden to soothe his hunger with a piece of bread? I tell you again, Jamil, my brother, that I was made to love creatures. I chose art for my party. Art is love and reason. It is a shield for me against the insanity of the world. I have accepted the flowers and the thorns in life, but my country is in turmoil, and Baghdad has gone out of its mind. I avoided the thorny pricks of the withering branch of flowers, but their points have entered my heart. My heart throbbed and leaked a drop of blood, and the passion rose to my head. Only recently, my mind began to struggle with my good heart, and I'm afraid that the struggle will ruin things for me. How could I voluntarily lose a thing as bright as the pure depth of my heart, all because of my rotten mind? My God! Are you listening, my brother Jamil?

I was between the hammer and the anvil. The sun was bright and had points like sword blades, and these bright blades of sunlight entered my eyes like fainting spells coming in waves. My brother Hesqail said, "Get going, Sha'ul! Take the Turkish delight and hold the pastry. The people in Battawin have run out of patience. They have a circumcision celebration, and we haven't brought the stuff to them yet. Go and come back fast!"

I would take it in a horse carriage or by taxi. There was no time to argue with Hesqail. I wouldn't cause pain to anyone. The celebrants are fixing their eyes on the road, waiting. I would extract the thorn from their joy caused by my brother Hesqail in the habit of asking, "Do you have enough money?"

"Enough. Six hundred fils." He offered me another dinar for the prick of pain, for traveling money. Hesqail wasn't usually so generous, but I was his brother, his flesh and blood, and blood can't turn into water.

'Abd el-Wahab and his "el-Gundul" song, or as you said, *el-shundul*, or "The Hymn of Art"—I beg you to play it for me. It's by the musician of our generation, Muhammad 'Abd el-Wahab, my master. It's liable to make me forget and revive the tyranny of my compassionate heart. It also lulls all the questions of my wounded mind.

I sang "The Hymn of Art" two years ago during a gathering at the Washshash Base before a big crowd of officers and soldiers. I was a reserve soldier then, stationed there for six months. I was a Jew with a golden throat. As it was written, " . . . and they labored hard in the Egypt of Pharaoh four thousand years ago," and now I was a Jewish soldier in Washshash Base. The other soldiers were on the front. After four thousand years—clay, mortar . . . the distant past and today. What a pity that I took off my military uniform, because otherwise I would have been able to cope with the nagging in my mind.

Yesterday I came back broken and didn't even have one fils in my pocket. I heard people singing "The Hymn of Art." I also sang it during the circumcision celebration. I thought it would be received excitedly like at the Washshash Base. Don't look at my sloppy appearance and think that I am the way I look. I have a genuine gift. Officers and soldiers were jammed into the hall to hear me singing in front of the microphone. When I reached the line, "Who honored and promoted art but King Faruq," I recalled I was in Baghdad, a soldier with a golden voice singing in front of high-ranking officers. When I sang that part last night, I didn't care because I left everything up to natural inspiration.

Are you listening to me, 'aini Jamil? I had taken a carriage, impatiently striving to get to Battawin on time. I probably kept them waiting. They cursed my brother a thousand times and probably me too; there's no doubt about it, my brother is negligent. They had ordered the pastry and the Turkish delight three days in advance and paid cash. But Hesqail left them worrying. Had I been in Hesqail's shoes I would have delivered the order before dawn. It was fated for me to eat my heart out and be the thorn in their joy.

The carriage driver asked, "Do you want to bargain?"

"How much?" I responded.

"Two dirhams," he said without hesitation. I almost left him to hire another carriage, but I remembered that time was not in my favor and that I had to arrive as fast as possible at the house in Battawin. To be fair, Jamil, do you think that two dirhams are enough from Taht el-Takyah to Battawin? I bargained with the driver.

"No, three dirhams. If you agree, that's okay with me. If you don't, don't be angry, we're just bargaining." The carriage driver scratched his head and said, "Sir, I'm afraid you didn't hear me well. I told you two dirhams only, not four."

"And I am telling you three now. If you don't like it, then forget it."
I'm not my brother Hesqail. I pay for what I get. I don't know how
to steal away the rights of a poor carriage driver who doesn't realize
that he deserves more for his service. Well, what about my rights?
That's a different matter. It's up to my brother Hesqail and me.

The stupid carriage driver shrugged his shoulders. Content with
the bargain, he said, "Board the carriage!" I obeyed and answered,
"Hurry up!" His two horses galloped at tremendous speed on the
melting street tar.

What was I saying, Jamil? Damn you, Jamil. My thoughts were
lost, but I quickly retrieved them. Speed was our common denomina-
tor. Our world is racing now. Inspired by my genial master, an intel-
lectual charge came upon me: "Art is love, life, and inspiration—not
politics."

Without stuttering or hesitation, I quickly began to sing, "Who
has honored and promoted art besides the prince regent?" If you
could have just heard the storm of applause, Jamil! The lieutenant
colonel gave me a huge collection of records that contained all the
songs of Hammuli, Darwish, and Sheikh Salamah. I'll keep it and
take it to my grave as a symbol of the brotherhood of peoples and
classes that art has achieved.

I sang "The Hymn of Art" again last night at the circumcision
celebration in Battawin. You're right, Jamil. But you really don't
know me and my pursuit of good deeds. Don't make fun of me,
Jamil! Please, don't tease me. Rushing to help when needed is more
than a duty. Does it take a fortune-teller to know the celebrants in
Battawin had neither myrtle nor the prophet Elijah's chair required
for the ceremony?

I volunteered and came back to downtown Baghdad and brought
the chair and the myrtle and rolled up my sleeves to assist the hosts.
Soon it was evening. I didn't know how the time passed so quickly.
I put the towel on my shoulder and ran to serve the guests. They
begged me to stay at the party. How could I turn them down? As
usual, I forgot myself and sang the Hebrew circumcision song "Besiman Tob" with the musical troupe—I hope you follow suit and have

children, my friend Jamil. There I sang "The Hymn of Art" or "The Internationale"—the hymns of my party and of my master, Art.

It was a full moon, and I satisfied all my senses and my conscience and left staggering with joyous intoxication. I had one dinar and change in my pocket, enjoying myself after telling such a good story like the one about the dog that struggled in the toilet while the rabbi's daughter opened her legs wide in the room, waiting for me impatiently. So, Jamil, don't be mad! All I want is to please you. Yesterday's story had an upsetting end.

Well, damn you, Jamil! I'll go back to our first story, okay? The important thing is that you don't get mad at me. Don't mumble, please! I said that I'd wrap up the story about my poor dog. Listen to this part only.

I was like a king without a throne, wrapped in darkness and intoxicating dreams. I stood by Nasr Square singing in a low voice to myself, looking for a carriage. Suddenly, a woman wearing ragged, shabby clothes appeared out of the darkness. No, no, you know I don't believe in demons. The poor woman had nothing to do with demons. If you had seen her, you would have started to cry. The whore of politics will demonstrate more things, and so will the female demon. But that is something else, neither a whore nor a demon, rather a poor human being who puts her mouth to my ear and whispers, "May God protect your honor! I have children in the hut with no dinner. I left them screaming and I'm ashamed to beg."

You're a Communist, Jamil, so what would you do? The joy of intoxication I had flew away, and no hope for the future remained; it quickly sunk into the mud of people's sufferings. I couldn't save the joy, the future, and myself unless I saved this troubled woman.

First, I emptied my pockets and gave her all my money. Would you consider yourself and keep a dirham to get home? If so, allow me to say that you're selfish. I couldn't have done otherwise in such a situation, and if I had thought about myself I would have been like you. I don't believe in shiny mottoes; I only have complete faith in my work.

I beg of you Jamil, tell me, is God good? Are people evil? This thought has been troubling me.

I had to walk for an hour to reach Bab el-Mu'azzam. I had only my feet and this other joy that would accompany me on my way. As soon as I covered the distance, I would be in my bed at an hour after midnight when the nightmares of the world couldn't disturb me any longer. No, I'm not a human hero. I'm just an ordinary person, a cheerful man singing parts of "The Hymn of Art." I reached Bab el-Sharqi and then everything went wrong.

Something like the Angel of Death appeared to me in the form of two soldiers. They were hunting, drunk. My appearance made me identifiable, and I was wearing civilian clothes. Where was my uniform? May their Adam's apples be silenced by disease!

"Give!"

I guess you were right sometimes. I should have slipped one dirham in my pocket and then started the journey. Should I have taken the bus or walked? I should have kept one dirham for an emergency, for the two soldiers. But to deprive hungry children crying for food of one dirham while riding a carriage like a sultan is unworthy, just as if I had never done anything good. But the dirham would have been useful.

"I swear by God, I didn't have even one fils in my pocket!"

Suddenly, I got hit in the head, and the intoxicating joy disappeared.

"So what are you doing at night? You're a Zionist spy."

"I, a Zionist? I belong to the Party of Art. Go and ask about me if you don't believe me. Everyone knows me."

"So, give!"

"I swear by God, I don't have any money. As proof, I'm going from Battawin to Bab el-Mu'azzam by foot."

"You bastard! Were you in a subversive cell in Battawin?"

"What cell are you talking about? I'm a good person, and just because I'm good, some call me crazy."

Another blow.

"Give us money! Otherwise we'll accuse you of Communism."

My mouth went dry. The brown soldier said to the black soldier, "Hold him, Abbas, don't let him go!" I wish he would fall ill for this Abbas-like cruelty! His first blow broke a bone in my arm.

"Search me and if you find anything, do whatever you please."

Abdalak, Jamil! What blows, fisticuffs, and slaps on the face I received in addition to getting frisked and accused of Communism or Zionism, or both! Then there were whispers. May he be beheaded! What an Abbas he was! That night there were both officers and non-commissioned officers in the audience, and everyone in the Wash-shash hall applauded me. The slaps and blows my body absorbed from their hands resounded all the way to Bab el-Sharqi. I wish that Abbas's hand be paralyzed! What a heavy hand he had! He broke my ribs and said to me, "You pimp! Where are you hiding your money? Do you want to laugh at me and cheat me? Can there be a Jew without money?"

Tell them, Jamil, you know. Isn't it true, that there are a lot of Jews in Abu Sifain and Hinnuni without dinner, tens of thousands who have wasted away and starved, spending the night with nothing more than a glass of water sweetened by a spoon of sugar? The soldiers looked greedy and threatening in their brutality. I already had a blow here and a blow there.

I wished the eyes of Abbas be swollen when he said, "Choose between being beaten and being taken to the police station. Two witnesses say you blasphemed Islam."

What would you do? Which choice is easier? I said to Abbas, "I'm at your disposal, do whatever you want with me, only don't take me to the police station."

They continued to beat me. The cup of my joy was smashed, and splinters wounded my insides. I tried to see what was in front of me and only saw a blackness where I had fallen and gotten lost. I hope you don't hear evil things anymore. I was led around a thousand turns and a thousand times I went from side to side. How should I get to Bab el-Mu'azzam from here? How? From where? From here—I was signaling to show the way, don't you see? Do you know what they said? I don't want to repeat it to you. I looked at the watch. It was a quarter to four and my heart couldn't stop nagging at me.

Please tell me, Jamil, did I do something bad? Why does God punish me like this? There is this fundamental debate between us.

You ask, "Where does God exist?" while my question is, "Why did God create bad people in the world?"

5—Ya'qub, 'Amam's Son

Let my face be smeared by the shit of my ass for what I have done to myself! But I doubted this self-slander and was embarrassed about questioning my past and present, about comparing what had happened with the events that were taking place now like two opponents standing on trial in the arena of my mind. And who was to judge? Who would look into the case and do justice to the oppressed and the vulnerable? Without being sure, I sensed that something was wrong and unnatural, which distorted the truth and changed people's behavior.

I was living at ease but circumstances cast me out and, in return, I cast out God's bliss and bounty. Then confused and painful shreds of longing took root, and I became content with the refuse of this world, but it rejected me and kept its distance. Still, everything became false and lost, the money, peoples' hearts and my life. Even the lucky 'Irq el-Sawahil bone charm turned false and could no longer make one piece of 'Aishah's bread fall to the bottom of her clay oven. The world became like a corpse with outstretched legs. Such devastating luck was choking me while everything was turning into shiny counterfeit money, into double-blank. The bad luck insisted on clinging to me, and the burning sun of Baghdad struck my life. Then I urinated on the bone of ill omen and threw it into the Tigris.

Was I deluding myself? What was the way out, Majid, my brother? Where was Majid now to silence them one by one? I was lying quietly on my bed thinking. Did I give in when the world spit in my face? So, here I am, just a worker sticking labels on juice bottles. Be ashamed of yourself, Ya'qub! The other day the chocolate burned, and I brought handfuls of it for Joudi. In the factory after the whistle was blown, the workers never stopped talking about the upcoming closure. My job there was as short as the apricot season. Was this job too much for me? I was content with being unfortunate, as if this were not enough. Was I really cheating myself and hiding away by denying what was going on inside me? Was I playing hide and seek with fate as imposed by the filthy gypsy whore? What's next? Am I blind? Don't I see what's ahead of me?

The continuous, wide gap between facts and lies bothered me, as if each of us were beyond such circumstances. This gap could welcome our end as a wonderful event stronger than fate. 'Alwan, our lifelong friendship has been deeply rooted for a long time, so why should the gap between Jews and Muslims grow wider now? Are the roots in the dust of this land uprooted so swiftly? These roots have become integrated into the history of this country more deeply than anything else. And my prayer, the pure, holy kiss behind which stands another spirit, has now become an impure stake driven into your heart. And the sword that once chopped off heads is defiled with hatred. It stains meek souls with blood and accuses us of treason. You may drink our blood to your fill, but will it quench your burning thirst, Mr. 'Alwan? Could the blood turn into water, 'Alwan, once my life-long friend?

I couldn't understand, for there was no stability, and I was swept up in a murderous disgust for everything around me, stemming from the obscurity of things, a disgust that widened the breach and allowed the poison to enter. I had heard about the Baha'i faith in the Alliance Club before I started to stick labels on the bottles in the 'Ulwiyah factory, and I sometimes frequented the club where a few Jews were engaged in various contemporary "opiates" like Freemasonry, Communism, and Zionism, but the Baha'i faith was something else.

I was still doggedly devoted to life, and nothing could dissuade me from the belief that life was stronger than becoming a mere straw in the mocking wind of the Gypsy Whore. So I was shocked by the rapid disintegration of friendship under the force of filthy politics. But my fingers were weary with fatigue and as pale as a lemon peel. The Baha'i ideas stuck in my mind like a stake, but different in a way from the bloody one. Could this stake succeed in uprooting the other one from the world? Spirituality and purity? The Baha'i faith, the other stakes! Was it possible that my heart could gather together the scattered fragments of love?

There exists love in religion . . . "And you shall love your neighbor as yourself." Majid is like my brother, so are Hamid, HamaDa, and the incredible Mahdi. The land seemed as spacious and compassionate as my mother, 'Amam. Shame on you, Ya'qub, I said to myself! You're an imbecile, a moron. Now you're looking back at the past—my father died here, so did my grandfathers and my forefathers. They were Jews who adhered to their religion and country. Where are the righteous people now? In fact, I'm religious too and I pray and fast, but why then should I dig into modern heresy when I already have the age-old tradition of "loving your neighbor as yourself." After all, love exists in Islam and Christianity as well. So who has gone bankrupt? Has man really declared the bankruptcy of a love so deeply rooted?

I was weary and collapsing on my bed in the evening while my mother remained silent and isolated in another corner of the room. The situation became worse, the gap grew wide, and the house, like my heart, continuously vomited its tenants and declared, like man, bankruptcy. No! I may have lost things, but I wouldn't lose my friends or my love for the country of my fathers and forefathers, even if the abyss would hold a sea of hatred, and even if the precious and pure jewel were taken away. I would be here forever, 'Alwan. And if only one Jew were to remain in Baghdad, know that I would be that one.

Pessimism penetrated and surrounded me and made me afraid. I was hiding inside myself and avoiding what was happening around me. My strength of decision wavered and shivered in the violent storm as my anguish increased. With trembling hands void of strength, I adhered courageously to my destiny, continuing to cling despite fatigue and a near inability to move. While jumping out of my bed with fear and hugging uncertain life in the violent storm, I said to my mother, 'Amam, who sat silently in the corner of the room, not fully aware of her own thoughts, "I'm going to see the fellows in the café. If I'm late, don't worry."

I really longed to see my friends, and with my heart and soul I desired to be close to them.

6—Joudi al-Qarawchi

Da, da, da! The beetle was afflicted with the black smallpox. Da, da, da! A human mind fell from the lofty Tower of Babel. Da, da, da!

"Stay home and don't go out! I won't be able to stand it if they were to take you and hang you. Your sisters' deaths were enough," 'Atiyah said.

For many days I roamed in order to find a hanged mouse, but I found the rotten skeletons of elephants instead. My friend with the pockmarked face and dented, fleshy eye was angry with me. He stuffed my head with images that he pulled from the throat of whales swimming quickly through the sky of Baghdad. I saw the pickax swinging in there.

"The mice gathered under your nostrils!"

I could feel those who had caught cold in the reaping swing of the sickle, then I used my ax to carve out a cellar from which I ascended to a hanging coconut. I struck it with my stick, and the grounded mountain split into two. Corpses of footless people and hundreds of midgets crawled toward the stone.

Da, da, da! Black smallpox afflicted the beetle. The Tower of Babel collapsed on the heads of the wise men and it was destroyed. I desired to eat the apple, and Adam gave me a golden quince. My mother said, "Don't eat the quince, otherwise they'll hang you."

The quince had the circular shape of a coconut, like the apple, the steel skull, the bow, the earth, the thoughts, and the ambitions of the wise men.

Da, da, da! The vicious circle with the hole, a sickle! I said to my insignificant friend, "Why is there the sickle and the pickax?"

I found fields of blood the eyes can't count amidst the nails of the devil compassionate. Then there were fields of harvested mice. My mother said to me, "It is good that you don't know how to love. If you did, you would cause troubles for me. Don't you know they hang anyone who loves?"

Da, da, da! I loved the worms despite the hoopoe bone. I extracted them from the golden apple and ate them. An anonymous woman gave me the apple. My friend, the whale, said, helping me, "Don't worry, no one will harm you if you forget names. The names are the wise men's invention."

Da, da, da! Is it true that the world is supported by the devil's two horns? "The devil entered this place and hasn't left," my mother said.

The devil! The dissipation! The fish! The germ! The worms! The gallows!

"Say, the reasonable man loves the sickle and the pickax," the one-eyed man with the twenty-one noses objected.

I was not confused, because children are no longer the devil's son. My mother said, "It's great that 'Aibah no longer picks on you."

Da, da, da! So 'Aibah will be hanged. I cried for the children and I laughed like a human. My mother said a thousand times, "Be careful, they'll hang you; they'll hang you!" She also said a million times, "The devil hasn't left yet."

Da, da, da! The pickax! The gallows! The sickle! 'Aibah! The devil! Does my stupid mother know what these things mean? I'm crazy and scream nonstop with my craziness. Da, da, da! Down with the wise men! My greatest love is the worms, the only love in the wise men's world.

7—Sa'idah Ghawi

I kept on looking into the dark corridor and saw piles of clothes in the room, heaps of rags, heaps of obliterated life hanging like dust particles on the walls. I was patching and stitching the clothes, daydreaming. I concocted the events in my mind. The eyes of my father, brother, and sister opened anxiously. During my struggle, Baghdad was overflowing and swaying back and forth.

After the resurrection of my soul from meaningless sleep, my mother said, "May their eyes be gouged out, those of your cousins from both sides, Ya'qub, and all the Jews."

Did I realize that there were high trees across the river in the Karkh District and that Karim's house there would soon become mine? When Karim crossed the river with me I was attacked by a feeling of ugly loneliness and estrangement, lost among the women's headbands, the tattoo marks, the black clothes, the smells of acid coming from bodies, and the filthiness of the wholesale farmer's market, and garages. Going home to visit "the in-law's," I saw unfamiliar faces and cousins. My mother knew that 'Aziz had vanished, and I saw 'Abdallah Ghawi among a herd of cattle driven by a Bedouin holding a rod. I also saw an army of flies humming continuously and clung to Karim.

Karim placed my hands on his heart and whispered, "What are you afraid of?"

Nothing! Love is stronger than this fear, but another fear was barking in Jewish homes, which never ceased fabricating illusions in their miserable and crowded rooms in the narrow alleys of Bani S'id. This other fear had reached me. It is the fear of confronting and discovering love that had overwhelmed me. Everything had fallen behind, leaving ghosts and a deep vacuum. Love was stronger than entire obstacles, but Latifah was hard-hearted. She could widen the crack in me—a crack through which a violent wind blows and caused me to cling to Karim. My conflicts would narrow and deepen, however. "You and I are the world" still resounded in my ears like successive echoes inside a forsaken cellar. It was a real voice reaching me once more, not just echoes, "So why dig up the graves of the dead?"

The two of us were alone in his home, but the ghosts rose from the graves, and without moving a finger dust flew from these graves. I had desired long ago to leave or pour piles of mud or even cement on top of them. But the devils' harmful spirits would resist. I was still fighting them by my love.

Karim gave me a book. "I brought you the Koran," he said.

I touched it—the other destiny. The Torah was there with the ghosts. I used to fast on Yom Kippur. From now on, would I fast during Ramadan? I embraced the Koran in order to escape from all the evil spirits. Karim surprised me when I yearned to escape only with love and no Ramadan and no Yom Kippur either. I clung to him hard and asked, "What has happened? Have you suddenly become God-fearing and pious?"

I heard his answer and escaped the smile of his lips and eyes. It was better for me to disregard this conflict and just flee. It was a good idea to block out my struggle with a thoughtless wall and only buttress it with the weight of Karim's love.

"Because of you I'll become pious, fast, pray, and stop loose living. No more liquor or women," Karim promised.

Undoubtedly, he meant her, Salimah. The time was right. I put Salimah in front of me like an amulet against my confusing fear. How strange was fate! Salimah. The agony perched on my heart. Salimah was a whore and Jewish; revenge and the Koran was my other destiny. I turned the pages and read with difficulty, "And we shall smite them with lowliness and humiliation."

"Who are they?" I asked.

"The Jews," he said in a natural manner.

"Karim, don't forget I'm Jewish."

"You were. From tomorrow you'll be my wife according to Muslim law."

Under the pressure of this accursed conflict, I let out a long sigh, and my thoughts dispersed in dense suffocating puffs of black smoke. They will say I converted, and Latifah would mercilessly throw coals on me, coals the devil uses to stone people. My father would kill me. I laughed. My laughter was a sharp and painful bone piercing my divided mind. Was everything really vile and evil? Really?

"Karim, my relatives are Jews. You can't separate the bone from the flesh!"

"Because of this they'll be safe. Have you forgotten tomorrow? In the second round, not even one Jew will be spared, but thanks to you, your relatives will be saved. Isn't that good enough?"

"Karim, how can the Jews have a country now? Though it is written in the Koran, 'And we shall smite them with lowliness and humiliation.'"

Did I forget about tomorrow? Did I forget the humiliations? Tomorrow! The other decisive round, my other destiny. That love was a wild fragrance that I hadn't experienced before. My first love was sincere and strong. Karim told me, "You and I and the world. Why dig up the graves of the dead?"

The humiliation! . . . I am deprived. Salimah was really vulgar and low, and her face was smeared over with a creamy falsity. By the same powerful falsehood my brother 'Aziz was deceived and humiliated. 'Aziz had been roaming aimlessly and walking with his head down, working as a busboy in a nightclub. Can't you see the difference between 'Aziz and Karim, I asked myself. Then a pinch of nausea as the heart of pale affection died . . . Wasn't that so? The rag! What a difference between a rag and Karim's stamen-like stature that fills my eyes with love, making the world's heart throb! Another stamen exists under his clothes, hardened like a stake. My fingers slipped quickly into this stem, into the other destiny. I wondered if there was a difference between Karim's stem and Ya'qub's. Did Ya'qub have a stem like this? Did Yusuf Abd el-Nabi have it—or my cousins, or those who were my cousins? Ya'qub was another lowly person who lost his life; he was another refugee from a miserable fate and humiliation. They all fled like mice.

Rags were hanging from the gallows in the crazy safety of humiliation. This disgraceful powerlessness made a most bizarre surrender to death, because there was no way out, because of the eternal stain—the curse. This was my previous destiny, and I ran away from it to love and power. The hands of 'Abdallah Ghawi would never touch me. On the contrary, I would pluck off his own facial hair, scratch his skin, and wipe away tears of shame and disgrace. I had mixed feelings of happiness and sadness. Love alone was a guarantee to heal me, and his love was indeed a great miracle, a miracle that steered feeling, appeased thought, and impartially guided my emotions. How now? I was lost again. Wasn't Karim my last hope?

I had already risen from the depth of the grave, and tomorrow the second round would take place, and real power would wipe away the humiliation of my family. My family would be safe. Well, what would happen if they were to leave the country and run away? I felt as if I were whipped.

Latifah was hard-hearted; all of them were selfish and mean-spirited. In a tone of haughty arrogance, Latifah said, "You're marrying him, and what will we do then? Who will marry us?" She was selfish and thought only of herself.

Karim said while tickling me, "Hush, come back to this world! Why are you daydreaming?"

"What?"

I paid attention. Why hadn't I stopped falling into the lap of love? My family wouldn't leave me behind. Certainly not! Humility gained the upper hand again: "Karim, don't you have cousins to marry my sisters?"

I sighed. All of Baghdad were my sisters' cousins. I would include those who were only relatives, those who were "my cousins," with my noble new relatives. By all means, the Ghawi family should be saved from repeated humiliation in the second round of Farhûd. Well, what would happen if they got fed up and left before the decisive round came? No, my mother wouldn't do this. She told me in a fighting spirit, "Let their eyes explode and their bellies split!"

I felt numbness invading my arms. Karim said, "Don't bring anything with you, I've prepared a trousseau fit for a queen." I was invaded by pride but couldn't get rid of the red dress and yellow nightgown I had worn the night he had banged on the door for the first time. I also wore the bracelets and the gold necklace with the dangling gold pieces. The jeweler had melted down the Star of David when I became trapped and humiliated by death. Despite the humiliation I didn't wish to die. Also the jeweler had melted down the Hebrew letters for El Shaddai, "God is my Lord." There was no doubt that the letters of the word Allah were stronger than the Hebrew El Shaddai. The numbness was still spreading like columns of crawling

ants. The night reigned with confusion in my heart, opening wide
my tangled emotions, which cried for Karim. I called his name for
protection, a love charm, and said, "Salimah" as a charm of hatred
and reason for revenge.

The snoring of my father coming from above and my brother
being lost were both signs of blindness yielding to humiliation, both
reasons to run. Latifah dreamed in her sleep. I fabricated illusions
and dresses day and night. I felt a twinge of affection—Latifah, don't
think I'm mad at you. I'll compensate you. Who knows what will
come of the unexpected?

Farhah Ghawi asked, "Have you already decided to go?" My
mother knew! I was silent. My chin and mouth trembled and contracted, and both joy and sadness informed my tears. My mother
asked again in corrosive despair, "You mean you decided?"

I wiped my tears. This other fear was actually stronger—you,
Farhah, gave your blessings for this love. I whispered to God for Farhah Ghawi not to give me up at the last moment, not to badmouth
the most pleasurable things I had ever lived for.

Do you remember, Mother, on Yom Kippur when you were opening your hands and praying upon opening the Ark in the synagogue?
You had prayed that an honest man would come and kidnap your
daughter, that the brethren would win in Palestine. But Karim came.
What was the difference? What was the difference really? And the
brethren did win in Palestine. But Karim was sure of another decisive
round.

"Karim! I kept begging in front of the Torah that God would
send me an honest man. He fulfilled my wish by sending you."

"And what did you think?" he said calmly.

"The Torah fulfills all wishes, why not ours?"

I was still Jewish, and with astonishment and innocence I asked,
"The Torah belongs to the Jews, doesn't it? I know the Torah is the
possession of the Jews and the Koran is yours."

"No, 'aini Sa'idah. When, God willing, we get married tomorrow, everything becomes yours."

We, therefore, were deceiving ourselves and claiming what belonged to others? I was compassionate when I saw how bankruptcy had overtaken the Ghawi family from everywhere.

"So the Jews have nothing?"

"They have money, and . . ." he stopped.

I knew that they also had submissiveness, humility, and the Jewish State. I veered again between his words and my relatives. Which one should I believe? Both promised me contradictory things. I drove away a fly that stung my cheek, and the fly buzzed away. But most likely I was attacking two flies at the same time; the other fly was inside my overworked head. The nagging humming became silent, and only a voice of thunder appeared and flew over me. "You and I alone," it bellowed.

Apologizing to Farhah Ghawi, I said, "I love him, I can't leave him." I imagined that I had a dream akin to a nightmare. Why was Farhah's face so gloomy? Didn't she support me during my love's journey so full of flowers and thorns? My mother had mumbled, "Both ill fortune and bad luck are predestined."

I fell on my mother. Her lap had always protected me. I burst into a muffled cry, "Mother, are you mad at me? Did I turn anyone else down who wanted to marry me?"

Farhah's eyes shone and said with resignation, "No, my dear daughter. Go! May God be with you. What can we do? It doesn't make sense for you to stay buried in your room as if you were keeping an eye on the dead. Go, let your relatives explode and boil in their juices."

Humility is written on their foreheads, on their fate until the Day of Resurrection. Latifah is miserable, and my brother is miserable too, and you, my mother, stand in the middle of us. Who is more miserable?

I glanced at Latifah's sleeping face, frowning and angry even in her sleep. I would be buried here after I left. I carried the bag containing my shabby clothes. He would laugh at me and ask, "What did you bring?" No! I saw the traces of my early life in that bag— memories that would stay with me forever. My second destiny would soon begin. I stepped toward the door hesitantly and slowly, with a mixture of joy, humility, and despair.

Farhah Ghawi whispered, "My daughter, did you forget your money?"

I turned around and stroked her cheek.

"No, Mom, I didn't forget, I left it for Latifah, I don't need it. Maybe she can use it for her marriage."

I had saved over a thousand dinars by hard labor. Farhah lingered, then followed me, as I left to follow my new destiny, carrying unknown things and waging a war within me that broke out into tears. My mother hugged me in the courtyard and shed tears of blood. I kissed her and said crying, "All your life you've been compassionate to others. Why hasn't God been gentle to you?" I then asked some questions of myself and suddenly remembered and fumed with indignation.

I was running, fleeing because I couldn't stand the pain of my conflict. I suppressed a confusing question that often bothers me. I wished to avoid it as long as I had no answer to the question, "Why did God create people as sects and make them Muslims, Jews, and Christians?"

Karim was waiting at the end of the alley full of doubt and fear that he finally overcame and replaced with determination. As for me, I put all of my strength into running without turning my back. Nothing should remain in this world except this absolute love.

Ten

1—Farhah Ghawi

The Day of Judgment! The wheel of the sewing machine stopped because another wheel with sharpened blades rotated, and I was ground by the teeth of the other machine. This is the Day of Judgment involving the hereafter and this world too. It's longer than a thousand years. Did I assassinate the world? Did I destroy the Holy Temple, 'Abdallah? Latifah? Bannutah? The whips of fire lashed me.

Yesterday, a customer said, "I wonder why Sa'idah isn't here, may evil stay away from her! I hope nothing bad happened to her."

Latifah was quick to answer. "She died, she died."

I closed my ears and longed for her—may I die before Sa'idah! You're all murderers! All of you are murderers. They killed me then placed me in the prisoners' dock in the other world.

I sighed heavily with great effort as if hot lava were rolling down my body, and saw fingers made of my flesh pointing at me, issuing the most terrible sentence. And this customer was cheerful upon congratulating me, "Now we're relatives. Why didn't you say anything or distribute one piece of candy or make cries of joy?"

I was embarrassed and mixed up because vengeful fate was getting ready to strike me. Every now and then, Latifah shot from her mouth a sudden lightning bolt, reminding me of my own sorrow and pain.

They lied by naming you Farhah—*joy*. I swallowed what was left of my mixed joy, and Sa'idah vanished in the darkness.

"We're busy now with something other than sewing, come back in a week or two," I told the customer.

Had Latifah heard what Khadijah Umm Tariq said, she would have been insulted and ashamed. I watched behind and in front of me and looked out a long way ahead. I ran away to nowhere, escaping from my shadow. What did I do wrong in my life? No sooner had I married than I bewailed my misfortune, toiling in vain and getting stuck in the mud. Is this my end? Is the world devoid of sense? The meanings of things became very unclear. Even motherhood had become a crime in a world of evil people. I put my hand on my cheek in contemplation and saw that I had lost my way in this peep show in a world of evildoers. The light of the dwindling candle had faded and extinguished. It had been pallid and blurred ever since I had chosen to be a caring mother forever—or say, since I, Farhah, had given birth to the firstborn. Latifah shouted and stepped on my torn heart, wanting to suffocate me as if I were the Angel of Death, as if I robbed people's souls and created death and destruction.

She told me to go to Sa'idah, "Wear a black headband and follow your daughter. Leave! We are motherless. What are you still doing here?"

I spent my life so that my daughters would dilute my blood and suffering. But Latifah is a criminal, a criminal. She attacks me from all directions. What a pity for all my hard work!

I was separated from my own children, cut off from the blood that used to pump life into my body. Now animals dominated my being, tore it apart, and bit inside my stomach and my lost soul. Suddenly, I felt ostracized and lonely roaming aimlessly alone and vulnerable. Does someone know when she is dead? Human beings are deceived just like my name was deceiving. The puzzles challenged me to the breaking point. Were the answers really there while I still didn't know what was happening? I pleaded to the wall of stiff, arrogant faces surrounding me. I experienced lean and gloomy years and kindled candles pleasantly burning to light the way for my children in an unknown desert inhabited by dangers. But is it my end to be thought of as a bad mother who can't tell good from bad and right from wrong? I know nothing; I don't know what the good and the bad things are anymore.

I searched in my mind and found a seed of insane rage growing in the heart of confusion, a dirty curse against Latifah, yes, Latifah. I was choked by my hostile and stiff attitude toward Bannutah and felt a blow in my sick soul. 'Abdallah, has your father died, and are you lamenting him like this? Your father died a long time ago, so why are you preparing so fully to bemoan him? On his face the stubble hairs and glistening tears were ash-colored thorns. He crumpled down in the ashes, not smelling joy but the odor of death instead in the rotten, cold, naked ground. What was good, what was bad, and what was right and wrong? I couldn't tell right from wrong in our criminal world. Answer me, 'Abdallah, whom are you mourning? Don't you see a bad omen about Latifah?

"My Latifah! Which trait of this family did you inherit?"

Latifah shouted back, "Sa'idah died and killed all of us with her. You killed her and killed us. Do you realize what you've done? Open your eyes and ears! Listen, look, feel!"

Why did Latifah cry after the turmoil was over?

"Latifah, Sa'idah left a thousand dinars for you in the box. Your sister loves you." But Latifah averted her glance from the Angel of Death, from me, because I had become the Angel of Death in her eyes.

"Don't mention her name in my presence," Latifah demanded.

Oh God! Sa'idah is the happiest person! The mix-up is as wide as the sea. What comes out of diving to the bottom of the lake? Very often the mind falls away and stops working. There are facts—do you deny them?

"'Abdallah! Your daughter has entered the shelter of married life. She is happy in a world where happiness is scarce."

'Abdallah raised his voice for the first time, "Shut up! May your face be blackened, the grave of your father be sacked, and your mother be burned."

What! The sheep suddenly had a tongue to shoot off his mouth.

"'Abdallah—if you were truly good for something, you would have been named Khairallah, *the bounty of God.*

"May your father be skewered in his grave!"

"What did my father ever do to you? Aren't you afraid he'll pull you next to him?"

Damn you! Damn you! This was doomed from all directions. Why? If Latifah had kissed my hands and feet, it would have drawn praise. You'll see! Jealousy and resentment now blind you. But what was right and what was wrong? You're a criminal, a criminal, I say. I devoted my life to you. I'm a burning candle lighting a safe way for you, and you say, "You killed us." I tried to discover my fault in the confusion of this mistake-ridden world. I know what I killed and why. No, my dear Bannutah, I killed no one, but I am fated to have bad luck. The deep, red illusion blinds the eyes. Nightmares are the world.

What was the use of talking as long as they looked at me as if I were just blindness and darkness? Why me? I shouted hysterically, "Why me, oh disgraced people? Where is God? Doesn't He have a will? And where is your father? And your brother? Do they have one? Bad fortune and rotten luck are like the dark world. I alone carried both the burdens and the charms of this world on my shoulders. I wish you had a good brother, a good father, and good cousins. I alone was the father, the brother, and the householder. I was mother to all."

'Abdallah Ghawi shouted out his sorrow and humiliation at me. "Shut up! May God disgrace your father's grave!" he yelled.

Deceitful visions, illusions were so dense and heavy! The confusion was thick. I thought that I had cast deceit underfoot. I thought I would reform the world, but whatever I did was in vain. Confusion was omnipotent. I didn't know how to solve the puzzles. Should I slap my own face? Should I kill myself and make them mourn? What did they want from me? There was one deterrent; I must first join the funeral ceremony of accumulated confusion and illusion.

Where was 'Aziz? A madam! My son thought his mother was a madam.

Who brought you, 'Aziz? What did your mother do? Did I really tell Sa'idah to leave from the bottom of my heart? This bewitched vicious circle is the outcome for all existing things, hanging over us like chronic disease and only conquered by death, like the unresolved puzzles that have existed from the beginning of creation and will exist until the end of time. Does love kill? Can it be I loved all of them without exception?

Latifah said to me angrily, with the sauciness of one facing the unexplainable mistakes of the world, "You, you're the only one responsible."

The curse! The world is full of sinners and fornicators. I'm the only one accused of killing all because of fornicating fate. Confusion is either shortsighted or blind. I search my way down on a road through a land whose branches lead nowhere. Of course, Jamil, the blind one, knows his way, but I don't know my next step down my far-reaching road through a land of puzzles and deceits. I'm a victim of selfish humanity.

'Aziz appeared to be held by misty illusions, and I moaned again, "I wish to mend the world." A hard ball was formed out of nothingness and fell in the center of the cobwebs breaking into it and creating a hole that soon thousands of spiders were to fill again with more cobwebs. The best thing to do is to go and bring Sa'idah back, but would she come back? Things seemed clearer to me now. Sa'idah would definitely come back, but I would spoil her happiness. As long as this was what they wanted, to hell with it all! Let her stay with them and bury herself there! No! No! The situation was not so. There must be something I was afraid to confess. Did I really tell her "Go away" with all my heart?

Every time I remembered this, the envelope of my heart tore. Sa'idah would return, Sa'idah must return. I was overpowered by fear. I was disappointed many times. All my dreams did not come true, and my delusions drove me to the present situation. Now I was a criminal, as cursed as a snake. But my dread was now everywhere, making me tremble at the shadows of ghosts. I saw now how my dreams had collapsed with the past and yesterday. I saw and heard my daughter. Did I really lose her? Why do they make me feel that it's only my fault? What did I do wrong? What's right?

I heard the incomprehensible echoes of mixed noises, similar to noises of vehicles moving slowly on the crowded Ghazi Street or to the terrible human jabbering in Shorjah Market. The grain of craziness swelled in my mind, and I was frightened, continuously repeating, "I'm going mad." The world was out to get me and grimly filled me with agonizing pain. There was no one helping here. The tenants—where was Na'imah? Where was Sabriyah? Where were the dead? Nothing was there except the echoes of things falling behind me in the abyss of right and wrong. My mind was concentrated on Sa'idah. No! May I die before Sa'idah! Maybe I didn't lose my daughter as I previously thought.

There were dreadful things resembling the knife of the Angel of Death. He lodged in my mind as a pleasant guest but slashed me mercilessly. I'm selfish. Everyone is selfish! Fear became fright with an open mouth, like an open grave.

I was in the courtyard defeated, searching with a candle for a person to guide me or put this crazy voice within me to sleep. I expected a magic word, any word that didn't bear this accusation and unforgiving falsehood. I wanted to hear any word said with joy and cheerfulness, with ease, in a good and plucky spirit that would flatter even a dog by addressing it as "Sir." Then I saw Ya'qub's mother, 'Amam, and felt dismayed. Yes, 'Amam knew how to rear bastards, but she was blind as far as my daughter was concerned. All the tenants and relatives ignored me and covered their eyes with black bands. As a result, I gulped down my dry saliva in a sign of terrible anger fed by blazing frustration, still dominant in its conversion of everything into hatred.

Hatred now overpowered me and made me feel a dire need for anyone, even for a dog that I could call "Sir." I despised it for this reason. My abundant anger sprung from an inexhaustible source, but now I controlled it because I needed a person to talk to. I approached Ya'qub's mother. I had to pretend to smile sweetly, force myself to gush and insert a note of affection into my voice in the style of flattering and hypocritical greetings.

This old woman, 'Amam! Suddenly she became invisible and avoided and ignored me. May her gray hair be smeared with shit—she was not really as good as people thought. May the good persons among them be cursed! All of them were garbage. I released my venom and spat on the ground with disgust, seeing the spit spread out and overflow onto everyone. Then I laughed frantically. All of them, not one of them could stand me anymore. I only wished I knew what I had done wrong.

I was scared. I was still deceiving myself and going to extremes. I spat on the dirty ground and watched 'Amam, the woman with the beautiful face like that of a puppy. No, could it be that even the ground had begun to hate me—or had I lost my mind? Was I starting to imagine all kinds of things? I was looking for a person, only a person to guide me. For heaven's sake, and in the name of all the whores in the world, do me a favor and explain what my fault is!

My eyes caught Lulu, Moshiyah's daughter, entering the house like a storm wearing shabby clothes. Her 'abayah reached her knees; she was gasping; saliva was pouring from her mouth. I asked myself, panting, "Why is she drooling?"

She was looking around bewildered when I asked her, "What's the matter, Umm Marrudi?"

She opened her mouth to talk and then recognized me; she recognized this outcast, this cursed snake. The moment she saw me she coughed and ran away frightened to that old bitch, 'Amam. Even this sloppy, shabby woman looked down at me, so there must be some fault, either in me or in others.

The devil didn't stop weaving his web around my heart and soul, and I realized I was caught with no apparent hope of freeing myself from the net. There was something as small as a mote carried by the sandstorm of events that had thrown Sa'idah from this house into the Karkh District. Sa'idah! I sweetened my bruised pride with hope and then recovered and let my caged thoughts fly again. I fixed my sharp eyes on the door. Three other pairs of eyes stared too. Suddenly my eyes saw the mote flying again in the sandstorm. I had a magnet that picked up this mote, but I still asked what I did wrong and what I did right. Sa'idah was undoubtedly coming and she would soon push open the door and come in.

2—Lulu, Moshiyah's Daughter

I felt the curse and ill omen of Farhah Ghawi. I saw her face when I left and saw the face of this bitch when I came back. I was breathless, exhausted, absent-minded, and melting in the heat of many fires. Oh God, save my mind! Fanning my face with my hands and puffing, I mumbled, "Why doesn't the heat wave break?" Perhaps I was just imagining it. My head seemed on fire. The burning sun penetrated my head, and the courtyard looked like dancing ghosts, and everything in front of my eyes flew like sparkles. Between Farhah Ghawi, the curse and the misfortune on one hand, and me like a pure angel on the other, there existed many differences. It was impossible to extract the impurity while my vision was swerving and dancing.

A refreshing and affectionate voice came near me. "Where were you? I waited for you impatiently, and Marrudi, may God protect him, couldn't bear it any longer and I worried about you. Oh dear, even if you had left to fetch the whole market, you couldn't have come so late," said 'Amam.

Why was the heat not breaking down? It's in my head, my eyes, and my ears. Woe is me! What happened to me today? How many hours was I out? "Do you have cold water from the *hebb* vessel?"

But the orange-blossom water came before the cold water. 'Amam calmed me down. What happened to me today should be recorded in history as a nightmare, or did I lose my mind in places out of this world?

"Relax, take a breath! Even a donkey would die in this heat after being out since the morning. Your face is swollen, and your eyes are as red as blood."

I collapsed, my lungs didn't function, and I wheezed constantly whenever I inhaled or exhaled. Of course the heat did ease up, but even then it burned in my head like the flame in a stove. What had happened? Even a donkey would die in this heat! A nightmare.

"I got lost, may the Name of God protect you, 'Amam! Such a thing never happened to me in my life. I was on my way to Shorjah Market to buy some items for Marrudi. Is there anything wrong with that? As usual I wanted to go to Qahwet el-Zgaygi and pass through it on the way home. Suddenly, I found myself in unknown alleyways where I couldn't make heads or tails out of the way. I entered one alley and saw a thousand alleys, one inside the other. I was alone, without a soul there, and my mind stopped functioning. I traced my steps back and found endless alleys and didn't know whether I was in the Fadil or the Uwainah Quarter. Well, how did I get into such twisted quarters? I've gone to Shorjah Market a thousand times before. Even if I'd been a blindfolded donkey I should have known the way. Oh dear!"

"Why didn't you ask for help?"

"I was afraid. They were forsaken, unfrequented areas, the strangest roads I had ever seen in Baghdad. I didn't know the source of the scented grill, but then it emitted an offensive smell of raw meat coming from the butchers' market. I followed the odor of the meat and saw an isolated herb shop at the end of an alley. In the center of the shop was a sayyid wearing a black turban. A few steps from him I saw another sayyid with a turban sitting and begging. He was blind."

"May evil be driven from us! Where was all this stored up for you? Woe! You suffered a lot."

"My soul was brought down by a slingshot, and the blind beggar chanted, 'Oh charitable people! Help the hungry and the thirsty! God will compensate you with the best with which He endows His most pious worshippers. Oh descendant of the Prophet! Oh God!' Visions of persons, iron chains, beating drums, and bleeding bodies crushed together in my eyes. Half-nude males. 'Ashurah and 'Azwat mourning ceremonies, beating for Husayn. My mouth was dry. The voice of the beggar filled the unknown quarters. I heard it as if a thousand voices were bursting out in unison, in harmonious eulogy. Then I perspired. From where was the smell of the grilled meat coming? The old blind man was alone next to the herb shop. I stretched my hand mechanically and slipped it between my breasts looking for coins. My purse was there but contained only bills. I pulled it out and gave the beggar a quarter of a dinar. He stuffed it into his pocket and opened his hand spontaneously begging again, thanking me, shouting, 'May God protect you for the sake of the faithful Caliph Ali Ibn Abu Talib!' I didn't open my mouth. I didn't say a word. How did the beggar know I was a Jewish woman without my saying a word?"

"They know, don't you think so? The blind are endowed with insightful hearts."

"I was afraid. A white bird flew in front of me, then climbed onto my chest wanting to perch on me, but soon slid down. It had a dark-red spot on its neck. Where was I? Have you ever seen such a bird? They say that the cities of Najaf and Karbala have such birds. They have a spot on their necks like a stain of blood. They say it's Hussein's blood."

A familiar pigeon cooed in the courtyard, an ash-gray pigeon with a black stripe around its neck. "*Coocoo ekhti*," it tenderly warbled. 'Amam commented tenderly, "The poor pigeon is thirsty. I put a bowl of water for the sparrows and pigeons in the courtyard. I wonder if that pigeon notices it and tries to drink." A crow perched beside the pigeon and began to crow.

"I said to the blind beggar with the turban, 'Please tell me where is Shorjah Market.' He cleared his throat, wiping the dirt from his eyes, and said, 'Oh dear! Shorjah Market is very far from here.' My fear grew. 'Where am I?' The beggar didn't answer and returned to the herb vendor shouting, 'Abu Kadim, may God bless the breasts that nursed you, show this Jewish woman the way to Shorjah Market!' I was out of my mind. How did he know I was Jewish?"

'Amam scratched the root of her gray braid from under the head-dress and asked, "Didn't you know where you were?"

"I felt a dream entangling my soul."

'Amam whispered in a sympathetic voice intermingled with fright, "God forbid! You didn't enter their home, I hope."

"Whose home?"

"The home of those beings who are better than us?"

It was about time for me to know. But I lost my mind and my reason roamed in a world of imaginations. The calming cooing of the pigeon reached me and almost made me feel safe. I was saved now and left the oddest nightmare behind me, full of astonishment, fright, and a lot of distressing uncertainties—who knows how long they would stay with me? 'Amam was a pure angel seeking under his wing to find shelter from her fears, but despite her efforts, her confusion broke up the past into pieces of terrible memory. Strange events, however, stayed in her memory, and the burden of the fresh event completely occupied her weary mind. Was it true that I used to experience ghosts for a while?

"Abdalek 'Amam, don't scare me! Do you really know what happened to me?" I asked.

"I cry for you for suffering so much. In your place, I wouldn't have been able to withstand it all and would have died," 'Amam lamented.

"I was lost and perspiring, and my thoughts poured out of a crack in my skull and forehead as from a bag of honey or yogurt with a hole in it. I rubbed that concoction of sweat mixed with filth and sediments of dust, licked it, and found it evil smelling with a bizarre taste.

"I was alone on unknown streets in strange neighborhoods with a blind beggar and an herb vendor who said, 'Look, lady! When you leave here, turn right, walk straight ahead, and you'll see a long alley in front of you. Enter it and walk until the end, then you'll come to a dead-end alley and a mosque. There's a water fountain next to the mosque. Enter the mosque's gate, walk straight, and exit from the other gate. Ask there and they'll show you the way.'

"I made a mad dash and got mixed up leaving one alley and entering another that led to nowhere. I was breathless, lost, scared, and alone in a Baghdad I didn't know—in another Baghdad. I was alone in the very city where I had first seen the light of day but in which I now felt like a stranger. At that moment it didn't occur to me that I was wandering aimlessly in a world of ghosts, not just demons or spirits. I was plainly lost and unable to think, driven crazy by the crazy trouble. Could there be places in Baghdad that I didn't know? Heavens, how would I get out of them?"

Thirst! I drank another glass of the invigorating, sweet rose water mixed with the bitterness of my mouth. I heard the chirp of the birds joining the cooing of the pigeons. More pigeons came into the courtyard, and then I heard the noise of the flock flying together. Suddenly, I remembered the other scene and trembled as if a pin had struck my body.

"Look at the hair on my head, 'Amam, how it's standing up straight! I saw the black coffin and the old people; there wasn't even the shadow of a woman among them. May the Name of God protect us!

"Harsh stammering gushed out in a flood of noise, while I was alone, lost in distant alleys. I found myself in an alley without a mosque, not as the herb vendor had told me. Could he have lied to me? Why wasn't there crying, slapping of faces? Suddenly, the black coffin slipped from the shoulders. The bier fell and got smashed. Many black things began to roll out from the bottom of the coffin. I then saw the mourners running and falling on each other. A dreadful but soft jabbering reached me. The mourners were scared, and I was even more scared. But why were they afraid? I was at the foot of a slope. Something like a black pomegranate with bulges and depressions rolled to my feet.

"I picked it up. Seemingly, it had the hard peel of a pomegranate with natural bulges. I stuck it between my breasts and stepped back. That black pomegranate looked weird and very beautiful. I said to myself, 'My dear Marrudi will be delighted with this.' Nobody sensed I had made off with the black pomegranate. How beautiful it was! I continued forward, entered one alley and exited from another in the terrible heat.

"Marrudi would play with the strange pomegranate. It was in my breast, black with square bulges, with valleys and mountains.

"Then suddenly I found myself near the Shorjah police station. Listen, Umm Ya'qub, I'm not through yet! I wouldn't want anyone to go through what I went through that day. Did I get there—how did I get there?

"I nodded with sadness. Marrudi was hidden in my scattered and fragmented thoughts everywhere I went. The front building of the police station was crowded and there was no room to stand.

"I saw a black pomegranate before me. A policeman held it in his hand, but I felt between my breasts and found my pomegranate there, guarding my heart in its embrace. Impossible! Could this strange black pomegranate multiply? I found this bomb in the street. At the same time, there were bombs everywhere in Baghdad, and my pomegranate turned out to be one of them. I carried the beautiful and strange black pomegranate between my breasts, frightened.

"I was amazed and startled before 'Amam Umm Ya'qub and the crowd that had gathered near the Shorjah Market police station. At that point, my nightmare rose to the top of a lofty mountain while I was caught in the fist of the demon. A crow was croaking in the courtyard disturbing the cooing of the pigeons. At that time there was a group of crows croaking in my head.

"I froze, afraid to go forward or backward. It was a disaster either way. If I had a little reason left in my brain it also flew away when my breast carried a deadly weapon. It was as if I lost my way just in order to find it, and in my ignorance I was overjoyed that I could bring Marrudi something unusual to play with.

"I was frozen. When I felt between my breasts again there was nothing except this sweet, black, bulging bomb attached to me. The heat around the pomegranate was fervent and became as unbearable as a furnace. The pomegranate seemed to pound in my head. Boom, it would explode in my hand! Boom, I would be broken into pieces, a million pieces! I thought of one question: who would stay with Marrudi and take care of him? I didn't know what to do; I wanted to throw it away, get rid of it.

"What did I do? If I had walked through the crowd I would have jostled people and they would have felt me. It looked like a bulging ball, very visible, threatening me with a strange death. My legs collapsed and became pieces of rags. My face looked like a corpse, and

I was on the verge of falling. Thousands of eyes stared at me. Then I lifted up my dress and pointed to my breasts. It was as if I had heard strong voices shouting around me, 'She's a Jewess carrying a bomb.' They would roast me, tear me to pieces, and make me into mashed apricots. All I worried about was Marrudi; he guided me around. He said, 'Go back!' and I obeyed his voice. I turned back and covered the way through the alleys until I arrived at Murjan Mosque. At that moment, I became sober once more."

Frightened, 'Amam said, "No matter what happened, God be praised! He's compassionate and merciful. I kissed my hand and then touched my eye in a sign of thanks to God. I would have brought death to my only son, but without my knowing, the Sublime and Benevolent guided me. I walked fast, a thousand racehorses wouldn't have been able to catch me. To where? I ran like crazy holding my 'abayah with my hand over my chest on the way to the old bridge. When the people were off guard, I threw the beautiful black pomegranate from the bridge and saw the Black Death sink into the depths of the Tigris. I recited, 'Hear, O Israel, the Lord is our God, the Lord is one.' My life was saved, and I felt relief."

I was relieved again and drank another glass of rose water. 'Amam was standing next to me, and Farhah Ghawi was still alarmed in her room. Little by little I gathered my tormented thoughts while various sounds rose from the courtyard. Pigeons cooed tenderly, birds chirped, and a crow cawed. I remembered Marrudi and trembled. "Umm Ya'qub, I left Marrudi without cooking for him or feeding him lunch."

"Don't worry. Where do you think I was the whole time? I called him and fed him lunch with 'Aibah. I cooked *kishri* and boiled a whole chicken. I wish you had been there, too. 'Aibah gave him an appetite, Marrudi ate his fill, and together they left to play outside. What about spooning out something to eat for you now? Abdalek, okay? Let me spoon out the food. I wonder how you managed all that without anything to eat or drink," 'Amam asked.

Farhah Ghawi's voice filled the entire house. I thought of 'Aibah, the devil's seed. I had seen the ill-omened face of Farhah when I left, and I saw it again when I returned, and I felt a needle sting in my heart—Marrudi. I did not see him when I came home. Where was he? I was on the brink of losing my mind again, but I remembered the great miracle that God had made for me today. I mumbled words of thanks and praise to the Creator and kissed the inside of my palm, then raised it to my eyes bathed with tears.

3—Marrudi and 'Aibah, the Two Boys

A reversal of fortune, a change of thought, a change of feeling, a change of face, even a shake or shiver, either silence or an earthquake. Marrudi didn't know whether a shock had leveled him with the rage stored inside. He stared at the fat 'Aibah, as corpulent as a bear, short with wide hips. He examined himself, as tall as a palm tree or a rod, as thin as a stick, or as strapping as sweet basil. The other boy shouted, teasing Marrudi.

"Hee-hee-hee! I won again even though you tried to beat me."

Marrudi was insulted. The sun disappeared behind the wall while Marrudi hid in the corner.

Where was his mother? Marrudi was enraged. "I wish she wouldn't come back forever!" he thought. 'Aibah was near him and held Marrudi's elbow with a little remorse. Angrily, Marrudi shook 'Aibah's "impure" hand away but failed to free himself. Shaking and pulling 'Aibah's arm away was as hard to do as casting the spinning top to the ground. Marrudi's top always landed on its side like a corpse lying sideways on the floor. The bottom tip of the spinning top "dies" instead of spinning.

"Are you mad?" asked 'Aibah. Marrudi was silent and angry. "Let's play jacks," 'Aibah suggested.

The attempt to reconcile Marrudi failed as he tried to cast the spinning top properly. May all games go to hell! His mother, Lulu, knew nothing of her son's boyish anger, and was unaware of his being controlled by 'Aibah. Lulu was the innocent victim of Marrudi's blind wrath. He was alone, with nobody near except the devil 'Aibah, the one who stole all his hopes. 'Aibah was both friend and enemy, the only one who continued to challenge Marrudi after losing. But Marrudi alone was paralyzed. Where was his mother? A few months from now he would be a man when he donned the phylacteries. She said to him: "Don't play with this bastard, he is a roughneck and cheats people like you."

Marrudi missed his mother and borrowed her tongue to shout resentfully, "I won't play with you anymore. You're a nagel—you were born out of wedlock!"

Marrudi received no answer and clung to his corner. A bit of remorse cast its shadow on his refusal. He summoned up his diminished hate, so his fortune and his aborted revenge came to him together with his conflicting thoughts, sometimes sweet, at times bitter, with and without encouragement. He waited apprehensively for 'Aibah to make peace with him again, but he only found silence. His conflicting thoughts clung to him all of a sudden. He chewed on them and they chewed on him in silence. His fury returned automatically to him and he said to himself, "I'll show him, just wait."

"Bastard!" 'Aibah retreated, distracted. Suddenly his thoughts grew gloomy; he was lonely with nothing to do except kill time playing games. He was among strangers, though 'Amam was like a mother to him, and Ya'qub, her son, was like a father. Where was Gerjiyi? Who was his father?

'Amam had said to him, "Don't worry 'Aibah, I'll put in a good word for you with Uncle Ya'qub. He'll buy you a prayer shawl and phylacteries and teach you to pray, and we'll make your Bar Miswah with Marrudi." But he seemed as if he were wandering in a dark and sad dream, and 'Amam was still patching over the crack of his ambiguous self when the welded seam had opened. But he was still cracked, and his thoughts wandered through the darkness of the alley.

There was a boy riding a bicycle and circling the open space at the intersection of the branched alleys, most of which were dead ends. 'Aibah looked as if from behind a dark-colored glass; the sun seemed white in his eyes, blinding him despite the darkness. His eyes caught the sweat from his forehead and he plunged into the dense fog of a dream. The bicycle rider fell suddenly. 'Aibah rushed to free him. In exchange, I might get a ride on the bike, he thought. He saw Marrudi in his impatient isolation but was afraid to call out to him. He was also hesitant to leave Marrudi alone.

Where is my mother? Why do they call me a nagel? he wondered. Why didn't Marrudi know how to ride a bicycle?

'Aibah never went to the movies or school in his life and he didn't know how to read. He didn't even know his father's name. The bicycle! I'll ride the bike and pedal and will roar down the street, he thought. Then I'll put Marrudi behind me—hold on to me well, Marrudi! I'll speed up r-r-r-r-r-r-r-r-r-r-r-r-r and let fly.

'Aibah would travel throughout Baghdad with the bicycle and would fly with two wings, head, and tail. A gray mare like an airplane would take him and Marrudi everywhere, and he would look for his mother and find the unknown father who shot the sperm into his mother's womb.

No, Marrudi would stay clinging to the wall, and I'll be alone, thought 'Aibah. 'Aibah would fly far, amid glittering stars that held no fatherhood nor motherhood nor bastards. He would read all the books in the world, go to all the movie theaters, and write books about Tarzan and Cheetah. He had heard a lot about Tarzan and his ape from the children with whom he used to play dice near Ya'qub's shop, when Ya'qub owned the shop. I am Tarzan and Marrudi is Cheetah, he used to imagine. I'll take care of Marrudi and love him, not tease him, and he'll have no reason to call me nagel.

'Aibah felt the coins in his pocket. Aunt 'Amam gave me money secretly, without Ya'qub's knowledge. There was a lot of money in my pocket. I'll gamble and become the richest man in the house, he thought. I'll bet Marrudi for a bottle of soda. We'll open it, and as always the foam will rise and overflow on the floor, and I'll win. He corrected himself: "No, I'll let Marrudi win once for a truce, and then he won't call me nagel anymore."

Suddenly, 'Aibah broke out of his dream and did not find the boy who fell from the bicycle or the flying horse. He approached Marrudi once more and said, holding him gently, "Hey, Marrudi, let's ride bicycles! Don't be afraid. I'll watch you, hold you from behind so you won't fall." 'Aibah felt that he, like a man, was responsible for a child needing care.

Marrudi's expression was like the crest of a wild bird disclosing his true mind, the colors of his face alternating ceaselessly with emotional strife and contradictions. 'Aibah wanted to reconcile with him again. Marrudi softened at first, willing to make up, but then he hardened, his head stuffed with angry words. You have become a man, he said to himself, gathering his thoughts. I could stay alone, but then 'Aibah would continue to win. Will I choose peace or war? War was rooted deep inside him.

"Come on, Marrudi! Let's ride bicycles and buy 'al-'oudah. It's on me. Look how much money I have!" He jingled the money in his pocket.

'Aibah was showing off, thought Marrudi, assuming I have no money, although I have more than he does. My mother gives me money while he begs from 'Amam, Ya'qub's mother. I go to school while he can't tell A from B. I know who my father is and he doesn't. His mother left him alone like a dog, and I have a mother—where did she go? It had been six hours since she left. May my mother's house burn! She stood in the agonies of his mind while he was stuck in the corner of a dark alley, stuck in a blazing oven. Marrudi wondered, where did that daughter of a dog go? I am a man! Between his manhood and his childhood, jealousy broke out fervently and as blind as his concealed hatred.

'Aibah said, "Come, Marrudi, don't make a fuss! If you're afraid to ride a bicycle we can go and fly a kite."

Was Marrudi afraid? No! He would punish his mother. He would never allow her to be like Gerjiyi, 'Aibah's mother. No way! An idea occurred to him, secretly numbing his faculties. Was his mother with another man? What does it mean to be with another man? Marrudi's mind exhausted all kinds of imaginings as he was consumed with jealousy, as if by fire. He would kill her. Just wait and see when she came back. He was on the verge of crying when the other boy begged him again, as if he had been dreaming.

"We'll fly kites with long tails, buy ice cream and 'al-'oudah bars, play coins, and beat the other boys," promised 'Aibah.

Marrudi took pity on 'Aibah and his dreams. He also took pity on himself. 'Aibah's mother was lost and so was his own mother. He was no longer a child. I'll be Bar Miswah in a short time, he remembered. My father was a swimming champion. Marrudi's mother told him repeatedly, "Your father used to sit cross-legged on the water as if he were sitting on the floor, where he would put the narghile between his legs and smoke." His mother had disappeared as suddenly as his father did. She had left six hours ago and hadn't returned. She betrayed him, betrayed his father, the champion whose face he had never seen. She used to say to Marrudi, "The water betrayed your father, and he went down quickly unnoticed." She was sad whenever she told him this, and she would burst into tears. Perhaps she had betrayed both of them—his father and Marrudi. She must have followed Gerjiyi Nati. Where was she?

His question was choking in his throat, blazing in the furnace of his being, in the furnace of the world. I'm a hero too, he thought, with affection for his father and his heroism. My father used to beat all the other swimmers. He would cross the river back and forth on only one breath. He used to dive from the bridge and stay under the water for an hour and go out near Layali Baghdad Casino. Lulu, his mother, used to tell Marrudi all these things.

His gloomy soul smiled amid the crushing chaos overcoming him. He shook off the miserable childhood still haunting him, like a ghost—I'm a man like my father. He took pity on 'Aibah and felt confident. In the process of freeing himself from the embrace of a silent hatred he had guarded as the last spark of a child's wounded pride, he quarreled with his mother and fought the ill fortune of games with 'Aibah. You've become a man, you've become a man, he quietly insisted to himself. I'll show 'Aibah and show my mother. This mute chatter was crushing his soul amidst the commotion, his humiliating inadequacy, and his consuming jealousy of 'Aibah. I'll be a man of worth, Marrudi reiterated silently. Proudly, he turned to his friend and rival and in commanding tones, said, "Come with me to the river, or else I won't talk to you until the day I die."

'Aibah was embarrassed. In his small mind something had erupted. He was, after all, the "seed of the devil," or so he had heard from Lulu, Moshiyah's daughter. In any case, people agreed that he was a wretched, harmful bastard. He recalled Lulu saying to Marrudi, "Are you playing again with that nagel, that son of the whore? You won't stop until he makes something bad happen and you get hurt."

But 'Amam made up with 'Aibah and also kissed him after wiping the tears from his chunky cheeks saying, "Don't worry, don't take what that woman says seriously. She's crazy, but you're a good boy, the best."

'Amam lied; Lulu was not the only crazy one.

Suddenly, 'Aibah was as enraged as a chained slave. He felt imprisoned and encircled by impurity and he burst into tears. He wanted to destroy everything, himself and the whole world. If my Uncle Ya'qub hadn't invented this name for me, people wouldn't have called me nagel, he thought. His thoughts crushed his hope and he slipped and fell into a world of unforgiving reality. Where was his mother, Gerjiyi, and who was his father? Where was that damn stinky bitch? If she were truly virtuous, she would not have abandoned me. Where did she go after she left that dirty Khoshi, the Persian? Do they think I don't know? She went to live with a man who wasn't my father. And people call me "nagel and a son of a whore."

Oh the river, oh the river!

"God forbid that nagel misleads you and tempts you to the river. Wasn't it enough that the river caused your father's death?" Marrudi recalled his mother saying.

The river! It was a cursed word, as devilish and dreadful as 'Aibah. Lulu had a fit whenever she heard the word *river*.

Marrudi said to 'Aibah, "Don't pay attention to that crazy woman! I already went to the river secretly a thousand times and learned how to swim. I have to become a swimming champion like my father. My mother has a screw loose because she thinks anyone who swims in the river is sure to drown."

Marrudi lured 'Aibah to follow the temptation invading his desire. Many times he forced him to disobey this taboo of swimming in the river. 'Aibah swam with him near the river bank without using carob pods or inner tubes to stay afloat. One time a young man, out of pity, gave them an inner tube with which they did move a few meters in the water.

'Aibah was at a loss when he found water flowing strongly in the middle of the tube and becoming like a whirlpool. It was a whirlpool of sins, of forbidden things, of devilish material mixed with his blood. So he believed he was a devil, and since he was a bastard, he should therefore be filthy. Filthiness was a characteristic of the devil, the ultimate bastard, according to Ya'qub. Games of chance and gambling were created by the devil and so they were strongly forbidden. It was for that reason that 'Aibah was attracted to them. They made him forget the world. In fact, he was a big winner in the forbidden games, and Marrudi got mad at him and reminded him of his origin. His destiny seemed a vicious circle. Could he escape it?

'Aibah felt stymied and weird, but at the same time he wanted to change his imposing, cruel destiny. How could he stoop to reconciliation with Marrudi when he was a man and Marrudi was only a child? A feeling of responsibility came over him now and then, a strange and unpredictable feeling toward his friend, a split responsibility, three parts of a single responsibility: the river and Marrudi's desire, the river and the devil's seed, the river and Lulu's fit.

Marrudi said, threatening, "Are you coming with me to the river? If not I'll go alone and we must part forever; I'll not know you and you'll not know me."

The river! It was the extinguisher of the world's fire, the fire of 'Aibah's being. The water danced and refreshed. He would splash water on his face, dive under, and then step out of the water. It would wash away the filth that had mixed with forgetfulness, such as the forbidden sweet sucking stolen from Sabriyah's sleeping mouth.

Where was Sabriyah now? Where was my damn mother now, 'Aibah wondered? What if Bannutah, Farhah Ghawi's daughter, were to come with us to the river and I were to float almost nude, wearing only my underpants? I have no swimming trunks. 'Aibah only had underpants made of a raw material that would show his genitals when wet. If Bannutah came he would show how smart he was when he floated, and he would pretend that he knew . . . the secret.

'Aibah had fallen into a filthy, stinky basin. He was filthy, a bastard, ostracized, and ill treated. Why? He was lost, not understanding certain things. Marrudi got mad at me when I beat him in the games and he teased me, calling me nagel. Why? he wondered. He yearned suddenly to put his head between Bannutah's breasts. He sighed. Now Marrudi sought to win 'Aibah over, giving him his sole possession: affection and friendship. 'Aibah hated the entire world except Marrudi. He also desired forbidden things, his own forbidden things.

He said to Marrudi, "Okay, we'll go to the river now, provided you don't tell your mother. We'll come back soon."

The river! It had lifted Marrudi's father to the rank of champion but had led him down to his death. His mother, though, had forgotten that first part, and she took her troubles out on the river and on Marrudi. People call me sissy, he thought. His desire grew more urgent to reach the river fast. He wished that all of Baghdad would become the Tigris so that he could challenge his mother and the river, quench his devastating jealousy and announce to 'Aibah, to the world, and to himself, "I'm no sissy."

The river!

'Aibah felt seething passion and gave in to Marrudi's wishes. High summer had come with the heat of the human curse—'Aibah's stained self, his flaming ambiguous yearning for human flesh, Sabriyah's flesh or Bannutah's. 'Aibah felt deprived of a female's flesh; all he had was the flesh of a mother who neglected him. He longed for the water too, his will bent to Marrudi's. The water would wash away the scars of shame with which he was born.

'Aibah, the bastard, had a filthy vein bound to throb and he yearned for the river as much as Marrudi. For Marrudi's sake, 'Aibah would violate prohibitions, take care of Marrudi, and make him love him and not call him nagel any longer. He would give Marrudi a chance; it was a childish joy with dark outlines and shadows. He felt this precious and wonderful sense of responsibility for Marrudi. It proved he was a good person and had nothing to do with the throbbing vein of the devil. He would be born anew, like playing a rematch of the game where children had cheated, but the cheating was discovered before it was too late.

The crowd next to the Shorjah police station dispersed, and Ghazi Street dozed languidly in the early afternoon hours under the burning sun of Baghdad, although not much of the summer remained. Driven by vicious whips of desire and the narghile-like bubbling of dreams, the two boys accelerated their footsteps.

My father used to cross the river with his legs crossed, putting the narghile between his legs and smoking, mused Marrudi. 'Aibah followed Marrudi like a mother hen and guide, simultaneously bearing his own dreams and hiding his fear from the wrath of Lulu, Moshiyah's daughter.

I hope a car hits my mother Lulu so she won't come back, Marrudi wished. I hope a car hits my mother and frees me from her shame. After all, I'm a man. But suddenly he felt overpowered by a sudden eruption of his painful and deprived childhood experiences. He was not yet aware of the ordeals required of those who had reached manhood.

'Aibah said to him when he saw a horse carriage driver in an empty carriage at the way toward Bab el-Sharqi, "Marrudi, let's hang onto the rear!" Marrudi hesitated but obeyed. The bank of the Tigris seemed closer to him now, especially since he was in a hurry. He hung onto the rear of the carriage with 'Aibah. "Hang on tight so you don't slip and fall!" Then 'Aibah heard the cracking of the whip and said, "Lower your head and don't stick your head out. We'll be there soon!"

The cracks of the whip speeded up, and a flood of curses showered in vain upon them, "Get off, get off, you sons of filthy mothers, you bastards! May your fathers and mothers be damned!"

'Aibah, in delight, suppressed a laugh.

Marrudi said to himself, "He calls my mother filthy. Just let that stupid woman of mine wait and see. I'll show her I'm brave." Lulu's absence stuck in his mind like a skewering stick, and his brain roasted like a kebob. Marrudi was consumed by jealousy and unacceptable taunts of devilishness were both intangible and real—his imagination was set loose galloping like the horses shaking his entire being just like the carriage.

From afar, Marrudi saw a barge approaching the dock. The temptation of the water increased, attracting him to the barge and to the *chardagh*, changing hut. Marrudi's eyes hung on the barge while 'Aibah's eyes were fixed on the hut. 'Aibah blinked along a line of shiny whiteness separating him from the hut. The bridge was not distant but it was hidden away and neglected, like the green palm trees on the other side of the river.

On the other side of the river, Sa'idah Ghawi's destiny was a tangible reality lived in an unrecognizable house among thousands of Muslim houses. Lulu, Moshiyah's daughter, was crazy. She stood on the pillars of a different bridge and threw the black pomegranate into the water trying to toss death to the bottom of the river. Then she ran home gasping.

May my mother's father be skewered! Where did my mother go? Marrudi said to 'Aibah, "Come on, I'm roasting in this heat. I want to be in the water."

The water was here; the water was everywhere! But it was more active near the *chardagh* and the barge. Marrudi talked to 'Aibah about the water with the voice of a drunken dreamer saying, "You know, 'Aibah, one time I came early in the morning, before summer break from school, and you know what?" Then he remembered and imagined many groups of boys at dawn, here and there, nude with carob pods—one, two, or three pieces—tied to their backs and bellies. Then they went to the water and you could only see heads bobbing like a group of ducks.

The swimming teachers led the boys and urged the swimmers, "Get going, boys!" Their loud and rowdy cries sounded like waves over the water, spreading like the fronds of palm trees. They would cross the river, over and back. My father was a swimming teacher once, thought Marrudi.

'Aibah, on the other hand, used to spend his days with his mother and Ya'qub in the shop, and Ya'qub used to curse him, "You son of a whore, where did you take that bracelet?"

Something disturbed 'Aibah inside. He didn't know what, but he didn't cry. His greatest joy was to win ten fils and sit in the alley with his legs crossed in a circle of boys who knew nothing except how to play dice, curse, and bad-mouth each other.

Marrudi urged him, "Come on, 'Aibah!" They walked fast toward the chardagh and the barge.

"Get going, boys!" the swimming teacher shouted.

"Do you want to see how I dive from the barge?" Marrudi asked 'Aibah.

"No, I don't want to. There's no need to show off, let's go to the water for a short while only," 'Aibah answered, turning his back on the view flooding over him like a river. He was hotheaded, his body and feelings filled with passion. I'm a full-grown man; I only came along to watch Marrudi, he reminded himself. What? He was responsible for Marrudi and promised himself to competently "remove this stain," this filth that was clinging to him, like a black blemish.

I'm really a man, thought Marrudi, though 'Aibah thinks I only want to show off. My father used to dive and stay in the water for an hour. I'll dive for only one minute.

The view there was wide and unrestrained, and the chardagh area seemed abandoned in those hot hours. Where were those dawn hours he was told about when the chardagh and the surrounding areas were supposed to be full of children? 'Aibah was a child again, and his mind was in flames with fresh images burning with unfulfilled desire, like a string of rosary beads spread and scattered in his head. The chardagh! 'Aibah said to Marrudi, "Come and let's take our clothes off in the chardagh!"

Marrudi ran with a group of children toward the chardagh, as on a racetrack where men and children compete. Everyone and everything was running, even the water in the Tigris. Even Lulu, Marrudi's mother, ran when she returned home troubled after getting rid of that black death in the Tigris. Marrudi ran to the barge with his strong passion and eagerness. He would jump from the barge and dive in the river like a fish.

'Aibah objected, "No!" Then Marrudi said, "No!" to himself, meaning that he must find another way to show both 'Aibah and his mother.

The sun disappeared, but behind it a lonely fragment of a cloud hovered over the river and cast shadows. For a moment, a white diamond-like beam appeared and green color came into sight on the top of brown trunks standing on the other side of the river. The barge looked black after being rusty brown. It was docked motionless at the bank of the river. Everything was still. Then a whirlwind of sand gained strength and blew hard at the bank. It took a jagged course and swept up straw and pieces of paper and debris, but soon it calmed down and vanished, and the sun shone again, spreading crystal whiteness mixed with dust.

Though he was a calm on the outside, conflicts, feelings, and desires oppressed Marrudi within. Here was the man! He stretched out his feet, one after the other, tossed his right sandal off, landing far away. The left sandal followed. He ran eagerly after the sandals he had removed, picked them up from the sand, put them on again and started to undress. 'Aibah shouted, "To the chardagh!"

In the chardagh, 'Aibah would finally get to take off his clothes ceremoniously; he had felt deprived of the ceremony and could imagine groups of noisy boys crowded on the mats at dawn. I am different from them, he thought. But he did not stand out at all. Then he realized with sadness, no, I definitely differ. I do.

'Aibah was different in all aspects, but his mind was flooded with sweet visions—the chardagh and undressing with hundreds of boys at dawn when the Tigris sent cold breezes to challenge the blazing furnace of day. He forgot Marrudi for a moment and crawled with his dreams into the walls of the chardagh. The mats were dingy and torn in a few places. They were placed on wooden pillars or rested on sticks and rods. The benches were filthy, stained, and loaded with sand.

"'Aibah, I'll go into the water. Keep an eye on my clothes on the bank."

'Aibah heard Marrudi's voice as if it came from the other side of the river, just an echo that no sooner stayed than disappeared. Now he forgot he was a man, forgot he was responsible, even forgot that he existed in the world. He was in the chardagh, dazzled and attracted by the noise and the scene. The overturned rusty black can was shaking and rattling; and the white ivory dice indented with red dots like moles rolled in the can amid a circle of tiny bodies roasting in the sun. One boy, two, three, four, five boys were avoiding the heat and sitting around the game completely engaged in it. 'Aibah saw red bills, jagged silver coins, felt his pocket, and licked his lips. He drowned in the temptation.

The barge! The temptation drowned Marrudi. My father used to jump from the piles of the bridge, so I'll dive from the barge. He examined the barge and found it high and long. His father used to dive from the bridge and go out near Layali Baghdad Casino. He was enchanted and stepped along the barge measuring it with his steps— ten meters, twenty or more? It was necessary to practice first.

Where was 'Aibah? Where was my mother? Someone was bound to see him. 'Aibah was human, though a nagel. 'Aibah would tell people about my courageous deeds and say, "Marrudi is a man, Marrudi dove."

Marrudi hesitated. Well, what if I don't know how? What will happen if I don't make it? I have to be sure. I must prove I'm a man of competence. I'll try first, then go and call 'Aibah. I'll climb the barge and jump in headfirst, then swim the breaststroke from one end of the barge to the other. It won't take more than a minute.

'Aibah was attracted by the game and enjoyed every minute of it. I am like my father, Marrudi imagined. He clamored on the barge and reached its deck. 'Aibah licked his lips and swallowed his saliva from the excitement of watching the game. Should I play or not? I want to play badly.

Marrudi jumped from the barge and dove in the water. Let my mother come and see me now! Doesn't she want me to step into my father's shoes? He treaded the water under his feet and swam under the barge.

Should I play or not? 'Aibah was confused and felt a strong desire to play. One boy jumped up and grabbed another by the throat, "Why are you cheating? Give me the money." The two boys grabbed each other.

'Aibah was dismayed. They would kill each other, but this boy was right. I saw the other one cheating, he thought. What a cheating game! I used to cheat too. The game was as corrupt and deceitful as his life. Still, whoever didn't cheat didn't win. All my life I've been cheating. I denied it, or rather I had already denied it, and then forgot.

'Aibah woke up. How did he become a child again without feeling it? Then he remembered—I'm a man. I must take care of Marrudi. The children's squabbles grew louder in the chardagh, and he rushed toward the bank of the river calling, "Marrudi! Marrudi!"

Marrudi's clothes were laid on the bank of the river. 'Aibah turned right and left. Where was Marrudi? He called again, "Hey Marrudi!"

'Aibah fell in a sea of confusion and embarrassment. Where was that son of a bitch? He was just here a while ago. 'Aibah looked at the ground and noticed traces on the sand and sandy clues on the barge. He held his breath. The noise grew in the chardagh and disturbed his thoughts. Then he stopped hearing all the voices except the fading murmur of the water. Despite his calmness he muttered devilish curses and anxiously shouted "Marrudi!" for the third time. Then he listened. Silence prevailed on the river and in the surrounding area. He only heard the echoes of his own fearful voice coming back to him and he rushed toward the chardagh. There he found five tanned children quarreling, shouting, and badmouthing each other.

Where was Marrudi? He ran back again and saw Marrudi's clothes piled on the bank, but where was Marrudi? "Marrudi! Marrudi!" After resting a while he listened closely and looked carefully. Nothing! He found no traces except footprint marks on the barge. Suddenly, a dreadful and frenzied storm wind threatened to blow him over and he began to moan and sob like a child scared of something unknown, unfair, and terrible.

4—'Amam, Ya'qub's Mother

What a calamity, what a disaster! Who would have believed what happened? Who could foresee it and who would dare talk about it? Our hearts went out to Marrudi and his mother. Is there anyone in the alley who has not wept tears of blood? We didn't expect this; after all, Lulu was supposed to celebrate his Bar Miswah, poor boy! I ask God, "Why didn't you take me instead of that child? Why didn't you take his mother? She would have preferred to die and not see what happened. Can injustice like this exist in the world? What a calamity, what a disaster!

He went suddenly; death devoured him in a second. Who can understand the deeds of God—may He be praised. How could I have known that such a disaster would happen? The poor boy came to me with this damned 'Aibah, and I fed them, and then they left together to play outside. Did I know he would be dead so fast? What a grave calamity! It's as black as the soot of the pot. 'Aibah had nothing to do with it. It was predestined. It would have been better had death taken me instead of the boy.

What did poor 'Aibah have to do with all this? That poor boy was ill-treated and has never stopped weeping. Didn't he love the late Marrudi? He swears that he didn't want to go to the river at all or cause Marrudi's death. The boy insisted and tempted 'Aibah to go there. The poor boy, Marrudi, exposed himself to the devil. We should not interfere if things are destined to happen! In fact, the death of the poor boy had already drawn near and he ran to the river so that the Angel of Death could catch him there. Nothing would have helped to prevent this from happening because his fate was already sealed. What a calamity! Oh God!

They say that He is an expert in destroying homes—God forbid! I no longer know what rubbish comes out of my mouth. Did this disaster make people aware of what they say? Woe is poor Lulu! Wasn't it enough for her to be lost for six hours, to have suffered, and then have come home weary and short of breath? Wasn't all this enough? I wish this had been all, because what happened later shocked everyone. It was as if He had set aside the disaster so that He could completely put her eyes out. What an ill omen! Things were bound to bring misfortune. Lulu never stopped nagging Marrudi. What Farhah did, and may her face be blackened, was no small thing either; she gave away her own daughter. But who must suffer the consequences? Since birth, the unfortunate Marrudi and his mother have suffered.

Are people wrong when they claim that every deed brings a consequence and a purpose? A mountain could fall only if it filled an empty pit. Nonetheless, we say again that God predetermines everything. We blame Farhah again and again. Nonsense! It's God, may He be praised. He knows what He is doing, but man's mind is beneath grasping what happened. Why does God, the Sublime, may His name be praised, hunt the poor and the oppressed? He doesn't let them enjoy the pleasures of life. Isn't there enough injustice in the world? Such a maddening calamity has never happened before. This is too much.

Even 'Atiyah al-Qarawchi tells me, "The calamity of this boy overweighs the calamity of my two daughters." 'Atiyah cried and beat her breast, "The poor boy used to bring the son of the Indian woman to reason. Also, he never insulted my son Joudi and didn't let anyone provoke him."

When poor Marrudi was furious at his mother, he only wanted
to be pampered. Poor woman, how she longed to see him grow into
manhood! She reared him with tears up to this age, happily awaiting
his Bar Miswah. My heart bleeds for him and her. The entire alley
has been turned upside down. What happened is no simple thing; it's
a major blow.

And Hamidah, 'Abdallah's mother! What did she do? She sat
among the women, and with 'Atiyah they held the Chaynah eulogy
ceremony. Her eyes were bathed with tears, and she bewailed him in
such a way that even professional mourners like Rimah and Azizah
were no match for her. She lamented him with proper words, suiting
the heart's wounds, as if she were reciting a eulogy from the Holy
Book for one of her own sons—may God protect them! She recited
a lamentation: "When the boys walked together, I saw them and
became powerless. He died in vain." She called on the feelings of
the mourners, arousing their sorrow, and 'Atiyah answered her, "Oh
sonny, you are the ring of my right hand. Oh, who made the world
bloom for me? Who will come to me after you are gone?"

And Farhah raised her loud voice in lament, and her woes split
hearts. What strong blows and slaps she delivered to herself! Her
heart was in agony for her daughter. One has to be fair and speak
one's conscience. She never gave away her daughter Sa'idah willingly.
She hit herself as if she were smashing down a wall. She was in pain
and sad for her daughter and Marrudi. It seemed that we had blamed
her for too much. If she hadn't felt pain for her daughter, Sa'idah, she
wouldn't have done this much. Would she have hit herself as hard as
she did? True, she was crying and beating her breast for the loss of
her daughter, Sa'idah. So what? Hadn't she given a lot by sacrific-
ing her daughter? It's true she didn't realize the seriousness of the
matter in the beginning. Now, after what had happened, after our
house had suffered a big loss, she revealed her good intentions. What
suffering she inflicted on herself and what tears she shed! She finally
realized that her home was destroyed. She insisted on serving food
during the first seven mourning days. She also covered her hair, and
on Friday night she stood before the oil lamp and stretched out her

hands, tearfully imploring God. She became strictly religious. Was it too late?

What happened was over, but it would have been better had his mother died instead. She didn't really need any more blows, but God gave this one as the ultimate sign. A person's heart burns for what happened so unexpectedly. Lulu came back tired from a six-hour journey. I wish her legs had been paralyzed and she had never been able to leave. Could it be that she only left so that this poor boy, who had seen nothing in his life, could lie under the dust? She left barefoot and her head was uncovered. Lulu was troubled, lost, and wandered back and forth. What kind of disaster did God inflict on her? She can no longer see, hear, or understand anything.

On Marrudi's burial day, she refused to go to his grave. She said no and meant no and whatever anyone did to convince her to change her mind didn't help. Her heart couldn't live with the thought of seeing her dear son buried under the dust. May God help her and not tear apart a mother's loving heart for her son!

I said to Ya'qub, may God and Elijah the prophet protect him, "We'll take care of everything as needed." He tried to object, "But the factory will be closed, and I'll sit like a blacksmith without fire. What will we and this son of a whore eat? Keep quiet and listen!" He was on the verge of slashing 'Aibah's neck, but I didn't let him touch one hair of his head. What did that poor boy have to do with what had happened?

I said to Ya'qub, "May God protect you, sonny! God will compensate you for your good deeds! Marrudi's mother lost her mind. I know our situation is not as good as it used to be, things aren't going our way, and you're short of money." I also told him, "They want someone to recite the Qiddish prayer for Marrudi but couldn't find anyone. I beg of you to recite it for him and continue to do so until the year of mourning is up." Do you think it was easy to say all this? In the beginning, Ya'qub had kept silent, afraid that bad things would happen to me. To hell with it all! Let me die today before tomorrow comes! Why should I live like this? Everywhere I turn I see the world as black as tar. Didn't I say to God, praised be He, "You should have taken me instead of this poor kid who never committed a sin"? What a catastrophe befell his mother too! I only wish God would put out the fire in her heart.

What do you think, hasn't she turned melancholy? Of course, after the panic and breast-beating of the first and second days, she calmed down and grew tired. At first, she stayed the same for a while but then would jump suddenly and become disturbed and demand, "For God's sake, take me! Take me there, merciful people! Take me to his grave!"

What a calamity! No one can grasp it. Never. On the other hand, all the tenants helped her—I pray they would need to help only on happy occasions. All of them helped: Ya'qub the believer, Jamil the musician who brought his friend, Efrayim, Sabriyah's husband—may God reward him and reconcile his wife to him and make them love each other. But the situation is bad. Efrayim has no job, and Sabriyah insists that he find one. Did he actually find one and turn it down?

What was I telling you? Yes, all of them helped, but I think about what happened and say again, "What is the use of all this? Unfortunate is the one who died; all of them are still alive, but the poor child who died had no joy, no enjoyment in life. Woe for him and for his mother! What a world is this? It has so many calamities. It's not worth living; it's not even worth one fils."

5—Jamil Rabi

Damn me, Jamil! I stopped suddenly, then walked and stopped again. Rumbles shook in my stomach. The snakes circulating inside me squirted poisonous gases. People stared at me with dismay and surprise. They didn't know the cause of my sudden stops and random starts. Then I would surge forward and turn red from exhaustion. Then I felt some relief.

"Abu Ghalib, they don't know whether it is so or not. They don't know whether it's true or false. They don't know what poisonous smells escape from my stomach. These days the gases are killing me. Do you think I'm getting old? I swear by God, Abu Ghalib, the time hasn't come yet. This is not the reason, my friend, my brother—what else do you want me to call you, Abu Ghalib? The troubles have increased a lot and become a permanent disease. The agonies, the torments of heart and mind, are to be blamed for that.

"Naji el-Jundi asked, 'Why is your face gloomy and sad again?' I admit it all and give up. This time I won't deny it. I felt my face with my hand and measured it. It had become longer, but at the same time its width shrank to two spans of a hand. I said to Naji, 'My face is not the only thing that is sad, because if you stab me now with a knife a thousand times, you won't find a drop of blood.' Excuse me, Abu Ghalib, do you understand what I'm saying or don't you understand either? By God, these gases will kill me; I have to release them. I must. Either I release them or I die. They're as piled together and crammed on top of each other as my troubles. I'm lost in an endless wilderness turning me upside down."

Abu Ghalib said to me, "What's wrong? I hope everything is all right."

I pulled him by his shoulder and told him, "Get up! Take advantage of this! I've found what you've been looking for. You'll chase it for a whole year all the way to China."

No! I don't know why, but suddenly the game of desires and contradictions had changed, and my heart was split with the collapse of my mind. My friend Abu Ghalib left. Marrudi left too, but how did he go, I wondered? I tried to understand how it happened. Was there some reason? There must be. Perhaps I was crazy in the past when I used to say that there was nothing at all, but now I admit that there is cursed injustice and a tyrannical power that ridicules pain and hope.

The poor boy disappeared like a drop in the sea, just like his father. It doesn't make sense that this was just a coincidence. My heart was torn for more than one person; wherever you turn you find people who are in dire need of compassion.

Ya'qub said, "Let me slaughter 'Aibah, slash his neck, drink the blood of this son of a whore." This Ya'qub wants to handle the affairs with muscles and slyness. All people look for relief. For instance, what can I do with these gases inside me except get rid of them and let them out, and when they're unable to take revenge on the unknown and abusive power, they have an 'Aibah to hang onto—he's available. Isn't 'Aibah the devil's seed? Let 'Aibah get it from all directions!

"Lulu is unlucky. 'Aibah is a poor boy. Marrudi was miserable, and I'm an unsuccessful man, Abu Ghalib! What's more, all of us are helpless people. 'Amam defended 'Aibah and so did I. Do you know why? It's because the devil's seed exists elsewhere, not only in Joudi's tears or in his fear and sorrow. Excuse me, Abu Ghalib, the killer gas is rising to my mouth. I can let it out and get rid of it, but is it a real solution? Man as a whole is flawed because of his weakness and inability and must give in to the power of the devil. I went with them to the graveyard and I heard Ya'qub praising and glorifying the Creator, thanking Him for His black deed. He recited the Qiddish prayer for Marrudi: 'Let the glory of God be extolled. Let His great name be hallowed and praised!'

"I said, 'No, I'll never say amen!' Do you remember, Abu Ghalib, the game called the human comedy, the sad plot with the happy ending? Is there such a thing? I only see an unfair and oppressive power against humanity. In fact, Abu Ghalib, tears shouldn't go for those who die; they must be for those who are still alive. Just let me die and have the stray dogs and cats eat me after my death!

"Is it so? Suppose that a few years later, this dirty government is changed. This government has conspired with evil powers to bring invisible and contagious death. I want it to be replaced by a good, sincere, and unbiased ruler who doesn't discriminate against people and will befriend our brethren in Moscow. Suppose that one day he wants to build a television station, and our fellows in Moscow come and check the ground and tell him that this Jewish graveyard is the most suitable place for building a television station. The ruler will feel the conflict because he is a good human being and doesn't want to antagonize anyone. On the one hand, serving the country is above everything, while on the other hand, he doesn't want to defile sacred places. Then he'll find the solution. 'I need the ground for the television station. I'll give you another plot of land where you can transfer your dead.'

"Suppose this happens, and all the graves are opened after the fresh wounds have been buried with the dead. What will poor Lulu say when Marrudi's grave is opened and a handful of small bones are taken from a bag weighing less than a kilo? Such is the end of man, Abu Ghalib—forty to fifty kilos and the contents of a beautiful life become a heap of bones and dust so decomposed that a hundred bottles of rose water can't mask the foul smell.

"The human being, Abu Ghalib, is a heaped handful of bones and dust. And still Ya'qub gives thanks and glorifies God. The dead are like a piece of wood, a pile of dust and bones without feelings. Weeping is for the living, Abu Ghalib. The curse befalls them. Remorse will haunt poor 'Aibah all his life. If I hate myself onefold, poor Joudi will multiply this hatred a thousandfold.

"Lulu was leaning on a cane anyway and needed only a light touch to fall. How will she live now, I ask you? Excuse me, Abu Ghalib. These gases are a result of our human curse and the dilemma of our own existence. Don't you know?

"Since the Marrudi incident I have not taught Shridah one lesson. I stopped teaching him the sad tune of Subayyah's melody because it was too much for me to carry the confusions and calamities of the world in my own head. We are facing one and only one fact. I said to Shridah, 'Don't worry, you're sure to learn, but now excuse me. You have reached the tune while I still have a sad and disturbing melody playing in my mind.' This melody is definitely in my head! It's a long lamentation for the living rather than for the dead. Our filthy, miserable, seething world is evaporating in my stomach like poisonous gases. The owl's wings flap, and the snake hisses inside me, spitting lethal saliva.

"Naji el-Jundi was accustomed to saying, 'Sufficient unto the day is the evil thereof.' Consequently, many people believe that a person can coexist with the world. My mind is leaving me though; my stomach squeezes me, and I press on. Lo and behold, the air escapes! Again the poisonous air is released. Don't be afraid, Abu Ghalib, soon the gases will form and accumulate, time after time, until my death—as long as this is the world and our life, and existence is the dominant game, the most terrible game we play with that invisible, tyrannical power.

"Between the grave of Marrudi and his mother stood Ya'qub conferring glory, blessings, and thanks to something unknown and unjust called "God" by His victims. In this case, how could one expect the poisonous gases not to accumulate inside me? Tell me, honored Abu Ghalib, don't these gases have a good reason for forming? I release them, and they came back again and they'll come again and again from now until I die."

Eleven

1950. Baghdad's frost melted. The month of April came again. A neglected child was on the edge of a road crowded by pedestrians. He cried "Nga, nga, nga . . . Here I am!" The voice of the child submerged in the noise and commotion. All the pedestrians were absorbed in current events. Time eventually made things elapse in April; then April died too. Sandstorms blew, and the coming of summer was announced.

1—Sabriyah, 'Abdush's Daughter

One, two, three.

Sabriyah's eyes moved alternately back and forth with the pendulum of the wall clock that swung left to right and right to left in constant monotony and rhythm; the hands of the clock were slow. There was a steady mechanical and circular movement above the swinging of the pendulum, and, only slightly aware, she stared at the two movements. But, she was alive to another circular movement not different than the movements of the hands. The pendulum swayed and everything moved around its own axis.

"I will think," she said to Efrayim.

As the globe turns around its orbit, human beings circulate around our own selves, as do our human thoughts. *The Blue Lagoon* was playing at the Ghazi Theater and *Little Women* at the Dayana.

'Afaf pinched her: "Sabriyah! I see you're behaving as you did before."

The couple was alone on an isolated island in *The Blue Lagoon*.

329

"Why? Who told you I've changed?"

"Naturally, you don't give up anything. You're as stubborn as a Kurd." Sabriyah and her sisters were together with the family in *Little Women*. Sabriyah was tensed and troubled, and she said to 'Afaf, "Please leave me alone with my troubles."

A loud cacophony of oud strings came from Amirah's room. Sabriyah thought, Amirah won't stop until she breaks the oud! Impulsively, she unloaded her anger at Amirah and at Selman, leaving his oud with her as a trust before leaving the country, gambling with his life. If she followed him and went to Israel, the distance between her family and her would be farther, and a barrier of fire would separate them.

How would Sabriyah see 'Afaf, Amirah, and her father? She had mixed feelings of sadness, grief, and anger.

Jumping up from her seat, she threatened, "Amirah won't stop unless she's beaten to death." She rushed to attack Amirah in the room and beat her, but soon collapsed back on the chair and was startled to see the pendulum still swinging. Everything was still moving in a circle.

"Dad!"

"Yes, 'aini."

I kept silent, knowing that talk was useless. After all, my father knows what he wants; he'll never leave. He also knows how to read my thoughts. He said, "Dear Sabriyah, take your time to think, but if you ask me, your husband comes first." He kissed me on the cheek.

'Afaf protested: "Only her? What about me? Why is Sabriyah the only one pampered and loved?"

"Brat! Are you jealous of me? You'll marry, and your husband will kiss you a thousand times a day."

Efrayim planted a thousand thirsty kisses on my body. Selman Hashwah was jealous. Selman Hashwah was miserable. He became sick and tired of the world, and his oud is still sounding in Amirah's room. He left me a souvenir, his oud. 'Afaf likes to kid. I wonder whom 'Afaf and Amirah will marry. How can I wait until I see them again?

Selman was pale, his face and hair as yellow as the *shaih* plant, like Efrayim's hair. Efrayim begged me to leave the country, and I told him that I would think it over. Amirah started to act up after he left. Selman left the oud with me before leaving the country. Amirah is still wild. She never grows, up and my love for Efrayim will never grow weak, but I know he will never change.

I longed for Efrayim, and when he came my heart fell. I said to Amirah, "Who is that? Efrayim?" She said, "What about the oud?"

My heart throbbed in a strange manner. A sigh and a desire for a troubled life buried in a hole in Bani S'id! Why do we let our lives fall back behind us continuously? Why do our relationships with things and the past change? Why does the nostalgia for our life in the past remain solely in mute silence? thought Sabriyah. My tears fell silently like a slow and steady rain. I wish I knew why. The oud never stopped making noises in Amirah's room. She would stop only when she broke it. She wouldn't stop unless I beat her to death and cut her flesh into pieces.

'Afaf said, "What happened? The minute you saw Efrayim you became sad. Don't deny it, Sabriyah! Do you think that I don't know that you still love him, that all the time you couldn't control yourself and wanted to see him?"

I cried and laughed. I lost my mind in longing for Efrayim—lost and in pain. My house is there, in Bani S'id. My life was dispersed among mummies, among angelic tenants that men don't understand. I was tortured, fed up, and now I sighed and in vain tried to pick up the pieces. How has the world changed so much in ten months? The past behind me still exists, and I turn toward it and try to piece it together. I yearned for him and said, "I'll think it over." But, the solution is hidden in the future. I must decide and take a stand. All the while I'm standing between the two, the past and the future, between the two loves in *The Blue Lagoon* and *Little Women*. Is it possible to compromise between the two? How?

"'Afaf! Tell Amirah to stop, she's drilling a hole in my head. She'll break the man's oud. By the Holy Book, if she doesn't stop now, I'll take out all my troubles on her and beat her up."

Why did Efrayim come? I had forgotten him for a while. I wanted to give in to the selfishness of humanity, to monopolize this one love. I owe my existence to my mother and father, to Bistan el-Khass where I grew up and my body blossomed. Then he showed up.

I was wrong. I haven't forgotten him. I covered myself with a blanket made of spiderwebs to protect myself against this other love of my childhood. I put myself at the mercy of people's unjust desires and of this tyrannical world. They say, "You can't have your cake and eat it too." In fact, the two loves are big and sweet. My God, to which should I cling and where should I go?

Efrayim will never change. He's weak and passive. I thought he could never endure the estrangement of distance, and my love would then breathe a new spirit into him, making him ready to undertake any job nearby for my own sake. A month, two months, three months passed. Nothing changed.

So why did you, Efrayim, come back? Why? Marrudi drowned, the barber's wife went to her parents, Sa'idah Ghawi ran away with Karim 'Abd el-Wahab and got married, and Selman Hashwah fled the border illegally to Iran and left his oud with me. Is it possible that all these events took place in ten months?

And you said, "I came back because I decided to give up our citizenship and leave the country. There's no other way out."

I said, "I'll think about it." That is what I said to him, and afterward I drowned in tears.

"You love him! You love him!" 'Afaf said.

Sabriyah's yearning for two loves bubbled like molten steel in the pot of an unsettled conscience. This yearning was deeply ingrained in her skin, like a mole or a tattoo. On her skin. Attacks of nostalgia swept through her heart with every breeze, smell, sound, and glance. All these were part of her. She began to water the tiger flower, the coxcombs, the Raziqi, and the purplish Banafsheh flowers. The colors were loud—red, white, green, and purple. Her nose was filled with smells of the oleander and the *butnaj* herb. She also smelled the food frying from the Armenian camp mixed with the pungent smells of smoke coming from the Mi'dan's place, where water buffalo were raised.

One Mi'dani woman pressed down the street carrying a tower of yogurt containers and a tray of thick clotted cream, calling "*Geimar yu, geimar yu!*" More smells, sounds, colors, and scenes crammed themselves into her imagination. She also saw the raspberries covered with green fig leaves in the basket balanced on the head of the peddler. She longed for a raspberry, eaten by pricking it with the yellow palm tree toothpicks, and for *abu-l-tobah*, the head of romaine lettuce she used to eat leaf by leaf on sunny days. She also longed for the golden-yellow dry figs, for the chirping of the birds and cooing of the pigeons, the stench of mud and water in Bani S'id.

She also envisioned the Mosul train and a man in khaki with his ticket puncher, swaying from one car to another. She longed for his golden hair and black eyes—his weakness, timidity, firmness, too. Efrayim was an untamable and untenable love. The fall of his hot breath was like the vapor from a teapot, a dwindling desire.

In the flashing lights in Bab el-Sharqi she saw the vibrant life of the rivers, boats on the Tigris, and *jazrah*, the small island. She saw an overflowing sea of entertainment, movie theaters, nightclubs, and bars. How beautiful the Tigris was! She saw the chardagh hut and happy people on the bank dancing around the circular pits of barbecuing fish. She heard the tickling of the ouds, the jangling of tambourines, and the singing. Efrayim had not changed, she mused; he was planning to escape and wanted me to run away with him.

Selman Hashwah's oud could still twang. He left ten months ago, and his oud is probably out of tune. Perhaps he's begging there. Who knows? The oud, I'll bring it to him. If he has no choice, he'll go back to playing the oud, and the oud will help him make a living. What? Why am I talking of Selman's oud while following Efrayim?

"If you ask me, your husband comes first," Sabriyah recalled her father saying.

"Why did you come? Why did you come?" She yelled at Efrayim with pain in her heart.

"We should give up our citizenship and leave. There's no other way. All the doors are closed for me to find a job." Efrayim was running away, incapable of taking care of his affairs. A miserable boy died, a young girl fled and converted to Islam, a good and generous woman returned to her parents' home in sadness—and a poor, one-eyed, desperate human being decided to change his fate. And the two loves were great and huge. Which would she choose?

She was like a child. Her father gave her puffy marshmallows and fluffy, colorful cotton candy on a stick. She licked it and ate it, and it melted in her mouth as quickly as an ice cream, leaving only the aftertaste. It was sweet, as sweet as sugar.

Papa pampered me too much. Yet he also gave me the strength and the freedom to choose my destiny. Still, I felt weakness and inability. Freedom became void, and it was impossible for me now to make a choice even if given the chance. How would I be able to do so when deadly fragments diffused and mixed inside me? How would I sort them out? Or, rather, how would I gather them together in this commotion?

Why did you come, Efrayim? Why? I forgot you for a while.

Suddenly, she rushed toward Amirah's room. She was mad. She grabbed the oud from her hands and slapped her on the face, but when she heard her sister screaming, she collapsed and hugged her tightly, sobbing with shaky, broken breath, "Oh God, what should I do? What should I do?"

*

Sabriyah would stay attached to Efrayim's love, hanging onto her marital bond. She would leave, but at the same time, she would still be tied by love for her roots—by the smells, sounds, colors, and yearning. Efrayim wanted her to go with him, to give up her citizenship. Just by the stroke of a pen, she would lose her identity.

No! I have a double identity and I'll never give up either one. The two loves exist inside me, she thought.

"Why did you come back?" Sabriyah asked.

"I missed you. I swear by the name of God, I yearned for you."

Efrayim would never change, never change. Still, if this ruthless reality could change, then Efrayim could too. And what would I do if I obeyed him and left? Would he even then keep me away from my relatives while he sits at home jobless? The worst thing that might happen to him is to go there and work in construction. But I forgot I had only been fooling myself all along. Everything turns around itself, the hands of the clock, and man and his thoughts. I forgot that a marital bond has bound me to Efrayim, that I am tied to him, that I am tied by something greater—love.

She shouted, "Divorce me, divorce me!"

A finger stained with blood suddenly stepped in between the two loves and separated them with a harsh dose of foreboding reality. Could the head be separated from the body? There was a wide and deep, dark gap filled with a hateful smell between the two loves. No, not at all. The two loves were as blended and interlocked as soul and body. Nothing could separate them but death. The mistakes, the mistakes! People's mistakes have not stopped raining on my head, Sabriyah thought.

Now, Efrayim had run out of patience. Now he was a woman disguised as a man. She hated him and was disgusted by his shortcomings. The oud became silent in Amirah's room. Silence prevailed everywhere, except in Sabriyah's head. It was everywhere. Could a place be meaningless when two lovers were intertwined? Someday this world will sober up and the selfish, lustful desires of madmen will listen to reason.

Excuse me Amirah, I adore you—I swear by father's name, I love all of you—you, 'Afaf, father, mother, and Bistan el-Khass. But do you want me to be a widow while my husband is still alive? I'm confused and distracted, and Efrayim is passive, unmovable, and stuck in the mud. Efrayim is God's lowest creature, but he is still my husband and you are my relatives. I have changed my clothes and here I am holding my purse to leave.

"Hey, Sabriyah, where are you going?"

I said to 'Afaf, "My voice is fading, broken—what should I do?"

I'll go to Bani S'id. I'll go with him to register and give up my citizenship—our citizenship. What a deceit as definite as death this is! But the two loves exist, and the world is bound to become sober again. And when that happens the two loves will unite and nothing will separate them. Nothing, nothing!

Sabriyah left her house with hesitant steps, pulling herself up by force with shackled feet, going to Bani S'id, to her relatives, her husband—the two loves. The world would become sober one day. She cried but did not wipe her tears. She was enclosed within a horrible, locked whorehouse waiting for the world to come back to sanity. People in the street looked askance at her and wondered.

2—Farhah Ghawi

The sun shone but it was dark inside and chilly. 'Amam, Ya'qub's mother, was rinsing the dishes in the kitchen. She held me by the shoulder and whispered, "Farhah, what are you waiting for? Why aren't you going to give up your citizenship and leave? For you, this is a relief. Maybe God, may His Name be praised, will give your daughters a lucky break and they'll find their bridegrooms there. He strikes but His blows have mercy. See how they look? Every one of them has become as thin as a stick. Isn't it possible that the Law of Citizenship Renunciation was issued just for these girls? Take them and leave. Your poor daughters! Maybe they'll marry there and enjoy life."

The shining sun set in the darkness of my existence, then faded. Sa'idah! 'Aziz! Woe if I had to leave them, and woe if I stayed with them here! Latifah, Bannutah, and 'Abdallah were still here to cause me pain.

"Listen to me, Sa'idah. If you do nothing and your husband doesn't do anything either, then I'll accompany your sisters and go to register to leave the country," said Farhah.

The time had come to run away from this awful situation and avoid a disaster. My heart wouldn't be saddened any longer. Enough of bowing my head because of my son and daughter. I wanted to be able to raise it and look people in the eye. I wanted to see them without dying a thousand deaths a minute.

"You are a noisy nag, Sa'idah! I am comfused, I have a trouble. Damn you! Whose disposition did you inherit, mine?" asked Farhah.

"Damn you Sa'idah, don't leave us hanging, tell us what you've decided to do so we'll know how to proceed. Are you coming with me? Otherwise, I'll take the girls and leave the country."

The cutting machine was slicing inside me. Let me bemoan my miserable luck. I'm caught between my family and my grief. Do these people really think that my life is as sweet as honey? I got up and washed the courtyard. 'Amam would probably be surprised and remark sarcastically. I stooped on the floor and rubbed the surface time and again just to pass the hours.

I impatiently sucked on the bitterness of humiliation as if it were candy, licking it repeatedly like a cow chewing its cud. Even 'Abdallah controlled me. So what was left to do? I was like someone who swallowed a razor blade. If I coughed it out I couldn't be out of danger. If I pushed it inside I wouldn't be safe either.

I remembered the shoe repairman who lifted his eyes to heaven every time he struck his hammer, and I often raised my eyes to the courtyard's gate hoping Sa'idah would come, praying that she would push the gate open. Sister, make way for your brother! People, have your hearts become as hard as stone?

Latifah yelled, "Let them go to hell and be burned."

The gate was paralyzed and unmoving. I was running after a mirage. My head was making a racket. I wished to run after Ya'qub, 'Amam's son, and grab him by the throat, but my wish quickly vanished. I picked on Ya'qub just as my relatives would pick on me. Wasn't there another man to marry Sa'idah except Ya'qub?

The big mistake was a hidden bone pierced through the center of Ya'qub's mind. It penetrated him maliciously, secretly, and slowly without leaving a trace. I felt dizzy looking for clues that might guide me to the source—if only I knew the source of my troubles. How was the bone formed? The mistake was like 'Aibah, the nagel, whose origin was mysterious. 'Amam passed by and praised me, "Well done Farhah, long live your hands, Farhah! The courtyard is so clean that one could lick it."

I wish man's mind were as neat as this courtyard, if only his soul could also be cleansed and become as shiny as a mirror! I didn't open my mouth to answer 'Amam. Bewildered and embarrassed, 'Amam said, "Enough! How many times do you have to wash it? Don't you see it is already shining like a mirror? You have started to pant with the effort. Don't you care about yourself?"

I washed the courtyard once, twice, three times. Perhaps by washing it more than once I would find my lost self. I had a headache so I got up to brew a cup of tea. I realized that the tea was no longer effective because it couldn't bind the fracture or fill up the vacuum, even if I drank a whole pot. The bone was stuck there and wouldn't shake loose.

I noticed a huge black cat wiping its face with its paws near the closed gate. Why was the cat washing its face? Suddenly I saw this was a good omen. Sa'idah would come. 'Aziz too. I jumped toward the gate, forgetting the tea and myself. My eyes remained fixed on the gate waiting in anticipation and watching the unknown. The gate was bound to move some time soon. Open it and come in! The gate remained closed and paralyzed, ridiculing and mocking my impatience. It had a stiff heart and was entirely made of hard wood, like people's hearts. The sun sank again, disappearing behind the unknown.

Why did the weather suddenly become cloudy? I raised my head toward the endless horizon and saw the sun sarcastically staring down at me. I looked at the earth, at the shores full of light and the shadows of seas. Then I looked for the cloud and found it. It was my own cloud, black, dense, formed inside me, and scattering inside the gate of the house. The wing of a giant crow would get larger until it encompassed the universe under it and wrapped itself around the world.

I sighed with painful despair. Every day I hoped they would come that same day or the next. I joined those who mocked me and became one of them. Woe is my mind! It was better if I were to trade it for crude soap. I was naive and stupid, waiting for them in vain as if I were waiting for my dead children, may God protect them!

I recalled the tea, the strong black tea with the sharp aroma penetrating my pores and numbing my ability to breathe. The tea would make me drowsy, either kill me or resurrect me from the dead. When I drank a few sips like poison I felt relaxed and took a short breath of relief.

I would go to her. There was no way out. It was necessary that my wish come true. I would go to Sa'idah early in the morning.

I secretly crossed to the other side of the river by boat. I left my home like a confused thief, wrapped from head to toe with my coarse black 'abayah. The address! Where was it? Sa'idah had given me the address before I left, and I always kept it. I feared I would lose it or be caught with it, which would give away Sa'idah's whereabouts. I was afraid of many things. My fear stretched to the end of the blue shore on the other side of the river, attacking me from behind, coming from miles away beyond the shore. No one recognized me. I crossed the river, but the fear and the other burning things remained.

I pulled out the address, which was written in bad handwriting on a worn-out crumpled piece of paper. I inquired about Karim 'Abd el-Wahab's home. I felt both estrangement and closeness and was told, "Are you asking about the man who married a Jewish girl?" Everywhere my distinctive mark clung to me, and I was weary because Sa'idah found me as if I had turned into a gold mine. Suddenly, my heart was darkened. I became like the coarse wool of my 'abayah.

"Mama! I can't believe my eyes!"

Sa'idah's head was wrapped with a black handkerchief. Her forehead contracted above her small, cute nose, and there was a fresh turquoise-colored tattoo mark on her face. She collapsed on a chair because her body could not carry the belly so big that it almost reached her mouth. Farhah fell gasping and fainted out of grief and sorrow.

"I have come to take you away," I said. "Your sisters and father are making a big fuss. They insist on leaving the country. I would like to leave too, if not for you and your brother, 'Aziz."

Sa'idah was holding a quilt and sewing it for the baby sleeping inside her tingling belly. The quilt dropped from her hands, and she looked gloomy. Fear alone overwhelmed the looks of us both.

"So you'll leave me, Yom. I beg you don't, Mama! Stay! Stay with me, Yom!"

My mouth became parched. I had counted every minute before seeing her, wishing to hear a different answer, hoping to hear, "Go ahead, Mom! I'm your daughter and will go wherever you, my father, and my sisters go. My heart is bound to yours until the end of the world."

"Please Yom, *lat-hiddini wahdi*, don't leave me alone! Stay here with me, Yom! Stay, don't go!"

Suddenly I searched for 'Aziz in my defeated imagination. He was like a ghost with unclear features. Only 'Aziz remained. I said, protesting to Sa'idah, "Woe! I see that you've already forgotten our Jewish dialect."

Where was 'Aziz? Why did his father refuse to look for him? What happened to make him unwilling to come home?

Sa'idah's face blushed, and she said apologetically, "I have forgotten nothing, Mother. No one forgets his relatives, but I'm now used to speaking the other dialect. I haven't forgotten you. By the Holy Book, all of you are still in my mind."

Could I believe her oath? By which Holy Book did Sa'idah take an oath? What did we do to 'Aziz that made him abandon us and leave?

Suddenly, I heard Latifah's voice, "Go to her! Follow her!"

Let them walk into hellfire. Because of their nasty remarks I have bent my head and it has stayed bent all the time. I wished a sickness stroked them and a fire burned them.

"My daughter, if you truly love us, come back with me, I beg of you. Your sisters are dying of grief and your father is in bad shape."

I was staring at Sa'idah's swelling belly where Karim's son was lying calmly and peacefully, inside my daughter, my daughter Sa'idah. She breathed a sigh as heavy as lead and felt a burning flame in her head and face. Farhah wiped her face with her palm, felt a hot vapor stinging it, and rinsed her face with water quickly and repeatedly.

"You, Mama, you gave your blessing to this marriage and murdered Sa'idah. You are to blame!"

This was what Latifah told me. No, no! I didn't bless anything. I cursed all of them. But the curse fell on me alone and excluded all of God's other creatures.

"My daughter, he who doesn't associate with his own kind . . ."

I swallowed the rest of the saying.

I didn't listen. I blessed this marriage, and now I saw before me the first fruit growing in the womb of my dear Sa'idah.

"Mom! What about my husband and my son? Abdalek! I beg you, stay with us! I beg of you, stay!"

Despite this, I didn't cry. There was something bursting inside me that was stronger than tears. Death was maliciously getting ready. Marrudi did well to die. Those who die are right. They die wisely, but my blind fate was destined for me since the day I was born. Where was my 'Aziz? I was angry at the world.

"Mom! I love you all. Don't blame me. Don't you see my situation?"

What did I see?

I answered coldly, "If you truly loved us, you would give him his son and leave with us. Your sisters have melted down completely and nothing is left of them. The same holds for your father and mother!"

Where is my dear 'Aziz? Who would guide me to him?

"If you truly loved me you would stay with me, Yom. I beg you, Mom, stay with me, don't abandon me and go!"

However, I walked toward the door and suddenly death lived the same way that Karim's son was living inside Sa'idah. 'Aziz was lost in the unknown, and my daughters had become skin and bone. Sa'idah leaned on the chair's arms and got up to follow me out of the room. She was crying.

"My husband said that he saw 'Aziz working at a calligrapher's shop in the Sinak Quarter. He didn't talk to him, but he made inquiries about him and was told that 'Aziz doesn't frequent Salimah's nightclub anymore."

I was about to turn around but didn't. Death lived in me. Mentioning 'Aziz's name didn't revive me. I was alone, doomed, motionless, dying amidst all the living.

There was something wrong. Tears burst out again for both 'Aziz and Sa'idah. 'Aziz was working as a calligrapher. He was not far from here, but to me things seemed as distant as a dream. I was as close to him as the heart's artery and as far as the other world and illusions. I was going away from my firstborn daughter to be close to my firstborn son. The water of the river was turbid, blue, mixed with a killing beauty. Death was living inside me. Death was in the depth of this water. The water was fresh in the mouth of the lucky ones and bitter in my mouth. Death, death!

The boatman said, "Where do you want me to drop you, Mom?"

"The best thing is to drop me in the water."

The boatman didn't hear me because I was talking about death and God. Both were as silent as the dead. Death was located in the depths, in the depths of all things, inside me, and in the depths of the water. Marrudi did well by drowning. I was jealous of him.

'Aziz was now in the Sinak Quarter, and Sa'idah was lost like me. If only Karim hadn't seen Salimah and loved her. If 'Aziz hadn't gotten drunk and been brought home by this damned guy! But things must be traced back to their source . . . If it were not for the honor and respect Karim had shown from the beginning . . . If Sa'idah hadn't loved him, or rather if there were a decent and merciful man who would marry her, like Ya'qub, for example . . . If only 'Abdallah weren't a sheep, incapable of even tying his shoelaces . . . If I hadn't welcomed Karim . . . Wasn't it poor 'Abdallah who used to tell me not to let Karim in or welcome him? It was my fault again. So I admit this to myself about myself. My mind has stopped functioning. I'm losing it, unable to tell right from wrong.

The water invited her in. The water was fascinating, tempting. It opened its arms for her as warmly as a sincere friend.

Death! To hell with it! Jump in, she thought. Death was better than suffering and being in pain, better than being lost and not knowing a thing. Sa'idah rejected me as if I were a beggar with an outstretched palm. And 'Aziz? If 'Aziz hadn't forgotten us he would have come every month or two. Why did you act like this, Sa'idah? 'Aziz, did I ever do anything bad to you?

The Tigris stared at her. It was all eyes, open and smiling at her in a friendly manner. "Come to me, come!" the water called. A piece of dung was floating slowly on the water. Confused and weary, she wondered where the water would take it. Was it a horse apple, a cow patty, a mule's turd, or simply a piece of human shit? She didn't know anything, but she saw the entire world in that filthy piece of refuse. Then she saw herself in it, and though it drifted away from her she followed it. Will my body join my soul? She wondered. Well, who would lose out in the end? I would expose myself to disgrace, and those who didn't already know would find out, and everyone would gossip about my daughters.

'Amam told Farhah in the kitchen, "Alas, Farhah! What are you waiting for? Take your daughters and leave."

Latifah said, "If you don't leave, I will take Bannutah, my sister, leave the country, and unpack these troubles."

'Abdallah treated her as if she were a piece of dirt and cursed her father in the grave. Sa'idah rejected her and robbed her of her dreams.

The dung floated off into the distance, and she forgot about it. There was certainly a different life in the unknown. Well, what about 'Aziz? Should I go and leave both of them? she wondered. Abandon my two eyes? How would I be able to see without them, as 'Atiyah, Joudi's mother, says.

The boat docked on the other side of the river. At home, there were three waiting for her to make a move. Her illusions were ripped apart, nothing left except death. Death. Why death? Latifah! Bannutah, my daughters, and 'Abdallah, my husband!

She paid the boatman double fare, and he helped her out of the boat to the shore of the river. She stood there watching the turbid water. But the depth was beyond the horizon, and there was another life beyond that. She turned her face toward one side of the river and back to the other. She was torn and in pain, guilt ridden, but not facing death. She intentionally missed the opportunity and went on to Bani S'id.

Was she dead or alive? She didn't know but couldn't stop whispering to herself, "To hell with it. What am I waiting for? Am I waiting for the dead to be resurrected from the grave? May 'Aziz and Sa'idah be excluded from the dead? I'll carry on and maybe what God destined for me will be revised."

She continued to whisper, and inexhaustible springs of tears welled up again and wet her pale face.

3—Ya'qub, 'Amam's Son

What is going on? So this is why you were whispering to each other! Could my words be doubted now? My eyes sparked fire. People take pity on me. Isn't it a pity that women run me when in the past no one dared to tell me to do this and not to do that? I rushed to my mother and attacked her like a wild, stormy wind.

"Damn you, and Fawziyah, my sister! Who does Fawziyah think she is now that she got our citizenship certificates and gave up our citizenship to leave the country legally, all the while keeping it hidden from me? Whoever told you that I wanted to give up my citizenship and leave? Have I become a coward, a scarecrow? The fact that I am jobless doesn't mean that you can run my affairs and stop listening to me."

They conspired with 'Alwan against me, obeyed the cursed voice of the whore, and followed the desire of this cruel world. I was mad, and when I'm mad I lose my mind. It was the first time I stood face-to-face with my mother and challenged her. In a low voice, she hung on, not to defend herself but to talk about the filth of this world. Her bravery made me look bad.

"Son, you wouldn't leave the country unless you were forced to," she said. "Tell me, what is it that makes you want to stay here? You're jobless and things aren't as good as before. People are afraid to walk in the street, and those who stay home don't know what will happen to them. And you tear off with your buddies to the café and don't see what's going on. Please, Ya'qub, open your eyes!"

I broke down. Everything has become upside down, and I became upside down too. "Look around and think straight," I said to myself, "Open your eyes! Look and see what's happening around you and stare straight into the sea of darkness! You're drowning in the depths of this world." My mother bent her head before me and exposed her lost courage to me, looking to restore it by her innate self-respect. She was sweating out of shame and disgrace. Perspiration made her bright forehead wet.

She said, begging, "Listen, son, don't blame me. I don't know how to cope with all this. I can't find a patch big enough to cover the hole—there just isn't enough money. Do you think I don't know that you don't like squash, but what can I do? I beg you to force yourself to eat. It's better to eat than go hungry."

I pictured the gypsy whore to myself, but I tried to avoid really seeing her and having to escape from this world. I covered my eyes with a black veil, but I couldn't control myself and shouted at the world, not at my mother, "What should I do? I even glued labels on bottles, but the factory is closing down now. Should I burglarize, steal, or enter the toilet and shit piles of dinars and then fish them out? May you die! May you die, Ya'qub! Everything seems black to me. The eyes of my luck have been poked out with a finger."

My mother asked me, "What happened? Did your luck turn upside down?"

Suddenly, I saw the gypsy whore in front of me again in all her astonishment. I was stunned by her insurmountable strength, stronger even than people's fortunes and desires. The world then appeared like putty in the hands of the oppressors, but I spat at it and ran away to my friends Majid, Hamid, and Mahdi!

"For God's sake, explain to me what I should do with this world?"

The world opened its mouth and breathed a hot sigh. I didn't silence my friends, but clearly my question did something more potent for them than astonish them. This fickle pain was that of an uncaring world.

'Alwan ran into me a few days ago. Sparks were struck on the anvil of his eyes with all the hatred of the world. He was entirely buried in the lap of the gypsy whore. All of him was absorbed by the dirty whispers of the devil.

"Hey you, what did I tell you? Didn't I say you were all traitors and bastards? Do you see now how right I was? All of them are leaving the country. They appreciated nothing. Now you leave! Go fly with them, fool, one way with no return!"

Should I have asked 'Alwan, my lifetime friend, "Should I be like you, denying the bread and salt and the brotherly feelings of our childhood when we ran together barefoot through the alleys of the neighborhood?" I should have said to him, "The day will come when traitors and loyal people will show their true colors."

No! 'Alwan couldn't silence me. Nevertheless, I kept silent. He was using the language of the filthy whore who had put a lid on the world, turned people's fates upside down, determined their destinies in lieu of God, and changed white to black. Did I silence the mouths of my friends again? I had gone to my friends with a bleeding soul. The bleeding was still inside me like a red river, like the overflowing Tigris in flood season. Mahdi el-Tubar, who once threatened to kill me because of my loyalty to 'Alwan, was right. This Mahdi was the purest and most decent of God's creatures.

"What happened, Ya'qub? Why do you look so upset?" he asked me.

I felt the stab of a dagger in my heart, a stabbing that came from someone who saw me with one soul in two bodies.

"Nothing, my brother Mahdi. Don't worry. It is not serious."

"Please Ya'qub, you have to tell me who upset you. How can I sit and do nothing when I see you upset?"

"Thank you, brother! I swear by your life, there's nothing to worry about."

"Please tell me who he is?"

"Every word 'Alwan says sounds like a howling wind."

"Don't worry, Ya'qub! Don't give a shit about him. Let him make a fuss! He'll shut up with his own strength," Majid said. He was right, but I wished there were only one 'Alwan in Baghdad! Mahdi stood up as if he were getting ready for something.

"If so, Ya'qub, just say the word, and I'll take the breath of air from 'Alwan. Take my word, you'll hear screams of mourning from his house. He won't see another dawn if you just say the words, 'kill him.'"

I laughed. Did it make sense for Mahdi alone to purge the whole world?

"No, Mahdi, my brother. How many people are you going to kill? Is there just one 'Alwan in the whole world? There are millions like him, millions."

I wished to be buried next to my father in order to enrich the good earth with my remains and make another layer of fertilizer, but the gypsy whore had pierced my heart with millions of daggers held by millions of people like 'Alwan—my friend for life.

Majid asked without being astonished, "What's ailing you today? You aren't yourself, Ya'qub. Is it 'Alwan again?"

With a little thinking and reasoning, yes. He was the very one, he and millions like him who had sown a bad seed in the soul and desire of good 'Amam, in the souls of thousands of millions of people like her. The tears burst out of Majid's eyes, from my friend and the world, clouding even Mahdi's fixed glance.

"For God's sake, explain to me Mahdi, how the end of this world will be."

"You're an experienced person, Ya'qub. Everything was designed and planned. Our government has sold you out. I tell you, one person sold you out and the other bought you. You're the goods."

I lost my feelings. It meant that there was no escape. The whore won out. 'Alwan won. Cunning won. In fact, treason also won, but I was forced into an admission. Okay, 'Alwan, you and I are still alive. If not today, tomorrow will tell who the traitor and the victims are.

For three hours I went around looking for Gerjiyi. It seemed that the daughter of the pimp took her boyfriend and left the country. She wasn't even concerned about her son.

My mother said with fear and pity, "And what about poor 'Aibah? He has no citizenship certificate. Damn his mother! Would they let him leave with us? I plead with you Ya'qub, don't stop trying to find a solution for him. He has become like a son and should go wherever we go. Abdalak! Go and raise hell to add him to our family."

I was disgusted with everything, irritated without knowing the reason. Sure thing! Isn't this Ya'qub's responsibility? Everything falls on my shoulders. If a woman desires a man, Ya'qub should marry her off, and if someone dies Ya'qub should recite the Qiddish prayer for the whole year. And this whore Gerjiyi Nati gave birth to this bastard just so poor Ya'qub could take care of him.

Days, weeks, and months passed like the life of a sick man whose death was foreseen by the doctors. I said to my friends, "I suddenly have a fervent appetite for everything." I also had a sad feeling of restlessness, only appeased when nursed out of its bewilderment.

I drank ten cups of tea and asked the tea vendor to bring me more. I swallowed water and felt it had a scent I hadn't experienced before.

It was the fresh water of paradise. It made me cling to my friends until daybreak, but I still didn't feel satisfied completely, though I was with my friends all the time. When I smelled the barbecue and the herbs in the markets, I felt refreshed.

'Aishah the baker said to me, "What happened, Aggubi Bey? Why is it that you show up all of a sudden for the hannunah bread after I haven't seen you all year long?"

The piece of bread was so hot that I had to transfer it from one hand to the other. Then I popped it into my mouth and devoured it greedily. I said to 'Aishah, "Please, 'Aishah, would you sing an *abudiyah* or an *atabah*!"

"Of course, 'aini. I will sing for you, dear Ya'qub, even if I have to pick up the song out of nowhere."

'Aishah would always listen to me and knew how to lose me in the fascination of her clear, feminine voice, singing in the Baghdadi dialect. God never created a voice like it in any other part of the world. I closed my teeth and bared them at 'Alwan and his friend, the gypsy whore. Then I took a boat and sailed against the current to my lost childhood beyond the calm waves of the Tigris, southward to the *ziyarah* pilgrimage in el-Ezair. I visited there and had a good time, then returned on the same boat carrying baskets of pressed dates and manna candy. Yes indeed, I loved many things condemned by other people. With ardent passion, I also inhaled the toilet smell in the baker's house and the stale, watery stench throughout his quarter remained in my nostrils.

All of this was part of me, but I never felt their presence until they were cut off from me. I loved them and was afraid to lose them when my turn came to leave. I loafed in the familiar streets and quarters, listening, smelling, picturing, and reviewing the events that had occurred throughout my life, including the most recent, painful events. First, I thought of 'Alwan, my enemy now, but my friend in the good old days.

Then I said to my mother, "I want to go to the graveyard and recite the Qiddish prayer for my father and Marrudi."

I was attracted by the collapsing, muddy graves. They were triangular, black and gray, and I loved them too. It was twenty years since my father had died and was buried in his grave, but I stood in front of it astonished and sad again, just as if he had died yesterday, as if he were to die again.

My eyes traveled across the mute and earnest graveyard. Years would pass again, and the earth of fresh graves would crumble to make a good soil. My eyes shed tears without warning, amazed how my tears watered so easily. I was not in the habit of crying and, in fact, I hated tears. I wiped them off, rubbing them on my father's grave, and began to address, "'Alwan, 'Alwan! You'll see me lying next to my father. My words are the promise of a decent man, not to be changed."

Suddenly, I woke up from my dreams and felt the collapse of my confidence into apathy and incompetence. My words did not seem to be my own, and I slapped my own face, saying, "May you die Ya'qub, if the political whore truly controls you and thousands of people like you!"

I felt sorry for myself and recited a chapter from Psalms at my father's grave, only cutting short the recitation to start the Qiddish prayer. I failed to gather the ten men required to perform the prayer because the graveyard was empty and deserted, calm and colorless. I sighed. Even the graveyard had changed with the world.

Then I was content to recite the Eshkabah prayer to myself and thought I alone heard the recitation. No, there were the souls of the thousands of my forgotten dead relatives around me, wandering and listening. I wished the souls could be embodied in front of me so that I could talk to them and bid them farewell by shaking their hands as living people do. My pain grew because my wish was denied like other wishes. Only 'Alwan's wish and that of the whore friend came true.

An absentmindedness full of sadness tormented me. To where would I run away? Would I run to the dead in the endless silence of my beloved ones from whom I was separated by nothing more than a wall? I felt the wall closing in on my breathing, tightening. What seemed like paper was actually thick steel or iron. I ran away to Marrudi's grave, stumbling while passing the muddy rows of graves.

I noticed from a distance a black ghost clinging to the gravestone. No sooner had I approached it than I felt lost and horribly dazed. I was confused, and my feelings disintegrated, but I tried to straighten her out more than once. However she pushed me around and however hard she fought, she could not overcome me.

I said to my mother, "May the Name of God protect you! Are you listening to what I was saying about this? Lulu, Moshiyah's daughter was sitting at her son's grave lighting candles. I saw her and tried hard to move her and bring her home, but I could not."

Full of pain and amazement, my mother's eyes widened, "We thought she had gone to her relatives," she said regretfully. "What are you talking about? They still have to find a solution for her and arrange for her to leave the country." With hot tears, she begged, "Abdalak, do a good deed and go to the community administration and tell them about her. Also bring her the room rent, since we haven't paid her for many months and it's forbidden for us to keep her money."

This time I was not sarcastic with my mother. I had a nagging, urging desire to unload this burden from my weary shoulders and broken back.

4—Lulu, Moshiyah's Daughter

Lulu, Moshiyah's daughter, woke up even before the birds. Like a bad habit, her engrained duties woke her up like an alarm clock. Those duties were black ghosts shaking sleep itself, moving in a defeating darkness, and struggling with the rise of light. She pricked up her ears. Silence still prevailed outdoors, then came the first sound of footsteps. Hannuni Market began to yawn, but it was not awake yet. Lulu got up quickly.

There was no time left. She lit the candle, and a yellow, ghost-like light shone at the saint's tomb covered by a silky pink cloth. Short of breath but not tired, she wiped off the tile and swept the shrine's floor. She heard the first footsteps of somebody coming from the market. She stood in front of the crypt, opened her hands, and pleaded, "Sheikh Ishaq! You know why I live. I beg of you to ask your Lord to give me the strength to stay near Marrudi until I die and can be buried next to him."

She whispered from the bottom of her heart, then felt the sorrow abating. She felt happy with Marrudi and pleased with her choice. She passed through a door to a corridor that led by the crypt. Then she turned right toward the synagogue. The worshippers began to pray everywhere. When she headed toward the ark a congregant wrapped with the fringed prayer shawl followed her.

"Wait, Lulu! I came to open the ark for you," he said.

She stared at him reproachfully. "Haven't you opened it yet? Don't make me wait long, please! I have done the sweeping, wiped off the courtyard, and lit the candles. I want to visit and kiss the scrolls, pray, and then leave for home."

He didn't say a word, but he inserted the key in the hole of the lock. She once had a key but she had lost it. The ark opened. Seven silver cylinder-shaped scrolls appeared on the top shelf of the ark. She kissed the scrolls one by one while saying incomprehensible words to herself. When she finished she closed the door of the ark and turned around. Heading to the hall, she faced a man with a shining face and a black beard. She stopped for a while.

"I wish you strength, good health, and long life, Lulu!"

He slipped a handful of coins in her hand. She was embarrassed and whispered, "What is this for, Rabbi 'Ubbudi? Don't I have money?"

She tried to give it back to him but he rebuked her, whispering, "Put it in your pocket and don't say a word. Come on, there's no time. We have to begin the praying."

She fell on his hand to kiss it, but he pulled it away with full force and stepped back without saying a word. Outside, the calls of the first vendors, "Fish! Fish!" were mixed with the ambiguous sounds muttered in the prayer hall. Lulu was the only woman among the pious male worshippers, all steeped in a special kind of sorrow. The prayer refreshed her, and a new feeling flowed over her that she was still alive.

An hour passed, and light prevailed everywhere. Both the noisiness outside and the commotion inside stirred her to leave. There was no time left. She followed her urge and left by another door. A group of blind people sat outside on the stony rubble. She drew near one chunk of rubble on which was seated a middle-aged man with lightly discolored patches on his rosy face. His lusterless eyes blinked timidly. He was speechless, and his hand was stretched open to take something he could not identify. He whispered as if he knew who it was.

"Lulu?"

She slipped silver coins into his open hand and said, "Abdalak, Abraham, don't forget to recite Psalms and perform the Eshkabah prayer for Marrudi as usual. I'll go and sit next to Marrudi's grave. I don't have much time left." Troubled, she walked through a large gate festooned with nails. She was engulfed by a network of alleys and marketplaces and soon found herself swallowed up by the crowd.

Lulu asked herself, what did Ya'qub, 'Amam's son, want from me? No! A thousand times no! Do they think I'm crazy? I wish I were. Everyone is free to do what he wants and I have chosen my way. Damned the house rent! Damned death and disaster! I fled the house. Now, I am here doing a good deed for my only son, not a favor. What do these discontented people want me to do—change my mind? No, a thousand times no. I'm free to do whatever I feel; I'm the one who lives my life. Have I ever hurt anyone? So what do they want, the rent? I laughed. This land was my home. Of course, God's land was large, and I had no home except His.

God said, "I am not giving the land as charity. It's yours legally."

No! A thousand times, no! I forgive you; I forgive all of you. Don't worry about the rent. What does Ya'qub want? He put the rent money beside Marrudi's grave, may he rest in peace. Fine, I'll be rewarded for this. I turned up my palms, looked at them and found them clean, yes, clean. It was true they're rough and coarse, but they shone.

I didn't kill Marrudi. Was there a person alive who would kill his hope? I didn't bring him the black pomegranate, I tossed it into the river. It had fallen from the black coffin, in the wilderness, in the hidden alleys, and Marrudi went to the river. How and why?

What do they want from me? They don't leave me alone; one enters on the heels of another's exit. I thought and thought and couldn't figure out how the two, the father and his son, were drowned in the river, and how I tossed the bomb into the river.

What do they want? What do all of them want from me? And why is the same thing happening that happened before? The candles cast a light illuminating both Marrudi's darkness and mine. It didn't matter if the candles were consumed. I would light more. After all, what else was I there for? Was it not to keep the candles lit?

They think I'm crazy because I sit beside his grave—may God have mercy on Marrudi! And here they came back, the wicked heretics came back.

What do you want from me? Leave me alone! This is my place; this is my soil. Why should I be forced to leave the country? Nothing is done by force. I won't leave even if the world turns upside down. I didn't hurt anyone. The bird didn't hurt anyone, so why is it driven away from its nest by force? Help me Marrudi, help me! They want to take me away from you by force. A thousand times I say no. I'll say, "This is my right, and the land is not yours. It is God's, and I invested my life and wishes in it.

I clung to you with all my might. I clung to my right but they said to me, "Where is your citizenship?" Citizenship? What good was my citizenship to them? Well, it was located where only God could reach it. I continuously scratched my head. Fine. If they found my citizenship and took it, what would happen? I would scream so loudly that the earth would split.

"Sir, have a heart for God's sake, I beg you! Don't let them take me. I don't want to go. I want to stay with my son Marrudi. If you force me to go I'll kill myself. I warn you. I'll kill myself and be buried next to him. I'm attached here, and the candles illuminate my darkness, and I cling to him and light another dozen candles."

They were afraid; they shivered and fled. Only then did I feel relieved. I forgave all of them. I pardoned them but would never leave this place. I would stay in it dead or alive. I wished they thought I was insane.

I was very sane and knowingly chose what I did. Determined, I rejoiced with mixed sorrow and happiness and said to myself, victorious and completely sane, "It's already evening. I have to go to Sheikh Ishaq later and hardly have time to wash and nap. I'll come back tomorrow."

5—Naji el-Jundi

Problems! Why did I walk on one side of the street and then suddenly find myself on the other side like the worst drunkard? Swaying between yes and no, my head was overloaded, not knowing which Egyptian magazine or newspaper to start with—*al-Nujum*, *Akhir Sa'ah!*, *al-Kawakib*, or *al-Ithnayn*! The room was full of these art magazines and tons of art news. Three weeks of confusion passed in waste until I sorted them. I thought over what I should take with me and what I should leave behind, as if I did not have enough problems.

Jamil, Rabi's son, exploded the biggest bomb of confusion in my head. Like the worst drunkard, I rolled and swayed between the two rows of the houses on both sides of the street. Why and from where did Jamil's deadly questions come? They confused me as if they intended to trap me in a lost world of thought.

Jamil! May ill fortune strike you! You never keep quiet. You poke your finger into the human brain in order to plant the devilish seed of confusion. I'm troubled with my magazines. Which package should I pack in the suitcase and which should I discard? I've been sifting and sorting them for twenty days. I went around for three days to find the latest issue of *Akhir Sa'ah!* until I found the last unsold issue. It would have been better if I hadn't found it at all, since a horrible picture shocked me. How did *Akhir Sa'ah!* dare to publish the picture of Camellia, the Egyptian actress? I couldn't sleep at night thinking about the magazines on the one hand and poor Camellia pressing me on the other. I took refuge in singing "The Soul's Lover." Then Jamil bombarded me with his questions, emptying out the rest of my mind, tossing it into the frantic storm and distracting me from everything.

He said the worst thing of all, "You have no party except the Art Party anyway, so why did you give up your citizenship to leave the country? What do you call this action of yours?"

My mind crashed like the actress Camellia's airplane. It was fascinated by my master's questions in his song, "The Soul's Lover," and by his oud, singing "Why? Why? Why?" Unaware, I found myself lurching to the other side of the street like the worst drunkard. Who can control Jamil?

I said to him, "Am I different from other people? All of them are giving up their citizenship and leaving. Am I as odd as you are?"

Jamil responded, "Do you mean that the minute a person decides something, anything, you carry it out? If he jumps into the river do you jump with him?"

Jamil always wanted to plunge me into confusion. When he made me doubt my existence he said, "You're not Naji."

I said to Jamil, "My brother Hesqail closed his factory and left, because he was afraid that the government may suddenly prevent the Jews from giving up their Iraqi citizenship and leaving the country."

Jamil laughed at me, "Will you stay faithful forever? Is your life in Hesqail's hands? Wasn't it enough he exploited you?"

No one can win over Jamil. I laughed and said to him, "Okay, I am not Naji, I'm Sha'ul."

He said, "Naji is Sha'ul and Sha'ul is Naji, and if you aren't Naji then you aren't Sha'ul." He used to make me doubt my existence, now he was making me doubt my decisions.

"My mother and father are also leaving," Naji said.

"I left my mother and father in adulthood, and you are now an adult, married and divorced twice. Aren't you ashamed to say 'my mother and father'? I wish you bad luck, Jamil!"

Whenever I try to silence Jamil he silences me. I have this trouble with my magazines. I don't know which to take and which to leave behind. The terrible pictures in *Akhir Sa'ah!* shocked me. My mind is as crushed as the body of poor Camellia. The echoes of the song "The Art Lover," I mean "The Soul's Lover," is still buzzing in my head.

"You want the truth, my brother Jamil?" I said. "The situation here is no longer bearable. Did you forget what the two soldiers—may they be afflicted with a disaster—did to me?"

Jamil said, "But you have forgotten how the officers admired you during the night of the party. You yourself said that one of the officers gave you collections of poems by Hammudi, Sheikh Salama, and Sayyid Darwish. There are good and bad people in this world."

I'll put the collection of poems in the suitcase right away even if I have to throw out my clothes to make room for them. These collections are a memory of love, brotherhood, and loyalty. Jamil astounded me, and I found myself on the other side of the street like the worst drunkard. Once he made me doubt my existence, and now he was making me doubt my mind.

"If you don't believe that you are not Naji then ask our friends and see what they say!"

I looked at the people present. "You aren't Naji," they said. I was overtaken by fear and astonished at myself. If two people tell you that you have no head on your shoulders, shake it to be sure. There were about ten people and they insisted, "You're not Naji."

Who was I then? Did it make sense that ten people would conspire together against one person and agree just for the sake of undermining his existence? So my past, my present, and all my life was voided by a decision made by ten people. Should I really undo my firm personal decision, based on an incomplete consensus, to belong only to the Art Party?

"You aren't Naji!"

I went on my way, without a personality, without existence, forced to sway between the two sides of the street without really being drunk.

I heard a voice calling, "Naji el-Jundi," and asked myself, "Where was Naji el-Jundi? Who was calling him?" I didn't know and continued on my way without feeling my being. I was exactly as much a drunkard as the day I doubted my mind and my existence.

Suddenly consciousness came to me accompanied by a heartbeat, a throb of love for humanity—for this blind man begging with his stretched hand. Two children clung to him. I slipped my hand into my pocket without thinking and felt cold, solid coins. I scooped them out and poured them into his open hand. Then I wiped the tears that had broken into the corners of my eyes, and a compassionate feeling moved within me, flapping its wings like a sparrow. I forgot about being lost and about not being Naji el-Jundi.

Whatever happens, Naji el-Jundi can't see a human being or an animal tortured without being tortured himself. My heart was beating, and in the throbbing of my heart I became myself again. Naji el-Jundi, why did the tears pour out from your eyes? I asked myself. May your back be bent, Jamil! You only like to joke about such things, though they are serious, agonizing, and sometimes tricky. I still belong to the Art Party alone. Do you doubt it? Why have I been taking such troubles over my magazines? I also feel that I'll get closer to my master. The separation between us can never continue. I'll be closer to him, and just when the way is open it will be only a jump to your place. Oh the musician of the generation, my master, Muhammad 'Abd el-Wahab!

6—Jamil Rabi

I was as alone as an empty cigarette box thrown on the street, neglected on the street corner.

"A box of cigarettes for me," I said.

The cigarette vendor was astonished, and I belched. The terrible rancid taste of the kebob had risen to my throat. I wondered if it was the fault of the kebob vendor or my fault? Did he make the kebob badly or was it that my stomach couldn't digest any more? The café was crowded with customers, but I was alone. I was drowned in a symbol of muteness and freedom. All the opposites were embodied in a lie of mute resignation and the fallacy of claiming freedom.

"Abu Ghalib?" I called out to him last night, then I remembered that he had passed away. Suddenly our night guard died. I missed him and longed for his companionship in the latter part of the night and for the shrill sound of his ghostly whistle. A high wall cracked and fell in front of me and I found myself weaker and tenderer than I had imagined. Abu Ghallubi! Why did you pass away and leave the quarter without its night guard? I laughed at myself. I should have said, "Why did you leave me alone?"

I talked to the walls of the café and kept away from people, not to protect them from my evil deeds, but to protect myself from their evil.

"Are you blind? Can't you see?"

Those good days with my friends had passed, and I was left alone to face my own pain as a result of other people's evil. But what was there inside? Emptiness, nothing! It was all just motion. Abu Ghalib, the world is hustle and bustle. And now there was more commotion. If our night guard were alive, I would have said to him, "My mind is now like a beaten egg where the white and the yellow are mixed up." But Abu Ghalib was dead and everyone—the musicians, Naji el-Jundi, and the good old days—had gone. Only the contradictions remained—and the beaten egg in my head.

"Are you blind? Don't you see?"

It was only yesterday. Everything was tender, soft and delicate, while today . . .

"Hey, are you blind? Do you want to be equal with people? You turned into a revolutionary and a Communist by your own doing. Go, go to Palestine! This land has spit you out. What is left for you to do here? Haven't you exploited this land's plenty enough? Now you're conspiring with traitors and Communists!"

I closed my weary eyes. I didn't see the officer's face. The sour taste became sharp in my mouth. A rocky hill fell on top of my collapsing existence. I felt I was rejected by all things.

I may be blind, but I do have insight. Abu Ghalib! Although you're dead now and you can't hear me, I'll still ask you, "Did I ever exploit the bliss and bounty of this country? Is it right for this land to vomit us, the Jews? Have we watered it with castor oil?"

I became disheartened. Even if Abu Ghalib had been alive he would not have known the answer to my question; he would have kept quiet and scratched his head. And now I am the one to scratch my head, looking for my roots and for anything that may have lingered behind the harsh sentence against me.

The beaten egg and the paradoxes! I looked for my roots in the poor, devastated quarters in *Les Miserables*, in the toilet where I used to hide from the children in my worn-out clothes, in dirty popular restaurants, in noisy deserted cafés, in the corners of alleys as dark as the light from my eyes. Were these my roots? Who gave birth to me? Who were my grandfathers? My forefathers? Were they like my mourning women and my barbaric father? Didn't my grandfather treat bald heads and blind my eyes?

I disowned all of them when I realized my tragedy. I had chosen to be lost. So I cut myself off from my roots; there remained no blood ties binding me to anything other than to this land. I possess nothing except this land. I toil on it bearing my opposites alone, sinking to the bottom of the glass, sinking in the game of illusion and opposites, without origin, uprooted with no friends, ostracized and exiled even from self and being.

"Hey, you, blind of sight and insight!"

Whatever I do, I go nowhere and fall. Abu Ghalib, you're buried in the ground. I was buried deep inside myself, and then everything was filled with filth and refuse. Don't I have any understanding of the situation? It's true that ignorance has blinded my eyes, but poverty has opened my mind and given me sharp insight. Do you want the land to vomit us? Can it be that the land would spit out its own people?

Where are Naji el-Jundi, Selman Hashwah? Where are my friends? Is it true that this land has slurped down castor oil? If so, who taught it where to aim its spit and whom to embrace affectionately? No! Despite the opposites and the beaten egg in my head, the illusion and the entanglement of all my desires, one never becomes two. I'll go back again to the origin of the tragedy, to ignorance, blindness, mass poverty, agonizing pain, hunger and impoverishment, cause and effect.

One thing leads to another in the logic of the succession of events. My grandfather said, "Put a little Kuppalli powder in his eye and it will heal and grow as healthy as a rose in spring."

Unfortunately, my eye turned into a white and red rose without light.

My friend, who was hanged, used to say, "Where there's an oppressor, there is an oppressed." But actually the one became two. I lost my insight and the land was watered with castor oil and spewed out people.

"Hey, are you blind with no insight? Do you see yourself equal to other people? You made a revolutionary of yourself! Go away. Scram. Go to Palestine! This land has vomited you out." Between injustice and the death sentence lies the fallacy of trying to cheat the world and history.

Do you hear me, Abu Ghalib, or did you become a piece of wood resembling my mind and the rulers' hearts? I still hear you. I hear the whipping of the egg inside my head. I'll go out of my mind! Was the officer right? Am I truly a coward, blind, and lacking all wisdom?

When I didn't respond to the officer, I delayed my sweet desired death, missed the opportunity, and allowed oppression to step on the facts. No, I don't lack insight. I'll say it right now, and then they can hang me on the gallows. They are the ones without insight; the hangmen are the source of the sickness in the bowels of this land. No, I never exploited the bounty and the bliss of this land or sucked the people's blood. Go back to Bani S'id and Abu Sifain and to all the alleys of all the needy people! There are hidden and misleading mouths that secretly eat the inhabitants of Baghdad. In addition, you blame the country for spitting out its own people. But the world and history will condemn those who falsify history. The needy children and these good people will spit you out; I exiled myself and completely alienated it. I live without roots. Should I vomit myself through continued shameful submission? I shouldn't, but I continue in my perpetual losing streak.

What will happen in this other land? The worst is that I would stay the same: alone, playing rotten games with the contradictions, with the greatest problem of existence. What's the difference? I'm sure there is no difference. It will pass . . . anywhere. Can I live forever? It will pass in illusion, in opposites, searching in the depth of puzzles, anywhere. Do, re, mi, fa, sol, la, ti, do. Truth comes out of illusion. Things have changed now. I press the watch stem now, and the lid jumps. I feel the hands of the watch with the tips of my fingers.

"Turn the radio on, Muhammad!"

Today is the last day to register for giving up citizenship and leaving the country. The land is spitting out some of its miserable Jews. I'm exiled from existence and myself, but still I taught Shridah to play the qanun. I hear the sweet melodies of the qanun coming from the radio, and the player is Shridah, yesterday's busboy in all the cafés of Baghdad and tomorrow's artist. Shridah will replace the musical troupe Ikhwan al-Fann. What a faithful and genuine memory, a fact in the tooth of deceit! I wonder if Shridah will remember or forget me during the fervent war of deceit, the campaign of distortion, the turning of white into black, and posing death sentences for deceptive justice akin to murder.

Abu Ghalib? Please listen to me, never mind that you're dead now. You must testify, you must. It is necessary for you to testify that I did, in fact, create something out of an illusion: the tangible fact is sounding from the Baghdad radio. I'm the illusion. My colleagues in the Ikhwan al-Fann troupe stripped me of myself and even exiled me from my own illusory dreams.

Today is the last day to give up my citizenship. Now I step toward the truth to give up a piece of paper, which they claim belonged to me and lent me existence. But I never possessed one, Abu Ghalib. I can never replace it. I admit that those lost steps of mine are taking me from nothing to nothing, from all things to all things. The opposites. Abu Ghalib! The opposites. The game of desires and contradiction is not over yet. The melodies of Shridah's qanun alone will overflow the world. This is the only fact that came out of the womb of illusion. Shridah? Will the master artist, the skillfully talented qanun player, the successor of the Ikhwan al-Fann troupe, remember me? What do you say, Abu Ghalib? What do you say about this?

7—'Aziz al-Salmawi, Formerly 'Aziz Ghawi

The word was flexible and facile in 'Aziz's hand, obedient, nothing but one word. It flew from his brush like fresh running water and came out of his secluded soul in order to teach him more about this new style of calligraphy.

Salimah! The real Salimah had gone far from here, forgotten, 'Aziz thought. I tried to create the word *Salimah* anew and reshape it in endless copies. The origin! For your sake, Salimah, I denied my relatives, but you betrayed even your denial. Still, Salimah, I swear by your eyes that I clung firmly to this denial.

I am amazed that I don't comprehend what's happening. I'm attached to shadows, to debris, roaming amidst the ruins of myself and of painful events, not daring to dig out the ruins even though they have been restored through my sufferings, like a lofty building pleasing to the eye, except to my one eye clouded by everything except your image alone. The other eye attacks my sacred places like a devil. I tell you that even a blind bitch wouldn't fall in love with me. Araksi is in front of me obedient to the strokes of my brush. And Araksi is not a blind bitch at all.

I often heard Salimah singing the words, "When he found out that I loved him he played hard to get." She crooned tenderly and made me listen. Her crooning overwhelmed me and I laughed at the same time, then ran away to Bab el-Sharqi.

Why had everything changed in Bab el-Sharqi? Even the bar of Yusuf 'Abd el-Nabi, this horse, this son of a horse, had changed. He and his bar had become merely a memory of the past. I long for the days gone by. A terrible, unjustifiable yearning has choked me inside. More than one thing collapsed inside me. The lofty building has fallen stone by stone and buried me under its debris.

Araksi, Jalal, my success and fame! My innocent sister Sa'idah, my rival and brother-in-law, Karim, the pimp! My cousins, Farhah

Ghawi, the horse, and 'Abdallah, the male buffalo, the black water-skin—all have changed. Salimah-choka-boka, and my life and death, the nightclub, and even the water carrier have changed!

"Why is Salimah-choka-boka not here?"

They laughed at me. "Ha-ha! Are you daydreaming? Salimah left for Palestine long ago."

She left and I'm sitting here. I'll never leave, I swear by your life, Salimah. I am not one of your kind. For your sake I changed, and my innocent sister Sa'idah denied her origin. I started all this. I didn't believe in my origin. A person is a coward who starts something and doesn't take it to the end, to the last heartbeat.

"Bring me two bottles of arrack and two packs of Gold Star cigarettes!"

This is my misunderstanding, and if it reveals anything, let it persist, but if it insists on continuing to grab me by the throat, then I'll force it into a pool of wine and drown it there. There is only one hour left to put an end to it. In one hour, I'll empty the two bottles. The ashtray will be full of Gold Star cigarette butts. And I'm just the butt end of a man swaying and spreading a filthy, offensive smell of arrack and cigarettes from his mouth.

"'Aziz! Move your face away. The smell in your mouth is murderous," Salimah used to complain.

A series of events was still fresh in my memory. It had not dried up yet like my attempts to explain and justify events and other things.

"Draw your face closer! I want to smell you like I smell a rose." Araksi is an obedient and hard-working girl. She is remarkable. Poor Araksi! I am afraid that the smell of my mouth will kill her like the smell of arrack and cigarettes. I stabbed her in the heart. But the deadly smell of wine in my mouth was ambergris to her nose. Poor Araksi! She was ready and willing, even to the point of changing her dialect, denying her origin, denying herself, like my sister Sa'idah. Then why was Araksi incapable of hating what I hated?

'Aziz Ghawi is the dispirited failure, the despised dead, but 'Aziz al-Salmawi is successful and lost, a ghost, an illusion woven from the remnant of the deceased 'Aziz Ghawi. We're the embodiment of two lost and filthy souls. Though Salimah is filthier than I, she is out of the way. Gone. Undoubtedly Araksi is purer than my sister Sa'idah.

"I only worry that you may get sick from too much alcohol and cigarettes," said Araksi.

I was impatient, annoyed, and upset. I brushed Araksi off as if I were driving away a blind and scabby bitch, "No, don't worry about me. What did we say before? Didn't we agree that you'd talk the way I talk?"

She answered with the obedience and submission of a lover devoted with heart and soul. "I am worried, 'Aziz. Do whatever you please, and I'll also do whatever you want me to do. I only want to see you comfortable and happy."

Jalal gave me a look, which I found astonishing, given what was happening around me. "What's the matter with you, 'Aziz? By Great Allah! I don't understand anything anymore. You're going to drive me crazy. I don't know why you're upset. After all, everything is going well for you and you have become famous, even more so than I. Thanks to you the shop can't hold its customers, your name is on everyone's lips, and you have a girlfriend on the floor above you. She's worth the entire world. She's beautiful and would die just to get a whiff of you. What more do you want?" I questioned myself.

I was plunged into a wasteland of silence sown with sighs. I didn't answer and didn't know what to say. I didn't want to know . . .

"Say something, 'Aziz! All I want to know is who caused you to be in this mood? Salimah? Your relatives?"

I wished I knew. No. I know and don't want to be aware that I know, I thought. What is this? I dug deep inside myself demanding the impossible. But its meaning was doubtful. I felt ambiguous and had to conceal the feeling so they wouldn't mock and blame me. Was it possible to restore and reshape things? For example, if I were to become a child again and start life off with a different fate and personality . . . If Farhah Ghawi were to become a meek pigeon, not a malicious snake, and 'Abdallah, the black bloated waterskin, were to come to me one day, begging, crying, kissing my hand and saying, "For God's sake, leave with us! After all, your mother has killed herself."

This was just the nausea that made me vomit at the thought of being 'Abdallah's son. But I've changed. I have weaned myself from their filthy basins of drunken vomit. I was born here, and we'll die here like mosquitoes. Can my father be a real and strong man? He said to me, "At least give me your address so we'll be able to contact you."

Leave me alone. I've had enough. I'm not one of you. I ran from my father, but Jalal gave him my address. I hated Jalal for that. My family and I were on the verge of parting forever. I had changed my name to 'Aziz al-Salmawi, and my brother-in-law stole my sister and my life. His name is Karim 'Abd el-Wahab. I feel an urge to become his friend and his idol. Why not? If we were only in different circumstances . . . If he hadn't stolen honor and deprived me of my life—Salimah. The man who dies for her is promised life plus a thousand conditions of neither death nor life.

Salimah's spirit has built a different life for me out of deprivation. So being deprived of Salimah has killed me and made me realize that even a blind bitch won't look at me now. Salimah's staggering denial of her Jewish origin overwhelmed me. I learned from her to wear new clothes. Salimah is another poisonous snake, a poisonous snake like Farhah Ghawi. Salimah left, and I stayed here. Did she repent? I wondered. It is impossible to become 'Aziz Ghawi again. I'm 'Aziz al-Salmawi, staying and watching the results of immediate events. Araksi is not a blind bitch but an openly devoted and loving girl. Why can't she become Salimah-choka-boka?

Araksi came running with joy and said to me, "'Aziz! I bring you good tidings!" If the good tidings were that Salimah had returned to Baghdad, I would stuff candy down Araksi's throat and sleep with her without showing boredom. She continued, "You have received a letter from London, most certainly from your relatives. How much are you going to tip me?"

I was disappointed and tense. Two evils, two despised things—the letter, and having sex with her. However, I opened the letter avidly looking to find just one word in it. There was only one word fixed deeply in me like a chronic disease and an original copied over on a thousand scraps of paper written with a thousand styles of calligraphy known only to me. I found nothing in the letter except offensive tears, nothing else except the same broken record, pleading, "Tell us about your situation. We miss you very much."

There was nothing about Salimah. They drained my life essence. They took it for themselves, stole it so that I lived in emptiness and triviality. It was a mirage, but I lived within it.

I stared at Araksi. Her eyes, her features, and her body—all of her was begging me. I whispered to myself, "You have on the floor above you a girl worth the entire world. She loves you. She undoubtedly loves you." She tells you, "I'll do everything just to make you at ease."

My eyes were fixed on her face . . . No, Araksi was no blind bitch. I saw her face as a crisp piece of bread made of bleached wheat. With their black irises her eyes looked like they had been darkened from birth with kohl cosmetic. Her eyelids were thick and black, resembling two crescents surrounded by a sky with scattered white clouds. On her delicate lips formed a wavering line, attractive to men. Her bright, milklike breasts carried two glowing coals. Her trembling fattish body looked skinny sometimes, but it held her remarkable, dedicated soul. This was Araksi.

Salimah was as thin and dark as a black skewer. She infiltrated my view, and I saw her in Araksi's tender body. Suddenly, I opened my arms, and the two images merged into one body, and I said, "Come!" Araksi gasped, but I was falling breathlessly at Salimah's feet. Araksi smiled at my face, but it was Salimah before whom I humbled myself in the nightclub. Araksi came begging while I kneeled and begged Salimah. Then Salimah laughed at me and I shook my head. These clinging images are evil.

Araksi rubbed her cheek against mine, "'Aziz, your mustache makes you look old, almost like an old man. Shave it off for me."

Salimah said, "May your mother celebrate your wedding. Go and sit in your mother's lap."

Salimah! I'm a man, I swear by your eyes I'm staunch and used to be firm about many things, but today I'm determined about just one thing. Suddenly, my senses ran mad. I smelled Araksi again and again. Rage was in my nose, brain, and feelings. I continued to smell her tender skin. I smelled a sweet sharp odor.

"Take off your clothes, undress!"

Poor Araksi obeyed me. She was hardly eighteen years old. Salimah was almost an old woman by now, as old as my mother. I wondered how Salimah's smell was. My rotten filthy soul! I kneeled at her feet but my nose was suffering from a severe cold. My body felt numb, pierced with a sharp and disgraceful pain. Damn Salimah and the one who gave her birth! Because of her I turned into a near pimp.

Come on, come on! Let me pamper Araksi, let her be pampered! I'll bury all my pain between her thighs and in the hills of her tender flesh. I've changed. I'm 'Aziz al-Salmawi, the greatest calligrapher in Baghdad, greater than Jalal. I'm the greatest deceiver, the greatest pimp, greater than . . .

"Shave off your mustache and answer the letter," Araksi said.

Poor Araksi! The poorest man deceived her. She didn't know that my nausea was chronic even though I'm able to change. But going to the source to correct mistakes is an illusion of drunkards and daydreamers.

She held my beard begging, "Have mercy, do it for me, 'Aziz. Whatever happens, your family is miserable." Whatever happens, let Araksi be pampered. I'm the pimp, the eternal beggar.

"As you say, Araksi."

I followed constantly Sa'idah's news from afar. I knew that she had given birth to another child by Karim 'Abd el-Wahab. I won. I responded, "What is Salimah doing there? I ask you with all my heart to let me know if she has repented, or was she still toying with hearts and destroying them. As for me, I'm still alive."

I fell and said to Araksi politely and with hope, "Please Araksi, take this letter, put stamps on it, and mail it."

Salimah was stuck in my mind, in my memory, in my dreams, and Araksi obeyed me without hesitation, "With pleasure, 'Aziz."

I was impatient for the letter to be received and didn't care about an answer. It would take a long time to get to London and from there to Israel. I was amazed at what was happening around me— Salimah, Araksi. The two women blended again. I was thankful to Araksi and I treated her with tenderness. Poor Araksi! I was alone in the room checking my face in a big mirror. I saw my thick black mustache and was more astonished. Whatever happened, Araksi would be miserable. I would shave it off. Perhaps Fayiq the Barber would be surprised again. I would tell Fayiq it's a question of life and death.

8—'Atiyah al-Qarawchi and Joudi al-Qarawchi

"Hamidah Umm 'Abdallah, haven't you seen Joudi?"

'Atiyah was a heap of bones wrapped in eternal blackness. Her head was a bowl of gray hair, and her stature was bent, an ugly old jinni crawling on the surface of the earth with inexhaustible energy.

"He probably didn't go far away. He'll come soon," Hamidah answered.

Sighing with anxiety, 'Atiyah began to look at the tenants' house. All the tenants had abandoned the house. Grief swallowed her, and dread crushed her. Why had they left without coming back—all of them, all of them? She whispered in a choked voice, "Everything is deserted, the café is closed and nobody is there, and the Abakhanah power plant is crying, looking for somebody to take care of it."

I'm tired of deceit. I have gotten fed up with the game of secrets, so take me to the worm's kingdom, to my sisters' world, to Qadriyah's and Wafiqah's world. My companions refused and said, insisting, "Impossible! However you plead, however you beg, you and your mother will stay here. If everyone leaves, the illusions will be spread about and all the deceitful games will come to light, but you and she are staying until the end of this world."

"Why, why, why?"

My anger is a volcano. My revealed fate is clearly determined as unbearable and unending pain. My friends deceived all the people and left the truth for me only. Cross my heart! This is unfair—unacceptable. Does what is happening in the world leave a kernel of mercy in your hearts? Don't you see the wise men are destroying the universe for unreal goals and crumbling illusions?

Why? Why? My companions said indifferently, "You gave an answer yourself, so stay with your mother because the truth will inevitably remain in this false world of yours, only the unshakable and eternal truth." Oh, to the ongoing bleeding in my head like a torture from hell, a cursed truth in a world immersed in superstition! Am I capable of rebellion? I'll explode the broken word continuously, Da, Da, Da—again and again with fervor and rebellion never subsiding . . . Da, Da, Da!

I became worn out, so why do I still insist on living? I'm bleary-eyed. Though one eye leaks dirt and tears, it never stops looking up the street, at the neighbors' house, at 'Amam's Umm Ya'qub, but in vain. Hamidah told me, "I vow to sacrifice an animal at 'Amam's feet when she comes back." Will 'Amam really come back or are we mocking ourselves? I'm afraid she has gone for good like Qadriyah and Wafiqah!

"Hey Joudi! Hey Joudi! Why do you say constantly 'Da, Da, Da' without even taking a breath?" Oh, those who know how to read have left and only the dregs have stayed, Joudi and his mother! Come, dear, come and sit before your mother and let's butt each other's heads."

"No, I don't want to stay, I don't! I only want you, Mom, to take me to my sisters."

They laughed heartily, mocking me, then they shook me with a thunderous warning: "Either you stop this nonsense or we'll sober you up!" No, no! I repent. I won't say it again. I fell before my friends' feet kissing and wetting them with my tears. Only then did they feel compassion for me and remove my fear. In fact, they cut its head off. They blinded the transparent eye in my soul, planted ten tongues in the large field between my mouth and brain. These tongues know only one word, my own word. My private world was crowded with ten tongues behind my lips. They pushed forth the word and I let it out in a spree that seemed endless, "Da, Da, Da." The word multiplied quickly, restricting my breath and muzzling my mouth. Then I hurled it uncontrollably and rushed it out in order to rescue myself from the world of the wise men. "Da, Da, Da!" Let me follow Wafiqah and Qadriyah!

What happened to your mind? You must have gone mad. Otherwise how could you say, "Like Wafiqah and Qadriyah." Well, who was that woman who came panting with thirst the other day? Could it be that she was one of my two daughters? Otherwise, why did she refuse to remove her veil? Could it be that she was afraid I had recognized her? She was choking to death but said to me, "I'm thirsty, Mom!" She drank water from the vessel until she emptied it; it was full to the top but not even a drop was left. After drinking she asked, "Where's the toilet? I want to get rid of the water."

I remembered my friend 'Amam Umm Ya'qub and started to cry. I long for her very much. She used to tell me, "My sister 'Atiyah, you're in the wrong for being shy. Our house is yours, the water, the toilet."

I said to her: "We used to go to the neighbors, but now they have left. Hamidah's house across from ours is full of young men, and I feel ashamed to use their toilet."

She said to me, "Don't pay attention, pour the shame down the drain!"

In fact, 'Atiyah rushed to Hamidah's house. No, no, no! This is impossible. My daughters wouldn't have dared to say, "Pour the shame down the drain." My daughters are honest and chaste. No one is equal to them. Well, how could she do it differently, being unable to hold it? If such a thing were to happen to me, I would even urinate in the Sultan's mouth. But I was embarrassed and didn't know what to say. She was one of my two daughters, wasn't she? If Joudi had been sane I would have asked him, but where is he?

"Hey, Joudi! Why are you barefoot? Didn't 'Amam bring you Ya'qub's new sandals before she left? He wore them just three or four times. What did you do with them? The slippers she brought me, where are they? Where is the bundle of clothes? I put it next to the stove, where is it? Say something! Shame on you! Where are the items that Umm Ya'qub had brought? I'm talking to you, am I not? No, I swear by God, I'm talking to the wall." Does Joudi hear? Does he read? He has become like the crazy barber who used to repeat, "I'll soap it, I'll soap it." Well, I'll get up and look for the items Umm Ya'qub had left me prior to her departure. Perhaps I put them elsewhere. Worry has made me forget where I put them.

Da, Da, Da!

Never!

Da, Da, Da!

I'll stay in a safe place away from the wise people's family.

Da, Da, Da!

Translator's Afterword

Samir Naqqash (1938–2004) is among the foremost Israeli authors from Iraq. It is notable that he writes in Arabic and in the dialects of both Jewish and Muslim communities in Baghdad. Though the political turmoil of Iraq in the 1940s and early 1950s forced his Jewish Iraqi family to immigrate to Israel when Naqqash was only thirteen, he wrote in Arabic for his entire career. The premature death of his father soon after the family's arrival, the loss of his family's prestige and wealth, and the hardships he experienced in Israel shaped his literary talent and his pessimistic outlook.

Naqqash's literary output in Arabic includes three plays, four novels, and five collections of short stories, beginning in 1971 with his first collection, *Al-Khata'* (The Mistake). They are better known in the Arab world and Europe than in Israel. Doctoral dissertations on his oeuvre have been written in the West Bank, Jordan, Iraq, Egypt, Italy, England, and America. He is likely to be classified as an Arab rather than an Israeli writer; for instance, a translation of the story "Tantal," from Naqqash's 1978 collection *Ana wa ha'ula' wa al-fiṣam* (Me, Them, and Schizophrenia), appears in Shakir Mustafa's *Contemporary Iraqi Fiction: An Anthology*.[1]

Writing in Hebrew would have meant for him the denial of his past and the adoption of a different identity, that of a society he rejected. In his words, "I cannot come to terms with this society. . . .

1. Shakir Mustafa, *Contemporary Iraqi Fiction: An Anthology* (Syracuse, NY: Syracuse Univ. Press, 2008), 115–29.

I reside here, but I don't feel within my spirit that I live here."[2] In an interview he said, "I don't exist in this country [Israel], not as a writer, a citizen, nor human being. . . . I don't feel I belong anywhere, not since my roots were torn from the ground."[3] He traveled abroad extensively, and continued to express himself in Arabic, with a linguistic sophistication and complexity praised by readers and critics. Using Arabic as his medium of expression served to keep his identity intact, link him with his past, and bolster his attachment to his mother tongue and its culture.

The pattern for most Iraqi Jewish writers in Israel was to write at first in Arabic, then as soon as possible in Hebrew. Writing in Hebrew enabled them to integrate into the mainstream of Israeli society, and that new identity enabled them to suppress nostalgia for Jewish life in Iraq, portraying an antinostalgic view of a home no longer safe and stable, while acknowledging the difficulties that have faced immigrants to Israel from Middle Eastern countries. Iraqi Jewish authors have criticized social injustice and discrimination against Arab immigrants by creating in Israel a new subgenre of transit-camp literature. Characters in these works are marginalized by Israeli ideals dominated by the European Ashkenazi. Even those who write in Hebrew have no place in the canon of an Israeli literature that prefers experiences that promote heroism, Zionist aspirations, and security. Neither the Hebrew transit-camp literature nor Naqqash's writing have appealed to Israeli literary tastes. Nonetheless, *Tenants and Cobwebs* won the Israeli Prime Minister's Award for Arabic Literature in 1986.

Naqqash was the first Iraqi Jewish writer to use Baghdadi Jewish dialect in a literary oeuvre, drawing from Iraqi proverbs, sayings, curses, and biblical allusions. Even the title *Tenants and Cobwebs*

2. Ammiel Alcalay, *Keys to the Garden* (San Francisco: City Lights Books, 1996), 108.

3. Nancy Berg, *Exile from Exile* (Albany: State Univ. of New York Press, 1996), 3.

(*Nzualah u-Khait el-Shitan*) is an example of Iraqi Jewish dialect. Aware of the frustration that some Iraqi as well as non-Iraqi readers might feel because of his use of local dialects, Naqqash provided a glossary. As Neri Livneh observes in an eloquent obituary in the Israeli newspaper *Haaretz*, "In some of his books, the pages are divided into two parts: On the bottom half, Naqqash himself translated the stories into standard literary Arabic."[4]

Tenants and Cobwebs cannot be classified in any accepted literary style without doing it injustice. While it portrays the everyday life of ordinary people, and one may consider it a realistic novel, such description does not account for the intricacy or sophistication of the novel's structure and its stream of consciousness style. Thoughts, experiences, and events are transmitted to the reader through internal dialogues that burst the narrow confines of time and place. It is difficult to describe the plot development of the novel or even to speak of plot in the usual sense. The story unfolds in a nonchronological, nonlinear fashion, with few distinctions of earlier and later. Events in the novel move in two interdependent, interactive circles.

Tenants and Cobwebs covers the years following the Farhûd (1941), the violent dispossession, or pogrom. While no extraordinary events occurred in this period, searches, denunciation, arrests, heavy sentences, imprisonment, and economic and educational restrictions, along with memories of the Farhûd, kindled fears that it could be repeated. The setting is an apartment house in Baghdad inhabited by Jews and Muslims. Close by the apartment house is a shack where a Muslim woman, 'Atiyah, and her son Joudi live. Even as a child, Joudi is considered insane in the world of those who think themselves sane.

At first, the focus is on the small circle of Jewish characters whose lives proceed smoothly while the memory of the trauma associated with the Farhûd hovers on the surface. The world at large with its

4. Neri Livneh, "Exiled from Babylon," *Haaretz*, August 5, 2004, https://www.haaretz.com/1.4776005.

seeds of violence remains on the margins. With gradual transgressions of the tenants' boundaries, the emphasis shifts to the conflicts between the two worlds. Resentment and prejudice grow, and the spider spins its web in which all are trapped. Disturbances intensify when anti-British demonstrations take place in January 1948. The situation further deteriorates when repercussions of the war in Palestine affect the lives of all the residents and the cordial relationships between Jews and their Muslim friends. The residents in the apartment house no longer live in peace.

When the time comes to leave for Israel, Jewish residents relish sharing flatbread and a cup of tea sipped with Iraqi friends, enjoying Iraqi songs beside the Tigris. Soon the apartment house is deserted. Neighbors miss their Jewish friends. Hamidah, owner and resident of the building, says, "I pledge a sacrifice to God at 'Amam's feet when she comes back." 'Atiyah asks, "Will she really return or are we mocking ourselves? The best have gone, and only the dregs are left!"

I extend my sincere gratitude to all who have encouraged me and participated in completing this English translation. Through many long hours the process of revising and bringing the translation to finished form was supported by the limitless assistance of my wife, Judy, my three sons, Elan, Ranon, and Amir, and my cousin Latif Bartov. I also appreciate the support of the writers Nadia Nagarajan, Lev Hakak, and Eli Amir. I worked closely with my editor, John Dotson, to review the full manuscript and smooth the translation. John provided a complete substantive and technical edit while maintaining the vividness of the novel's mood and tone in order to provide access to Naqqash's powerful work. In an early phase, Judy Willmore edited and improved the manuscript. My thanks go also to Suzanne E. Guiod, editor-in-chief of Syracuse University Press, who agreed to publish this book and facilitated the process of obtaining permission for publishing this English version from the Association for Jewish Academics from Iraq.

Despite my enthusiasm to translate the novel, I was at times made uncomfortable hearing from those who felt that it would be impossible to translate the work into any language without doing the author an injustice. On the contrary, I decided to prove to myself that I was ready and willing to face this challenge and carry out the work to completion and thus to offer this text for those readers of English who may now begin to hear the tellings of Naqqash.

April 2018

A Short History of Iraqi Jewry

Glossary

A Short History of Iraqi Jewry

The Jews of Iraq are among the oldest organized communities of Jews in the Middle East. The majority of Iraqi Jews are direct descendants of those Judeans whom Nebuchadnezzar exiled from Judah to Babylonia in 586 BCE. This group joined Israelites already exiled by the Assyrians in 719 BCE. Over the years, Babylonian Jewry grew in culture, wealth, and power. When allowed to return to Jerusalem in 538 BCE, they refused to go. In subsequent centuries their region in Iraq became more hospitable and home to some of the world's leading academic centers in Sura and Pumbedita. Baghdad was the center of Jewish learning and scholarship where the Babylonian Talmud, the collection of Jewish law and traditions, was produced between 500 and 700 CE.

Following the rise of Islam after 632, and especially during the reign of the Abbasids dynasty in Baghdad from 750 to 1258, the Jewish community experienced ups and downs. Like other non-Muslim subjects of the state, Jews were considered *Dhimmis*, meaning that they were permitted, on payment of the jizya poll tax, to practice their religion and participate in their communal organizations. The closing of Jewish businesses on Sabbaths and holidays did not arouse any envy worth mentioning, and for many generations the majority of Baghdad's Muslims tolerated Jewish traditions. In exchange for tolerance and protection, the Jews had to put up with certain restrictions and many humiliating regulations that asserted the social superiority of Muslims over non-Muslims. It is said that the caliph al-Mu'tasim, ruling from 892 to 902, ordered the abolition of the jizya for the Jews. However, one of the wealthiest Jews of Baghdad opposed this order and told the caliph: "By the payment of the poll tax, the Jews become protected subjects. Were the poll tax to be abolished, Jewish blood would be shed freely."[1] According to this story, the caliph made this Jew responsible for collecting the tax.

The range of tolerance and intolerance varied with the rule of different caliphs. Under tolerant ones, Jews enjoyed freedom in their social and economic activities. Under intolerant ones, all non-Muslims were subjected to decrees of social discrimination. Special taxes were collected from Jews, and they were required to wear yellow clothes and patches to identify themselves. Some caliphs considered friendship of Muslims with Jews and Christians to be sinful. Jews were subject to forced conversions to Islam during the Mongol invasion of Baghdad by Holagu (1258–1335).

During the period of Ottoman domination of most of the Middle East (1517–81), the Jews of Iraq, like other non-Muslim residents, enjoyed relative freedom, and their economic situation was good. Most of the Jews were engaged in commerce with neighboring areas, as well as with Yemen, India, and other countries. They were still required to wear special dress and pay higher taxes than the rate imposed on Muslims. Generally speaking, Ottoman rulers readily enabled the Jews to observe their religious duties and hardly restricted them as to their means of earning their livelihood. Although Jews did not have equal rights with Muslims, some of them acquired important jobs in the courts of the Ottoman sultans, in the foreign service, and as civil servants, advisors, bankers, and physicians.

Between 1831 and 1917, the Jews found themselves under the rule of Turkish governors, or walis. Some of them mistreated the Jews in particular, but between 1839 and 1914 the legal status of Jews improved. When Midhat Pasha ruled Iraq (1860–72), he not only brought order among the various Iraqi states but also complete emancipation for Iraqi citizens. With Pasha's reforms, the Jews were no longer required to pay the jizya and became Iraqi citizens with equal rights, able to manage their lives with autonomy. They also benefited from the opening of the Suez Canal in 1869. Basra became an important port with business and economic opportunities opening for many employees. Iraqi Jews engaged in small businesses and developed trade links extending to England, India, and the Far East.

In 1908 the reforms brought by the Young Turks, establishing a new constitution in 1909, guaranteed full citizenship and officially granted

1. *Encyclopaedia Judaica* (1971), s.v. "Jewry in Iraq."

equal rights and freedom of religion to non-Muslims. Several Iraqi Jews were elected as Iraqi delegates to the Turkish Parliament. Jews were also appointed in government courts, district municipal councils, and civil service positions. They played important roles in all branches of trade, especially in those of silk and other textiles, pearls and precious stones, porcelain, and liquors.

Before 1909, Jews had paid a collective tax exempting them from military service, but beginning that year, they were required to serve in the army like other citizens of the empire. A difficult period for the Jews began with the outbreak of the First World War. Many Jews were recruited into the army and dispatched to the front. Money was extorted from them, at times under torture, to finance the military.

The Iraqi Jewry were not only engaged in trade but also in cultural activities. In the twentieth century, Jewish intellectuals—authors, poets, journalists, educators, doctors, lawyers, jurists, and engineers—made important contributions. In the field of Arabic language and literature, Jews wrote books and essays, and translated Western masterpieces into Arabic. Between 1909 and 1948, Iraqi Jews published eight newspapers, only one of them, *Yeshurun*, in Hebrew. In Baghdad, there were more than six Hebrew printing presses, which in these four decades published about five hundred books and pamphlets. Among the Jewish musicians favored by the Iraqi royal family were Salimah Pasha, who played in the first Iraqi film *'Aliyah wa-'Isam*, and musicians Salih and Dawood al-Kuwaiti, who were brothers. In the 1930s, the first musical band formed with the advent of radio in Baghdad consisted mainly of Jews.

After the end of World War I and the fall of the Ottoman Empire, Iraq was under British occupation (1917–21) and mandate (1921–32). The British offered many opportunities for Iraqis who knew both Arabic and English. Iraqi Jewry benefited not only from these opportunities but also from the facilities of the Alliance Israelite Universelle and the Anglo-Jewish Association that helped raise even further the educational standards of the Jewish community. During the British administration in the 1920s, many Jews attained an Arab education in tuition-free state schools and also studied in Jewish schools, before finding substantive employment. Attending Arab schools and working for foreign oil companies on Saturdays led to laxity in preserving religious observances and customs, but dietary laws were followed. Self-employed Jews did not work on the Sabbath.

When the country gained its independence in 1933, Faysal I, the first king of Iraq, proclaimed freedom of religion and promoted education. The Jews flourished and enjoyed unusual feelings of security and prosperity as the largest ethnic and religious group in the capital. They were an integral part of Iraqi society and played an important part in Iraq's welfare and progress. Jewish delegates were elected to the Iraqi Parliament. Because of their high educational standards, Jews occupied important positions in the government, especially in the administration of posts and telegraph, customs and excise, and elsewhere in civil service. Authorities depended heavily on the talents of well-educated Jews with their proficiencies in foreign languages in the transport sector, in railway, and in maintaining ties between Iraqi petroleum companies and other foreign companies in the port of Basra. Of Iraq's total imports, 95 percent were managed by Iraqi Jews. Iraq's first minister of finance, Sir Sasson Heskel, was Jewish. David Samra was appointed vice president of the court of appeals and played a vital role in the development of the Iraqi judicial system. Ya'qub Ezra (Elkabir) served as accountant general of the Ministry of Justice from 1921 until 1956, when he was discharged after the second Israeli-Arab War.

When King Faysal died in September 1933, his son Ghazi succeeded him, and the regime weakened. Ghazi was young and unable to unite various factions of the population or to control the nationalistic forces and organizations of Arab refugees from Syria and Palestine who had found asylum in Iraq. Ghazi was unable to secure protection of the minorities.

During Ghazi's rule, ending with his death in 1939, five military revolts occurred in Iraq. Although only one Jewish senator and a few deputies represented the Jews in parliament, the attitude of the government and the Arab masses towards the Jewish community deteriorated. In 1934, the Ministry of Economics and Transportation fired its Jewish employees and their Christian coworkers, although the latter were soon re-instated.

Between 1918 and 1935, various activities in Iraq gathered funding for Zionist education and activities. While the variety of opportunities and public policies accounted in large part for the secularizing trend of Baghdadi Jewish life, a number of societies taught Hebrew and for a short time published a Hebrew Arabic weekly. In 1935 Zionism was prohibited, and Jewish teachers from Palestine were expelled. The study of Hebrew language and literature was forbidden, and Jewish studies were restricted to lessons in the Hebrew Bible. The number of Jews in institutions of higher education was limited. Non-Muslims were forbidden to smoke tobacco in public during Ramadan. In September 1936, on the eve of the Jewish New Year, several Jews were murdered when leaving a club, and on Yom Kippur, a bomb exploded in the Jewish area.

It is important to note that the end of the British Mandate and the coming of Iraqi independence on October 3, 1932, coincided with Hitler's accession to power. While Iraq had gained independence before many other countries in the Middle East, antagonism toward Britain fostered support for the propaganda machine introduced by the German envoy, Dr. Fritz Grobba. With the rise of Nazi propaganda, the issue of Palestine became the most convenient instrument of anti-Jewish agitation. As Baghdad became the active center of Arab nationalism, the Palestinian problem became a major concern in Iraqi politics. The inciting presence of the Mufti of Palestine and of Syrian and Palestinian teachers in Baghdad led to the dismissal of many Jews from government posts and to the setting of quotas for Jews in government and in state schools and colleges.

From 1934 to 1941 attacks and murders of Jews became common occurrences in Baghdad. Hitler's doctrines were propagated throughout Iraq. In 1937 a large and violent anti-Jewish demonstration broke out in Baghdad. Jews closed their businesses; two Jewish merchants who remained in their shops were killed by the mob. Acts against Baghdadi Jews worsened in 1938 when nitric acid was cast on Jewish passersby. In the spring of 1941, a coup against the British led by Rashid 'Ali al-Gaylani brought anti-Jewish elements to power in the army and among politicians, including Yunus al-Sab-'awi, known for his hatred and hostility toward Jews. While celebrating the Feast of Pentecost, the Baghdadi community was subjected to looting and killing by a mob including members of the police and army. These incidents eventually led to the two days of attacks known as the Farhûd, the violent dispossession of Baghdadi Jews, on June 1–2, 1941. Jews were cruelly tortured and murdered, their property was looted, and synagogues were profaned. Many Jews were saved by Muslim neighbors who risked their own lives to protect them, some of whom were also killed. Casualty numbers would have been much higher otherwise. The intervention of the British subdued the situation.

There are no reliable figures of Jewish casualties or of property looted. An ad hoc committee appointed by the head of the Jewish community reported that 179 Jews were murdered, 450 were injured, and more than

900 homes were robbed; stolen property was valued at one million dinars. One member of the government committee held that the police; the German Embassy and Dr. Fritz Grobba, the German envoy; the Mufti of Jerusalem, Haj Amin al-Husayni; and Syrian teachers were responsible for the Farhûd pogrom.

The Farhûd terrified the Jewish population. With their sense of security shattered, some Jews were convinced that life in Iraq was no longer safe or bearable. A few left for Palestine, Iran, and India; however, the majority of these émigrés came back in 1942 when the political climate calmed down and the economy improved. A small number of Jews developed the theory that the Farhûd had occurred when Iraq was without a government and claimed that in the first year or two after the Farhûd the authorities stopped harassing Jews. Others considered the Farhûd to be a result of outside instigation, and they continued their daily lives as usual. There is evidence that between July and September 1941, a number of individual Jews acquired weapons for self-defense.

The aims of the Jewish emissaries from Palestine who came to Iraq until 1941 were mainly to sell memberships raising funds for the World Zionist Organization, and to collect contributions for the Jewish National Fund (JNF) in Palestine. In 1942, an underground Zionist movement in Baghdad was founded both by emissaries from Palestine, who came to the city legally and illegally, and by a few local Jews. Their main purpose was to instruct Jewish youth in the use of firearms for self-defense against the possibility of another Farhûd. Another purpose was to organize emigration, legal and illegal, from Iraq to Israel.

At the same time, the head of the community, Rabbi Sasson Khaduri, other leaders, and wealthy Jews opposed Zionist activity in Iraq. They did not want the Jews of Iraq to be considered a national minority, because such action could either expose the Iraqi Jewry to discrimination or incite the local population to violence against the Jews. At that time, the underground Communist Party began to gain strength in Baghdad, and Jewish and non-Jewish youth joined and were active party members. They believed that the rise to power of a Communist Party in Iraq would bring equality and freedom. In 1942, three Jewish high school students in Baghdad founded the Free Jewish Community. During its one year of existence it attracted about three hundred followers and acquired ten guns. Ostensibly the purpose of this organization was to teach Hebrew, to encourage emigration to Israel, but also to take self-defense measures. Nevertheless, it constituted a threat to the activities of the emissaries from Palestine, who eventually succeeded in exerting pressure on this organization to join the Zionist underground movement.

The operation to smuggle Jews out of Iraq suffered setbacks when in August 1942 Jewish emigrants were caught and returned to Baghdad while heading from Mosul to Qarmeshli in Syria. Other emigrants who tried to cross the border with British soldiers were robbed or handed over to the police. All these incidents had a demoralizing effect on Iraqi Jews ready to leave for Israel. In addition, the majority of the Iraqi community were not Zionists, basically, and stayed aloof from the Zionist movement. For some Iraqi Jews, attachment to Palestine had a messianic and religious character expressed in prayers and various aspirations, including the desire to be buried in Palestine. While the majority of the Jewish Hebrew societies that sprang up in Iraq during 1920s were in Baghdad, it was not until the government actions of 1935 that the Baghdadi Jews began to doubt they could ever live as Iraqis with equal rights. In fact, these Hebrew societies were no more than small, enthusiastic groups that desired to learn Hebrew, promote the welfare of the Jewish community, and broaden knowledge of events in Palestine; none promoted Zionist ideology.

When the British Army returned to Baghdad immediately after the Farhûd, the Jews again held cultural activities and resumed building a broad network of medical facilities and new schools. Yet this flourishing environment abruptly ended in 1947 when the United Nations supported the partition of Palestine and the war for Israel's independence began. In 1948, the Iraqi government passed a law establishing Zionism as a capital crime, with Zionist activities punishable by a minimum sentence of seven years, or by execution. It also forbade Jewish merchants from engaging in banking, bank transactions, or foreign currency. Anti-Jewish rioting broke out in Baghdad. After this, thousands of Jews fled illegally to Iran. Some immediately made their way from Iran to Israel, others did so later. In 1947, with Operation Michaelberg, three planeloads of Iraqi Jews were smuggled to Israel. In a most daring and risky activity, "empty" Iranian Airways jets were flown to Cairo and Beirut with "emergency" landings in Haifa to deposit their secret cargos of Iraqi Jews.

Many obstacles blocked the activities of the Jewish emissaries from Palestine. They did not master the local dialect, and Iraqi Jews did not want to go to Israel because they feared that they would have to take up agriculture and physical labor. Links with leaders of the local Jewish community in general and with wealthy Jews in particular were weak. The emissaries lacked leadership and administrative skills in managing their affairs in the Jewish community. Despite the difficulty that faced the Zionist underground, it succeeded in smuggling hundreds of Jews out of the country to Iran.

From 1935, the government had requested that every Jew who traveled to Palestine leave a deposit of fifty dinars until his or her return. This deposit was later increased to three thousand dinars. In 1948 the departure of Jews from Iraq was forbidden until future notice. When the state of Israel was proclaimed on May 14, 1948, martial law was declared in Iraq and military courts were set up. Hundreds of Jews were arrested, and their houses were searched. On July 14, 1948, two months after the promulgation of martial law, the Iraqi house of representatives passed an amendment to Article 51(a) of the Baghdad Criminal Code classifying Zionism, together with Communism, to be subversive and criminal creeds, punishable by death, hard labor for life, or imprisonment up to fifteen years. Since military courts could make judgments based on the testimony of two witnesses, it was easy for anyone dedicated to taking revenge on a Jew to engage a second witness to corroborate an allegation that a particular Jew was a Zionist. There was no appeal against these sentences, and military courts imposed heavy fines or terms of imprisonment on Jewish detainees. During the week of September 14, 1948, military courts delivered thirty-two verdicts against Baghdadi Jews, the lightest sentence being one-year imprisonment with a fine of ten thousand dinars. Sometimes the judge would humiliate, curse, and kick the accused. In less than nine months, forty-nine Jews were sentenced without stated charges while barred from visits with relatives. It was natural in such circumstances that Jews should want to leave Iraq and go where they might feel safe.

In 1949 Iraq was placed under martial law; the penalties prohibiting Zionism increased. Shafiq 'Adas—Jewish businessman, millionaire of Basra, and an anti-Zionist—was arrested, allegedly for selling arms to Israel. He was accused simultaneously of Zionism and Communism and was charged with organizing and financing Communist demonstrations and strikes in order to incite public opinion against the government; he was hanged in public. Two Jewish leaders of the underground Communist Party, Sasson Dallal and Yehudah Sadiq, were also sentenced to death and hanged. At the same time, authorities conducted searches of Jewish homes and imposed more educational restrictions and fines. The government forbade its local Jews to leave the country or emigrate lest they go to Israel.

On March 4, 1950, the Iraqi Senate suddenly passed a bill allowing Jews to leave the country provided they would relinquish their citizenship within a year. The law did not specify when such departures would begin nor the routes of transportation by which Jewish emigration would be conducted, nor did it indicate whether the Jews would be permitted to take their belongings and funds with them. It was quite clear to the Iraqi press and the local Jews that the only destination country the Iraqi government had in mind was Israel. Many Iraqi politicians believed that the sudden massive exodus of Iraqi Jewry would put economic pressure on Israel. The government justified the bill by claiming that many Iraqi Jews had already left the country illegally, and since the presence of the remaining Jewish citizens in the country was bound to adversely affect security and create social and economic problems, it was found that there was no alternative but to deprive them of their Iraq citizenship. The government failed to explain how Jewish citizens choosing to remain in the country posed a security threat. In the Chamber of Deputies, only 5 of 138 representatives voted against the bill and criticized the government for supplying Israel with additional manpower. In the Senate, the bill was debated and vehemently criticized by the right wing with warnings that approval would enable Iraqi Jews to join the Israeli Army. It was only after many long but superficial debates during which Parliament had been given sufficient assurances that the measure was entirely in the best interests of Iraq that the government was able to pass the bill.

Some attempted to explain this sudden move of the Iraqi government by claiming that the government intended to acquire Jewish property and get rid of Communist Jews. Others believed that the government desired to replace Jewish merchants and clerks with Muslims. Also, it was possible that the British wanted to get rid of the Jewish Communists and those Jews who loaned money to the Iraqi government to pay its civil servants. Zionist leaders in Iraq claimed that their activities were the prime cause for the law permitting the 2,700-year-old Jewish community to leave Iraq for Israel. Yet when this law was announced, the Zionist movement had already reached its lowest point, as most of the Jewish emissaries from Palestine had left, and the leaders of the underground movement had been arrested, tried, or imprisoned. When the bill was announced, the gates of Israel were open to accept more emigrants, and members of the Iraqi Jewish community were in dire need of finding refuge.

Many in the Jewish community believed that by enacting the law allowing the Jews to leave the country, the government wanted to round up and trap suspected Zionists. At first the number of Jews who registered to emigrate was very small, about four thousand, but in May 1950 the legal mass exodus to Israel began. By the end of 1950, sixty thousand Jews, half of the Iraqi Jewry, had registered. Numbers increased in January 1951 after bombs were thrown at Jewish businesses and meeting places, including Mas'udah Shem-Tov, the synagogue from which designated emigrants left for the airport. The Iraqi government claimed that Zionist agents threw the bombs in order to incite the rest of the Jews to leave the country. The issue of who was behind these explosions was raised many times in Israel, and Prime Minister Ben-Gurion set up a committee to investigate the accusation made against the Zionist movement in Iraq. In its report, the committee acquitted the active Zionist Ben-Porat and the rest of the Zionist movement and concluded that an Iraqi officer was seen throwing the bomb at the crowd near the synagogue and that the eyewitness died in the hospital before being able to give his testimony. Beliefs persist among many Iraqi Jews that this bombing was the work of Mossad, with the objective of encouraging emigration before the opportunity for legal registration expired. Scholar Elie Kedourie writes that "this may be so for the Zionists were capable of using such tactics."[2]

After long deliberations, the Iraqi government granted permission for transporting Jewish emigrants by air to the Near East Air Transport, Inc., a fictitious American charter company connected to El-Al Israeli Airlines, on condition that planes did not fly directly to Israel but would land first in Nicosia in Cyprus. The Cyprus authorities granted permission to land at their airport provided that the passengers immediately be flown to Israel. The agreement was signed by the Iraqi premier Tawfiq al-Suwaydi, by Heskel Shem-Tov, head of the Iraqi Jewish Community, and by a representative of Near East Air Transport, led by the Iraqi-born Zionist agent

2. Elie Kedourie, *The Chatham House Version and Other Middle Eastern Studies* (Chicago: Ivan R. Dee, 2004), 311.

Shlomo-Hillel. Shlomo-Hillel arrived in Baghdad carrying an American passport under the name of Richard Armstrong. He realized that his presence in Iraq involved high risk because he did not look like an American named Armstrong. Not only was he born in Iraq and was formerly an active member in the Zionist underground in Baghdad, he also had a highly visible scar on one cheek, caused by the so-called Baghdad boil, easily recognizable to a native Iraqi. At a dinner held in the home of a Jewish dignitary, Suwaydi approached his friend Shem-Tov and asked him, "Do you want me to believe this man is American? I swear by the Holy One he is an Iraqi recognized by his complexion and the scar (ukht) on his cheek." An Arab friend soon informed Shlomo-Hillel that the police suspected him of being a Jew, and the next day he left Baghdad on the first plane leaving for Cyprus.

Negotiations with Iraqi authorities to transport the Iraqi Jews by American companies were difficult, since two British companies were competing, and the director of Iraqi Airways, who was the son of Iraqi prime minister Nuri al-Sa'id, resisted an American monopoly. Near East Air Transport paid Iraqi Airways thirty dinars for each flight departing for Cyprus. Near East Air Transport increased the transfer of emigrants from an initial monthly rate of 2,500 to a rate of 13,500. From the beginning of the operation on May 19, 1950, until its conclusion on December 31, 1951, the number of Iraqi Jews airlifted totaled about 114,000.

On March 10, 1951, the day after the deadline of registration, the Iraqi Parliament met overnight in a secret closed session and passed A Law for the Control and Management of the Assets of Denaturalized Iraqi Jews, and The Fifth Law for Supervision and Management of Assets of Jews Who Have Lost the Nationality, which ordered the freezing of bank accounts and property of Jews who had renounced their Iraqi citizenship and applied for immigration to Israel. The funds of frozen accounts were estimated at six million dinars, and the value of frozen property amounted to twelve million dinars. Later the government also froze the assets of Jews who had left Iraq after the beginning of 1948 and had not returned by May 1951. Hence, this once wealthy community was instantly and unexpectedly impoverished. Later attempts to recover these assets were not successful.

When the exodus ended, the large majority of the Iraqi Jewish community had left for Israel; approximately six thousand Iraqi Jews remained in the country. Their situation returned to normalcy to the extent that they could conduct their businesses, maintain their communal and educational institutions, apply for Iraqi passports, and leave the country anytime. Many departed for Iran, Europe, the United Kingdom, the United States, and Canada, and did not return. In 2004, approximately thirty-five Jews were living in Baghdad. By 2008, there were fewer than ten.

Glossary

(JD) Baghdadi Jewish dialect
(MD) Baghdadi Muslim dialect

'Abakhanah. Structure built in Baghdad as a textile factory by the Ottoman governor Midhat Pasha. A siren was blown at start and end of the workday. During the British Mandate (1922–32) it served as a power plant.

abdalak (m.), *abdalek* (f.). Term of endearment used by Iraqi Jews for pleading or when frightened (literally, "may I be your substitute," i.e., "be a ransom for you"). In initial position, *abdalak* may mean "oh my gosh," "please," or "I beg you." (JD)

'abayah. A black, loose-flowing, robe-like outer garment with arm holes rather than sleeves, worn by women. (MD)

'abudiyah ('ubudhiyah). Type of love song popular in the countryside. (MD)

abu-l-tobah. Head of lettuce (literally, "the thing that has a ball"). (JD, MD)

Abu Rubain. Name of a Baghdadi Jewish family whose members were known for having six fingers on each hand. (JD)

'afsah. Gallnut (from gall tree) etched with gold stripes, hung on a child for the first forty days after birth to keep the evil eye away.

'Aggubi. Term of endearment for Ya'gub/Ya'qub. Iraqis often use nicknames derived from proper names as terms of endearment; for example, Ghallubi for Ghalib, Nahhudi for Nihad, etc.

'aini. Term of endearment used frequently in conversation as "dear," to mean that the addressee is as dear as the eyes of the speaker (literally, "my eye").

'Ajmi. A Persian person; the term, a loan word from Arabic, is often used by Iraqis referring in a derogatory way to an unsophisticated and a backwards person.

almanah. A widow (Hebrew, *almanah*). (JD, MD)

'al-'oudah. Ice cream bar.

'alucha. A candy that thickens as heated and kneaded, like taffy.

aruhlech fedwah (f.). "May I be your ransom!" (MD)

aruhlak kepparah (m.). "May I be a sacrifice for you" (Hebrew, kapparah, "sacrifice"). (JD)

'Ashurah. The tenth day of the first month of the Muslim lunar year, on which the Shi'ah perform passion plays commemorating the death of Husayn in 680 CE. Representations of his tomb are carried in procession accompanied by elaborate gestures of mourning, often flagellation.

'atabah. Love song.

'Azwat (sing. 'Azwah). Segment the Shi'ah mourning procession commemorating the death of Husayn, whose horse is recognized by blankets and arrows fixed to the harness.

barbug. Whore (literally, "flask with a wide mouth that does not sink in the sea"); said of someone who knows how to find clever solutions.

Beith ha-Miqdash (Hebrew, Bait ha-Mikdash). First Jewish temple, destroyed in 568 BCE.

"Besiman Tob" (Hebrew). Song performed by Iraqi Jews in circumcision ceremonies.

Bint al-Sudan. Name of perfume.

butlah. Special charm made by a mullah to cancel a magic spell over a person.

butnaj. Herb used by Iraqis to garnish cooked fava beans.

chardagh. Hut, like a cabana made of woven mats, used by swimmers for changing clothes and protection from sun.

chirag. Cake rolls. (JD)

choka-boka. Onomatopoeic term of endearment, as with "honey bunny."

damghah. A crushed white stone mixed in a drink and used as magic. Some Iraqis believe that the drink causes a loss of willpower, and the person who drinks it comes under the control of the person who prepares it.

dayram. Inner bark of a walnut tree used as a lipstick.

dinar. Monetary unit in Iraq valued at $2.80 in 1950.

dirham. One-twentieth of a dinar, valued at fourteen cents in 1950.

dishdashah. Ankle-length robe with a buttoned opening halfway down the front. The dishdashah is standard dress for children and adults not wearing Western clothing.

effendi (Turkish). An educated man who wears Western clothes; a gentleman.

El-Ezair. Small town south of 'Marah on the Tigris.

Elijah. Prophet of the ninth century BCE. Frequently referred to as the promised precursor of the Messiah and dynamic helper in times of stress. During the circumcision ceremony, Iraqi Jews place "a chair for Elijah" as protector of the infant.

El-Shaddai (Hebrew). "God is my Lord."

Eshkabah. Prayer for the dead in a burial service.

Ezekiel. Prophet-priest of the sixth century BCE and author of the Book of Ezekiel. Iraqi Jews believe he is buried at Kifel near the city of Hillah. The annual pilgrimage to his tomb is celebrated with dancing and songing.

Ezrah the Scribe. Priest and scribe who reformed Judaism toward the end of the fifth century BCE. His tomb in el-Ezair is visited annually by thousands of Baghdadi Jews.

Farhûd. In June 1941, Rashid 'Ali al-Gaylani formed a neo-Nazi cabinet in Iraq that included Yunis al-Sab'awi, well known for his hostility to the Jews. For two days, while the Jewish community in Bahdad was celebrating the festival of Shavu'ot, a mob and several members of the army and police attacked and looted Jewish homes and properties. The Farhûd was not perpetrated by Muslims against their Jewish neighbors but rather by mercenaries and vagrants who exploited the situation. An ad hoc committee appointed by the head of the Jewish community reported that 179 Jews were murdered, 450 injured, 586 stores and warehouses looted, and 911 homes robbed. Some non-Jews died as well. The committee found that the police; the German Embassy in Baghdad, especially Dr. Fritz Grobba, German envoy; the Mufti of Jerusalem; and Palestinian and Syrian teachers in Baghdad were responsible for the pogrom.

fedwah. "Please, I beg of you" (literally, "sacrifice," see *aruhlech fedwah*); often used to express an admiration of beauty. (JD, MD)

fils. Coin worth about three cents in 1950.

gawwad. Pimp; often used as an insult.

gawwadah. Prostitute in a whorehouse.

geimar (Turkish, *kaymak*). Butterfat remaining on top of water buffalo milk after boiling and cooling, usually eaten in the morning with date honey and bread.

gol-bahar. Type of backgammon.

hannun. Iraqi flatbread. (MD)

hannunah. Piece of Iraqi flatbread.

hebb. Large, porous vessel for cooling water on rooftops during summer nights.

hinni. Henna.

ibin halal. A kind person.

ibn-el almanah (Hebrew, *almanah*). Son of a widow, used as a curse wishing that the addressed man's mother should die.

ibn-l mal'unah. Son of the damned, cursed one. (JD, MD)

'Irq el-Swahil. Charm made from a pair of brown sticks (associated with Bedouins), sometimes with the bone of a hoopoe, thought to bring the owner respect, prestige, and success.

izar. Attire covering from head to toe, usually made of silk having a hem decorated with silver or gold threads, worn only by Jewish women in Baghdad.

jamkhanah. Wooden room with at least one glass wall.

jazrah. Island formed in certain spots along the Tigris in summer as a result of low tides. Baghdadis picnic and hold parties there.

Jubah. An old district in Baghdad where those who raised water buffalo lived.

ka'ak. Pretzel-like pastry. It was customary among the Jews of Iraq to serve *ka'ak* and Turkish delight, a candy, when celebrating circumcision. (MD)

kafishkan. A small storage room with a low ceiling located on the second floor of an Iraqi house, used for storing bedding and tools.

Kallachiyah. Former neighborhood in Baghdad that contained brothels, a red-light district.

karab (sing. *karbah*). Carob pods grown on palm trees. Beginning swimmers tied these to their chests and backs to help them float.

Karbala. A city southwest of Baghdad, site of the massacre of Husayn and his band of followers in 680 BCE. It is one of the Shi'ah sacred places, containing the Shrine of Husayn, a place of pilgrimage. The word combines, according to folk etymology, the Arabic *karb* (agony) and *bala'* (grief).

kepparah (Hebrew, *kapparah*). Ransom.

khailiyah. Square veil made of horse tail hair. (MD)

khatiyah. Used to express sympathy; "what a shame!" (MD)

kheswah. Genitalia.

kirr. Big bowl or pool where a Shi'i cleanses himself and his utensils when a non-Shi'i person touches him or his utensils. A faucet may also used for this purpose. (MD)

kishri. Cooked rice with lentils. It was a custom among the Baghdadi Jews to cook kishri every Thursday, and when a boy reaches puberty. (JD)

lat-hidini wahdi. "Don't leave me alone." (MD)

liwan. Area facing the courtyard of a house.

mahbus. Variant of backgammon in which pieces of one player are blocked by those of another player landing pieces on the same row.

m'aidi (pl. *mi'dan*). People who raise water buffalo and who are considered to be inferior.

mal'un (m.), *mal'unah* (f. sing.). Damned, cursed.

maykhalif. "Never mind, okay." (MD, JD)

meswah (pl. *meswoth*). Good deed. (JD)

mezuzah (Hebrew). Parchment scroll containing Deuteronomy 6:4–9 and 11:13–21, which the Jews fix to doorposts in a wooden or metal case.

midan. Red-light district.

miswah-khiswah. Vernacular expression for nonsense, with structure of "willy-nilly."

mullah (m. sing.), **mullayah** (f. sing.). Muslim religious leader.

nagel. A child born out of wedlock, a bastard. (JD)

nazzah (pl. *nazzahin*). Man who empties cesspools, usually located under a courtyard. After draining the water with buckets, he undresses himself and descends to the bottom of the cesspool to clean the residue.

Orozdibak. Well-known Baghdadi department store.

oud. Stringed instrument similar to a lute.

pachah. Stew made of meat taken from the head, feet, stomach, and neck of a sheep or a cow.

qanun. Stringed instrument similar to the Persian *santur.*

Qiddish. (Hebrew, Kaddish). Prayer for the dead.

qran. Iraqi currency equal to twenty fils.

riyal. Iraqi currency equal to two hundred fils.

salam. Peace.

salonah. Iraqi Jewish dish made of baked layers of fish and vegetables.

salwah. A black crushed stone mixed in a drink, believed to cause weakness and emaciation, eventually leading to death.

sammun (*sammunah*). Diamond-shaped sourdough roll.

sayyid. Title of a descendant of the Prophet Mohammed through his daughter Fatimah.

shaih. Yellow dye.

shakarlamah. Soft peanut cookies.

shaku beeha? "What's wrong with that?"

Sheikh Ishaq. A famous rabbi, head of the Babylonian Academy, buried in Baghdad inside a synagogue named after him. Jews and Muslims frequented his tomb, especially single girls who implored his help in accelerating the search for a spouse, and sick people asking for cures.

shundul. Penis. (JD)

sidarah. Typical Iraqi hat worn until the 1940s.

soney yisrael (Hebrew). One who hates Jews.

takhtahbosh. A wooden-floored room above the cellar, reached by a ladder.

Talmud (Hebrew). The large collection of writings containing a full account of the civil and religious laws of the Jews. It has two parts: the Mishna, or "second law," containing a compendium of the whole ritual law, and the Gemara (i.e., the supplement, completion).

tashrib. Dry bread cooked in water, fat, and a little lemon.

teffillim (Hebrew, *teffilin*). Phylacteries. These two small leather cases containing slips of paper inscribed with certain texts from the Pentateuch are worn by male Jews for prayer, one fastened with leather thongs to the forehead and one fastened on the left arm.

tfak. "Damn you, woe to you" (literally, "may you extinguish"). (JD)

ukhut. Sister, or Baghdad boil, a skin scar or depression caused by a mosquito bite. (MD)

ukhti. Form of addressing a female stranger (literally, "my sister").

Umm. A term of respectful address for a mother, usually paired with the name of her eldest son or, if there are no sons, the name of her eldest daughter.

wadhah. Distortion of *wallah*, "by God!" used jokingly.

walad 'aza. Sissy.

wammah. Oath; distortion of *wallah*, "by God!" used jokingly.

Yosef Hiyyim. Famous rabbi of Baghdad (d. 1909).

Yum (or *Yummah*). Mother. (JD, MD)

ziyarah. Pilgrimage to the tomb of Jewish saints, especially that of the prophet Ezekiel. Iraqi Jews believe that Ezekiel is buried near Hillah.

zneef. Type of domino game in which the number five and its multiples score points.

Samir Naqqash (1938–2004) is among the foremost Israeli authors from Iraq. He wrote in Arabic for his entire career in the dialects of both Jewish and Muslim communities in Baghdad. The political turmoil of Iraq in the 1940s and early 1950s forced his Jewish Iraqi family to immigrate to Israel when Naqqash was thirteen. The premature death of his father soon after the family's arrival, the loss of his family's prestige and wealth, and the hardships he experienced in Israel shaped his literary talent and his pessimistic outlook. Naqqash's literary output in Arabic includes three plays, four novels, and five collections of short stories. They are better known in the Arab world and Europe than in Israel. Doctoral dissertations on his oeuvre have been written in the West Bank, Jordan, Iraq, Egypt, Italy, England, and the United States.

Iraqi Jewish authors have criticized social injustice and discrimination against Arab immigrants by creating in Israel a new subgenre of literature. Characters in these works are marginalized by Israeli ideals. Even those who write in Hebrew have no place in the canon of an Israeli literature that prefers experiences that promote heroism, Zionist aspirations, and security. Neither the Hebrew transit-camp literature nor Naqqash's writing has appealed to Israeli literary tastes. Nevertheless, *Tenants and Cobwebs* won the Israeli Prime Minister's Award for Arabic Literature in 1986.

Born in Baghdad, Iraq, in 1934, **Sadok Masliyah** attended Jewish elementary school, middle school, and two years of high school there. In 1951, as a teenager, he emigrated with the mass exodus of Iraqi Jews to Israel, where he earned his high school diploma. At the Hebrew University in Jerusalem he earned his BA in Arabic language, literature, and Middle East studies. Sadok served as senior interpreter for Arab delegates in the Knesset (Israeli Parliament) from 1960 to 1964. He completed his MA in Hebrew studies at the University of Wisconsin–Madison. In 1973, he obtained his PhD from the University of California, Los Angeles, with the dissertation topic "The Life and Writings of the Iraqi Poet Jamil Sidqi Al-Zahawai." He has taught Arabic at UCLA, Hebrew and Arabic at Oberlin College, the University of Utah, the Defense Language Institute, Presidio of Monterey, CA, and Arabic at the Monterey Institute of International Studies (now Middlebury College). He has numerous publications on Iraqi culture and spoken dialects, the most recent of which is *The Formation of Quadrilateral Verbs in Iraqi Dialects* (Oxford University Press, 2017). He currently resides in northern California.